KERRY BARRETT is the author of thirteen novels, including *The Secrets of Thistle Cottage*, and *The Smuggler's Daughter*.

Born in Edinburgh, Kerry moved to London as a child, where she now lives with her husband and two sons. A massive bookworm growing up, she used to save up her pocket money for weeks to buy the latest Sweet Valley High book, then read the whole story on the bus home and had to wait two months for the next one. Eventually she realised it would be easier to write her own stories . . .

Kerry's years as a television journalist, reporting on *EastEnders* and *Corrie*, have inspired her novels where popular culture collides with a historical mystery. But there is no truth in the rumours that she only wrote a novel based on *Strictly Come Dancing* so she would be invited on to *It Takes Two*.

When she's not practising her foxtrot (because you never know . . .), Kerry is watching Netflix, reading Jilly Cooper, and researching her latest historical story.

Also by Kerry Barrett

The Secrets of Thistle Cottage
The Smuggler's Daughter
The Secret Letter
The Hidden Women
The Girl in the Picture
The Forgotten Girl
A Step in Time

The Could It Be Magic? Series

Bewitched, Bothered and Bewildered
I Put a Spell on You
Baby, It's Cold Outside
I'll Be There for You
A Spoonful of Sugar: A Novella

The Book of Last Letters

KERRY BARRETT

ONE PLACE. MANY STORIES

HQ
An imprint of HarperCollins*Publishers* Ltd
1 London Bridge Street
London SE1 9GF

www.harpercollins.co.uk

HarperCollins*Publishers*
1st Floor, Watermarque Building, Ringsend Road
Dublin 4, Ireland

This paperback edition 2022

1
First published in Great Britain by
HQ, an imprint of HarperCollins*Publishers* Ltd 2022

Copyright © Kerry Barrett 2022

Kerry Barrett asserts the moral right to be
identified as the author of this work.
A catalogue record for this book is
available from the British Library.

ISBN: 9780008481117

MIX
Paper from
responsible sources
FSC™ C007454

This book is produced from independently certified FSC™ paper
to ensure responsible forest management.

For more information visit: www.harpercollins.co.uk/green

Printed and Bound in the UK
using 100% Renewable Electricity at CPI Group (UK) Ltd

For nurses and carers everywhere.

Prologue

Elsie

Summer 1941

I woke with a start, my heart thumping, and it was a minute before I remembered where I was. I'd had the nightmare again – the same one that had plagued me since I left London. In my dream, the book had been uncovered and passed around. Everyone knew everything that had happened. Everything I'd done.

'How could you?' they said to me, their faces twisted in hatred, fingers pointing in accusation. 'How could you do such a terrible thing?'

Knowing I'd not be able to go back to sleep after such a sudden wake-up, I wiped my clammy brow and swung my legs out of bed. Uncomfortable now that the baby was getting so big, I smoothed my nightdress over my rounded midriff and went to the window, looking out over the quiet city. It was peaceful. Everyone was still sleeping, though the sun was beginning to rise over the horizon.

Feeling my heart rate begin to slow, I took a deep breath,

thanking my lucky stars that I was here, safe and sound, away from the bombs and the sirens, and …

It was over, I told myself firmly. The book was gone. It was buried beneath the rubble, never to be found. No one would ever know what I'd done.

Chapter 1

Elsie

1940

It was astonishing, I thought, as I clambered up the few steps from our neighbour's Anderson shelter, how quickly we'd all got used to something that would have seemed unimaginable a year ago. I couldn't believe that I'd slept through what Mrs Gold, our neighbour, told me had been another bad raid.

'I barely slept a wink,' she'd said when I'd woken. 'Didn't drop off until I heard the all-clear.'

I straightened up, hearing my spine click in a very satisfying fashion, and looked round. Things weren't as bad here as in the East End, but the bombers seemed to follow the railway line that ran along the backs of the houses and we'd had some hits. I could see smoke in the distance and the air felt gritty with brick dust. But the houses in our street were still standing.

'Thank you,' I said to Mrs Gold who had followed me out of the shelter and was blinking in the dim early morning light. 'I'm working tonight so I won't be here.'

'What about Nelly?' she asked, brushing a bit of something from the arm of my coat – I'd learned very quickly that it was better to wrap up warm when I was spending the night in the shelter.

'She's worked an extra night shift,' I said. 'Someone on her ward was bombed out so she had to cover while the other nurse got herself sorted. But she'll probably be home now actually.' I checked my wristwatch. 'Gosh it's much later than I thought. I can't believe I slept so well.'

Mrs Gold, who was barely ten years older than me but who treated Nelly and me like her daughters, clucked fondly. 'You work so hard, you girls,' she said. 'I'm not surprised you're tired.'

She grinned at me, adjusting one of her curlers under her hairnet. 'Right, must get on. Don't want those chaps in the office to be forced to type their own awfully boring documents, do I?'

I smiled back, taking in her innocent gaze. I was fairly sure Mrs Gold wasn't actually "just a typist" like she claimed, because I'd seen her with some very important-looking papers, and she was often away for long periods of time. But I didn't argue. Instead I waved as she hurried off up the garden path towards the kitchen where I could see Mr Gold making tea. I'd not even heard him get up and leave the shelter, I'd been sleeping so deeply.

Still feeling slightly snoozy, I went up the side passageway round the side of the Golds' house and out on to the front street. We had a side door out to the back garden, but I liked to go in at the front after a night in the shelter. I liked to see what had happened while we were safely tucked away at the bottom of the garden.

Now I marvelled again – as I seemed to every morning – at the resilience of London and its people. It was just like a normal day, if you pretended you couldn't smell the smoke in the air, and see the rubble at the corner where last night's raid had taken out three whole houses and half of the Evans family's home, in the street next to ours, leaving their living room sliced clean in two.

A bus rumbled past – more normality, even though it was covered in dust – and I stepped back to avoid being splashed as it drove through a puddle, and then I headed up our path, feeling in the pocket of my coat for my key so I could let myself into our maisonette.

'Nell?' I shouted, bending down to pick up the post from the doormat.

'In the kitchen,' she called.

I took off my coat and hung it from the bottom of the bannister, then went to find Nelly. She was sitting in a chair in the kitchen, still wearing her outdoor clothes, with her face streaked with dirt and her eyes red with tiredness.

'Letter for you,' I said, handing it over. She took it and glanced at the front then dropped it on to the table. 'Bad night?'

'Just never-ending.' She sighed. 'I need to go to bed, but I'm running on adrenaline.'

'I'll make you tea,' I said. I filled up the kettle and lit the hob with a match. 'Why don't you have a bath – see if that relaxes you?'

Nelly shook her head. 'Too much effort,' she said. 'I'll have my tea, then I'll have a wash and go to bed.' She frowned at me. 'You should get your head down later if you're on nights now.'

'I'm going to work early to help with the blankets,' I said. We had a bewildering lack of blankets at the hospital and it seemed to be a full-time job to sort them out and allocate them to wards. I'd heard friends at other hospitals talk about nurses going into bomb sites and taking them. We'd not got to that stage yet, but I sometimes thought it wasn't far off. 'Aren't you going to read your letter?'

Nelly sighed. 'No point. I know what it says.'

'How can you know if you've not read it yet?'

'Because my mammy writes the same thing every time,' she said. 'She tells me how it's so peaceful in Dublin, and you'd barely know there was a war on, and Dr Connalty says there's a job for me at the Sisters of Mercy hospital whenever I want one …'

5

I grinned at her. 'Maybe this time she's written to say you're doing a grand job here in London and you should stay as long as you want.'

Nelly laughed. 'Maybe.'

'She's just worried about you,' I said softly. Even though Nell's mother sounded overbearing and fussy, I knew it was because she loved her daughter, and I envied Nelly's family connections. She had brothers and sisters all over Ireland, and relatives in America, and she was always getting letters and once – thrillingly – a parcel from her sister in New York with stockings and a lipstick inside. I'd got the occasional note from Billy of course, and then I'd got the telegram, and now I got nothing.

Nelly got up from the chair with a groan. 'I'm going to sleep,' she said. She leaned forward and kissed me on the cheek. 'I'll see you later?'

'You will.'

I waited until she'd gone into her bedroom and then I took the letter from her mum and put it in the drawer in the sideboard, where I put all the other envelopes that came from her home and that she didn't open. I knew Ireland wasn't involved in the war and that Nelly's mammy was safe in that way, but I also knew bad things happened in wartime too, and that perhaps Nelly would want to see her mother's handwriting one day, and read her caring words.

I could really do with a bath myself, but I didn't have time if I was going to help with the blankets before my shift started. I settled with a proper wash in my bedroom, even though the water was cold and made me shiver. I found a clean uniform dress in my wardrobe and folded it up neatly and put it in my bag – I'd get a fresh apron when I got to the ward.

Then I went into the kitchen to look for some food. There wasn't much choice. Nelly and I still hadn't really got to grips with rationing and because we ate at odd times, we were often left with empty cupboards. Luckily there was half a loaf in the bread bin, so I stuck a couple of slices on the end of the toaster fork and toasted it over the fire, warming myself up at the same time because I was still shivering after my wash.

I worked in South London District Hospital. It wasn't far from where we lived. Before the war I had often cycled to work, but now I was usually too tired so I normally jumped on the train for two stops. We worked long shifts and we'd doubled the number of patients we looked after since the bombing started. We were a casualty clearing hospital now, and took in people who'd been injured in air raids. Most of them were local, but sometimes if it had been an especially bad night, we got casualties from Central London too. They would arrive in specially converted buses, because there weren't enough ambulances to transport all the patients.

With my bag packed and my tummy full, I finished my cup of tea, and left a note for Nelly saying I'd see her later, put on my coat and a hat because there was a definite nip in the air now, and headed outside to walk to the station.

I'd not walked more than a hundred yards, when someone fell into step beside me.

'All right, Elsie?'

My heart sank. It was Timothy Jackson – an old schoolmate of my brother Billy. As far as I knew, he and Billy had only really been acquaintances, but Jackson – as everyone always called him – seemed to think they had been great pals.

I scowled at my feet and then turned towards him – still walking – and forced a smile. 'Hello.'

'Are you off to work?' he said, keeping pace easily with my quick stride, despite the flat feet that he'd told me had kept him from enlisting on medical grounds. 'You're not due at the hospital until later, are you? I thought this was your first night shift?'

I felt a tiny shiver of unease. How did he know my shift pattern? Jackson always appeared when I was out and about and it wasn't the first time I'd suspected he was watching me. But Billy had always said he was a nice enough bloke. A bit of an oddball, perhaps, but harmless. I found him more sinister than strange, but I didn't want to be unkind.

'I'm doing some extra work for my matron,' I explained, quickening my steps a little bit and loosening my top button because walking so fast was making me sweat.

'You're not overdoing it are you?' Jackson's expression darkened. 'I don't want you wearing yourself out.'

'I'm fine.' I gritted my teeth, resisting the urge to say it was nothing to do with him, and anyway, weren't we all worn out right now with the bombs dropping every night and Nelly working extra shifts and us all just doing what we could for the war effort?

'Billy wouldn't want you tired out.'

'I need to catch a train, Jackson. It's been lovely to catch up.'

'Because I promised him, didn't I? That I'd look after you.'

I stopped walking so suddenly that Jackson kept going for a couple of paces before he realised, and then scurried back.

'Are you all right, Elsie?'

'What do you mean you promised Billy you'd look after me?'

Jackson scratched his nose. 'It was the last thing he said.'

'Unless you were at Dunkirk, then I very much doubt that.'

My sharp tone didn't seem to bother Jackson in the slightest. 'The last thing he said to me.'

'What?'

'He was here, actually. Or maybe a little bit further down the road, more towards the bus stop …'

I glared at him and this time he did understand. 'Anyway, he was going to catch the train, and he was in uniform, all smart, with his kit bag on his shoulder. And I said was he going to the war, and he said yes, and I wished him luck and he said thank you, and then I said I'd look after you for him, and he said I'd better.' He took a deep breath and looked at me, triumphant. 'And then he got on the train.'

The train. I glanced round and with relief, saw the smoke

of the approaching engine. 'I have to go,' I said to Jackson. 'My train is coming.'

I hitched my bag further up my shoulder and took to my heels, running down the street in a most unladylike fashion to the station. I got to the platform and straightaway the train pulled in. I hurried aboard, slamming the door shut behind me and slumping on to an empty seat. How dare Jackson lay claim to my brother's final words? I thought. I wiped my clammy brow and leaned forward to open the window as the train chugged across the bridge over the road. Down below I saw Jackson standing where I'd left him, shielding his eyes from the low autumn sun and scanning the carriages, clearly looking for me.

I shrank back into my seat, for some reason not wanting him to spot me. And then I chided myself. He was being nice, I told myself. He was just lonely. After all, there weren't many men his age around now, his parents had moved away shortly after war was declared, and I knew he didn't have siblings. Perhaps we had more in common than I liked to think. I should be kinder to him. More understanding.

I leaned my head against the firm seat back and closed my eyes, thinking about Billy. I wondered for the hundredth time what his final thoughts had been. If he'd said any last words. Had he been scared, I wondered, when the German bomb landed on the beach as he was waiting to escape? Or had he not had a chance to be frightened before the darkness took him? I'd had a letter from his commanding officer, but he'd not been with Billy when he died. He simply said he'd been a fine young man and a credit to his fellow soldiers. It was true, I was sure. Billy was a hard worker. Brave and steady.

But I remembered how frightened he'd been when our mother died, a few years ago. How for a minute, his stoic expression had dissolved and his eyes had filled with tears. Back then, I'd put my arms round him and promised him we were a team and that he'd be all right because he had me by his side. I couldn't bear the thought of him being scared in France, looking out to sea as the little boats came to their rescue and feeling hopeful, not knowing what was round the corner. Or worse, bleeding and in pain, frightened and all alone. I sighed. I would never know what was in his head when he died, and I was going to have to come to terms with that.

Chapter 2

Sometimes I looked back at when I'd started nursing, before the war began, and marvelled at how I ever thought it was difficult, or tiring, or that shifts were busy when we had five beds on each ward and they were all full. Because it was a different kettle of fish now and no mistake.

I always felt tense when I was getting ready to start a night shift. I could feel my jaw clenching and my shoulders tightening, as I prepared myself for what the evening would bring. Today I felt even worse. I was unsettled by bumping into Jackson and I felt a bit off kilter.

Nelly and I worked on different wards, but I was hoping to see her before our shifts began, after I'd finished sorting out the blankets.

Sure enough she was in the cloakroom when I had delivered all the bedclothes to the right wards and had gone in search of a clean apron before we started work properly. She was looking much livelier than she had earlier.

'You look better,' I said.

'Amazing what forty winks can do for a girl,' she said. She opened her locker and pulled out a mirrored compact, checking her reflection.

'Is Dr Barnet working tonight?' I teased, as she pinched her cheeks to make them glow.

'I have no idea what you're talking about.' She shut her compact with a snap and gave me a wink.

'Then you won't be interested in the dance at the Pig and Whistle,' I said, turning away from her. 'Never mind, I'll find someone else to go with.'

Nelly shot out her arm to stop me leaving. 'You wait a minute, Elsie Watson. What's this about a dance?'

'There's an advert on the noticeboard in the nurses' accommodation,' I said. 'I saw it when I was looking for blankets.'

'You're stealing blankets from your fellow nurses now are you?' Nelly shook her head sadly. 'Sure that's terrible.'

I nudged her, laughing. 'Do you want to hear about the dance, or not?'

'I do.'

'It's on Friday week.'

Nelly's eyes gleamed. 'We're off.'

I nodded with enthusiasm. 'Exactly. It's downstairs at the Pig and Whistle – you know, the big pub on the main road? It's got a huge cellar apparently and they've done it all up for dances. There's going to be a band playing.'

Nelly's eyes lit up. 'And will there be soldiers?'

'Undoubtedly.'

'Will we go?'

'We'll have to double-check our shifts – you know how things can change – but it could be fun.'

Nelly clutched my arm dramatically. 'I can't even remember what fun is.'

'Then we will definitely go.'

I tied my apron round my waist and checked my own reflection in the spotted mirror on the wall. My cap was wonky so I straightened it. I loved that Nelly brought out the fun in me. I'd always been rather quiet when I was young. And losing my mother when I had barely left school made me grow up fast. Billy and I learned to look after ourselves when she was poorly, and there wasn't a lot of time left for nights out when you had to do the cooking and cleaning and the laundry. I'd met Nelly when we lived in the nurses' accommodation when we were training. Billy had stayed in our house, fixing cars in a garage nearby. He had loved engines, my Billy.

When Nelly and I qualified and the war began, there were so many new nurses jostling for spaces in the hospital digs, it made sense for us to move back to our old family home. And heaven knows I'd been glad of her company when I got the news that Billy had been killed. Living with Nelly had shown me that there was more to life than housework and worrying about money. She always said I'd rediscovered my youth, even though I was only twenty-one.

'I saw Jackson again on the way to work,' I told her.

She made a face. 'I don't like him, Elsie.'

'I don't like him much either,' I admitted. I pinned my watch – a present from Billy – on to my apron and checked the time. Then, making the most of the couple of minutes before the shift began, I sat down on one of the battered armchairs in the staffroom, and sighed. 'He said he saw Billy as he was leaving, and he asked him to look after me.'

'Well that's not true,' Nelly said immediately. 'Billy knew you could look after yourself.'

I smiled, but it was a bit of a sad smile. 'He did.'

'And if he'd wanted someone to look after you, he'd have asked me.'

This time my smile was bigger. 'That is very true.' Billy had adored Nelly. He always said she was a "right card". 'If there's anyone you want in your corner,' he'd said to me more than once, 'it's Nelly Malone.'

'Well, there you are.'

I nodded. 'It just made me feel a bit prickly, you know? Him having spoken to Billy when he left.'

'Because he spoke to Billy more recently than you did?'

'That's it.'

Nelly came over to where I sat and gave me a hug. I had never been much of a hugger before I met her either. But she was so affectionate and open, that I'd soon had to learn to love her impromptu expressions of friendship. 'Your Billy knew how much you loved him,' she said. 'And you know that he thought the world of you too. Nothing Jackson can say can change that.'

'You're right,' I said. 'I just wish I'd had the chance to tell him, that's all.'

'I know.' Nelly looked thoughtful. 'I was thinking that last night. There was this man brought in, and he was bleeding so badly, and he knew he was going to die – you know how some people just know? And he was saying "tell Susie I love her" over and over.'

I found myself blinking away tears, even though we dealt with death every day. 'Did you?' I asked. 'Did you tell Susie?'

'Ach, no. How could I? I didn't even know his name, let alone who Susie was,' Nelly said. 'He was brought in wearing his pyjamas.'

I felt desperately sad for the man who'd died without telling Susie what he wanted her to know. Was she his wife? I wondered. His daughter? Maybe even a secret lover. But she'd never know that this man had been thinking of her in his final moments.

'This war,' I said, my voice slightly croaky. 'This awful war.'

'Ladies,' a voice said. 'Should you be sitting in here, or should you be on the wards?'

We both looked round to see the matron from Nelly's ward at the door. She sounded cross but she was smiling.

'Just going,' I said.

'Nurse, there are tin hats on every ward now,' Matron said. 'Make sure everyone puts them on when the siren goes.'

I groaned. 'Really?'

'Really. We've got more sandbags being delivered and the

14

operating theatre downstairs is up and running now, but we can't be too careful.'

I nodded and Nelly did too.

'Go on then,' Matron said. 'Off to the wards please, Nurse Malone and Nurse Watson.'

*

I worked on a women's ward. It was meant to be a surgical ward, but all bets were off now we were a casualty clearing station and part of the Emergency Medical Service. We were already double the capacity we'd been before the war, and they'd put up huts in the grounds too that were going to be used as more wards. The children's ward was now where the dining room had once been, and the staff canteen, which had been in the basement was – as Matron had said – now the operating theatre. It had taken some getting used to, and things were still changing. I kept thinking that these nightly raids couldn't last much longer, but the Luftwaffe didn't seem like they were giving up. And I was fairly sure the powers that be wouldn't have made so many changes to the hospital if they were expecting the bombs to stop. That thought made me shiver every time something new was built, or more alterations were made.

'This war has made them do more for this hospital in ten months than they'd done in the previous ten years,' Matron was fond of remarking, pointing out the new equipment we had, and the extra staff. Though the fancy new bits and pieces weren't much use when the electricity went out in a raid and we had to sterilise equipment in a saucepan of water heated on a Primus stove.

It was dark outside already and the windows were covered. I cast an experienced eye around the ward. We had three empty beds, which was unusual.

'Calm before the storm,' said another nurse, Phyllis, coming to stand by my shoulder.

And she was right. It wasn't long before the siren was wailing and we knew our steady evening routine, giving the patients their medication and settling them down for the night, would soon come to an end.

We didn't move the patients when the siren went. We didn't have enough room to transfer them all downstairs to the basement – and even if we had, some of them were so poorly they wouldn't have lasted the trip. Anyone who was able went to the hospital shelter, but our patients were normally too weak. So we just kept going. When the siren went we pushed the beds into the centre of the room, away from the windows even though they were boarded up, just to be on the safe side.

'Hats please, nurses,' Matron called, handing out tin helmets just like the ones the ARP wardens wore. Feeling faintly ridiculous, I strapped mine on, making a face at Phyllis as I did so. She grinned back, rapping her knuckles on the top of her head.

The planes were overhead now, and I could sense everyone holding their breath, while we pretended to be normal. Phyllis and I were giving one of our patients a bed bath, and changing her sheets, so we carried on our jovial conversation.

'I reckon a couple more days and you'll be back home, Mrs Marsden,' Phyllis said, raising her voice over the sound of the anti-aircraft guns. 'What do you reckon, Nurse Watson?'

I reckoned poor Mrs Marsden wasn't actually a missus, for one thing. She'd got a nasty infection from a backstreet abortion and the ring she wore on her left hand had gone green underneath. But that was none of my business, so I smiled at Phyllis and then at Mrs Marsden.

'You'll be up and about in no …' I breathed in sharply as I heard the whistle of a bomb falling. 'In no time.'

Mrs Marsden winced as something crashed nearby. 'You think?'

'I know,' I said, gently sponging her face. 'The infection's gone.'

She gave me a small smile. 'That's good. I like your helmets.'

'I think they make us look like ARP wardens.'

She chuckled. 'That's right.'

Another huge rumble made us all shriek. We were on the ground floor, but the boards beneath our feet shook with the impact.

'Lord, that was close,' Phyllis said. 'Must be aiming for the railway line.'

'If it's this bad here, think how it must be in the East End. I can see the smoke hovering over the docks from my bedroom window each morning.'

'My sister lives in Oxfordshire and she says they can see Coventry burning,' Mrs Marsden said. 'It's miles away but they can see the flames every night.'

'You should go and stay with her,' Phyllis told her. 'Sit up and I'll do your pillows. Much safer than here.'

'I think I might,' Mrs Marsden agreed. She twiddled the ring on her green-tinged finger. 'Not much point in staying round here.'

In the nurses' station at the end of the ward, the phone rang and Phyllis and I exchanged a look. We knew that meant more casualties were on the way. Sure enough, Matron called: 'Nurse Watson? Can you go and meet the ambulance please. Only one for us at the moment.'

'Will do.'

I left Phyllis looking after Mrs Marsden, and walked down the ward and out into the corridor. The main entrance of the hospital was already in chaos. There were people everywhere in the corridors. Doctors and nurses dashing from ward to ward. Injured people on chairs, looking dazed. Someone crying. And more patients about to arrive. I had no idea where we'd put everyone.

Bracing myself I pushed open the door to the outside and went out into the chilly evening air.

It was pitch-black, of course, but the darkness felt heavy with smoke. Every now and then the sky was lighting up with flashes as bombs exploded in the distance, and there was a red glow to the night air in front of me that I knew meant some-thing, somewhere was burning. There were tall trees around the perimeter of the hospital grounds, and as the sky brightened with the explosions they appeared, silhouetted against the light, and then disappeared.

I shivered, wishing I'd thought to bring my coat out with me and wondering if I had enough time to run back to the staff cloakroom and grab it. But then there was a rumble from the road and I could see the faint outline of the bus-turned-ambulance coming. It pulled into the hospital grounds and stopped in front of the doors where I was standing. The driver, a woman about my own age with a streak of dust across her face and a tin helmet like mine, jumped down from the front of the bus. 'Three casualties,' she said. 'Two men, one woman. Crush injuries.'

I nodded and next to me, two other nurses I knew by sight added their voices to mine. The bus doors opened and there was a flurry of activity as we got the patients out of the ambulance and into the hospital.

'Will there be more?' I asked the driver as I signed the sheets she gave me, and she signed mine, in a vain attempt to keep track of patients. She rubbed her nose with the palm of her hand and nodded.

'Oh there will definitely be more. It's a bad one. This lot are all from the same place – direct hit on a pub full of dock workers. They were all in the basement but it collapsed.'

And then she pulled herself up into the driver's seat and started the engine. With the help of a porter, a lovely chap called Frank who we were all ever so fond of, I took my patient along to the ward and we got her settled. The poor woman was in a bad way. She had been crushed by a falling beam that had pinned her to the ground. One of her arms was broken and needed to be set and put in plaster. It was in a sling with a splint holding it firm, and I was glad that the ambulance team had managed to do that at least. Her other arm, though, was simply a terrible mess. It was covered in blood and hanging limply at her side. Clearly the emergency team hadn't thought it was worth even trying to fix it.

'She's going to lose that arm,' Phyllis said as she helped me take the patient's vitals.

I nodded grimly. 'Sooner rather than later too. Don't want it infected.'

The woman's eyes flickered open and I grimaced. I hoped she hadn't heard us talking about her like that.

'My kids,' she croaked. 'The kids.'

We were used to families being separated. 'We'll find them,' I told her, frowning slightly because hadn't the driver told me the casualties were all from a dockers' drinking den, which didn't seem like somewhere children would be. I looked at her notes. 'Violet is it? Where were your children, Violet? Were they with you?'

She shook her head slowly. 'They're in Wales.' She groaned in pain, trying to sit up. 'They were evacuated.'

'Stay still, Violet. The kids are safe – don't worry.'

Violet gritted her teeth. 'But they won't know what's happened or where I am.'

'You can write to them when you've had your op, and you're in the convalescent hospital,' Phyllis said cheerfully. I kicked her, hard, on her ankle, looking meaningfully at poor Violet's useless arms. 'Ouch,' Phyllis grumbled. Her eyes widened as she realised what she'd said. 'Well, someone can write for you.'

'I'll do it,' I said. 'Do you know the address?'

'Course I do.'

I felt in the pocket of my apron for a pencil and then got a fresh sheet of paper out of Violet's notes. 'Tell me.'

She reeled off the address, breathy and clearly in pain but determined to pass on the information.

'What are your children's names?'

'Winifred, Ray and Jimmy.'

19

I scrawled that on the top of the page. 'I'll write to them as soon as I'm finished on the ward,' I promised. I saw Violet relax a little bit.

'Thank you,' she said.

Chapter 3

Stephanie

Present day

It was raining again. Of course it was. I looked up at the sky, wondering whether to risk it or go back inside and find my waterproofs. A distant rumble of thunder made my decision for me, so I darted back up the stairs at the side of my tiny flat and hurried inside. I took off the battered leather jacket that had once belonged to my brother, and instead pulled on my bright yellow cagoule and managed to cover my rucksack in a plastic carrier bag so everything inside wouldn't get soaked. Then I dashed back outside again.

My flat – if you could call it that, which you couldn't really – was above the detached double garage set slightly to the side of the big house where my dad's friend Bernie lived with his wife and teenage kids. Bernie owed my dad a favour, which was why he let me live in the flat that had once been used by a succession of au pairs. I hadn't asked what the favour was, but it must have been a big one because Bernie let me stay there for a tiny amount of rent – which I still struggled to pay.

I clattered down the metal staircase and opened the garage door to get my bike out, keeping my gaze away from the corner where all my canvases were stacked against the wall, and my art equipment was gathering dust in the bags for life I'd stashed it in.

After adjusting the straps of my rucksack, I wheeled my bike outside and came face to face with Micah, Bernie's teenage son.

'No,' I said, wheeling past him.

'Oh come on, please.'

'No. Go to school.'

I was not Micah's au pair but he seemed to think I was. Or at least he thought he could use my flat whenever he wanted, to hide out when he should be at school. But when Micah bunked off, it was me who got the blame. I had a suspicion that Bernie's wife, Jan – nice as she was – had been forced into welcoming me into their annexe. She'd had plans to convert the garage into a gym before I landed on their doorstep, so I didn't want to give her any excuse to get rid of me. I couldn't risk losing this flat, even though it was tiny and cramped.

Micah scowled at me and I scowled back, but good-naturedly because he was a nice lad really and I saw something in him that reminded me of myself. A fluttery anxiousness that made me want to look after him.

'The thought of going to school is worse than it'll actually be when you get there,' I told him, as I got on my bike. 'It's never as bad as you think.'

'Is that how you feel about work?'

'Totally,' I lied, because while I didn't dislike work it was always a bit of an effort. 'I'm working with Tara later. If you come by after school, I'll give you the key and you can hang out at mine all evening.'

Micah gave me a dazzling smile. 'Thanks, Steve,' he said.

'It's Stevie,' I said with an overexaggerated sigh. Micah had been thrilled when he discovered my friends and family all shortened

22

Stephanie to Stevie, and he delighted in giving me his own version of my nickname.

'Okay then, Steve.'

'It's Stevie,' I called over my shoulder as I rode off down the drive and out of the automatic gates. 'Stevie!'

*

Tall Trees residential home was surrounded by a low hedge, a red-brick wall, and absolutely no trees, tall or otherwise. It was a large building shaped like an L with the long bit of the L parallel to the road and the gravelled car park, which I'd long ago learned not to cycle across, at the front. I locked my dripping bike up in the empty rack, and took my helmet and my shopping-bag-covered rucksack into the staffroom.

'You're late,' said my boss, Blessing, hurrying past the door to the room with a pile of clean towels as I peeled off my wet outer layer. Then she stopped, and grinned at me. 'Here.'

She threw me a towel and gratefully I caught it and wiped my face.

'It's still raining then?'

'Actually it's stopped.' I squeezed my damp ponytail with the towel then hung it over the door of my locker while I got out my clean uniform tunic.

'But …'

'Bus,' I said wryly. 'And puddle.'

Blessing raised an eyebrow. 'You're on the bottom corridor today. They've all had tea, but they'll need you to help get them up for breakfast. Then when you're ready and if the rain's holding off, can you take Mr Yin out into the garden? He wants to see if the peonies have flowered yet.'

'Will do.'

I finished buttoning up my tunic, tidied my hair, shut my locker, and hurried off to the bottom corridor.

'Morning, Val,' I sang as I went into the first room. 'How are you today?'

'I wish I was dead,' said Val who was ninety-five, and who spoke her mind without hesitation. 'Can't even get a proper cup of tea in this rotten place. Is it too much to ask for an Earl Grey of a morning?'

I grinned at her. 'Ready to get up?'

'What's the point?'

With a flourish, I pulled two little Twinings sachets – like the ones you got at a hotel breakfast buffet – from my tunic pocket and waved them at her. 'Would you get up if I promised to make you a cup of Earl Grey?'

Val smiled at me suddenly and uncharacteristically. 'You know what you are?' she said. 'One of the good ones.'

I busied myself filling her little kettle so she didn't see the tears that had sprung into my eyes at her kind words. Just about anything made me well up these days. Tears were never far away now.

'Right then, shall we get you out of that bed?' I said, falsely jolly. 'What would you like to wear today?'

*

Once all five of the residents on my corridor were up and dressed and in the dining room for breakfast, I went to find Mr Yin. He was sitting in the lounge, drinking coffee and looking out of the window. 'This building was once a hospital,' he said.

I nodded. 'It spooks me a bit if I think about that when I'm on a night shift,' I admitted. 'When it's quiet and dark, the corridors give me the willies.'

'The willies?' Mr Yin raised an eyebrow. He was a clever, distinguished man who had spent his younger days jetting between the UK and Hong Kong, but sometimes my South London idioms made him scratch his head.

'Shivers,' I said. 'Give me the shivers.'

Mr Yin nodded and I knew he was storing away the knowledge for another day.

'How are your legs today? Do you want me to get a chair?'

With a sigh, Mr Yin nodded. 'I think that would be easier.'

Some of our residents were in wheelchairs all the time, but others – like Mr Yin – only used them when they had to, so we had a line of them by the reception desk.

'Two mins,' I said to Mr Yin, heading out of the lounge to grab a chair. A man – my age or perhaps a bit older – was signing in at the front desk. I'd never seen him before and I wondered which resident he'd come to see. He looked a bit like Louis Theroux. All tousled hair and thick-rimmed glasses.

'Morning,' I said, and he looked up at me and smiled.

'Morning.'

I got the chair, and helped Mr Yin into it, and we went out the front door and round to the side of the home. The gable end of the home was painted white – a dirty, peeling white, but plain enough to be a tempting canvas for any passing graffiti artist.

As I pushed Mr Yin round to the garden, I noticed that today some scumbag had scrawled "f*ck the govermant" in red spray paint, right across the gable end. I couldn't say I entirely disagreed with the sentiment, but the spelling made me wince.

Some of the other residents were on the terrace.

'Want to join your mates?' I asked Mr Yin. 'You can see the peonies from there and keep dry if the rain starts again.'

'Thank you, Stephanie,' he said.

I pushed him over and got him settled and then, just as I was about to sit down myself and have a chat with them all, Blessing leaned out of the window.

'Stephanie, you can go and see your nan now, if you like.'

I shook my head. 'I'm just with Mr Yin at the mo.'

'I'm fine,' said Mr Yin, giving me a puzzled look. 'Unless you

25

don't want to go?' He studied me with his sharp eyes and I made a face.

'I know I should, but it's so hard. She doesn't always remember me.'

'My wife's mother was the same. It's very cruel.'

I looked away from him and blinked to stop the tears coming again. 'She's not going to be here forever,' I said. 'She's really gone downhill recently. I should go.'

'I agree.' Mr Yin nodded. 'You'll regret it if you don't.'

'Are you sure it's okay?' I called to Blessing.

'Go on,' said Blessing. 'I'll send someone else out to stay with the residents.'

With a stifled sigh, I nodded. 'Right then.'

The dementia unit of Tall Trees was at the far end of the building, behind locked double doors to stop anyone wandering off. I walked slowly towards the entrance, because much as I loved my grandmother, and lucky as I was to be on-hand and get to visit her all the time, it was hard seeing her there.

'You look like you've got the weight of the world on your shoulders,' said the home's handyman, Cyril, as I walked past where he was mending a fence. 'When you should have the world at your feet.'

'Going to see my nan,' I told him, and he made a face.

'Worse is she?'

'Good days and bad days,' I said. It was that I found difficult really. I didn't like not knowing how she would be when I got to her room. 'Have you seen the graffiti round the side?'

Cyril rolled his eyes. 'No. What is it this time?'

'Very badly spelled. Fairly offensive.'

He shrugged. 'Well it'll have to wait. This fence needs mending, then I've got to do the leaky shower on the top corridor, and that new lady down the end's got a window in her room that won't open, and another one that won't shut.'

'Can't you just paint over it? It won't take long.'

'You're supposed to be the artist,' said Cyril. 'You do it. There's paint in the shed.'

'Maybe I will,' I said, ignoring his comment about me being an artist. 'I'll see you later.'

'Not if I see you first,' said Cyril, like he always did, and I carried on to the dementia unit.

I found my grandmother in their lounge – much smaller than the one at our end of the building because other than the occasional choir, they didn't have much entertainment – looking out of the window. I wondered what she was seeing, because she didn't seem to be focusing on the cloudy sky or the plants outside.

'Hello, Nan,' I said. I sat down next to her and took her hand. Someone had painted her fingernails and that touch of kindness made my eyes fill with tears again. She'd always been really smartly turned out, my nan. I'd written that on her "all about me" form that was kept next to her bed for her carers to look at.

'You look nice,' I told her. She turned to look at me, with her sharp eyes searching my face.

'Stephanie,' she said.

My heart leapt. 'That's me, Nan. How are you?'

'I've been dancing.'

'Have you?' They often played music for the residents in this part of Tall Trees. 'Who did you dance with?'

She leaned towards me. 'Just myself,' she said. She patted my knee with her manicured hand. 'Never rely on a man,' she said. 'Independence. That's what a girl needs.'

'You're right, Nan.'

'I've got a granddaughter,' she said. She sat up a bit straighter, looking proud. 'Stephanie, her name is. She's independent.'

I nodded. 'That's me, Nan. I'm Stephanie.'

She blinked at me. 'Well I never.'

I looped my arm through hers, giving her a squeeze. 'It's good to see you.'

'They're twins, you know? Stephanie and Max. A pair. A right pair of Charlies, I always call them.' She chuckled and I breathed in sharply.

'I know, Nan.'

'Stephanie?' Nan said. 'Where's Max? When is he coming to see me?'

I'd known it was coming but it never got any easier. One of the nurses in the unit had told me to go along with Nan's forgetfulness, telling me it was distressing for her to be corrected all the time. It was certainly distressing for me to have to tell her the same awful thing over and over. And so I tried to smile, even though my mouth didn't want to move in that way.

'Max is …' I breathed in deeply, trying to think of the right words. 'Busy,' I lied. 'He's busy.'

Nan looked at me fondly. 'He's such a good boy,' she said. 'Is he on holiday?'

I rolled my eyes. It wasn't exactly a holiday and Max wasn't exactly what you'd call a good boy. 'He is away, yes.'

'He'll come and see me tomorrow.'

I pinched my lips together, feeling anxiety pulse in my chest as my forehead grew clammy with sweat. It was getting harder and harder to lie to her, but I thought her knowing the truth would be even worse. 'I'm not sure, Nan,' I said quietly trying to catch my breath.

'Maybe he'll come tomorrow,' Nan repeated. 'My grandson, Max.'

I swallowed. 'Maybe.'

With a nod of satisfaction, Nan turned her attention back to the window and for the hundredth time I cursed my stupid, selfish brother who'd managed to get himself sent to prison and left me to pick up the pieces.

Chapter 4

'You're late,' Tara said as I rushed into The Vine that evening. She was sitting at the end of the bar, reading a book. There was one customer, a man who was hunched over a coffee in the corner, looking glum.

'Are you busy?' I said, glancing round the empty bar in an overdramatic fashion.

Tara raised a well-groomed eyebrow.

'Sorry, sorry, sorry. It's been a bit of a day.' I was still wearing my bike helmet and my cagoule, so I began unzipping my jacket as I went towards the tiny back room where we stashed our belongings.

I threw my coat and my rucksack inside, then I took off my helmet and balanced it on top, checked my reflection briefly in the mirror on Tara's desk, and quickly pulled out my ponytail and brushed my hair with my fingers.

'Were you at Tall Trees today?' Tara asked as I emerged from the office, twisting my hair up into a bun because it was tangled and knotty from my helmet and the rain and my fingers couldn't make it look better. I nodded.

'How's your nan?' The word sounded funny in her drawling Californian accent, but I quite liked it. I shrugged.

'Same,' I said.

'Did she ask about Max?'

I pinched my lips together and nodded again.

'Don't you think you should tell her the truth?'

'No,' I said feeling very tired suddenly. 'I don't want to upset her.'

'I don't see why you have to cover for him.'

'I'm not doing it for him.'

'Good,' Tara said. She didn't think much of my dysfunctional family, which I quite liked. She was protective of me and I appreciated it. 'What did you say to your nan?'

I held my hands out, showing that I was at a loss. 'I just said he was away.'

'It's not an outright lie,' she said with a small smile. 'But that's tough for you. I'm sorry.'

'It's fine,' I muttered.

Tara's expression darkened briefly. 'What does your dad say?'

'He just pays the Tall Trees invoices,' I said with a barb in my voice. 'He doesn't get involved in the emotional side of it. Things have always been tricky with him and Nan. Since my mum sodded off anyway. And now he says it's too risky to come home in case he ends up inside, like Max.'

Tara rolled her eyes. 'He's such a drama queen. What exactly has he done wrong?'

I hauled myself up on to a stool next to her and rested my chin in my hands. 'Not a clue,' I said. 'Fiddled a bit of tax, perhaps? He lost his business but a lot of that was because he bailed Max out and paid a fortune for his solicitor and that. I'm not completely sure it was all legit but I think the worst that would happen is that he'd get a big bill. He's hardly Donald Trump.'

'It's an excuse?' Tara said.

'Probably.' I sighed. 'At least he came back for Max's trial.' I closed my eyes briefly, remembering how my parents hadn't even put their differences aside to support their son in court. Not that it had been the first time he'd been in the dock, but this time we knew he wasn't going to get off with a slapped wrist.

My mother had shown up wearing drapey white trousers, a floaty shirt and sandals even though it was November. She'd not said a word to anyone – not even me – when she arrived but when Max had come into the court, flanked on either side by the security officers, she'd gasped loudly and theatrically, and stood up, clasping her hands to her chest. My father's face had grown red and his eyes bulged a bit and he'd started muttering about "what gives her the right" and "she would have walked past him in the street" which wasn't entirely true, but felt it.

Before Dad exploded and got himself arrested, I had edged over to Mum on the shiny wooden bench where families sat, and gently made her sit down. She'd sat with her eyes closed throughout the whole thing, and I'd fixed my gaze on Max, willing him to glance in my direction. But he didn't look up. Not even when he was taken away to the cells. Afterwards, when we loitered outside the court building, like awkward strangers, my mother looked at me properly for the first time.

'Stephanie,' she said. She gave me a tight hug, her bangles jangling, and said: 'How did this happen?'

But I thought what she was really saying was: "How could you let this happen?"

Even though she clearly blamed me for Max's "troubles" as she called them, I was pleased to see her. I clung on to her, desperately, because she was still my mum and I'd not seen her for so long. But she'd carefully backed away from my embrace. 'I can't stay here,' she'd said, looking round at my dad and his partner Chrissy, talking to Max's – very expensive – solicitor.

'I need to be alone,' Mum added. She was like that, my mother. Ethereal. Impossible to pin down. She had never been one to go along with the normal trappings of everyday life or to be bothered by things like parents' evenings, or graduations, or court cases. 'This is not where Max would want me to be.'

And I'd nodded, sympathetic even though I thought Max didn't really care where she was. I wanted to go with her, away from this murky autumn street, and the people in suits spilling down the stairs of the court building. Away from the guilt. But I knew if I asked to go with her, she'd say no, and that would be worse than not asking at all. So I'd watched her leave, wafting down the dingy street like a shaft of sunshine breaking through a cloud. It reminded me of when teenaged Max and I had pressed our noses to the living-room window and watched her dance down our front path with a rucksack and her passport in her hand.

'I need to be me,' she'd told Dad at the time. 'Not a mother, and certainly not a wife.' She'd not even looked up at us though I was pretty sure she knew we were watching.

Of course Max had thought it was brilliant. 'Yes, Mum,' he'd breathed, doing a little air punch. He'd always been far more accepting of her "free spirit" than I was.

I had watched from outside the court, as she reached the end of the street, where she climbed into the passenger seat of a battered camper van parked in a disabled space, and embraced the driver who was wearing a cowboy hat and looked vaguely like our old next-door neighbour Graham. I'd not seen her since.

'What about your mum?' Tara asked, reading my mind. 'Could she help with your nan?'

I snorted. 'She never liked Nan anyway,' I said. 'Which was a bit rich, to be honest, seeing as Nan was the one who looked after us when she went off to find herself.'

Tara looked at me carefully, like she was weighing up what to say. Then she slid off her stool and took a step towards me. I held my hand out to stop her.

'Don't,' I warned. 'Don't. You know it'll make me cry if you're nice.'

'I wasn't going to be nice.'

I narrowed my eyes. 'You were going to hug me.'

'Was not.' She reached a hand out towards me and I batted it away.

'Stop it.'

'Stevie, Jesus. You've got something in your hair. I was just going to pick it out.'

'Really?'

'Really. I promise not to be nice to you, okay? God forbid I show you a bit of affection.'

I gave a small laugh. 'Sorry,' I said. I leaned my head towards her. 'Go on, pick it out.'

Tara reached out her hand again and yanked a strand of my hair.

'Ow!' I jerked my head away. 'No need to be so heavy-bloody-handed.'

She grinned. 'Got it,' she said holding up her fingers so I could see.

'And half my hair.' I clasped my head. 'What is it?'

Tara rubbed her fingers together. 'Oh my God, Stephanie Barlow,' she said in wonder. 'It's paint. Have you been painting? This is brilliant.'

'Don't get excited,' I warned her. 'It's emulsion. I've been painting a wall.'

Tara went round to the other side of the bar and washed her hands in the metal sink. 'I thought you were a carer, not a handyman.'

The gloomy customer had finished his coffee and was heading to the door, just as a group of women who I recognised as teachers from the local primary school came in. It was Friday so I knew we'd be busy and I was glad we'd had a chance for a break before things got too hectic.

'I am a carer.'

'Then why …'

'Painting over some graffiti,' I said. I stood up and went to get the empty coffee cup and give the table a wipe while Tara served the teachers who all greeted her like an old friend.

The Vine had once been a run-down backstreet boozer whose only regulars had been a bedraggled stray cat and an elderly lady called Vera, who came in every day for three neat whiskies and then left again showing no signs of being any the worse for the drinks. It had been owned by Tara's ex-husband and when they divorced, instead of packing her bags and heading back to the Californian sun – which was totally what I'd have done – Tara had negotiated for him to sign over The Vine to her, and stayed put in this rainy corner of South London. She'd transformed the place and made it a quirky bar with good drinks – and enough craft beer to attract a hipster crowd. I'd been working there since I was at college and Vera – who still came in every day but who had taken to drinking artisan gin instead – was the only customer. So I'd been thrilled when Tara took over. She was like my boss, my best friend and my favourite auntie all rolled into one. And it seemed the customers felt the same way I did.

'Can I have the key?' Micah was standing at the end of the bar, managing to look awkward and bullish at the same time.

I turned to him. 'Please?'

'Please can I have the key, so I don't have to spend all evening listening to my mum and my sister talking about *Love Island*?'

'Shouldn't you be hanging out in the park and drinking cider?' I dug my hand into my pocket and found my keyring, then began sliding my bike lock key off it so I could get home later.

'I'm a teenager, not a tramp,' said Micah. He held out his hand. 'Please.'

'Don't make a mess.' I held the keys over his palm. 'And no booze.'

He gave me a look of total disdain. 'I'm going to be gaming.'

'Fine. Unplug your thingy when you're done. And don't put your feet on the coffee table.'

'It's a PlayStation. And your coffee table is an old trunk you nicked from my dad's garage.'

'I like it and I don't want your feet on it.'

'Okay,' he said reluctantly.

I dropped the keys into his hand and to my surprise he gave me a very quick hug, which was mostly elbows. 'Thanks, Steve,' he said.

'Stevie,' I called to his retreating back. He ignored me.

'You're too good to him,' Tara said disapprovingly, watching on from the other end of the bar.

'He's a nice kid.' I looked out of the front of The Vine where Micah was slouching along the road, hunched down in his hoodie even though it was quite warm now the rain had stopped. 'I don't think he's very happy. He's kind of tightly wound and he doesn't seem to have any friends.'

Tara frowned. 'He's not Max,' she said. 'You don't have to rescue him.'

'I know that. That's not what this is. Don't make it weird.'

She held my gaze defiantly and I looked away. She was sort of right. Max had a wild side. He was reckless and sometimes self-destructive – very much like our mother – and I'd spent my life trying to fix his mistakes. And now he was someone else's problem and I wasn't quite sure what to do about that. I swallowed.

'It's getting busy,' I said, hoping Tara would leave me alone. She glanced at the customers choosing where to sit and turned her attention back to me.

'Sooo,' she said. 'Now you're painting again …'

'I'm not painting again; I painted over some rude graffiti at Tall Trees.'

Tara shrugged, as if to say it was all the same thing to her. She looked over to the customers who were still rearranging themselves and moving chairs around, then picked up her iPad from the side.

'Look at this,' she said, tapping the screen and turning it round for me to see.

'Community art grant,' I read aloud. 'Tara, this isn't really …'

'It's £10,000,' she said.

'What? Give me that.'

I took the tablet and in amazement read the notice. The local council had been given some Lottery money and wanted to spend it on an art project.

'Presents from the Past,' I read. 'Artists from the borough are invited to apply for this grant, intended to cover living expenses for four months.'

I made a "wow" face at Tara who grinned.

'You could live like a queen,' she said.

'I could pay off Max's credit cards.'

Tara snorted, showing me exactly what she thought of my darling brother who'd taken out not one but two credit cards in my name, and whose debts I'd been paying since he went to jail.

'What does Presents from the Past mean?' she said.

I scanned the page. 'The project has to be based on a story from the local area that is relevant to the past and the present,' I said. 'The rules are it has to be in a public space, or somewhere it can be seen by the public without payment.'

'You could do this,' Tara said.

'I don't know any stories from the local area.'

She shrugged. 'You've literally lived here your whole life. There must be something. Ask your nan.'

'I suppose …'

'And think what you could do with that money.' She looked at me intently. 'You could cut your hours at Tall Trees and concentrate on your art for a while. Get your mojo back.'

I bit my lip. My creativity had taken a nosedive, what with the trouble with Max, and Nan declining, and Dad moving to Portugal permanently.

I'd done an exhibition, not long before Max was arrested. Not on my own, of course, but with a few other young artists in a great space right in Central London. We'd attracted quite a lot of attention and I'd loved it. It felt like the start of something big. Like all my hard work was paying off.

But then Max had turned up at my tiny flat, begging me to let him stay. And of course I had, even though he was edgy and acting weird. And then one day I'd come home and found my flat trashed and my laptop, my TV, anything of any value, gone. Which wasn't much, to be fair, but it was everything I had.

And I had a horribly knotty suspicion that Max was behind it. But I'd had to tell the police, because I couldn't claim on the insurance if I didn't. And Max had vanished. His phone was unobtainable and I had no idea where he'd gone. I'd actually spent days worrying that he was dead. That he'd finally got on the wrong side of the wrong people and that was it.

But I'd carried on with my exhibition, telling myself Max would show up eventually because he always did. He didn't though. Not this time.

I'd been standing in the middle of the gallery, looking around with wonder at the walls where my paintings were hanging, and thinking that I'd finally made it, when the police had arrived. And for an awful, horrible, terrifying minute I thought they'd come to tell me Max was dead.

In fact, they'd come to let me know they'd picked Max up in a stolen car, with a fairly hefty amount of cocaine in his bag, and my laptop on the back seat.

He blamed me for it, of course. Told me if I hadn't reported the burglary to the police then he'd have been home and dry. He could have paid off his debts and started afresh.

'All you care about is your crappy painting,' he'd said. 'You've let me down.'

And everything had fallen apart after that. It was like all the years of worrying about Max had finally exploded. I'd always been anxious but now I struggled to get out of bed each day, crippled with fear about the possibility of bad things happening.

I didn't go back to the exhibition and I'd not had the energy to follow up any of the contacts I'd made. When my canvases – my huge abstract paintings – had come back from the gallery,

I'd stacked them in Bernie's garage and ignored them. That was months ago now, and it didn't seem like anything was changing any time soon. Ten grand, though ...

'Applications have to be in by the end of the month,' I said. 'I can't do that. That's not long enough.'

'It's June 1,' Tara said. 'You've got the whole month. Why not just see if you can come up with some ideas? No pressure.'

I felt a bit sick at the thought, but I nodded. To my relief someone approached the bar and I leapt over to serve him.

'I'll think about it,' I said to Tara. 'What can I get you, sir?'

Chapter 5

Elsie

1940

I wrote to Violet's children the next day, sitting in the staffroom at work watching out of the window as porters put new beds into the huts they'd built in the grounds of the hospital.

'*Your mother was worried you'd wonder why she wasn't writing, so I wanted to let you know she is all right. I'll write again when I know where she is and you can send her all your news,*' I wrote.

I checked my watch. I had a while before my shift began; I'd come to work early in an attempt to avoid Jackson. I didn't want to be rude to him, but I didn't want to see him either.

I put the letter into an envelope and sealed it, then I wrote the address on the front, checking it carefully to make sure I'd not spelled the unfamiliar Welsh words wrong. I intended to post it on my way home, so I put it into my locker for now. Then, still with time to kill, I wandered over to the window, watching the activity below. The new huts would give us another two wards, judging by the size of them. I wondered if we'd get more nurses to cover them, or if we'd all be spread even thinner.

'They're for soldiers,' said a voice behind me. I turned to see Nelly, her cheeks flushed.

'Where have you been, Nell?' I'd not seen her since yesterday. I gave her a good-natured shove. 'I was worried.'

'Were you?' She clutched her chest dramatically. 'Sure that's the nicest thing you've ever said to me.'

I made a face. 'Well, maybe not worried. Interested.'

Nelly stuck her tongue out at me. And I laughed, pretending to think. 'Actually, interested is a bit strong. Mildly distracted maybe.'

'So you don't want to know where I was?'

I feigned indifference for about three seconds, then caved. 'Well of course I do,' I said, clutching her arm. 'Were you with Dr Barnet?'

'I was,' she said. 'He's a dream.'

'He's a rat.'

'I'm not marrying the fella. He's just a bit of fun.'

'Really?' I said doubtfully, because the look in her eyes told me otherwise.

'He says he's never met anyone like me before.'

'Since the last girl.'

She prodded me. 'Ah stop it, will you? He's a good man.'

'With a terrible reputation.'

Nelly rolled her eyes. 'He gave me a book.'

'A book?'

'Of poems.' She looked triumphant. 'Love poems.'

'Bleurgh.'

'You have a heart of stone, Elsie Watson.'

'Is he coming to the dance?'

'He's swapped his shift,' she said in triumph. 'Because of me.'

I was a bit disappointed because I wanted to have fun with Nelly at the dance, not spend the whole night feeling like a gooseberry, but I didn't say anything because movement down below caught my eye. 'Look,' I said. 'They're taking in the bedclothes. The patients must be arriving soon.'

'Already? Can you see them? Are they soldiers?'

I laughed at her eager expression. 'Aren't you supposed to be swooning over Dr Barnet?'

'Hedging my bets,' she said, shoving me out of the way so she could see out of the window.

'Nurse Watson and Nurse Malone?'

We both stood to attention as Matron appeared in the doorway. 'Nice to see you here so early. Do you have some time before your shifts begin?'

'We do,' I said, nodding.

'Then could you go down to the huts please? The patients are arriving and the beds aren't yet made. It's all hands on deck to get things ready.'

'Of course,' I said as Nelly added: 'Absolutely.'

'Thank you.' She gave us both a small smile as we passed her in the doorway. 'Airmen,' she said. 'There was a bomb at Biggin Hill.'

'Lord, was it bad?'

Matron nodded. 'Quite a few killed as far as I know. We mostly have the walking wounded though.'

I felt dizzy for a second thinking about the loss of those lives. Men cut down before they even got started living. I steadied myself on the doorframe and Nelly, bless her, obviously realising how I felt, took my arm and hurried me down the corridor.

'Airmen,' she said, as we went, fanning herself with her hand.

'Nelly Malone, you are incorrigible.' But I was laughing. I was so grateful to her for being there and letting me lean on her – physically and mentally.

'They'll be fun to have around.'

'They're injured, Nelly.'

'Ah didn't Matron say they were the walking wounded? They'll be up for some fun, I've no doubt.'

She was right. The airmen were arriving as we were making

the beds, tossing pillows and sheets to each other in well-practised fashion. They were battered and bruised, there was no doubt. I heard someone say they'd been dug out from under the rubble and it was clear they'd been through the wringer. Some of them were on crutches, some had broken limbs – quite a few had both arms broken. A few were quiet and still, lying on trolleys outside the hut while they waited for their beds to be ready. They were accompanied by a handful of Red Cross nurses who were efficient and jolly and who, they assured us, would be looking after this bit of the hospital.

As Nelly had predicted, most of the patients were in good spirits. Shouting support as we threw bundles of bedding to each other and spread sheets smooth, and making cheeky comments whenever one of us bent over.

'We'll have none of that, thank you,' said one of the Red Cross nurses firmly, removing a wandering hand from her behind. 'You behave as though we were all your mothers or your sisters, or we'll turf you out on the streets and see how well you fare left to your own devices.'

'Sorry,' the airman muttered, looking suitably chastened. I felt a bit sorry for him. He was so young, and one side of his face was in shreds – bandaged but clearly causing him a lot of pain.

'Here, your bed's ready,' I said, pulling back the sheets and helping him up. The whole side of his body was bandaged but I could see blood seeping through. I caught the eye of the Red Cross matron and she gave me a little nod to show she knew.

'Thanks, Nurse,' the airman said. I plumped up the pillow behind him and resisted the urge to pull him into a hug. These lads had given so much. Just like my Billy. And they may have been in good spirits now, giddy with the adrenaline of being survivors. But I knew that when darkness fell the nightmares would come. Or the guilt of having made it out alive when so many others – so many of their friends – hadn't. So I didn't hug the lad, but I smiled at him and he smiled back.

'Did you write to those kids?' Nelly asked me as we moved on to making up the next bed.

'I did. I'll post it on the way home tomorrow morning.'

'That's a good thing you've done there,' she said, shaking out a sheet and deftly folding it under the end of the bed. 'Getting that message will mean so much to them.'

'Did you send someone a message?' asked the cheeky airman. 'Could you send one for me?'

'You can send your own, you lazy oaf,' I said.

'*I* can't,' another airman said. He was being helped into bed by one of the Red Cross nurses. He had both arms in plaster and one leg was bandaged too. 'Is that what you do? You write messages for people?'

'No,' I said. 'I did it for one patient who needed to let her kids know where she was.'

'But you could do it for me?' he said. 'Just a quick note for my mum? They'll have told her about the bomb and she'll be so worried.' He had a nice face, this chap. Warm and friendly, with furrows between his brows. 'My uncle was killed, you see? Her brother. Last time round. She'll be thinking the worst.'

I felt myself soften at the thought of his poor mother worrying, so I checked my watch. 'I can't do it now because my shift is about to start,' I said. 'But you'll be here a while, I assume? I'll come back and you can tell me what to write.'

'Would you really?' He gave me a beaming smile that made my stomach turn over in a rather pleasing way. 'Promise?'

'What's your name?' I asked.

'Harry.'

'I promise, Harry.'

'What about me?' Across the hut, another man was looking concerned. 'Could I write something?'

'Well, of course you can. That's nothing to do with me,' I said. He was one of the less injured men, with just cuts and bruises as far as I could see.

'I know. But I'll be going back before I know it, won't I?'

'And?'

'And when the bomb hit, I thought about all the stuff I'd not said. All the things I wanted to tell my wife, and my dad. Even my sister. I had so much I wanted to say to her. I just thought maybe I could write it down for you and I don't know, perhaps you could keep it safe. Just in case …' He rubbed his nose. 'Nah forget it. I'm just being sentimental, that's all.'

I sat down on the edge of the cheeky airman's bed, clutching a bundle of sheets. Nearby Nelly stood, watching me carefully. 'No, you're not,' I said in a slightly shaky voice. 'I think that's a lovely idea.'

Suddenly there was a clamour of voices.

'My house was bombed and I don't know where my wife is. Can you get a message to her?'

'I want to write down what happened before I forget everything. For my kids to read later.'

'Can you get a letter to my girl?'

And then the sentimental chap spoke up, his voice clear over the hubbub. 'Will you help us?'

'What's your name?' Nelly said to him.

'Davey.'

'Davey, we're really busy as you can imagine. But I promise, Elsie and I will do whatever we can.'

'We will,' I agreed. 'Honestly.'

I met her glance over the bed and she smiled at me. 'It's important,' she said.

*

I didn't have a chance to think about the messages during my shift because it was another awful night of raids but when I was walking home from the station – alone because poor Nelly had been held back to aid in the operating theatre and very slowly

44

because my legs were aching after another night on my feet – I wondered if it was even possible to help these men. I popped the letter to the children into the pillar box and walked on. They all wanted different things, I thought. Messages to their wives or their girlfriends, memories recorded, final thoughts before they went back to fight. It just didn't seem like something we could do. I shook my head, concentrating on putting one foot in front of the other. I was so tired the pavement was swimming in front of my eyes and I was desperate to get to bed. I couldn't think about this now. Once I'd had some sleep and some food, I'd be in a better position to come up with a plan. Perhaps.

I turned the corner into our street and almost cried to see Jackson sitting on the wall outside our house. I didn't want to see him now. Didn't want to deal with his inane chat when all I could think about was climbing into bed.

I wondered wearily if I could avoid him somehow, but my legs were still carrying me towards him and I couldn't stop.

'Elsie,' he said, spotting me and jumping to his feet. 'I've been so worried about you. I didn't see you leaving yesterday, so I knocked on your door and you didn't answer.'

I looked at him through drooping eyes. 'I was at work.'

'I know that, silly. Did you change your shifts?'

I shook my head, feeling my hair coming loose from its pins. I must look a right state, I thought. Dusty smudges on my face and arms, mucky uniform, a ladder in my stocking. But Jackson was looking at me fondly.

'You look so tired,' he said. 'Are you getting enough rest?' He reached out and tucked the loose strand of hair behind my ear, letting his fingers brush my cheek as he did. I froze. I didn't want him to touch me. I didn't want him near me. But how could I say that? He was just looking out for me.

'You're so pretty, Elsie,' he cooed. 'You'd be even prettier if you smiled more.'

'I have to go to bed,' I said. My mouth was dry with discomfort.

'I could come with you,' Jackson said, then he gasped and put his hand over his mouth in an overexaggerated fashion. 'Not like that, Elsie. I meant to check you get in all right. I didn't mean anything untoward.'

But the way he looked at me suggested he meant exactly that. My heart began to beat a little bit faster because I wanted rid of him and I didn't have the energy to tell him to leave.

'I'm very tired, Jackson,' I said weakly.

'Elsie! Oh, thank goodness!'

I looked round to see Mrs Gold hanging out of her living-room window on the ground floor of our maisonette. She was wearing a dressing gown and she had a headscarf covering her hair. 'Elsie, could you help me?'

Next to me, Jackson stood up straighter, his chest puffed out. He had heard a woman ask for help, and he was ready to answer the call. I wanted to cry because I knew he was getting ready to go inside and then I'd never get rid of him.

'What can I do?' he said in a slightly deeper voice than he usually used.

'Oh, thank you, darling,' said Mrs Gold. 'But it's Elsie I need.' She bit her lip and gave Jackson a meaningful look. 'It's women's troubles.'

Jackson stepped back like she'd hit him.

'I'm coming,' I said. I darted round the side of Jackson and up the path before he could stop me, then I let myself into the front door and slammed it shut, leaning against it to catch my breath. Mrs Gold appeared in the hallway, next to her own front door.

'Are you all right?' she said.

I made a face. 'Yes, are you? You said you needed help?'

'I'm absolutely fine.' She took off her dressing gown revealing she was fully dressed underneath, and then peeled off her head-scarf too. 'I thought you needed an excuse.'

I stared at her in astonishment. 'I really did.'

She draped the dressing gown over her arm and smiled at me

in a conspiratorial fashion. 'Men like that are terribly scared of the workings of women,' she said. 'I knew if I looked like I'd just come out of the bathroom, he'd scarper.'

'You're amazing,' I said in awe.

'You're tired. Off to bed.'

I nodded. 'Thank you.'

She waved a hand like it was nothing and I started climbing the stairs to our flat, pulling myself up on the bannister.

'Mrs Gold,' I said, turning to her. 'Do you think it's important for people to say things? Before they die?'

She looked up at me, her blonde hair shining in the light of the hallway. 'I suppose it depends who they are, and what they want to say.'

'My brother Billy died,' I said suddenly. The Golds hadn't yet lived downstairs when I got the telegram and I'd never mentioned it. 'And Jackson – the chap outside – he says Billy asked him to look after me.'

'Did he?'

I sat down on the middle step with a thump. 'Not really. I think Jackson offered and Billy just said yes in a kind of jokey way. But then he died and now Jackson seems to have this idea that he's my guardian angel.'

Mrs Gold rolled her eyes.

'I'm angry that Jackson spoke to Billy after I did,' I admitted. 'And these men at work – airmen – they want me to keep messages for them, for their families in case they don't come back. And I know how much that would mean to them, but I feel a bit ...'

'Resentful?'

'That's exactly it. I didn't get a message from Billy – I just got Jackson. And I know I'm being petty but I feel rotten about helping other people.' I leaned back against the worn stair carpet. 'Gosh, that's awful. I'm awful.'

Mrs Gold came round to the staircase and sat down on the bottom tread. 'I don't think you're awful; I think you're sad.'

I nodded. 'I'm so very sad.'

'Maybe writing these messages for your men would help you feel less sad?'

I gave her a tiny smile. 'They're not my men.'

'It might help.'

'It might.'

She reached up and patted my leg. 'But for now, you have to sleep. Go on. Up to bed with you.' She sounded so much like my mum that for a second I was dizzy with sadness and loss, but then I heaved myself to my feet and smiled.

'Thanks,' I said.

Chapter 6

Stephanie

Present day

I couldn't stop thinking about the ten grand. I didn't have any trouble sleeping usually, but that night it took me ages to drop off, because I kept doing sums in my head, and working out what I could do with the money. Or at least the bit of the money that was meant to be for my living expenses. The luxury of not having to count every penny was very tempting indeed.

I had been so distracted that I hadn't even minded that Micah was still in my flat when I got home, not long before midnight, and the whole place smelled of pepperoni pizza.

'Can I leave it all plugged in?' he asked, turning off his console. 'I'm playing again in the morning.'

'Here?' I leaned over him and took a piece of cold pizza from the box next to him on the sofa. 'You're playing in my flat on my day off?'

He shrugged. 'Didn't think you'd mind.'

I tried to mind but I was too tired. I shoved some more pizza into my mouth. 'Go home, Micah,' I mumbled.

As soon as I got into bed, though, I couldn't sleep. It was raining again, hammering down on the flat roof above my head. 'Ten thousand pounds,' I heard in the rhythm of the drips from the blocked gutter. 'Ten thousand pounds.'

If I had the grant money to live on, I could use my salary from Tall Trees and The Vine to pay off Max's debts. My debts, actually, seeing as he'd taken out the credit cards in my name. I could even reduce my hours at Tall Trees a bit to concentrate on the community art project and maybe if I was forced to paint again, then I would eventually start doing my own work. The thought made me feel scared but also a little bit excited.

I'd not painted since Max stole all my stuff. It was like as soon as he landed in my life again, all my creativity just drained out of me. Back then I'd been working – I had a proper job, teaching art classes at a local adult education centre. Because I got free classes as a perk of my job, I'd been taking counselling lessons and I'd been thinking about training in art therapy. Which now seemed completely ironic as if anyone was in need of therapy, it was me.

Then though, I had studio space at the education centre, which was a huge Victorian school building with high ceilings and amazing light. I'd done one small exhibition, where I'd sold a satisfactory amount of paintings, and then landed the bigger one in the centre of London. Things were going well.

And then Max landed on my doorstep and I was furious with him. Because he always did that. He always arrived at my door when he needed me to bail him out or to lend him money or to give him somewhere to sleep for a week before he sodded off again. But this time, I felt in control – like a proper grown-up with a job and a plan and I didn't want him to mess it all up for me.

I let him stay but I made sure he knew I wasn't happy about it. I said some awful things to him about his selfishness and the way he used me. So when I rang the police about my burglary, he was convinced I'd done it on purpose – that I'd got him banged up to get him out of my life.

And the awful thing was, I thought he might be right.

But after that my life gradually fell apart anyway. Not all at once. It just happened slowly and because I was worrying about Max and feeling guilty, I found I didn't have the energy to stop it. I knew it sounded pathetic, but it was like I didn't have the strength to hold everything together.

First of all, I didn't follow up on my exhibition because I couldn't bear to go back to the gallery. I kept thinking about the police officers showing up and the lurch of fear that Max was dead and the last thing I'd have said to him was that I wanted him out of my life.

And then there was the guilt of knowing he wasn't dead but he was in prison because of me. The weight of it all meant I didn't show up to the many press evenings, launches, parties and viewings. I missed all the chances to make contacts and spread the word about my art.

I found that I couldn't quite bring myself to apply for my teaching post for the next academic year. We always had to sign up before the holidays to say we were available next term. It was a formality rather than anything arduous. We said what courses we could teach, and the hours were shared out. But it was just after Max had stolen all my stuff, and the anxiety that had always fluttered around inside me since I was a little girl grew stronger and made me weaker and I didn't do it. So I didn't get a course to teach, and I couldn't carry on with my therapy lessons, and suddenly I didn't have enough money coming in to pay my rent.

When I swallowed my pride and rang my dad and told him I was going to be evicted and could he lend me some cash to tide me over, he said no. He had a bit of a cash-flow problem himself, he said, because he'd been helping Max and solicitors didn't come cheap, you know.

But thankfully, he sorted out my room over Bernie's garage,

which meant when I found out about Max's credit card debt, I didn't have to move again. Instead, when I was visiting my nan, I spotted an ad for a carer's position at Tall Trees and I got the job. So with that and my shifts at The Vine, I kept my head above water. Just. But my creative spark, my ideas, my love of art, had all vanished.

I shifted in bed, listening to the rain pattering down on the roof. Perhaps this grant was just what I needed to give me a kick up the bum. Get me going again. The only problem was the application form asked for a lot of details and I didn't have any ideas. Not one. I wasn't even sure what "Presents from the Past" really meant.

Outside I could hear shouts and laughter as a group of loud drinkers went past. I put the pillow over my head. What kind of weirdos stayed out so late in the pissing rain? I thought. Clearly they were up to no good. Probably they were heading to Tall Trees to write rude slogans on the wall I'd painted over earlier.

With my head still under the pillow, I gasped. The wall at Tall Trees! I pulled my head free then sat up, hugging the pillow to my chest, and feeling my heart beating a little bit faster. The bloody wall. It was easily seen from the road, so it was definitely public. And it was like a blank canvas, just waiting to be painted over – as the local graffiti "artists" kept proving. Could I use that for a community art project? Paint a huge mural perhaps? I loved working on a big scale, though my usual style was more abstract.

I thought for a moment, frowning in concentration and thinking about the phrase "Presents from the Past". It was like one of those advertising slogans that didn't mean anything, but perhaps I could design something based on the history of Tall Trees? I'd never been very interested in historical stuff but hadn't Mr Yin said Tall Trees was a hospital during the war? That was something. I could paint some poppies on the wall or a few soldiers. I leaned back against my headboard and closed my eyes. It would have to be more inventive than that, I knew; a £10,000 grant wasn't just going to be handed out to the first person who applied for it. And there was no guarantee Tall Trees would let someone like me scribble all over their property anyway. But perhaps I had the very beginning of an idea.

Despite the sound of the rain and the shouts that were now fading into the distance, I felt sleep creeping up on me. I wasn't working at Tall Trees tomorrow, but I thought I might go round anyway. I could see Nan, and have a look at the wall. Maybe once I was there, inspiration would strike.

*

And so, the next morning, I got on my bike and cycled through the quiet streets to Tall Trees. I didn't go inside at first. Instead, I stopped on the pavement outside. The home was behind a low wall, just a bit higher than my waist. It was easily jumped over, which was why the tempting white gable end got daubed in graffiti so often. Now I leaned my bike against the wall, put my hands on the top, and with a bit of effort, clumsily pulled myself up so I was sitting on it. Then I stood up and studied the gable end. It was the perfect place for a mural, I thought. It really was a blank canvas. It was visible from the street, and from every bus and car that went along the busy road. I stood on top of the wall with my hands on my hips and took it in. It was perfect. And also absolutely impossible. It was such a big space to fill – way bigger than the canvases I used to paint – and I had no ideas. Not one.

'Are you breaking in?'

I gasped at the interruption, wobbling on my perch, and luckily managed to keep my balance. Annoyed, I turned and looked down to see the floppy-haired man I'd seen in reception, grinning up at me. 'Are you casing the joint?'

'Busted,' I said. 'I'm planning on nicking a load of bed pans and flogging them down the Queen's Head.'

The floppy-haired man laughed loudly. 'You work here, don't you? I saw you the other day.'

'I do,' I admitted.

'But you're not working now?'

'I'm not.'

Fed up with balancing. I sat down with my legs dangling into the grounds of Tall Trees. To my surprise, the man clambered up on to the wall next to me and sat with his legs astride the wall.

'So what are you doing?'

In the face of such enthusiastic questioning, I could only tell the truth. 'I'm thinking about painting a mural,' I said.

'Brilliant,' He took his bike helmet off and ran his fingers through his hair, studying the gable end. 'It's the perfect place for a mural.'

'I know.' I was pleased by his approval.

'What will you paint?'

'Now that I'm less sure about,' I said, shaking my head. 'There's a community art grant up for grabs but I need some ideas. I thought if I came here and looked at the space then inspiration would strike.'

'Has it?'

'Nope.'

'I always think you have to let an idea settle into your mind,' he said. 'Don't think about it, and let it take root, and something will come to you when you least expect it.'

He rested his bike helmet on the top of the wall and leaned on it, his eyes still fixed on the gable end, and nodded in appreciation. 'It's definitely a good spot.'

'It is,' I agreed. 'The only trouble is that it gets graffitied all the time. This wall is easy enough to climb over, as you can see.'

The floppy-haired man bit his lip thoughtfully, staring at the wall and the ground beneath, where there was an overgrown flowerbed that was always trampled under the feet of the graffiti artists. 'You need to plant some prickly bushes,' he said.

'The pricklier and bushier the better. That would stop people standing there.'

It was so simple that I couldn't believe no one had thought of it before. 'That's amazing,' I said. 'You're right.'

He smiled again, showing dimples in both his cheeks. 'Is that what you do here, then? Are you an art teacher? Or a therapist?'

'I'm a carer,' I said, feeling oddly like I'd let him down. So I added: 'I did teach art for a while, adult education classes. And I've thought about training to be an art therapist.'

'You should teach classes here,' he said, tilting his head towards Tall Trees. 'I reckon they'd love it.'

I glanced at him in astonishment. All these months I'd been coming here and that had never occurred to me. 'I might do that,' I said truthfully. I turned to face him. 'Who are you?' I asked. 'Besides some sort of good idea fairy?'

He let out his loud laugh again, and I found I was pleased to have amused him. 'Good idea fairy,' he said with a chuckle. 'I like that.' He stuck his hand out for me to shake. 'I'm Finn Russell. I'm a historian.'

I stared at him, unable to believe my luck. 'Are you serious?'

'Yes,' he said, a little uncertainly. 'You sound like my mother.'

'Do you know what "Presents from the Past" means?'

Finn frowned. 'Precious artefacts, like archaeological treasures?'

'Maybe.'

'Or lessons we've learned from history, perhaps?' He looked at me curiously. 'Why?'

'It's the theme for the mural I'm considering.'

'Ooh,' said Finn. 'Interesting.'

'Is it, though?'

He laughed again. 'It could be. There's so much to learn from the stories of the past.'

I liked his enthusiasm and I wondered if he was a teacher. Perhaps I'd be more interested in history if I'd had teachers like him instead of Mr Goodfellow who dictated passages from textbooks and made us write them into our books while we all quietly died of boredom.

'Is being a historian an actual job? Do you teach?'

'Now you really do sound like my mother. Yes, it's an actual job. I'm a lecturer at the university and I do my own research, too.'

'Into what?'

'The Second World War.' He looked pleased with himself. 'But not the battles or military strategy. I'm a social historian. It's the people I want to know about.'

'That sounds interesting,' I lied, because it didn't really. Then I frowned. 'So what's that got to do with Tall Trees? Why are you here?'

'Tall Trees was a hospital during the war. Did you know that?'

I almost laughed at the serendipity of it. 'I did actually. One of the residents was talking about it the other day.'

'It was what they called a casualty clearing station during the Blitz.'

'The Blitz?' I said, genuinely interested this time. 'We're quite tucked away here in suburbia, aren't we? Was this area badly bombed?'

'Yes and no,' Finn said. His eyes gleamed with enthusiasm in a way I found quite appealing. 'There were bombs dropped here. Sometimes the planes just dropped them on the way to Central London, or the way back. But often they were following the railway lines.'

As if on cue, a train rattled across the railway bridge just along from where we were sitting. We both laughed.

'This hospital was dealing with injuries locally, but it was also being sent casualties from the East End. The organisation was impressive.'

I looked over at the quiet building, trying to imagine it busy with doctors and nurses, and people with terrible injuries. It seemed a world away from how it was now.

'Were there trees?' I asked suddenly.

'Pardon?'

'It's called Tall Trees but there aren't any trees,' I said. 'Were there trees back then?'

'Actually, back then it was called South London District Hospital,' Finn told me. He looked at a spot somewhere over my head, obviously thinking hard. 'But I seem to remember there were trees, actually.' He swung his front leg over the wall and jumped down on to the ground. 'I've got some photographs. If you want to see them, I'll be around most of the day. They've given me a desk in the back office.' He gave me that broad smile again. 'Well, it's more of a cupboard really.'

To my surprise, I found I did want to see them. 'I'm not working today,' I said. Was it my imagination, or did Finn look disappointed? 'I should go and visit my nan though, as I'm here. Can I come and find you after that?'

He pushed his hair back off his face and smiled up at me.

'I'd like that.'

Chapter 7

Elsie

1940

The next week was one of the worst we'd had so far. There were raids every night. Terrible, awful raids leaving people burned and crushed and dead. Nelly and I, and all the nurses on our wards, worked long shifts, and even slept at the hospital a few nights because we couldn't leave in case we were needed. Nelly and I resigned ourselves to not going to the dance, because things were so bad we couldn't possibly take our days off.

'There will be other dances,' I said, hoping I was right. In these dark times, it was hard to remember what it felt like to have fun.

But finally on the fifth night, there was a respite. There was a raid but there were fewer planes and they came in up the river, so while we knew we would get casualties from the East End later in the night, for now things were calmer.

'Maybe even the Luftwaffe need a night off,' Matron said, looking serious despite her tin hat.

'Could I pop over to the huts if things are under control?' I asked. 'The airmen asked Nelly and me to write messages to their families for them and we've just not had a chance. I wanted to let them know we'd not forgotten.'

I thought Matron would say no, but she nodded. 'Go on then,' she said. 'Five minutes.'

The ward was quiet and dark when I arrived and the men were sleepy humps huddled under blankets. I rubbed my forehead feeling silly – day and night were all muddled in my head now because we'd been working such odd hours. I'd not expected them all to be asleep.

I tiptoed to the nurses' station and found one of the Red Cross nurses there, filling in a medication chart.

'I was here the other day,' I whispered, not wanting to disturb the slumbering men. She looked up at me and nodded in recognition.

'We were talking about writing messages for the men?' I said.

'That was such a kind offer.' She smiled at me. 'They've been talking about it a lot.' She glanced round to see if anyone was listening. 'It's been hard for them, these last few nights. A lot of them struggled when the bombs were falling nearby.'

'Gosh, I can imagine,' I said. 'We have patients the same. People who have been injured by bombs and then have to listen to the raids, feeling the beds shake as the bombs fall. It's so hard for them.'

The nurse nodded. 'They're good lads,' she said fondly.

I bit my lip thoughtfully. 'We'll definitely come back and write their letters for them,' I said. 'Nelly and I work the same shifts and we've got a couple of days off coming up. We'll come back then.'

'I think they'd like that.'

'Could you let them know? I don't want them to think we've forgotten them.'

'Of course.'

I turned to go and noticed one of the men was awake, sitting up in his bed watching us talking. It was the chap who had both arms in plaster and who'd told us his uncle had been killed in the last war. He smiled at me and I smiled back and felt a little tug of connection between us.

*

The smiling airman stayed in my thoughts the next day as Nelly and I got ready for the dance.

'Dr Barnet said he'd be there around eight o'clock,' she said, adjusting one of the grips in her hair as she stood in the doorway of my room. She looked beautiful, as always. Her dark hair was shining and there was mischief sparkling in her eyes. She was wearing a dark red dress that had once been mine, but suited Nelly perfectly.

'You look lovely,' I said with fondness. 'I never looked that good in that dress.'

Nelly gave me a twirl. 'You look lovely too,' she said. I was wearing a blouse with a skirt that swirled round my legs. It had once been two skirts but I'd unpicked the seams and stitched them together, making them billow in a most satisfactory way when I danced. I was rather pleased with myself because I wasn't very handy with a needle – at least, I'd not been before the war began. Now we were all being thriftier.

'I thought if we go to the pub soon, we could have a couple of drinks first before we go downstairs.'

'How many drinks are you planning to have?' I said, frowning at my reflection in the mirror in my bedroom. 'Why does my hair never go right when I want it to?'

Nelly came over to me and stood behind me as I sat at the dressing table. She twirled a lock of my hair round her finger and pinned it firmly into place.

'There,' she said, looking at me in the mirror over my shoulder. 'Perfect.'

I put my hand up and touched hers where it rested on my arm. 'Ready to have some fun?'

'I can't wait,' Nelly said with a little bubble of laughter. 'It's been so long.'

With a sudden flurry of excitement, we both gave our reflections one last approving glance, then we whirled round the flat, finding our bags and coats and scarves. It had been ages since we'd been out dancing. When the bombs started dropping everything stopped for a while. People were nervous about being out late, and at first we thought it would just be a couple of nights of raids. But it had been almost three months now of bombings and sirens and there seemed to be an urgency among people to get on with living their lives. I understood that. When you were surrounded by death and destruction every day it seemed important to make the most of the time you had.

The Pig and Whistle was a large pub on the corner of two roads. I'd been in there with Billy before he went off to fight and as we approached it, I felt my steps slowing.

Nelly, who had her arm looped through mine, realised I was drawing back.

'Thinking about your Billy?' she asked astutely.

'A bit,' I muttered.

'He loved a dance,' she said, which wasn't exactly true, but Billy had liked being with friends, having a drink, and chatting. 'We need to make sure we have some extra fun for him tonight.'

'We do.'

Hand in hand, heels clattering on the pavement, we danced across the road – the light from our torch bouncing – and into the pub.

Going from the dark and cold evening, into the cosy, warm Pig and Whistle made me feel like Alice arriving in Wonderland.

The pub was full of people our age and there was a real buzz of laughter and chatter in the air. I could hear the music playing downstairs in the cellar.

'There's a band,' I said in delight. 'A real band.'

Nelly grabbed my hand.

'Come on, let's get a drink before it gets too busy,' she said, pulling me towards the bar.

But I'd seen the back of Jackson's head. He was sitting at a table with an older man. I didn't think they were together, partly because they weren't talking and the older man was reading the newspaper, and partly because I never saw Jackson with anyone.

'Jackson,' I said in Nelly's ear. She looked in the direction I nodded and made a face. 'Let's go round this way,' I said, tugging her to the other side of the bar. 'I don't want to talk to him tonight.'

We ducked round a group of men in Army uniform and I hoped Jackson hadn't seen us.

*

The dance was wonderful. We had so much fun.

The cellar of the pub was enormous, with curved stone arches so there was plenty of space to dance. The landlord had put chairs and tables round the edge and even made a little stage out of wooden pallets. I thought he'd been very creative. The war was forcing people to adapt in ways they'd never have thought possible.

And there was a real band. Well, there was a pianist, and a drummer, and a woman singing who Nelly and I both agreed was simply marvellous.

'How did they get the piano down here?' I wondered aloud as we queued up for a drink. A man in the queue ahead of me turned and gave me a dazzling smile. 'They lowered it down on ropes, through the hatch where they drop the beer barrels.'

'How inventive.' I sighed.

'Fancy a dance later?' the man – who I recognised vaguely as one of the doctors from the hospital – asked.

'Why not?' I said and giggled as he blew me a kiss.

Nelly and I danced together at first, enjoying the music and the sheer thrill of not being at work.

Then Dr Barnet showed up and was actually much nicer off duty than he was on the ward. He was very handsome and clearly besotted with Nelly, and I found myself warming to him. He had lots of friends with him, who were all eager to dance so I found myself being whirled around the dance floor by a succession of chaps, which was enormous fun if a little exhausting. We drank some gin and the men had beer, and I saw a few friends from nursing training that I'd not seen for ages, and I was glad the music was too loud to talk properly because it meant no one would ask about Billy, so I didn't have to worry. All in all it was a lovely evening.

As the crowds in the basement began to thin out, the band struck up a slower song. Around me, couples found each other in the dim light and started to sway along with the rhythm. Feeling a little like a spare part suddenly, I sat down at the side of the dance floor. My feet were aching and I didn't really want to dance anymore. It was odd that despite all the men I'd spent time with this evening, the person I kept thinking about was the airman with the two broken arms and the sweet smile.

'Sitting this one out?' Nelly appeared next to me, with her face flushed and her eyes sparkling.

'I'm beat, and my shoes are rubbing,' I said, sticking one foot out in front of me. 'I honestly don't think I can dance another step.'

I smiled at her. 'It's been fun, hasn't it?'

Nelly sat down next to me and clutched my arm in excitement. 'Percy has asked me to go on somewhere with him and his friends.'

'Who's Percy?'

She nudged me. 'Dr Barnet,' she said, shaking her head at me. 'Percy.'

'Percy?' I raised an eyebrow. 'That's not as romantic a name as I was expecting. I thought he'd be called something like Humphrey.'

Nelly giggled. 'Humphrey?'

I laughed too. 'Errol?'

'Ah shush,' Nelly said. 'I like Percy.'

I looked over to where Dr Barnet was leaning against the wall of the cellar, gazing at Nelly with admiration. 'And he definitely likes you too.'

'Are you coming with us? Percy said he knows somewhere there's jazz and cocktails.'

'Really?' Our part of South London wasn't known for its fancy night spots.

'That's what he says.' Nelly stood up. 'Coming?'

I shook my head. 'I'm whacked, Nell. I think I'll just go home.'

'Want us to walk you back?'

'Nah, you go on. Have fun, be careful and go to a shelter if the siren goes.'

'Yes, Mammy,' she said. She bent down and kissed my cheek. 'Love you.'

'Love you, too.'

She dashed off and I found my coat and scarf draped over the back of a chair, and then – walking rather awkwardly on my sore feet – went up the stone steps from the pub cellar. As I reached the top, with a little lurch of annoyance, I remembered Jackson had been there so I scanned the room for him and there he was, standing by the door of the pub looking for all the world as though he was waiting for someone. Was he waiting for me? I wondered with a shudder.

Not wanting him to walk me home, but not sure how I'd get out of it if he spotted me, I darted round the bar and out of the side door of the pub. I'd walk the long way home. Go round the block and arrive from the opposite direction. My feet may have hurt, but the thought of walking further on my uncomfortable shoes was still preferable to Jackson taking my arm and making his odd comments.

I hurried down the street, flicking on my torch because it was so dark and for the first time, taking comfort in the blackout, which meant Jackson wouldn't be able to see me if he came out of the pub now.

It was freezing, the wind sharp on my cheeks, and I pulled my scarf up to cover my chin as I hurried along. I crossed the road, and turned right down the street opposite where there was another pub – a smaller, less well-heeled place than the Pig and Whistle. As I approached, hunched down against the cold, the door to the pub opened, spilling light on to the pavement, and out came a woman with a hat pulled down over her ears. She stood still for a moment, silhouetted in the light from the door, then unsteadily she began walking in the same direction as I was going, vanishing into the darkness as the door shut again.

But she looked familiar. Something about the way she held her head, even if she did look as though she'd had one too many. And I'd heard stories about lone women coming a cropper during the blackout. So I quickened my pace on my blistered feet and, knowing I was risking a telling-off if an ARP warden was around, I lifted the beam from my torch to see if I could spot the woman. She was standing on the corner, looking this way and that, clearly not sure where she was. As the beam of my torch hit her she raised her arms to stop the light dazzling her and I realised it was Mrs Gold, our neighbour.

'Oh,' I said in surprise, because she was standing very straight and upright, waiting to check for traffic before she crossed the road. She didn't look remotely unsteady now. 'Mrs Gold,' I said, lowering my torch beam so she could see. 'It's me, Elsie.'

'Elsie.'

I hurried over to where she stood. 'I thought you were the worse for wear,' I said. 'You looked a bit wobbly.'

She grinned at me. 'Not at all, darling,' she said, looping her arm through mine. I wondered if she'd been pretending to be tipsy and if so, why. But I didn't want to ask because I had a feeling she wouldn't tell me.

*

We walked home through the night, arm in arm and I filled her in on the dance and Nelly and Percy.

Just as we reached the front door, the siren began to wail.

'What good timing,' I said with a sigh. 'Is Mr Gold here?'

She shook her head. 'No. He was called away.' She looked a little fed up as she said it and I felt sorry for her. 'We should go to the shelter.'

'I need to take my shoes off.'

She rolled her eyes. 'Quickly.'

I pulled off my painful shoes and hurried upstairs in my stockinged feet, where I put on my wellington boots because they were easy, and headed back down. Mrs Gold was waiting obediently by the back door, looking worried.

'Sounds like it could be another bad one,' she said.

I shrugged as we made our way outside and into the safety of the shelter. They were all bad, I thought. We were just getting used to it. I wondered where Nelly was and if she was safe. I hoped Dr Barnet would look after her.

Mrs Gold settled down, and feeling the effects of the gin I'd drunk earlier, I got myself as comfortable as I could on the hard bunk. I went straight to sleep and when I woke up the next morning, Mrs Gold wasn't in the shelter anymore. She must have gone to work early. I got dressed, wondering for the millionth time exactly what it was my neighbour did.

Chapter 8

Stephanie

Present day

I slid down off the wall and wiped the dust from my hands on my thighs.

'She's not Irish is she?' Finn said.

'Who?'

'Your nan?'

'Nope, Londoner through and through. Why?'

Finn began wheeling his bike towards the entrance of Tall Trees and I followed.

'I met one of the residents the other day and you remind me a bit of her.' He looked over his shoulder and grinned at me. 'She wasn't impressed by my job either.'

'I wasn't not impressed. I just questioned whether it was, in fact, a job.' I frowned. 'She was Irish, this resident?'

Finn nodded as we went through the entrance of the home and I shut the metal gate behind us.

'There are no Irish residents,' I said.

'Well this lady was definitely Irish, definitely a resident, and definitely not happy to see me.'

'Oh,' I said, remembering my conversation with Cyril. 'I think she's new. Sometimes they're a bit prickly when they first arrive. It's no wonder really, it's scary for them. Like your first day at school but a million times worse. I usually try to find something they like, or something we have in common and use that to help them feel more at home. One of my ladies likes Earl Grey tea so I always bring her some teabags.'

Finn gave me a little sideways look that I couldn't quite read.

'That's kind,' he said. 'You're kind.'

I ducked my head, embarrassed by the praise. 'I need to go to the dementia unit,' I said. 'That's where my nan is.'

'Come and see me before you leave, and I'll show you those pictures.'

'Okay,' I said with a nod. 'I will.'

I pushed my bike to the rack and locked it up.

'Hey!' The shout made me turn. Finn was standing a little way away, shielding his eyes from the sun.

'You didn't tell me your name,' he called.

'You didn't ask.'

He laughed loudly again. 'What's your name?'

'Stephanie,' I said. 'But my friends call me Stevie.'

'See you later, Stevie.'

I waved to him and then I wandered up the path to the unit, to see my nan.

To my delight, today was one of my nan's good days. She knew who I was straightaway.

'Stephanie,' she said. I went to where she was sitting in her usual chair by the window. 'Hello, dear.'

I braced myself for the normal barrage of questions about Max, but it was my father who was on her mind today.

'Where's that useless dad of yours, eh?'

'He's in Portugal, Nan.'

'Portugal?' She looked pleased with herself and then she began singing about going to sunny Spain and clicking her fingers like castanets.

'That's right, Nan,' I said, laughing. 'Just about.'

She settled back in her chair. 'Useless.'

'Do you remember the Blitz, Nan?'

Nan turned her dark eyes to me and for a moment I thought she'd gone again. That happened sometimes – she'd have a period of being lucid and then it was like a cloud had descended and she was back to not remembering. And even when her mind was clear, her thoughts danced about. But then she nodded.

'I was only a nipper.'

'I know.' Nan had been born in 1935, so she would barely have started school when the bombs began falling. 'You stayed in London, though? You weren't evacuated?'

Nan shook her head. 'I stayed with my mum.' She laughed. 'She was a right piece of work. She went to prison.'

The word made me widen my eyes in alarm. Had she heard about Max and got confused?

'What? Your mum didn't go to prison.'

Nan folded her arms. 'Me and Auntie Sandra went to visit her.' She smiled fondly. 'You can't just take stuff that belongs to other people though. She needed to be punished.'

'She went to prison? Really?' I said. Perhaps Max's recklessness didn't come from our mother after all.

'My old mum could sell sand to the Arabs. My Geoff's the same.'

'He is,' I said. I had to be honest, she was right about my dad. He was a born salesman.

'We'll go to the bombsite and see what we can get,' Nan said in a sort of sing-song way, like she was talking to a child. 'See what we can sell.'

'Did your mum steal from bombed-out houses?' I asked. 'That's terrible.'

69

She gave me a sudden grin. 'I had a hat with a bow on it. I loved that hat.'

She put her hands on her head like she was putting on a hat, and I watched, feeling strangely disappointed. I liked the idea of the Blitz spirit and everyone being nice to everyone else. I had thought the war was all singing songs and eating powdered egg and huddling together in the tube. But times were tough back then. Perhaps people did what they had to do to get by.

Nan leaned forward and patted my hand. 'The horses all died,' she said.

I blinked at her, not knowing what she meant. 'Which horses?'

'In the dairy. The horses all died when the bomb fell. Lying there on the cobbles, they were.' Her eyes glazed over. 'I cried and cried.'

'I'm not surprised, Nan.' I wished I hadn't asked. 'That's awful.'

'I had a hat with a bow,' she said again.

'Sounds lovely.'

'Where's Max?' she asked suddenly. 'Is he coming to see me today?'

I shook my head, feeling sad. 'He's busy, Nan,' I said.

*

I stayed with Nan for a while, and I chatted about the flowers in the garden and the rain and everything that wasn't Max's whereabouts, and then I went to find Finn.

He hadn't been exaggerating when he said that he had a cupboard to work in. His cubicle, which was off the reception area of Tall Trees, fitted a tiny desk and that was it. He was surrounded by boxes, because clearly he was sharing his space with Cyril who was using it to stash supplies of loo roll and cleaning products and a broom.

I tapped on the door lightly and Finn, who was bent over a book with his back to me, turned round and smiled.

'Stevie,' he said, closing the book. 'Perfect timing.'

'Are you sure I'm not disturbing you?'

'Not in the slightest.' He gathered together some papers and a thick folder. 'Shall we go into the lounge? I can spread everything out on the table in there and the residents quite like seeing the pictures. It gets them talking and I love to hear their stories.'

I nodded, thinking how nice his enthusiasm was. It seemed a long time since I'd been so enthusiastic about anything. 'I was asking Nan about the Blitz earlier. She told me some things she remembered. She could tell me more about the bombs than she could about yesterday. But she was so young – she wasn't even at school when the war began.'

'There aren't many people left who were there,' Finn said, handing me a bundle of papers. 'Can you take those? That's why I love hearing these stories now because in a few years there will be no one left alive who can remember.'

'It's important,' I said, meaning it. 'We need to write this stuff down.'

We walked along the corridor to the lounge. Inside a few of the residents were watching *Cash in the Attic*, and a couple more were reading, or chatting quietly.

'Hello, Finn,' a resident called Kenny bellowed as we walked in. He was deaf as a post but he hated his hearing aids. 'How's that book on Millwall coming along?'

'Slowly,' said Finn. 'Very, very slowly.'

'Too busy writing about Charlton's glory days are you? Mind you, that won't take you long.'

'Rude,' Finn said mildly. Kenny chuckled in delight and I looked at Finn questioningly.

'Kenny's a Millwall fan,' he explained. 'And I'm Charlton.'

I grinned. 'You've found something in common,' I said. 'Like me and the teabags.'

'You're right.'

Finn put his papers down on the table and I did the same, then we both sat down and I looked at him expectantly.

He didn't disappoint me.

'Like I said, Tall Trees was originally the South London District Hospital,' he said. He opened one of the folders and took out a photograph. 'Here.'

I looked. There was the main building, looking very similar to how it did now, except the far side of the building looked different. And at the end, where the dementia unit now stood, was a row of very large poplar trees.

'Tall trees,' I said triumphantly. 'They must have cut them down to make space for the dementia unit.'

'I guess so.' Finn pointed to the part of the building that was different now. 'And this bit of the hospital fell down after a bomb.'

'Tall Trees was bombed?'

'Sort of.' He sat back in his chair and grinned at me. 'And that's why I'm here.'

'Spill.'

'A bomb fell on the road outside, in early 1941. The hospital's foundations became unstable. Word is that they'd dug out the basement to fit more beds down there or an operating theatre – I can't remember the details – and hadn't supported some of it properly. Anyway, that part of the building collapsed in on itself.'

'Oh gosh,' I said. 'Were the patients killed?'

Finn shook his head. 'By some miracle, not one patient was hurt. There was one chap who was injured and he did die later on but he was a member of staff, I think. And he was the only casualty.'

'That's amazing,' I said. 'It must have been very frightening.'

'Must have been.'

'So what's all this got to do with you?'

'When they rebuilt the damaged part after the war, they shored up the basement obviously, but they left the rubble as it was because it was too costly to dig it out again. A couple of years ago, they were renovating the home, and they considered expanding into the basement.'

I shuddered. 'Who'd want their room down there?' I said. 'I can't see that being popular with the residents. They all love looking out into the garden.'

Finn shrugged. 'That's probably why they decided against it. But as part of the plans, they had some of the rubble left over from the bomb cleared. And they found this.'

He opened the biggest folder and from inside he produced a large, A4-size book. It was bound with a stiff spine and thick covers – it looked like the old family Bible I remembered Nan having, or an old-fashioned photo album.

'What's that?'

'It's a sort of scrapbook.' Finn did a little bounce on his chair like an overexcited schoolboy. 'There was a nurse who worked at the hospital, whose name was Elsie Watson. She kept this note-book for most of the Blitz. As far as I can tell, she gave it to her patients and they wrote in it.'

'What did they write?'

'All sorts of things. Some of them wrote messages for loved ones. Others wrote down their memories of the time. They had huts here, round the back, where they looked after injured airmen from Biggin Hill.'

'Oh that's not far from here,' I said.

'Exactly. So they were in the hospital along with injured civil-ians and they all seem to have embraced the idea. A couple wrote poems. Or Bible verses. There are thank-you notes to the staff. Some of them drew pictures of the view from the windows or places they'd been.' He smiled at me. 'A few drew Elsie and the other nurses.'

'Oh my goodness,' I breathed. 'That's amazing.'

'I know.' Finn put his hand on the book in a territorial way. 'I've had a look through but I've barely begun to read all the notes inside. It's a treasure trove.'

'How did you get it?' I said.

'We just got lucky really. When the book was found by the contractors, they passed it to the bosses at Tall Trees – not Blessing, the people who run the company. And one of them is a bit of a history buff so he brought it to my department for us to have a look at. Obviously with everything that's happened recently, it's taken us a while to get it organised but now I've got my mitts on it.'

'So that's why you're here?'

'Yes. I could work in my office but I like being here. It makes it feel more alive. I'm planning to read the whole book and then maybe write my own book about it. There are so many stories in here just waiting to be heard.'

'What about the nurse?' I said. 'Elsie, did you say? Is she still alive?'

Finn shrugged. 'No idea.'

I was doing sums in my head. 'I suppose she could be over a hundred now.'

'Well,' said Finn slightly dramatically. 'No one really knows what happened to her.'

'What do you mean?'

'I mean, she kept this notebook through most of the Blitz and then she disappeared. I can't find a record of her.'

'Oh gosh, was she killed in an air raid do you think?'

'Maybe, but I can't find a death certificate.'

'So she could be alive.'

'I doubt it.'

'Are you going to track her down?'

He made a face. 'She's not important really. It's the letters and notes I'm interested in.'

'Poor Elsie,' I said. 'Aren't you curious about where she went?'

'A bit, but I've learned over the years not to get side-tracked,' he said. 'If I start looking for her, I'll end up down all sorts of rabbit holes and I'll never get my own research done.'

I thought about Max, who often went AWOL for weeks at a

time, and my mother, who was also fond of disappearing when things got difficult, and I wondered if Elsie was the same sort of person. Somehow I doubted it, but I found I wanted to know more about her.

'Maybe you could ...' I began.

'You're here again then, I see?'

I turned to see a woman with piercing blue eyes studying us.

'Hello again,' Finn said. He turned to me. 'This is Helen. I believe she's a new resident.'

'Hi, Helen.' I got to my feet and stuck my hand out to her. 'I'm Stephanie. I'm one of the carers.'

'Not in uniform?' She looked me up and down, and then – as though I'd passed some sort of test – she shook my hand with a firm grip.

'I'm not working today. I just came to visit my grandmother.'

She huffed as though that was terribly inconvenient. She was relatively young to be one of our residents. She only looked to be in her late seventies or early eighties and she was straight-backed and steady on her feet. Still, it wasn't for me to judge.

'How are you settling in?' I asked, giving her a cheerful smile.

'Fine thank you.' She turned away from me and focused on Finn. 'I wanted to use the table,' she said.

'Oh sure. We're pretty much done here anyway.' He began picking up his papers again. I was disappointed, because I'd been enjoying hearing him talk and I was itching to have a look inside Nurse Elsie's book. But now I'd seen what Finn was doing, I knew he would be around Tall Trees for a while to come.

With the table cleared, Finn stood up and Helen sat down. She got out a little box of note cards and a pen, and began writing. I looked at Finn and raised an eyebrow. The table we'd been using was a large one, used for buffets at birthday parties and occasionally for large jigsaw puzzles.

Finn gave me a little shrug of his shoulders. Clearly Helen wasn't impressed by his research.

'We'll get out of your way,' he said to her. She didn't respond. I gestured to the door. 'I'm going to get off. I'm working later.'

'I thought it was your day off?'

'I work at a bar too. The Vine. Do you know it?'

Finn looked blank and I grinned. 'It's not really a student place.'

'I'm not a student.'

'Whatever you say.'

He rolled his eyes and chuckled. 'Good luck with your plans for the mural,' he said. 'Let me know if you want to throw some ideas around. Sometimes it helps to have a sounding board.'

'That's nice of you,' I said, torn between wanting to spend more time with this cheerful, interesting man, and not wanting to talk about my art – or lack of it – ever.

'I'll be in my cupboard. Come and find me, any time.'

'All right then, Harry Potter,' I said. 'Maybe I will.'

Chapter 9

Elsie

1940

Nelly was smitten with Dr Barnet. Perfect Percy, as I liked to call him. I'd heard every detail of their evening listening to jazz. I'd heard how when the siren had gone, Nelly had thought they would go to the public shelter in the park, but Dr Barnet said no.

'I thought he'd lost his marbles,' she told me. 'But he said it wasn't safe. So he took me to the railway arches and there was a shelter under there. I didn't even know it existed.'

She looked dreamy for a second. 'And he wrapped me up in his coat to keep me warm and held me all night.'

She'd even given me chapter and verse on their first kiss. I pretended to be horrified, putting my hands over my ears and begging her to stop telling me all the details, but I liked it really. It felt normal. Like life before the war. And Nelly was so happy, and now I'd met Dr Barnet he seemed to be much less of a rat than I'd expected him to be given his handsome looks and charming manner. In fact, I couldn't help thinking it was all rather romantic.

'Do you know what Percy said, when he walked me home this morning?' she said. And, she was off again, telling me all the sweet nothings Percy had whispered into her ear.

*

There was still no sign of Mrs Gold, nor Mr Gold, when Nelly and I left the house later that day. We were going to the hospital, even though it was our day off, because I wanted to see the airmen and help them write the letters. Nelly had promised to help, too, though she was worried she'd be no use because her handwriting was untidy and she always splattered the ink.

I stayed quiet as Nelly chattered about Percy, feeling a little thrill when I thought about seeing the sweet smile of the airman – Harry – who wanted me to write to his mother for him.

At the huts, the airmen were all in rather raucous spirits. They cheered when we went inside, which made Nelly and I laugh. The Red Cross nurse rolled her eyes. 'Good luck,' she said.

I'd brought the writing paper so I pulled it out of my bag and waved it.

'We're going to write letters to your families for you,' I said. 'But only if you promise to behave.'

They all murmured their agreement and I turned to Harry, who had the bed closest to the door. 'Shall I start with you?'

'Yes please,' he said. 'Hello.'

'Hello.'

'I'm Harry.'

'I know,' I said. 'I'm Nurse Watson.'

'I remember you.' He smiled at me and his whole face lit up. He wasn't what you'd call handsome, not as such, but he had the loveliest smile and eyes that sparkled with fun. I had the strange thought that if I stayed here, looking at his face for the rest of my days, then that would be enough.

'You said you were going to come back and write a letter for me. I've been waiting.'

'Well, like I said, here I am. Ready to write.'

'Really?' He looked sweetly eager.

'Really.'

'You're like an angel,' he said. 'An angel sent from heaven to bring us joy.'

I looked at my watch. 'An angel who needs to be home before blackout, so we should probably get on,' I said briskly. Harry stuck his bottom lip out like a sulky schoolboy, though his eyes still flashed with mischief.

'Sounds like a plan,' he said. He had a northern accent and I liked the way it sounded. I gave half the notepaper to Nelly who went off to the other end of the ward to start writing, and I sat down next to Harry's bed.

'Fire away,' I said, then I winced. 'Sorry, that's an awful expression to use for you.'

He grinned. 'Don't worry.'

'I just meant what do you want to say?'

Harry thought. 'Dear Mum,' he dictated. 'I know you'll have heard that I was injured by the bomb at the base. But I wanted to let you know I am doing all right. There is a lovely nurse here called Nurse Watson who is writing this letter for me because my arms are both out of action, but hopefully not for long. Also ...'

'Hold on,' I said, writing as fast as I could and feeling my cheeks flush because he'd called me lovely. 'Let me catch up.'

Harry paused until I'd finished.

'Also, I saw a dog the other day who looked exactly like Macauley. It made me really homesick and I wished I was there with you to throw a stick for him on the beach.'

The sweet honesty of his words made my eyes prickle with tears. I kept my gaze fixed on the notepaper.

'Hope you and Dad are doing well. I miss you. Love, Harry.'

'Is that it?' I said.

'That's it. Oh no, hang on. Can you add a PS: I am looking forward to getting back into a plane.'

I wrote the PS then I held the letter up so he could read it and he nodded.

I slipped it into an envelope and Harry gave me the address in Lancashire.

'Are you really looking forward to getting back in a plane?' I asked as I tucked the letter into my bag carefully.

'So much,' Harry said. His whole face lit up. 'I love it.'

I shuddered. All I knew of planes were the ones that flew overhead every night, bringing fear and destruction. 'What's it like? Flying?'

Harry looked far away at a spot somewhere over my shoulder.

'It's magic,' he said, and I smiled because the dreamy way he spoke sounded like Nelly when she talked about Dr Barnet.

'Don't you get scared?'

'Sometimes. But that's all part of it.' He looked at me again. 'When I was little, my bedroom was right at the top of our house. And I'd sit by the window and watch the swifts riding on the thermals, swooping and diving, and I'd wish I could be like them. When war was declared I knew I wanted to fly. Most of the lads from school joined the Navy, because we'd grown up by the sea. But I wanted to be in the air.'

He gave me that sudden grin again. 'And I get right seasick.'

I laughed. 'Is it how you imagined?'

'Sometimes when I'm in the plane, it's like being one of those birds, and I want to scream with the joy of it,' he said. 'And other times it's so frightening I think I might faint.'

'But you don't.'

'I don't. Because we've got a job to do and what use would I be if I fainted, eh?'

'I think you're ever so brave.'

He shrugged, but he looked pleased. 'We're all doing our bit.'

I looked at the notepaper on my lap. 'You should write this

down,' I said. 'Write about what it's like to fly. Maybe when your arms are better you could start keeping a diary.'

'We're not supposed to,' he said, tapping the side of his nose. 'It's all top-secret business.'

I rolled my eyes. 'I don't mean sharing anything that would get you into trouble, I just mean writing about what it's like to fly. One day, when you're older, you might like to look back and remember. Or someone might.'

'Maybe,' Harry said.

'Oi, Harry, are you done?' the airman in the bed next to him called over. 'Stop taking up all this nurse's time. I need her to write to my Marjory for me.'

'Righto,' I said to him. I got up from the chair next to Harry's bed and picked it up to take it round to the other chap. Harry reached out his arm, stiffly because of the plaster cast, and put his fingertips on my hand. 'Thank you, Nurse Watson,' he said.

*

'He likes you,' Nelly teased as we walked home later. We were both feeling quite giddy because we'd written lots of letters for parents and siblings and sweethearts, and it had been emotional and heartbreaking but also really rather fun.

'Who likes me?' I said now, even though I knew who she meant.

'Harry, was it? The airman with the sparkly eyes.'

I snorted. 'They all look the same,' I fibbed. 'I don't know who you mean.'

'Sure you do,' said Nelly. 'I saw the way you looked at him, Elsie Watson.'

'Rubbish,' I said, but I couldn't hide my smile. We'd walked all the way home from the hospital because, though it was cold, it was bright and the sun was shining, and we weren't in a hurry for once. But the air was thick with dust from buildings and though we'd not walked far, my eyes felt gritty. As we turned the corner, we saw several houses that had taken a direct hit and been reduced to rubble.

'Jesus,' said Nelly looking at the pile of debris. 'Didn't whatsit from the hospital live round here somewhere? That doctor – what was his name now?'

I had no idea, so I just shrugged, finding it hard to tear my eyes away from the bombsite. A woman in a thin coat was standing on top of the rubble, a little girl by her side. She couldn't have been more than four years old, five at the most, and she was gazing round in wonder. She wouldn't remember a time before bombs, I thought. How awful that this was her childhood. As we walked by I saw something catch the little girl's eye. She bent down and when she stood up again, she was wearing a hat with a large bow on it and looked very pleased with herself.

I nudged Nelly. 'Look, she's found her favourite hat.'

Nelly smiled. 'That's sweet,' she said. 'Her mammy's found some bits too, see?'

The woman was rummaging through the debris, throwing small items into a suitcase she'd perched on the remains of a dining-room table. But as we went past, a shout from an ARP warden nearby made her look up.

'You there,' he yelled. 'Get out of it. This isn't your house.'

The woman shut the suitcase, took the little girl by the hand and hurried away. Nelly and I exchanged a glance.

'Thieves,' I said in disappointment.

'People are doing what they have to do,' said Nelly and I admired her empathy. She was so kind – always seeing the best in people.

As we got close to the house, I groaned. 'We've got no bread,' I told Nelly. 'We need to go to the shop.'

'I'll go and get some. I've got some other things to pick up, too.'

'If you're sure?'

'Course.'

She wandered off in the direction of the shops and I went inside the house.

Mrs Gold was in the hall. She was wearing her coat on her way in or out – I couldn't be sure. She looked pleased to see me.

'Thanks for keeping me company last night, Elsie,' she said.

'I was glad you were there. I don't like being in the shelter alone.'

We smiled at one another.

'Where have you been on your day off? Have you been up to something fun?'

'Nelly and I have been at the hospital,' I said. 'But not working.' I explained about us writing letters for the injured airmen and she beamed at me.

'What a marvellous thing to do. Well done.'

'One of the chaps was telling me about how he felt when he was flying. It really was marvellous. I said he should write it down in a diary but he said he wasn't allowed.'

Mrs Gold leaned against the doorframe. 'You could do it.'

'Keep a diary?'

'I remember hearing that in the last war, lots of the nurses who looked after the wounded soldiers kept books – big sort of scrapbooks – and they let their patients write in them.'

I was intrigued. 'And what did they write?'

'All sorts. Memories of the war, accounts of battles, poems, Bible verses. Some of them drew pictures even. They're real treasures, I believe.'

'What a lovely idea,' I said. 'Like a book of memories.'

'Yes, exactly.'

'Maybe Nelly and I could do that? Get a book and let the patients write in it.' I frowned. 'Our patients aren't soldiers, though.'

'Everyone has a story to tell,' said Mrs Gold wisely.

'You're right,' I said. 'I'll talk to Nelly about it when she gets back from the shops.'

She grinned at me. 'Let me know if you need any help,' she said.

Chapter 10

Stephanie

Present day

'So there's this huge book, and apparently it's full of stories and letters and drawings about the war,' I told Tara at The Vine later. She was polishing glasses and I was watching her. Now as I talked, she handed me a cloth and pushed one of the glasses towards me. I screwed the cloth up in my hand and ignored the glass.

'Finn had to go so I didn't get to have a proper look inside but he says it's unbelievable. It should be in a museum or something, not an old people's home.'

'Where did it come from?' She frowned. 'Was it just stashed in a closet somewhere.'

'It was in the basement apparently. They found it a couple of years ago when they were doing building work.'

'And this guy – this Finn – he's the one who found it?'

I scoffed. 'No, he's a historian.'

'That's not a job.'

I threw my head back in triumph. 'That's what I said! But apparently he teaches history or something.'

'And he has the book now?'

'Yes, and it's amazing.'

'Now you sound like a historian.'

I leaned on the bar, looking out over the tables so I didn't have to meet Tara's gaze. And ever so casually, ever so quickly, I said: 'I thought it might make a good subject for the community art project. You know? Presents from the Past and all that stuff?'

'What?' Tara bellowed, so loudly that two women sitting in deep conversation to the side of the bar both looked up.

Shaking out the cloth I still held in my hand, I pretended to wipe a non-existent mark from one of the beer pumps. 'I thought it might be a good idea for the grant application.'

Tara squeezed my arm. 'Yes! This is perfect.'

She took the cloth from me and gave me a little nudge in the small of my back. 'Go on then.'

'Go where?'

'Home.'

I looked up at the clock on the wall. 'I'm working until ten.'

'Not now you're not.' She looked round the bar. 'It's quiet, and Lucas is working at eight. I can hold the fort until then.'

'Why do you want me to go?' I was confused.

'So you can get started.'

'No.'

'Go on.'

'I don't want to.'

'Stevie, go home now or I'll fire your ass.'

'You wouldn't.'

Tara folded her arms and stared at me, unsmiling. 'Try me.'

I wasn't about to test her resolve.

'I'm going,' I said, skirting round her and lifting the hatch to get out from behind the bar. When I was safely out of arm's reach, I added: 'But I'm not happy about it.'

She threw the cloth at my retreating back and I ran.

*

I knew if I went back to my flat and got comfortable, I'd never venture back down to the garage. So when I got home, I didn't go up the stairs. Instead I left my bike leaning against the wall outside, and taking a deep breath I opened the garage door and went in.

It took me a moment to get accustomed to the dim light inside so I had to blink a few times as I slowly approached my stack of canvases, nervously as though they might come for me – like a lion tamer approaching a lion.

'Come on, Stevie,' I muttered. 'Come on.'

My forehead was sweaty. I wiped it with the back of my hand, annoyed at myself for reacting so badly. I reached out for one of the carrier bags that I'd shoved all my equipment into. I didn't need paints or anything like that at the moment. I just needed a sketchpad and some pencils really. All I wanted to do was to start getting some ideas on paper. 'It's no biggie, Stevie,' I told myself. 'Stop making such a meal of it.'

Obviously all my pads were at the bottom of the bag. I reached inside, wishing I had the cash to just buy new stuff instead of going through this trip down memory lane. But I didn't, so I had to grit my teeth and get on with it.

I pulled out a tin box, which I knew had tubes of acrylic paint in, and put it down on the concrete floor of the garage with a clatter. A tray of watercolours followed. And underneath that was a stack of tiny canvases. I caught my breath. Normally I painted big. Not as big as a mural, perhaps, but I painted on canvases the size of fence panels, swirling the paint across them. They were kind of landscapes but not. And they had been the paintings that got me noticed and had been in the exhibition.

But when things started getting complicated in my life – Dad moving abroad, Nan's dementia, and Max being Max, my paintings got smaller and smaller. By the time Max stole the contents of my flat I was painting tiny squares of canvas, the size of a ready-meal container. Tight, dense pictures, which I could see now as I pulled them out of the bag, were really not very good. And then – after the police arrived at the gallery and I had that heart-stopping moment when I thought my brother was dead – I couldn't paint at all.

I dropped the little canvases next to the paints, and as I did, a photograph fluttered to the ground and skittered across the smooth floor. It was my favourite photograph of Max and me, taken when we went to Glastonbury together, years ago. I was looking straight at the camera, beaming at whoever had taken the picture – I couldn't even remember now. And Max was laughing and looking at me with such love that it made my heart skip. We'd been such buddies back then. He'd been my best friend in the world. And now he was in prison and I was on my uppers and he hated me. How had everything fallen apart so completely?

My hands began to shake. My chest tightened and I felt my breathing get shallower. I'd been standing, leaning over the bag as I rooted around, but now I sank to my knees because my legs were suddenly unable to support me.

'No, no, no,' I breathed. 'Not again.'

I had thought the panic attacks that had plagued me after Max's arrest were in the past. I'd not been able to afford counselling but I'd learned some basic strategies in the little bit of the therapy course I'd completed, and I'd also done a lot of googling and some of the techniques I'd found online had helped. I'd not had one for ages.

But here I was, crouched on the dirty garage floor, trying not to be sick as my forehead grew clammier and my breathing more rasping. My heart was racing and I thought I might pass out. I put my head down onto my knees, squeezing my legs tight, and tried to concentrate on breathing in through my nose and out through my mouth, counting to five each time just like I'd seen on one of the websites.

With my head still on my knees, I put my hands down on the floor, feeling the dust on the rough concrete, I could smell the washing powder I used to clean my jeans and engine oil and I could hear my breath, more regular now.

I kept breathing and counting, and as I felt my pulse return to normal, I lifted my head and, to my shock, saw Micah sitting next to me, watching me with a concerned expression. He reached out a hand and put it on my arm gently. 'I didn't want to scare you,' he said. 'Panic attack, yeah?'

Surprised by his insight, I could only nod.

'How you feeling now?' he asked.

I breathed in deeply. 'It's going,' I told him. 'Better.'

He gave me a little smile. 'That was a long one.'

'Do you …?'

He shrugged his skinny teenage shoulders. 'School's not always easy, you know?'

I felt a rush of affection for this gawky man-boy. 'I know.'

'Gaming helps,' he said. 'It stops me thinking about all the stuff that's in my head.'

'That's good.'

'Fancy it?'

'Gaming?'

'Yeah, I'll show you what to do.' He unfolded his long legs and stood up, holding his hand out to me to help me to my feet.

'You're very kind,' I said.

He rolled his eyes. 'Don't tell no one.'

I saw him glance at the photo I'd dropped and my bags of painting bits and pieces. 'Do you want me to bring that bag?'

I shook my head. 'I just needed a sketchbook.'

Efficiently, Micah scooped up the picture from the floor and wiped the dust from it on his behind. 'I'll put this in the bag and keep it safe,' he said. He dropped it on to the equipment, making me think we had different views of what constituted keeping something safe, and then reached down and pulled out a sketchbook. 'This one?'

'Perfect.'

Feeling stronger, I spotted a pack of pencils in the other bag, along with a case that I knew had coloured pencils in, and pulled them out too.

'So,' I said to my school-uniform-clad saviour. 'What are we playing?'

*

It turned out, Micah was absolutely right. Gaming did stop me thinking about my troubles. We played two matches of a football game, which I lost so thoroughly, Micah laughed like a drain. Then he showed me a cowboy game that was almost a film, because the story was so gripping. And I found a strange satisfaction in shooting all the baddies. As we played, eyes focused on the screen in front of us, Micah occasionally chatted.

'I worry about big tasks,' he said out of the blue, scoring another goal against me. 'Get in! I freak out and I can't get started.'

I didn't reply, not wanting to put him off.

'I've had some … help at school and stuff,' he added. 'And now I know to start with one bit of it. So if I'm worrying about doing, like, my chemistry homework or something, I just tell myself to do one question. That's all. Because that's manageable, innit?'

'It is,' I said, impressed. 'That's good advice.'

'So whatever you're worrying about, maybe just start small.'

'Maybe I will.'

I thought for a second. 'Have you ever done any art, Micah?'

He looked dubious. 'Like colouring in?'

I laughed. 'Maybe. Anything really.' I adjusted my position on the sofa so I could see him better. 'I was learning about art therapy before I lived here. Before things got messed up. It can really help.'

'I'm rubbish at drawing.'

'Doesn't matter. It's not about what you end up with, it's about doing it. And it doesn't have to be drawing. It can be finger painting or sculpture or collage.'

Micah looked vaguely interested. 'So I do art and it makes me feel better?'

'I'm not sure it's that simple. But the idea is you focus on your worries while you're working, and it should help. Sometimes it's good to get things out of your head and on to paper.'

He fixed me with a hard stare. 'Sounds like you should take your own advice.'

He had a point.

*

Later that night, as I lay in bed, I rolled over and took my sketchbook and pencils from the floor where I'd left them. I sat up against the pillows and thought about Micah saying to start small. And I began to draw a tree – one of the proud poplars that I'd seen in the photographs and which were obviously where Tall Trees got its name. I had a vague idea that the mural should be framed by the trees. And perhaps I didn't yet have a plan for what would be in the middle, but I could work on that later. For now, I was starting small. I let my pencil sweep across the page and tried to lose myself in the rhythm of the shading. It wasn't anything like the paintings I used to do, and that was good. It made it easier.

When I woke up the next day, the pad was next to me on the bed and the pencil was on the floor. Wiping the sleep from my eyes, I picked up my drawing and looked at it with some trepidation. But it was okay, I thought. Not amazing. But it was okay. I smiled to myself. Maybe I would draw another tree later. In fact …

Surprising myself, I turned to a clean page and began to sketch one of the peonies that were in the garden at Tall Trees. For more than an hour, I drew and coloured the petals, trying to capture the exact shade of pink that warmed the bushes and the heaviness of the blooms. When I'd got it right, I looked at it with satisfaction. Not perfect, perhaps, but not disastrous. And perhaps I did feel a little bit better. More clear-headed. I put it into a folder and put the folder into my backpack, and then I got ready for work.

*

It was busy at Tall Trees. There was a lot going on today – the bingo man was coming in that afternoon, and the mobile library, which normally came on a Tuesday, had arrived today instead for reasons that I didn't properly understand but which had thrown the residents into great fluster.

'I'll go and choose you something, if you trust me,' I told one of my favourite ladies, Joyce, as she hunted for her shoes because it was raining again and she didn't want to get her slippers wet when she walked across the car park to the library.

'I can't remember the last time I wore them,' she muttered, peering under her bed. 'Maybe I left them in Mr Yin's room?'

I smiled at the thought of Joyce being so comfortable in Mr Yin's space that she took her shoes off. 'Tell me what you want and I'll take back the books you've read and choose you some more.'

Joyce straightened up with a groan. 'My returns are on the coffee table,' she said. 'Anything along those lines really.'

I picked up the books she'd read. One Stephen King, one Shirley Jackson and two detective novels. I'd been expecting Catherine Cookson or Jane Austen.

'Vampires, ghosts and murderers?' I said.

'All three preferably,' Joyce said, giving me a wink.

I took the books, and her library card and went down the corridor, past Mr Yin's room. I stuck my head round the door but he wasn't there – perhaps he was getting ready for bingo, because I knew he was a fan. I took out the picture of the peony that I'd drawn and left it propped up beside his television. I hoped he'd like it.

Then I went out into the miserable afternoon. Inside the library truck it was quiet and warm with the rain pattering on the roof. One of the librarians, a nice woman called Sindhu, was showing a book to Kenny. I put Joyce's books on the pile of returns and went to browse the shelves marked "horror".

Sindhu turned her attention to the returns as Kenny took his book and left. I watched him go through the rain-lashed windows of the truck. He sheltered in the entranceway of Tall Trees as Helen – the odd new resident – came the other way. Intrigued, I watched as Kenny showed her the book he'd borrowed and she looked – to my astonishment – interested and friendly. She bent her head over the book as Kenny turned the pages and I wondered what it was that had captured her attention. As though sensing my eyes on her, Helen looked up at the library van and I stepped back from the window, not wanting her to see me watching.

'Kenny looks pleased with his book,' I said to Sindhu.

She smiled. 'It's about football during the Second World War.' She gestured proudly to one of the shelves. 'We've been bumping up our local history section because they go like hot cakes when we visit the care homes.'

I followed her gaze and to my delight noticed that the shelves were full of books all about this part of South London during the Blitz, and beyond. Perfect inspiration for my mural project.

Putting down the Dean Koontz I'd chosen for Joyce, I went to go over to the history section, just as Helen climbed up into the van. She flicked her gaze over me, then made straight for the wartime books.

Without even properly reading the titles of the books on offer, she began taking them off the shelf and piling them into her arms.

'Oh,' I said, too startled to be polite. 'Are you taking them all?'

Helen turned her steely gaze on me and then smiled at Sindhu. 'I believe I can borrow ten books on my ticket?'

'That's right,' Sindhu said. 'And you can keep them for six weeks. It's an extended loan period as we're not here every week.'

'Thank you so much,' Helen said. She picked up a book called *Bombs and Bandages – London's Hospitals in Wartime* and tucked it under her elbow. I wanted to reach out and grab it from her arms.

'Does that mention Tall Trees?' I asked. 'It was a hospital during the war.'

'Was it?' said Helen.

I nodded. 'I'd like to know more about it.'

'Well then, I'll be sure to let you have this book when my loan period is up,' she said. 'In … six weeks was it you said?'

'Six weeks,' Sindhu said. 'And if that's not long enough, you can renew.'

Helen added the final book about the war to her pile. 'I may have to,' she said. I thought her tone was triumphant, but I couldn't understand why. 'I have a lot here to get through.'

I looked at the now empty shelf where all that remained were two books about the Sixties, which did look interesting but weren't going to help me, and something about the Industrial Revolution. I forced myself to smile at Helen over the top of her pile of books.

'You must be interested in local history, huh?'

'I am indeed.'

'But you're not from here?'

She looked guarded suddenly. 'No, I'm from Ireland. I have some …' she paused '… family links with this area.'

She turned away from me and gave the pile of history books to Sindhu to check out. I waited for her to go and then borrowed Joyce's books.

'She's a big fan of history,' Sindhu said, tilting her head in the direction Helen had walked, back to the main building.

I raised my eyebrows. 'Apparently so.'

With Joyce's books in my arms, I hurried back to the main

building and shook off the rain. I could see the doorway to Finn's little cupboard as I walked through reception, but I couldn't see him. I felt ratty and cross that Helen had taken all the books from under my nose. But I was nothing if not contrary. So what if Helen was making things hard for me? I was going to do my own bloody research. Maybe I'd even track down Elsie Watson myself.

Full of determination, I ducked behind the reception desk and went inside Finn's tiny room. He wasn't there, but there was a pad on his desk. So I picked up a pen and wrote: 'I'm going to base my mural on Elsie's book. Any help you can give me gratefully received.' And then, after a moment's thought, I added my phone number. I hoped he'd call.

Chapter 11

Elsie

1940

Nelly was decorating our flat for Christmas, even though it was still three weeks away. She was singing "Deck the Halls" at the top of her voice as she tried to pin holly along the mantelpiece without pricking her fingers.

'Fa la la, ouch,' she warbled. I couldn't help laughing.

'That's God's way of telling you you're too early,' I said.

'Tsk, don't we deserve a bit of Christmas cheer? Ow.'

'Here, let me help you,' I said. 'Maybe we should put gloves on, to stop the prickles hurting so much.'

'Good plan.' Nelly went to find our gloves and, giggling, we put them on and finished arranging the holly.

'Where did you get this?' I asked. 'There's none in our garden.'

'Park,' said Nelly. 'Percy and I went on a twilight raid.'

'Nelly Malone, you awful thief.'

'It was such a hoot,' she said. 'We had to climb over the fence

95

and Percy got stuck. Honestly, I thought I was going to fall over I was laughing that much.'

'You really like him, don't you?'

'I really do.'

I gave her a hug. 'I'm so glad.'

She hugged me back. 'There's lots of mistletoe in the park too,' she said with a cheeky glance in my direction. 'Perhaps we should take some to work.'

'I'm not sure there's much call for mistletoe on my ward,' I said, pretending to misunderstand.

'There might be in the huts.'

My cheeks flushed. 'Stop it,' I said. 'Matron would be furious if she thought I was parading round the wards trying to kiss patients.'

'Not patients,' said Nelly, emphasising the S. 'Just one patient.'

'I'm not sure that would aid his recovery.'

'Bet it would.'

We both laughed again as Nelly looked at the clock on the mantelpiece. 'Ah, I need to go. I'm meeting Percy before work.' She kissed me on the cheek. 'See you at the hospital later?'

'I'll be there,' I said.

She rushed around, doing her hair and putting on some rouge, and then I heard her shout goodbye as the front door banged shut. I watched from the window as she went along the path and out on to the street, where Jackson was walking along very slowly. He stopped Nelly as she went and I saw them exchange a few words. Nelly had been practically dancing along but as soon as she stopped to talk to Jackson, she folded her arms and her shoulders hunched. I couldn't blame her. He had the same effect on me. They both looked up at the window where I stood and I leaned back a bit, even though I knew they wouldn't be able to see me watching. Nelly was shaking her head and shrugging. I got the impression she was telling Jackson she didn't know where I was and I found I was grateful for her lie.

Nelly looked at her watch and rushed off. Jackson, though, stayed where he was and then, as Nelly went round the corner, he walked up our path and rang the doorbell. It was loud in the quiet flat and made me jump. I stayed very still, hoping he'd go away. The bell rang again and I waited and waited until eventually I saw him walk down the path with a backwards glance up at the window where I stood, hidden behind the curtain.

'Honestly, Elsie,' I chided myself aloud. 'He's just a man.' But even though I knew Jackson was just looking out for me, maybe even doing as Billy had asked him to – though I still doubted that – I still didn't want to spend any time with him.

A knock on the door to the flat made me jump again. But when I'd gathered myself, I realised it had to be Mrs Gold because I'd seen Jackson walk away and it was the inside door, not the main front door. Even so, I felt nervous. It wasn't like me to be so jumpy.

Carefully I put the chain on the door and opened it a fraction. Just as I'd thought, it was Mrs Gold. Sighing with relief, I opened the door properly and she came in, carrying a large paper bag.

'That chap was outside again,' she said. 'The odd one.'

'Jackson. I saw him.' I gave her a little worried smile.

'He's gone.' Mrs Gold gave me a reassuring pat on the arm.

I sat down on the sofa with a sigh. 'He just makes me feel uneasy, but I don't want to be rude to him. Billy always said he wasn't a bad chap.'

'Hmm.' Mrs Gold looked unconvinced. 'Sometimes men don't see other men in the same way we do.'

A movement outside the window caught my eye and I looked round sharply, but it was just a pigeon swooping past. Goodness, I really was jumpy.

'You're worried about him, aren't you?' Mrs Gold said.

'I just know he'll come back.'

'Want me to get Albert to warn him off?'

I thought of quiet Mr Gold with his tweed jackets and dark-rimmed spectacles and shook my head. 'Jackson means no harm,'

I said though whether I was trying to convince Mrs Gold or myself, I didn't know.

Mrs Gold looked like she was going to say something else but she didn't. She looked round at the holly on the mantelpiece. 'It's looking delightfully Christmassy in here.'

'Nelly loves Christmas,' I said. 'She's getting ready even though it'll be different this year, and we're both working on Christmas Day anyway.'

'Do you remember last year, how people kept saying the war would be over by Christmas?' Mrs Gold said, rolling her eyes. 'And here's another year come and gone and things are worse than ever.'

'I think that's why Nelly's so determined to make the most of celebrating,' I said.

'She's got the right idea,' Mrs Gold said, digging into the paper bag she held on her lap. 'Ta-da.'

She pulled out a large box tied with a ribbon. It was very pretty, like a present in a shop window.

'This is for you.'

I was so pleased that for a moment I couldn't speak. 'For me?' I said eventually. 'Really?'

'An early Christmas gift.'

She handed me the box and I gazed at it in wonder. 'It's too pretty to open.'

'No it isn't. Untie the ribbon.'

I pulled the ends of the knot and it came undone. Then I eased off the lid and looked inside. It was a big scrapbook and some pencils.

'I thought you could use it for your patients,' Mrs Gold said.

'This is wonderful,' I breathed. 'You're so kind.'

She waved her hand as if it was nothing. 'I think it's a good idea and I wanted you to be able to get on and do it.'

'Thank you,' I said. 'I think it's a good idea too. I think if the patients write about what happened to them it might help them recover better. Because sometimes writing things down helps make sense of it in your head. Like writing a diary.'

'And it's history isn't it? It's very important to record every-thing.' She gave a little laugh. 'Though at work we spend a lot of time destroying papers.' She turned her attention back to the book. 'The pages are blank because I thought some of them might prefer to draw than write.'

'Yes, that's perfect. I can just give the book to the patients and let them do what they want.' I studied the book on my lap. It was large with sturdy covers, and the pages were thick. It would with-stand a lot of being passed around. Mrs Gold was very thoughtful.

'And if they want to write a message to someone to read if the worst happens, to a loved one perhaps ...'

'Or a sworn enemy,' I said, and Mrs Gold laughed.

'Yes, either or. If they write a message, you could deliver it. If you have to.'

'This isn't just a Christmas present for me,' I said. 'It's a present for every patient in the hospital.'

Mrs Gold's cheeks went a bit red and she gave me her most dazzling smile.

*

Later, when I was leaving to go to the hospital, Mr Gold pulled up outside in a motor car. I'd never seen him driving before – he and Mrs Gold always took the train to work – and now petrol was rationed lots of people had stopped driving. He got out of the car, looking rather pleased with himself, and gave me a cheery wave.

I waved back. I'd not spent as much time with Mr Gold as I had with his wife but he seemed nice enough.

'Are you off to work?' he called, patting the roof of the car. 'Would you like a lift?'

'Really?'

'Of course. I borrowed this from work. They said I could use it for as long as I needed.'

'That's kind of them. They must think a lot of you.'

'Oh I'm just a small cog in a large wheel,' he said. He opened the passenger door. 'I'll take you to the hospital.'

'If you're sure?'

'Clara would be furious with me if she knew I'd seen you and not offered.' He gave me a little smile and tipped his head towards the window. 'She's probably watching us now.'

'That's very nice of you,' I said. 'Thank you.'

I got in while Mr Gold held my bag – which was extra heavy because it was full of the new notebook and the pencils Mrs Gold had given me – and I arranged my coat so it didn't get stuck in the door, and then he handed the bag back for me to hold it on my lap.

He got into the driver's seat and started the engine. 'I wanted to say thank you for keeping Clara company when I have to work,' he said, pulling away from the kerb slightly jerkily. 'She doesn't like being in the shelter on her own.'

'Nor do I,' I said. 'We help each other.'

'Well it means a lot to me,' he said. 'To both of us.'

'Likewise.'

He nodded. 'What do you think of the old girl?'

'What do I think of Mrs Gold?' I asked in alarm and he laughed heartily.

'No, what do you think of the car.'

'Gosh, thank goodness.' I laughed too. 'It's very nice,' I lied because one car was very much like another in my mind.

'I can't believe you thought I called my wife "the old girl",' said Mr Gold, still chuckling.

I smiled at him, though his eyes were fixed on the road as we turned the corner. Still smiling, I looked out of my window and there, standing at the end of the road, was Jackson. He was watching the car as we passed, and his face was twisted in fury.

I felt a sudden lurch of fear. Was it me he was angry with? Had he seen me get into the car with Mr Gold? Was that what had made him look so full of rage?

I watched him grow smaller in the car's wing mirror as Mr Gold drove away from home. I wished that Jackson was really that small and I could squash him with a rolled-up newspaper like a fly.

'All right?' Mr Gold said. 'You looked worried there for a second.'

I forced a smile on to my face. 'Just thinking about work,' I lied.

'Must be hard in the hospital. Busy.'

'Busier than I could ever have imagined. I can't believe how many extra beds they've squeezed in.'

'And extra staff to help?'

'Not enough,' I said. 'We always need more nurses, and porters, and cleaners. It's tough.'

Mr Gold nodded as he slowed down at a junction. 'These are strange times indeed,' he said. 'Strange times.'

Chapter 12

Stephanie

Present day

Finn didn't call, but he did message me. He said he was very excited about the mural and that he would help me in any way he could.

I read his message, gripping my phone tightly. I was relieved he'd not said it was a silly idea, or made excuses about why he couldn't help.

I breathed out slowly. Maybe this could work, I thought. And probably I wouldn't get the grant – I had no doubt there would be other more experienced artists applying – but I felt like even managing to get the grant application written and sent before the deadline would be a victory of sorts.

My phone buzzed in my hand again. It was another message from Finn.

He wouldn't be around for a while because he was marking dissertations, he said. "But," he added, "try this link." Straightaway another message arrived with a password.

I was in the staffroom at Tall Trees because I'd been helping Tara with a stocktake at The Vine and there wasn't time to go home before my shift. So now, intrigued to see what Finn had sent, I sat down on one of the saggy armchairs and clicked on the link.

It took me to a basic website, and after I'd typed in the password, it took me a moment to understand what I was seeing. It was the book – Elsie's book of letters and messages and memories. All the pages that had been scanned in so far.

"This is amazing," I replied to Finn. "Thank you."

"Let me know if it sparks your creativity."

"I will."

It was infuriatingly hard to see on the tiny screen of my phone, so I got up and wandered to the main entrance of Tall Trees where Vanessa, one of the receptionists, was on duty.

'Can I use the computer?' I asked.

She dragged her eyes up from the book she was reading and gave me a hard stare. 'Are you looking up something dodgy?'

'No,' I said, not sure if she was joking or not. 'It's about the history of Tall Trees.'

Vanessa raised an eyebrow and tilted her head towards the computer at the end of the desk. 'Go for it.'

I pulled up a chair and sat down next to her. Then I opened the internet, typed in the link from Finn's message, and entered the password.

On the bigger screen it was easier to see the pages. It was a real mishmash of different things. I got the impression that Elsie had simply handed over the notebook to the patients and told them to write whatever they wanted.

The first few pages were accounts of a bomb that had fallen at the air base at Biggin Hill. I hadn't known about that before Finn mentioned it the other day, though I'd known it had been an RAF base before it became the busy airport for private jets that it was now. I zoomed in on a message and started to read, and once I'd got used to the old-fashioned handwriting, I was quickly engrossed.

The soldiers – airmen I guessed they would be called – had written all about how they'd been having their dinner when the bomb had dropped, with no warning. One of them had written a detailed description of what he'd eaten, which made me smile. Others listed the people who had died – lots of them women, to my surprise. One of them drew pictures of the friends they'd lost, which I found very moving. Another wrote a vivid account of dragging survivors from the rubble, rescuing them in daring and dramatic fashion. It was so thrilling, I found myself biting my lip as I read.

'Interesting, is it?' Vanessa said. I looked up from the screen and saw her watching me curiously.

Oddly, I found I was reluctant to share what I was reading. I felt a bit territorial over this book already. So instead I just shrugged. 'Local history,' I said.

'Is that what that Finn's doing?'

'Sort of.'

Vanessa nodded. 'He's cute.'

I looked at her. She was younger than me and she was related to Blessing in some way – a niece, or a cousin, or something. I couldn't remember the details. Vanessa was a student and working at Tall Trees on the side. She liked covering reception because she could do her uni work at the same time. I admired her work ethic, and I envied her stunning good looks, and I suddenly felt as territorial over Finn as I did over the book.

'Cute?' I said, ultra-casually. 'You think?'

'Hell yeah.' Vanessa glanced at me sideways, pouting her lips like she was getting ready to snog an invisible Finn. 'I love geeky men like that. They're like Clark Kent.'

I laughed. 'He's a history teacher, Vanessa, not Superman.'

She raised one perfectly shaped eyebrow. 'We'll see.'

I felt a bit prickly, like she'd stolen something of mine. 'He's not going to be around much for the next few weeks anyway, because he's busy at work,' I said.

'Shame.'

I shrugged, trying to show her that it didn't matter to me what Finn did, and Vanessa gave me a little knowing half-smile and turned her attention back to her book.

The next few pages of Elsie's book were hard to read. Not the writing – I'd got used to that now – but the words themselves. Some of the airmen had written letters to their families and sweethearts in case they didn't come back.

"I wanted you to know that I treasure the time we spent together," one man had written to someone called Ginny. I wondered if he and Ginny had ended up together or if they'd gone their separate ways.

"I hope you'll be proud of me, Mum and Dad," another wrote. "Because that's all I ever wanted, you know. To make you proud." He'd signed it, and added "age 19".

I felt tears in my eyes, at the thought of this young man – just a few years older than Micah – who'd gone off to war, hoping to make his parents proud. Making my own parents proud had never been one of my goals. Mum was much prouder of Max – turning his back on "normal" life – than she'd ever been of me. And Dad, well … I usually just got the impression that he was a little confused by me. I always felt my presence made him feel guilty, as though I reminded him of his shortcomings somehow. And obviously that meant he didn't want to spend much time with me. I wasn't even sure if he'd told his new friends in Portugal that he had children. Mind you, on the odd occasions when someone asked me if I had any siblings now, I would always be a bit vague and say I had a brother but we weren't really in touch.

I took a deep, slightly shuddering breath in and Vanessa looked up at me but didn't say anything and I was glad.

Maybe this was too much for me, I thought as I clicked on the mouse to open the next page. I was definitely on the mend, but I wasn't the same person I'd been before and I wasn't sure I ever would be. Maybe this wasn't the right project?

The next letter was a sweet note to a new wife, who was pregnant with the writer's first baby.

"Please tell our son or daughter that they were so loved by me, their father," he'd written. I pinched my lips together. "I hope you aren't working too hard and please if you get the chance to be evacuated, you must go. It's not safe for you to be in London when the bombs are dropping and things are so bad."

Underneath the letter, someone else – Elsie, I assumed – had added a note: "AC1 Rogerson killed in action 19 December 1940". And then, in a different colour of ink, there was another note adding: "wife killed in bomb in Stepney 11 December 1940".

I covered my mouth with my hand, feeling the loss of this family like a sharp pain, all these years later. I wondered if he'd known his wife had died before he was killed. Perhaps not. I wasn't sure how long news took to filter through in those days. It wasn't as though people could just email.

'Okay?' Vanessa said, looking at me in concern. 'What's wrong?'

I shut the website down. 'Fine.' My voice was shaky. 'It's fine. I need to start my shift now. Thanks for letting me use the computer.'

She gave me a dazzling smile. 'Any time.'

Feeling slightly wrung out, I hurried off to the staffroom to read the rota for my shift. I couldn't do this, I thought. I was too fragile and wobbly. The idea of painting a mural about the history of Tall Trees was a good one, but not for me. Not when the history was so sad, and so raw.

I was on the late shift tonight, but though our residents went to bed early, it wasn't time to start getting them into their night clothes quite yet. In fact, a lot of the people on my corridor were playing cards in the lounge. I left them to it and, grabbing a pile of information leaflets Blessing had asked me to make sure were given out, I went along the hall, just checking in on the ones who were settled in their rooms.

Val was one of the women who gave the card games a swerve.

I couldn't blame her really because they did get very raucous and extremely competitive. So I knocked on her door and went into her room, where she was watching *Four in a Bed* on the little portable television on her chest of drawers. Someone – probably Blessing – had told me Val had worked in hospitality when she was younger and I'd scoffed at the idea, because she was really very prickly and I couldn't imagine her running a hotel. But perhaps I'd been wrong.

'Blessing asked me to give these out to the right people,' I said, putting down one of the leaflets. 'Make sure you at least glance at it, won't you? Or she'll have my guts for garters.'

Val looked at the leaflet without interest, then at me, more carefully this time.

'Are you all right, Stephanie?' she said.

I eyed her with suspicion because she didn't often enquire as to how I was. 'I don't have any teabags,' I said.

Val tutted. 'I didn't ask.'

Immediately I felt guilty. 'I know, I'm sorry. I'm a bit out of sorts.'

'I can see that.' She nodded to where I'd put the information leaflet, which I saw now was about prostate screening, down on the table at the end of her bed and I screwed up my nose, and scooped it up again into the pocket of my tunic.

'What's got you so rattled?' Val asked.

'Nothing.' I smoothed out her bedspread, which was made from very pretty patchwork.

'Liar.' I stared at her in surprise, and she gave me a tight-lipped smile. 'You're obviously upset about something, and unless you want to give Mr Yin my osteoporosis medication, I suggest you get it off your chest.'

'I don't really want to talk about it,' I muttered.

Val picked up the remote control and turned off *Four in a Bed* with a click. Then she turned her head, regally, so she could look straight at me.

'Fair enough,' she said. 'Close the door on your way out, will you?'

I sat down on the pretty patchwork quilt. 'Do you remember the war, Val?'

'I thought you didn't want to talk?'

'Do you remember?'

She nodded. 'I was still at school when the war started. By the time it ended I was virtually a grown woman.'

'Did you …' I swallowed. 'Did you lose anyone?'

'I was one of the lucky ones. I had three sisters. We all did our bit, but none of us were ever really in danger. And my poor old dad, he'd been in the trenches of course, first time round, but he was too old to enlist. My mother was pleased that he didn't have to go.'

'Did you have a boyfriend who was off fighting?'

Val winked at me. 'I had several. But they all came back.'

'You really were lucky,' I said, more harshly than I'd intended. I ran my finger along the edge of one of the patchwork squares where I sat. 'Tall Trees was a hospital during the war.'

'I know.'

'A nurse who worked here kept a book where the patients she looked after wrote messages for their families. In case they didn't come back.'

'That was kind.'

'It was.'

Val looked far away for a moment. 'I had a friend,' she said eventually. 'Well, he was more than a friend. I loved him very much. But he was married, and he had children. He had a very important job, and I worked odd hours, which didn't fit with a conventional family life. So we had an arrangement that suited us both, you know?'

I wasn't completely sure what she meant, but I thought I could get the gist. Was she telling me she had been someone's mistress? A bit on the side? I nodded.

'We were together for a long time. Years and years. Until his children were grown and had children of their own. But no one knew. And when he died, of course, no one told me. It took me a while to find out.' She gave me a little sad smile. 'That was back in the days before the internet. In the end, I saw his obituary in the *Daily Telegraph*, over someone's shoulder on the tube.'

'I'm sorry – that must have been very hard.'

She nodded. 'I'd have liked to have had a message from him,' she said. 'One last message.'

'He didn't leave you anything?'

'Nothing.' A shadow crossed her face. 'Though, I think his son always had an inkling about us, and it wouldn't have surprised me if he'd kept anything he did leave from me.' She gave me a little sad smile. 'That was the decision I made when we met. I knew he wouldn't choose me over his wife. He was very protective of her.'

Not that protective, I thought to myself, if he'd been carrying on with another woman the whole time. But who knew what went on in people's marriages? So I simply nodded again, because I thought saying the right thing before someone went away was important.

'My brother …' I began slowly. It was always a bit nerve-racking, saying that my brother was behind bars. 'He's in prison. And I said some awful stuff to him, before he went.'

Val reached out and patted my hand and the simple, sympathetic gesture made tears spring into my eyes. I blinked them away and she pretended not to notice.

'Perhaps he deserved it,' she said.

'I think he did.' My voice was a little croaky. 'But I still feel bad about it.' I breathed in deeply. 'I thought he'd died, you see? When the police turned up, I thought he was dead and the last things I'd said were horrible.'

Val gave me a long, steady look. 'I think we all need one of those books to write in. In case we don't come back.'

'We really do,' I said, picking at a loose thread on the quilt.

Then I stopped still as an idea came to me, and I stared at Val. 'That's it.'

'What's what?'

'Presents from the past,' I said in excitement, ignoring her blank look. 'I could do a book for the residents here. Everyone can write their own messages to special people. And I could use some of the words from Elsie's book on the mural – base it all around the nurse and her idea.'

Val simply looked at me, but I thought I saw a spark of interest in her eyes.

'And,' I said, triumphantly, 'I could find out what happened to Elsie. Make it part of the project. Imagine if I could track her down – that really would be a present from the past.'

'I have absolutely no idea what you're talking about,' Val said. She picked up the remote control and turned *Four in a Bed* back on.

Dismissed, I slid off the patchwork quilt. 'I'll come back later and help you get ready for bed,' I said.

Val nodded. And then, as I reached the door, she said: 'Perhaps you could tell me more about this Elsie, too.'

I grinned. 'Definitely.'

Chapter 13

Elsie

1940

Thanks to Mr Gold taking me in his car, I got to the hospital early so I decided to make the most of my time and take the book round to the airmen. Because they'd all been eager to write letters to their families, I thought they would embrace the idea of writing in the notebook and I hoped their enthusiasm would rub off on the other patients. It was worth a try anyway.

So, as soon as I arrived, I hurried out to the new huts where the airmen were.

'I'm Nurse Watson,' I said to the Red Cross nurse who was filling in forms at the nurses' station just by the door. She was an older woman, probably in her early fifties. I recalled her being efficient and caring on the day the airmen had arrived. 'I helped set up the beds when the patients arrived?'

She looked up and me and smiled. 'I remember. I'm Nurse Cassidy. Call me Judith.'

'I'm Elsie,' I said.

'What can I do for you, Elsie?'

I showed her the book. 'My friend Nelly and I wrote some letters to the families of your men who were too injured to be able to write for themselves,' I explained.

'I heard,' she said with a smile. 'That was very kind.'

'Chatting with the men that day, and writing the letters, made us think that some of the patients might want to share memories. Or have some words written down in case of the worst. So I've brought a notebook for them to write in.'

'What a lovely idea. They'll be so pleased. And I'm pleased they'll have something to do.' She leaned over the desk and lowered her voice. 'Some of them are feeling better already and between you and me, they're beginning to get a bit cheeky. Pushing the boundaries, you know?'

That made me think about Jackson who didn't appear to have any boundaries, and I felt a little queasy. 'They're not bothering you, are they?'

Judith rolled her eyes. 'Nothing I can't handle, bless them. They're just boys, aren't they? Most of them are younger than my own kids. Poor lambs.'

I felt my shoulders relax. Honestly, I'd got myself in such a tizz over Jackson when he was the same. Just a young man, coping as best he could in a strange situation.

'Go on in,' Judith said. 'They'll be pleased to see you.'

Nodding my thanks, I took my notebook and went into the ward. There was a buzz of energy there. Some of the airmen were sleeping. Others were reading, lying on top of their bedsheets. A couple were sitting on adjacent beds playing cards. I looked for Harry and was pleased when I saw him in his bed. He was sitting up but his head was resting on his pillow and his eyes were shut.

'Hello?' I said, hoping they'd all pay attention to me. The airmen all quietened down and looked up at me obediently and I sent silent thanks to their commanding officers who'd clearly trained them well. Harry opened his eyes and looked at me and I felt the weight of his gaze like a warm shawl around my shoulders.

'Hello,' I said again. 'It's me again, Nurse Watson. Do you remember my friend Nurse Malone and I were here the other day, writing letters for some of you?'

'As if we'd forget you,' one of the men called from the end of the room. 'I never forget a pretty face.'

'That's enough, Eric,' said Judith from the desk.

I grinned. I liked these men, even if they were a bit cheeky.

'When I was here before, some of you shared some memories and stuff with me.' I caught Harry's eye and gave him a little smile. 'And some of you said you'd like to write messages for your loved ones, in case … well, in case you don't make it back.'

The quiet in the ward grew more intense for a moment as the men all considered my words.

'Apparently during the last war, some nurses kept books of memories for their patients,' I went on. 'And I thought it was a lovely idea. So I'm going to do the same.'

'A book of last letters,' said Eric.

'Yes,' I agreed. 'But not only last letters. Anything at all. I'm going to leave this notebook here with you and you can just write whatever you feel like. Anything at all.'

'What did you say your name was?' one airman shouted.

'Nurse Watson.'

He cleared his throat. 'Dear Nurse Watson,' he began, and the other men all groaned and laughed. I smiled too, enjoying their good spirits.

'Like I said, just write or draw whatever you want. You can write about your experiences at Biggin Hill, or what it feels like to fly.' I saw Harry give a little nod and I was glad. 'Write letters home if you want, or notes to your sweethearts, or draw a picture or two. Messages, poems, Bible verses, tributes to friends you've lost …' I looked round at them all. 'Writing is a good way to get your thoughts in order.'

113

'Anything at all?' said a boy who was studying the newspaper though he barely looked old enough to know how to read.

'Anything at all.' I smiled at them all.

'And if we write messages, you'll pass them on, will you?' said another airman, his brows drawing together.

'Of course – if you want me to. Or if you don't want to, that's fine too. You don't even have to put your name to what you write if you don't want to. It's up to you.'

There was a ripple of conversation and I put my hand up to quieten them.

'I've got to go now. Can I trust you to look after the book?'

The men all murmured their agreement. 'Good. And please help each other to write if there's anyone who's unable to hold the pencil.' I glanced at Harry again and he grinned at me and I felt a little flicker of something, deep down inside me. 'I'll come and collect it in the morning.'

'Thanks, Nurse,' said Eric. 'This is a really good thing you're doing.'

My eyes felt hot with tears suddenly, and I blinked them away. 'Who's first?' I said.

The newspaper-reading lad raised his hand politely and I went to him and gave him the notebook and pencils.

He opened the pad to a clean page and tapped it with his fingertips. 'Now I just have to decide what to write,' he said, picking up a pencil.

'Good luck,' I said. 'Pass it round and I'll come back and get it tomorrow.'

I left them all chatting, pleased that the notebook had received such a positive response. As I walked along the ward, I noticed that the bed I'd helped one of the more injured airmen into – the lad with the shredded face – was empty.

'What happened to the chap in bed 2?' I asked Judith as I made my way to the door of the ward.

She screwed her nose up. 'Vinny? He didn't make it.'

I put my hand over my mouth, shocked even though I saw death every day.

'Poor lad. Sepsis it was. Takes them quick.'

I shuddered. 'Such a shame.'

Judith nodded. 'Thanks for bringing the notebook for them. I'll make sure they don't write anything too bawdy.'

I glanced over my shoulder over to where the men were laughing uproariously about something. 'Good luck with that,' I said.

*

It was another busy night shift, but throughout the chaos I found my thoughts drifting to the men in the huts and wondering if they were busy writing in the book. So when I eventually handed over to the nurses on the day shift, I raced round to the huts.

Judith wasn't there, but there were other Red Cross nurses working, who were just as friendly. And when I walked in, the airmen all began calling to me, a cacophony of voices that made my head spin.

'Nurse, I wrote a note for you!'

'I've drawn some pictures, Nurse!'

'I don't know where my family are, Nurse. Can you find them?'

I looked around me, unsure where to start, and I couldn't see where the book was. Harry clearly saw me looking lost and raised his voice.

'Oi,' he growled and the men all fell silent. 'Nurse Watson here is doing a nice thing for us. Let's be polite, shall we.'

I smiled at him and he smiled back and I felt something pass between us, almost like recognition. 'I've got the book here,' he said, picking it up from his bedside and holding it aloft. 'The lads have almost filled it.'

I felt a rush of satisfaction and happiness. 'Have they really?' I looked round the makeshift ward. 'Have you all written?'

'Think everyone wrote something, or got someone to write for them,' said the cheeky one called Eric. 'Except for Mark. But he's not so good with words.'

A man at the end of the ward, whom I assumed was Mark, grumbled and then let out a hearty laugh that delighted me. 'True,' he said, unabashed. 'My letters always get jumbled up. But I drew a picture of Vinny.'

Vinny – the fellow they'd lost.

'It felt good,' Mark went on. 'To have a chance to honour him.'

I nodded, moved by how well they'd taken to the idea.

'We enjoyed it and we reckon you should take it all round the hospital,' Harry said. He pronounced "take" like "tek". I liked the way he spoke. 'I've heard there are patients here from different parts of London. The docks and that?'

'There are. They bring them down from the East End when the raids happen.'

'And Nurse Cassidy said some of them don't stay here?'

'No, they often go to safer hospitals, down in Kent or Sussex.'

'Maybe their families won't know what's happened then?'

'It's possible.'

'You need to let them write in the book, too. Not just us airmen. Everyone.'

I smiled at him. 'I will. That's exactly what I'm planning to do. And now you've started things off, others will follow.'

'Will you come back and tell us about it?'

'Of course.'

'Right, men. The dinner trolley's on its way so how about you let Nurse Watson get home, please?' said one of the nurses, who looked like a film star with huge blue eyes, but had a gruff, earthy voice that carried over the clamour of the men's questions.

'Bye then,' I said to the men.

Harry winked at me and I felt my cheeks redden. 'Bye, Nurse Watson,' he said.

*

I had intended to take the book home and have a look inside, but I couldn't wait. So I went to the staffroom, sat down and opened it up.

It was better than I'd ever dreamt possible. The airmen had completely understood what I wanted them to do, and the result was astonishing.

I read, open-mouthed, through messages to parents telling them they loved them, to wives asking them to look after children, and to sweethearts saying they were to be brave without them.

Mark's picture of Vinny was wonderful. He'd captured a glint in his eye and a proud tilt to his chin that made my eyes burn with tears.

And on the next page, he'd drawn me – in a very flattering way and with just a few strokes of his pencil. He was a real talent, I thought. I would tell him so when I saw him next.

'What you got there?' Nelly appeared in the doorway. She looked tired but her eyes were bright. I'd not seen her since we decorated the flat with the holly earlier on, so I'd not told her what I had planned.

'I've got a book for patients to write messages in,' I said, holding it up so I could see. 'Mrs Gold got it for me.'

'Oh, you clever thing.' She came over. 'It's such a good idea.'

'Apparently lots of nurses did it in the last war, for the soldiers they looked after.'

'But you're going to give it to all the patients?'

'We're going to give it to all the patients,' I said, emphasising the "we".

'Ah.'

'What does "ah" mean?' I looked at her in alarm. 'You're not going anywhere, are you? Are you going back to Dublin?'

'Don't be daft.' She sighed. 'Remember I said I'd like to have a go at working in the operating theatre?'

I widened my eyes. Nelly had wanted to assist in the theatre for months. 'You've got a chance?'

'I have. I'm going to be a theatre nurse.'

I hugged her. 'That's wonderful, Nell. Well done.'

'We'll be on different shift patterns now, though.'

I shrugged. 'We'll still see each other.' Then I grinned. 'We can leave each other messages.'

'Absolutely.'

'Look at this picture of me,' I said, showing her Mark's drawing.

'Now that's gorgeous.'

'It's very flattering.' I sighed. 'These boys are all so talented.' I turned the page and chuckled as I saw a limerick printed there. It wasn't signed.

'Nell, listen to this,' I said. 'There was a young airman named Ted, who struggled to get out of bed ... Oh heavens, I'm not reading the rest of that. It's too rude.'

We both laughed.

'Are you coming home now?' I said to Nelly.

She shook her head. 'Not quite yet. I have to go to the offices and sort out my transfer, and then I've got to go and meet my new matron. What about you?'

'I'm going to take the book to my ward and see if anyone wants to write in it.'

'Good idea,' said Nelly.

She leaned over and picked up a pencil. Then she wrote "see you later" in her messy writing at the bottom of one the pages. I rolled my eyes and she blew me a kiss as she hurried away.

With the book in my arms and a stack of pencils in my pocket, I headed towards my ward, where another nurse stopped me in the corridor, just by the entrance to the ward 2. It was where the really badly injured patients were cared for.

'Is that it?' she asked, nodding towards the book. 'I heard you were collecting memories in a book.'

'Oh is that the memory book?' called another nurse who was walking into the ward. 'Come and show us.'

Pleased that people were talking about the book, I followed her to the nurses' station at the entrance to the ward. It was quiet in there, and very still. All the patients were extremely poorly and no one really stayed on ward 2 for long.

'So, you get patients to write their memories in your notebook?' the first nurse asked me.

'No, it's not memories, it's messages,' said another nurse, who was making a bed with fresh sheets and who I recognised from when we'd trained together. Her name was Barbara, I thought. 'Messages between soldiers and their sweethearts. Ain't that right, Elsie?'

'I heard you were finding missing families,' said Matron, who was sitting at the desk. 'I heard there was a woman on your ward who didn't know where her children were and you found them.'

I looked from one to the other and held the book out in front of me. 'It's a bit of everything,' I said. 'That's what I said to the airmen – you know the chaps in the huts? I gave it to them and said they could write whatever they wanted.'

'And what did they write?' Barbara asked. She was from up north somewhere, Manchester I thought. Her accent was a little bit like Harry's. She took the book from my hands. 'Eh, it's heavier than I thought.'

'They wrote all sorts. Some wrote messages, like you said. But others drew pictures, or wrote poems. It's wonderful.'

We all went quiet for a second as we looked round at the patients on the ward where we stood, who were all too poorly to be writing anything at all.

'Can I take it to my ward?' Barbara said. 'I'm just helping out here, but I'm normally on ward 5. My men would want to contribute, I'm sure. Some of them were in the trenches, last time. I reckon they've got lots to say this time round.'

Ward 5 was where the elderly patients were cared for. I shuddered to think how Barbara's patients were coping with living through a war for the second time.

'That would be perfect,' I said. 'Thank you, Barbara.'

'I'm starting my shift in a minute. Can I take it now?'

'Why not. I was going to take it to my ward, but it doesn't matter what order it's in. And I'm off now until this evening.' I handed the book over. It felt a bit of a wrench to leave it in her hands, but I gave her the pencils from my pocket, too. 'Tell them to write anything at all. They'll get the idea if they look at what's been written already.'

'I read a book about how your brain adjusts to awful events,' said the matron, who was resting her chin in her hand and looking thoughtful. 'A few books actually. I'm rather interested in how our minds work. This is an effective way of helping our patients work through their injuries, I think.'

'I think so too,' I told her. 'Writing things down really does help.'

'I'll head up there now,' Barbara said. 'Shall I pass it on when my men are done?'

'Absolutely.' I nodded. 'I'll find it when I come back tomorrow sometime.'

'Grand.' She hurried off towards the stairs and, feeling a sense of achievement, despite the dragging tiredness I always felt after a long night shift, I wandered down the corridor and out of the main entrance.

'Night, Elsie,' one of the porters called as I went. He was pushing a trolley.

'Are you still here, Frank? That's a long shift for you.' Frank normally worked the same hours as I did.

'I'm doing a double because we're short-staffed, love. Half of the crew have joined up. Fancy a stint with us?'

'Think I'll stick to nursing, thanks,' I said, chuckling as I walked.

'Hello.' Jackson appeared without warning, looming up at me through the gloomy winter morning.

I let out a little gasp. 'Oh Lord, Jackson, you startled me,' I said.

To his credit, he looked horrified. 'I'm so sorry, Elsie,' he said. 'I really didn't mean to frighten you.'

Still happy about the book making its way round the hospital,

I pulled my shoulders back and forced myself to give him a smile. 'It's fine. What are you doing here?' I looked him up and down. 'Are you hurt?'

'Came to walk you home,' he said, puffing his chest out. 'I knew you'd been on the night shift. Though you're later than I thought you'd be. I've been waiting ages. I didn't want you going home by yourself.' His expression darkened. 'Or getting a lift off someone. That wouldn't be right.'

'My neighbour Mr Gold brought me to work in his motorcar,' I said firmly, wondering why I felt the need to explain myself to Jackson. 'It was very kind of him.'

'He's not here now?' Jackson looked around.

'Well, no.'

'So, I'll walk you home.'

'I was going to get the train.'

'Then I'll come too.' He offered me his arm. 'Billy would be pleased.'

I did not want to take his arm, nor did I want to walk home with him, but I remembered the angry look on his face when Mr Gold had driven past him and I was strangely nervous about how he'd react if I said no. So I looped my hand through his arm, and we walked to the station. Jackson talked all the way, and when the train arrived, and when we got off again, telling me how he was planning to join the ARP wardens so he would be doing his bit, or perhaps he would try to join up again. Maybe they'd let him enlist this time, despite his flat feet. I let his words wash over me. I'd heard it all before and I didn't really care whether he joined up or not. Though, if he did, at least he wouldn't bother me anymore.

'I think that's a marvellous idea,' I said.

He looked at me with shining eyes.

'Do you really?'

'Absolutely.'

We'd reached the end of my road. I turned to him. 'Thank

you so much for walking me home,' I lied. 'Good luck with it all. Must dash.'

I spun on my heels and raced off along the road towards home, pleased with how well I'd handled him this time.

Chapter 14

Stephanie

Present day

The idea of getting everyone at Tall Trees to do their own version of Elsie's book stayed with me all through my shift. I thought about it as I helped the residents get ready for bed, and when I popped over to see my nan before the rest of the staff headed home. Then I thought about how I could find out what happened to Elsie. And when I'd thought about that, I started thinking about the mural itself.

And I kept thinking about it as I settled down in the staffroom for the night, one ear listening out for any bells from the residents. Once upon a time I would have had a sketchbook and pencils in my bag, ready for inspiration to strike, but not now. Instead, I dug around in the drawers in the staffroom and eventually I found a paper bag that had one lonely drawing pin in the corner. I shook the pin out and stuck it to the noticeboard, where I found a scratchy biro that was stuck to the board with a fraying piece of string, and sat down at the table. I smoothed out the paper bag and carefully tore it down one side and along the bottom so I had two pages to draw on. And then I picked up the biro, thinking of the tree I'd drawn at home.

I could use similar branches as a frame, I thought, roughly drawing two tall trees on either side of my paper bag. And maybe I could draw Elsie too if there was a picture of her that I could copy. I added the outline of a figure to one side.

And then, perhaps I could pick out some of the words from the book, and add them to the design. Making a pattern perhaps. I drew a sort of rainbow made from nonsense words and frowned. Hmm. Perhaps not. Or flowers? Or anything really. The words were the important bit. I would have to find the perfect notebook and let the residents have it to write their own messages inside. A modern version of Nurse Elsie's idea.

I felt a flicker of excitement. Maybe, just maybe, this could work.

The alarm on my phone buzzed, telling me it was time to go for a walk around the corridors and check everything was as it should be. It was usually my least favourite time of a night shift, but today I found I was actually looking forward to it. The quiet corridors would let me imagine how the building had looked when it was a hospital. I got up from the table and put my paper bag drawing carefully into my bag. Then, I went off to start at the top of the building and work my way down, as was my habit. As I went upstairs, I typed a message to Finn, knowing it was late and he was probably in bed.

"Going to base my mural around Nurse Elsie specifically," I wrote. "Have lots of ideas."

Before I'd even got to the second floor, my phone vibrated in my hand with his reply.

"Amazing. Can't wait to hear about them. Need to pop to Tall Trees tomorrow actually. Are you working?"

I stopped on the top stair and sighed heavily. No, I wasn't working. We always had a couple of days off after a night shift.

"Not at Tall Trees," I wrote hopefully. "But I'll be working in The Vine from 5 p.m."

Finn sent back a thumbs up. 'What does that mean?' I said out loud, pushing through the double doors on to the top corridor. 'Not helpful, Professor Finn.'

*

As it turned out, though, the thumbs-up sign meant Finn was planning to come to The Vine. I was making cocktails for a group of older women when I saw him arrive. He sauntered up to the bar, pushed his hair off his forehead, and studied the beer pumps with a slightly furrowed brow.

Tara went over to serve him and I tried to catch her eye and let her know who he was. But it wasn't until Finn gave me a little self-conscious wave, while I handed over the final apple martini, that she twigged.

She turned to me, eyebrow raised and nodded. 'Nice,' she mouthed. Then when Finn took his beer and looked round for an empty table, she said: 'Stevie, it's time for your break. Why don't you join your friend?'

I had only been working for an hour, but I wasn't going to argue. 'Really?'

'Sure.'

So I gladly untied my apron and went over to where Finn was settling into a booth.

'Hi,' I said. He looked very at ease, and – I couldn't help noticing – rather handsome. That made me think of Vanessa saying he was cute, and that made me feel a little bit awkward so I hovered by the side of the booth until he nodded to the seat opposite. 'Sit down, please. I hate drinking on my own.'

'I'm not drinking,' I said just as Tara appeared next to me with a gin and tonic and put it on the table.

'You are now,' she said with a smile. 'Take as long as you want.'

I slid along the bench and Finn smiled at me. 'She's nice.'

'She's amazing,' I agreed. 'She's always got my back.'

'I like that.' He sipped his beer, looking thoughtful as he did so. I liked the way he looked as though he was carefully considering everything he did. It was very unlike how I lived my own life, in a state of total chaos and bad choices.

'So tell me about your ideas.'

I grinned. 'Final words,' I said. 'Last letters.'

'Mine? Or …'

'Well, you know that Elsie's book has lots of messages in it from soldiers, and other people. Messages she passed on if they didn't make it through the war.'

'It was really only the very early months of the war,' Finn pointed out. 'The darkest days of the Blitz.'

'Yes, okay, but the idea is the same,' I said, not letting his pedantry get in the way of my excitement. 'She collected people's last letters for their loved ones. I want to use those words in the mural. And I want to do my own book.'

'For the residents of Tall Trees?'

I loved that he'd got the idea straightaway. 'Yes, I thought I could do a book for them, like Elsie did.'

Finn nodded.

I put my hands flat on the table, either side of my G&T glass. 'So what do you think?'

'I think it's a wonderful idea.'

I let out my breath slowly, relieved. 'I thought I'd include Elsie on the mural. Do you have a picture of her?'

Finn shook his head. 'Not a photograph, but there are some sketches of her in the book. You could copy one of those.'

'Perfect.' I did a little wiggle in my seat. 'And I also thought I'd try to find out what happened to her. This book really is a present from the past – she's a local hero. Do you know much about her?'

'Not really,' he said, screwing up his nose. 'Like I said, she only kept the book for a few months. I think it was late 1940, to the spring of 1941. Just the worst days of the Blitz.'

'Maybe she didn't think there was any need for it after the bombing raids weren't so bad?'

He shrugged. 'I think she left the hospital around then, and I don't know where she went after that. I can't find her.'

'But she definitely didn't die?'

'No, not in the war. At least there's no record of her death.'

'That's good.' I felt strangely pleased that Elsie had made it through the conflict unscathed. 'Maybe she joined up? She could have gone to be a nurse in the Army or something.'

'Maybe.' Finn looked unconvinced.

'What do you know about her?'

'Just what was on her staff record from the hospital,' Finn said. 'Her parents were both dead by the time the war began, even though she was quite young to have lost her mother and father.'

'Poor Elsie. Did she have any other family?'

'A brother. But he was killed during the evacuation of Dunkirk.'

His casual words jabbed my heart. 'Oh gosh,' I muttered, taking a large mouthful of gin and swallowing it quickly, feeling the icy cold liquid swill down my throat. 'Goodness. That must be why she was keen to collect people's messages. Maybe she was thinking about the last thing she said to her brother?'

Finn nodded. 'She might have had things that she had always wanted to tell him and didn't get a chance.'

I swirled my finger in a pool of water left by my cold glass on the table. 'That's really sad.'

Finn was looking at me oddly. 'Are you okay?'

I forced my gaze upwards and met his eyes, which were furrowed in concern.

'My relationship with my brother is tricky,' I said carefully. Then I sighed. 'He's in prison.'

Finn raised an eyebrow. 'Okay.'

'It was really messy, and it's complicated to explain, but we had a huge argument and I said some horrible stuff. And then, for a little while, I thought he'd died. And then he went to jail and I felt a bit responsible.' I swallowed. 'I sort of know how Elsie felt.'

'That's a lot to deal with.' Finn put his hand on mine and squeezed my fingers gently and quickly, then let go again. 'I'm sorry to hear that.'

'I know how important this is,' I said, trying not to think about how cold my hand felt now he wasn't touching me anymore. 'I'll do the grant application when I get home later. Strike while the ideas are hot.'

'I always think it's best just to do these things,' Finn agreed. 'Don't overthink them. Write it down like you've told me all your ideas. Just let them all flow.'

'Flow?' I said. 'Okay.'

'Good for you.'

We looked at each other for a moment, and it was almost like the rest of The Vine vanished, until the doors opened, bringing in a burst of cold air and the five-a-side football teams who always came for nachos and beer after training.

'God, I forgot that it's Thursday,' I said. 'I need to go and help Tara.'

Finn drained his pint. 'I have to head off anyway. But keep me posted on how you get on with the application, won't you?'

'Of course,' I said.

I slid back out of the booth in a slightly ungainly fashion and went to help Tara pull ten pints of lager.

'He's cute,' she said to me. 'Really cute. And he likes you.'

'Do you think?' I glanced over to the door, where Finn was just leaving. He saw me looking and raised his hand in farewell.

'Hell, yes.' Tara nodded vigorously. 'He's all shy and blushing when you talk to him like a young Hugh Grant.'

I scoffed, putting another pint on to the bar for the thirsty footballers and picking up a clean glass. But I was secretly quite pleased. Because I liked Finn too.

*

When I got up the next morning, Micah was in my kitchen eating my cereal.

'Why are you here?' I said, looking bleary-eyed at the clock on the wall. 'It's school time.'

'I'm going to an appointment.' He held his spoon up to his face and studied the Cheerios floating there. 'About my worries and stuff.'

'Oh well done.' I was pleased he was getting help.

Micah made a face. 'Don't want to go.'

'Why not?'

'It's embarrassing, like.'

'Just tell everyone you went to the dentist.'

'Yeah.' He looked at me, seeming very young suddenly. 'But it's scary too, innit?'

I reached around him and picked up the kettle. 'Really scary. But most things are, I reckon.'

Micah grinned at me. 'We're a right pair of scaredy-cats.'

'Totally.' I filled up the kettle and turned it on. 'What time's your appointment?'

'Half ten, but Mum says we have to leave at quarter to, even though it's literally round the corner.'

I thought that perhaps his mum was scared about the appointment too. I didn't know her very well – Micah was really the only one of the family that I had anything to do with – but she seemed nice enough. More engaged than my mother had ever been, at least. Though judging anyone's parenting skills by my mum's was a fairly low bar for them to jump.

'So we have almost an hour,' I said now. 'Can you do something for me?'

'Is it your phone again?' Micah said with an exaggerated sigh. 'Because I've told you how to download those apps so many times, Steve.'

'Stevie,' I said automatically. 'And no. Why not try some art? I'll do it too.'

Micah drank the milk left in the bottom of his cereal bowl and put it on the side. 'What kind of art?'

'Whatever you want. How about collage? You can tear some pictures out of magazines.'

He looked alarmed. 'Like sexy pictures?'

'No, urgh,' I said. 'Stop being such a teenage boy. Fancy it?'

'No.' He wandered over to the sofa and threw himself down. 'Maybe.'

I'd raided the recycling pile at Tall Trees where the residents were still committed to reading printed editions of newspapers and magazines and now I put them all on the coffee table. 'Here,' I said. 'Have a look. Think of it as a kind of creative meditation.'

'Riiight.'

'Do it for me,' I said. I plonked a sheet of paper and some Pritt Stick down too. 'You're helping me.'

'Fine.' He smoothed out his sheet of paper and picked up the *Sunday Times Magazine* from the top of the pile.

For about forty minutes, we tore out pictures and stuck them down in companionable silence. My own collage was a mishmash of stuff. Pictures of drinks and elderly people and rainy streets – a glimpse into my life, really. But Micah's was lovely. He'd gone with colours, starting with dark pictures at one end of the paper, fading into light at the other end.

'This is amazing, Micah,' I said, looking at it in awe. 'Did you find it useful?'

He shrugged. 'Bit.' He stood up. 'I should go. Mum will be doing her nut.'

'Do you feel less worried about the appointment?'

'Bit,' he said again.

I stood up too. He towered over me in his gangly teenage boy way, and shrugged once more. But then he gave me an awkward hug. 'Thanks, Steve.'

He headed for the door.

'I'm proud of you,' I called as he went down the stairs.

'Shut up.'

Chuckling to myself I sat down again and picked up my laptop. I was going to write my grant application.

Chapter 15

I didn't hear anything at all about the application for a couple of weeks. I tried to put the grant out of my head and concentrate on Nan, and Tall Trees and The Vine, but I kept checking my emails and picking up my phone to see if I'd had a missed call. The closing date had been and gone and I thought it was probably time to accept that it had been awarded to someone else. It was no biggie, I told myself. No big deal.

But I was still disappointed.

'So you've not heard anything?' Tara asked one day at The Vine when I was gloomily wiping down the tables. 'Is that why you're moping?'

'I'm not moping, I'm distracting myself.'

She tutted. 'Is it working?'

'No.'

I sat down at the table I was supposed to be cleaning and sighed. 'I really thought this might be the beginning of something for me. A new start.' I reached out and picked up a beer mat, spinning it on one side absent-mindedly.

Tara came over and picked up the empty glasses I'd stacked up. 'It still could be. Even the fact that you got it together enough to apply is a new start.'

'I suppose.'

'And you got to meet your hottie professor.'

'I've not heard from him, either. He's doing exams.'

'Surely he's done with all that stuff?' Tara frowned.

'He's not taking the exams himself; his students are doing the exams and he's got to mark them.'

'Thrilling.' Tara shifted the glasses to her other hand and knocked the beer mat from my hand. 'Come on, misery guts. I've got you for thirty more minutes and I'm going to work you hard.'

I groaned. I'd not been sleeping well and the thought of going straight from a lunchtime shift at the bar to an evening shift at Tall Trees made me feel tired. 'Can't I just sit here until it's time to leave?'

'Not if you want me to pay you.'

'Fine.' With an eye roll to rival Micah's best, I got up as my phone buzzed in my back pocket. 'Hang on.'

I took it out and read the message. It was from Blessing. "Please come and see me when you arrive for your shift," she'd written. "I need to speak to you about your community grant art application."

'Weird,' I murmured, showing the screen to Tara. 'I don't think I've even told her about the application.'

Tara put the dirty glasses on the bar and gestured to them. Obediently I followed her and started stacking them in the glasswasher.

'You didn't tell her?'

'No. Why would I?'

'Erm, how about because she manages Tall Trees and you've just applied for a load of cash to cover one of its walls with paint?'

I put my hand to my mouth. 'Oh God, you're right. I was so busy worrying about books and rough sketches that I didn't think to check it would be okay.'

Tara raised an eyebrow. 'I guess she found out somehow.'

'Do you think she's going to sack me?'

'Maybe. I would if it were me.'

I felt sick. 'I need this job, Tara,' I said, beginning to panic. 'What will I do if she sacks me?'

Tara reached out and caught my hands. 'Calm down,' she said, looking straight at me. 'Sorry, I was just messing with you. I should have made it more obvious. Breathe. Are you breathing?'

I nodded, feeling the panic subside. 'Sorry,' I said.

Tara squeezed my fingers and let go and I leaned against the bar. 'I'm such a loser,' I said, mostly to myself.

'You've been having panic attacks again, huh?'

'A few, but not as bad.' I felt a bit embarrassed admitting it. 'Micah's been helping me.'

'Micah the teenager?'

'He has anxiety. We're helping each other.'

'That's cute. Are you using the stuff you learned in your course?'

'I didn't learn much, but I guess so. He's started doing some collages and stuff.'

Tara gave me a look that suggested she was impressed. 'And he helps you, how?'

'He goes to a therapist and then he comes home and tells me all the strategies she's told him.'

'Trickle-down psychiatry,' Tara said with a wry smile. 'If it's working for you, honey, then that's great.'

Suddenly self-conscious, I turned away from her to shut the glasswasher and fiddled with the controls.

'Go on,' Tara said. 'Go and see Blessing. She'll be fine.'

'Do you think so?'

'Totally. She needs you more than you need her. Good care home staff aren't easy to find.'

'I suppose.'

'Go on. Text me when you're done.'

Spontaneously, I kissed her cheek. She stayed still, but she looked pleased.

'Thanks, Tara,' I said.

*

Probably because I wanted it to be slow, my journey to Tall Trees was quick and easy. I locked up my bike and before I could get distracted by anything or anyone else, walked straight to Blessing's office and, with slightly shaky hands, I knocked on the open door.

She was at her desk, surrounded by paperwork, which made me smile. I knew we were supposed to be paper-free now, but she kept printing stuff out anyway.

'Hi,' I said, trying to sound casual and not like a woman about to grovel to keep her job. 'You wanted to see me?'

She looked up and pointed at me. 'Yes! Sit down. Let me find what I was looking at.'

I slid into the chair she'd gestured to and focused out of the window. I could see Helen, the new resident, walking in the grounds. Even though Tall Trees – my bit at least – was a care home rather than a nursing home, she was still quite young to be here. She was probably about a decade younger than Val or some of the other residents. In fact, striding across the grass, she looked both young and fit compared with some of our residents. I wondered if she had a condition I hadn't yet been told about. Something degenerative, perhaps. It was possible.

'I had an email from the council,' Blessing was saying. 'Here it is.' She pulled a piece of paper from under one of her piles. 'And they said you'd applied for a grant to paint the wall.'

She tapped the end of her biro on the print-out and turned it round so I could read it. Except I couldn't really make the words out because my eyes were filling with tears.

'I'm so sorry, Blessing. I didn't think to ask. I was sort of bursting with ideas and excitement and Finn – you know Finn? He said I should just do the application without overthinking it too much, so I did.'

Blessing held her pen up to stop me talking and I shut my mouth. 'Sorry,' I said again.

'It's a good idea,' she said.

'It is?'

'You don't think so?'

'Well, yes, I do. Because that wall is always graffitied, and I thought we could make it look better.'

Blessing nodded. 'I didn't know you were an artist.'

I ducked my head, embarrassed. 'Well, I'm not really,' I said apologetically. 'I mean, I sort of was beginning to be, but then, well, I had some trouble with my brother … you know? And now I mostly just work here.'

Blessing looked at me with her chin resting in her hand. I wasn't sure what she was thinking. But then she smiled. 'Women need to shout about what they do more often, don't you think? We are very good at staying quiet about our achievements. Men go on about them enough.' She leaned over the desk like she was sharing a secret. 'And most of the time, they have nothing to boast about.'

I looked at her, unsure if I was supposed to answer. She chuckled. 'Nothing at all to boast about,' she said. 'You're on the top corridor today. And we're one down in the canteen, because Marie's off sick, so can you help serve dinner, too?'

'Oh,' I said. Did that mean our conversation was over? 'Yes, of course. Thank you.'

I hurried away, feeling like I'd dodged a bullet and still slightly confused. It was only when I was checking the dinner menus a bit later that I realised I hadn't actually read the email from the council, and I still didn't know what it said.

'Probably another reason to turn me down,' I muttered to myself. 'Not having proper permission.'

I should tell Finn, I thought. Warn him that the project was a no-go. I felt a bit sad about not having an excuse to spend time with him after all, but at least he'd still be around. Though summer was coming and didn't universities have really long holidays? He'd probably vanish after the exams were over and not reappear until October.

Suddenly struck with self-pity I slumped into one of the dining chairs and pulled my phone out of my tunic pocket, planning to message Finn and let him know the bad news. Maybe I'd make it sound positive, like thank goodness it wasn't happening because I didn't have time anyway because I was working at The Vine. And that way it was a subtle reminder about where I would be if he ever fancied a drink. I unlocked my phone and saw, with a lurch of nerves, that I also had an email from the council.

'That's it, then,' I said aloud. 'Game over.'

I jabbed my screen with my finger to open the email and stared in amazement at the first word.

"Congratulations!" it read.

'What the …?'

With growing astonishment I read on: "Dear Stephanie, thank you for your application for the Presents from the Past community art grant. I'm pleased to inform you that you have been successful. We'd love you to come in and meet the committee and have a chat about your plans. As we're eager to get things going as soon as possible, please give the office a ring when convenient and we can find a date that suits us all."

I closed the email and took a deep breath. Was I dreaming? Had I misread it? I opened it up again and read it through once more. No, I hadn't misread it. The grant was mine. I was going to be able to do the mural, and start my own book, and find Elsie. Blessing's email had obviously been to tell her the news and now she'd probably told Vanessa and all the other staff would know.

And every time anyone walked past Tall Trees or drove along the road, or trundled by in a bus, they'd see my artwork looking back at them.

'Oh shit,' I gasped as the enormity of what this meant hit me. 'I can't do this.'

My chest tightened in panic. I'd have to ring them and tell them I wasn't able to take on the grant after all. And then I'd have to leave. Go somewhere else, so I didn't have to live with the embarrassment of turning it down. Maybe I could go and live with my dad in Portugal? But then who'd look after my nan? Who'd visit her and check she was doing okay? My breathing was shallow and my head was swimming. I gripped the edge of the table tightly, thinking of Micah and his strategies for dealing with his anxieties. *Focus on your senses, yeah?* I remembered him saying. *Think about something you can smell, or touch.*

I rubbed my fingertips on the tablecloth I was clutching. It was soft cotton that had been washed hundreds of times. I always thought it was silly to use tablecloths when it would be easier just to wipe down the tables, but Blessing said the residents liked them. And right now I was glad of it. I concentrated on the feeling of the fabric under my fingers. Soft, I thought, and tightly woven.

My breathing began to feel more normal. Maybe, I thought, maybe I could do this. Micah would be there to help. And Finn, hopefully. And Tara would do what she could. And frankly giving it a go would be much less humiliating than walking away. I smoothed out the cloth with my palms. And perhaps it could help other people say the things they wanted to say, before it was too late?

'I'm going to do it,' I whispered.

'Do what? Where is everyone?'

I turned in my chair to see Mr Yin standing behind me, looking round at the empty dining room. 'I'm early for dinner,' he said in confusion. 'I think my watch must be fast.' He shook his wrist and gave me a little grin. 'Can I get mine now? I'm hungry already.'

I stood up and gestured for him to sit down in the chair where I'd been sitting. 'Make yourself comfy,' I said. 'I'll get you something to keep you going. Dinner won't be long.'

'Thank you.' He sat down and neatly folded his hands on top of each other on the table. 'But don't let me keep you. Didn't you say you had something to do?'

'I did.'

'What was it? Something important?'

'I'm going to paint a mural on the end wall that's always covered in graffiti.'

Mr Yin looked delighted. 'That's marvellous. Well done.'

'Yes, it is marvellous,' I agreed. 'At least, I hope it will be.'

'I have faith in you, Stephanie.'

I beamed at him. 'Thank you,' I said. 'I hope it's not misguided.'

Chapter 16

Elsie

1940

My good mood lasted all day, even though Nelly and I didn't get much sleep before our night shifts because we'd been so busy.

'You left the book with Barbara?' Nelly asked as we walked to work later. There was no sign of Jackson, for once, and I was glad.

'I did. She was going to take it to her ward because she thought some of her patients might like to write about this war compared with the last one.'

'God, poor buggers, living through this twice,' Nelly said. 'At least they're old enough not to fight this time round. One of the surgeons was telling me yesterday that his brother was at Amiens, when he was only fifteen, and he's joined up again this time. He said his mother is beside herself with worry.'

'Crikey. The poor woman.'

Nelly put her arm through mine. 'I know. It made me think of my mammy, you know? I get annoyed with her fussing, but it's only because she cares.'

'That's what I keep telling you.'

She smiled at me. 'Maybe I should read her letters?'

'You should.'

'I'm staying here, mind you.'

'Glad to hear it.'

As we walked into the hospital, Frank was there chatting to the girl who worked on reception.

'How are you still here?' I said. 'You have to go home, Frank.'

'I'm heading out now,' he said with a grin. 'Don't you worry about me.'

I laughed and he gave me a nudge. 'Everyone's talking about you.'

'Are they?' I gave Nelly a slightly questioning glance and she shrugged. 'Why?'

'Not you personally, it's your book they're talking about,' he said. 'Every ward I go in, people are chatting about it. Everyone wants to write in it.'

'Where is it?' I said. 'Do you know?'

'Last I heard one of the Red Cross nurses had taken it.'

'In the huts?' I frowned. 'I thought all the airmen had written in it already.'

Frank shrugged. 'That's what I heard.'

'I'll go and find it.'

Frank gave me a little mock salute and wandered off. I turned to Nelly. 'Coming?'

'I would,' she said. 'But Percy should just be finishing his shift so I thought I'd see if I could say a quick hello.'

'My book and I can't compete with the charms of Dr Barnet,' I teased.

Nelly kissed me on the cheek.

'You're brilliant, but frankly, no you can't,' she said. She sashayed away from me and I laughed as I headed to the hut, wondering why the airmen had wanted to write more in the book.

Judith was just coming out as I approached, her arms full of sheets for the laundry crate, which was outside. She threw them in and turned to me, looking worried.

'Oh, Elsie,' she said. 'We lost Eric.'

I put my hand to my heart. 'Sweet Eric?' He was so full of life, I couldn't quite believe it.

She nodded her head, sadly. 'Sweet Eric.'

'But he seemed to be recovering well. What happened?'

'Internal bleeding,' she said. 'And then his heart gave out.'

'Lord.'

We stood for a moment in silence. I was thinking of how quickly a life could be snuffed out, and how glad I was that Eric had the chance to write a message.

'How are they doing?' I asked eventually, nodding my head towards the hut.

'Sad and a couple are angry. But they're resigned mostly. That's what's so awful. They just expect to go.' She reached out and took my hand. 'Your book has already helped so much.'

My eyes filled with tears again. I seemed to be doing nothing but crying these days. 'I'm really glad,' I muttered. 'Is it here? Do you have it?'

'It's on the desk. I went to fetch it when Eric died. I wanted to check he'd written in it.'

'He had written, hadn't he?' I screwed my face up, trying to remember if I'd seen something from him. 'Something to his wife?'

'Yes, he wrote to his wife.'

My legs were shaking. Knowing it was totally unprofessional I sat down on the wooden steps leading up to the hut. 'So we can send her the message,' I said. 'That's exactly what I hoped. I can copy it out from the page, and put it in the post for her.'

Judith bit her lip. 'Eric was from the East End. And the telegram that was sent to his wife telling her he'd been injured was returned.' She shook her head. 'No one knows where she is.'

'Blast.' I leaned back, looking up into the grey sky. The sun never seemed to shine anymore. A layer of grime covered everything. 'Is she dead?'

'I don't think so, because I think we'd know if that were the case. I think it's more likely she's been bombed out and had to move.'

'I didn't think of that,' I admitted. 'It didn't occur to me that we'd struggle to send the messages.'

'I might be able to help.' Judith sat down next to me.

'You can?'

'The Red Cross runs the Missing, Wounded and Relatives department,' she said, sitting up straighter as she spoke. 'They might be able to track her down.' She turned to me with a sudden grin. 'I know a chap who works there. I can pull a few strings.'

'Do you think so?'

'He's my husband,' she said. 'He'll help.'

*

When I was back at the hospital a couple of days later for my first day shift, Judith came to find me on my ward.

'Mickey – that's my husband – he found Eric's wife,' she said.

'And does she know?'

Judith nodded, her lips a tight line. 'She does.'

'It's so sad,' I said.

'Mickey told her Eric had left a message for her, and she took a lot of comfort in that.'

'Really?' I put a hand to my chest. 'Then I'll make sure I send it today. Do you have her address?'

Judith pulled a slip of paper from her apron pocket and handed it to me. 'She's staying with a friend's mother, or her mother's friend, one or the other, who runs a boarding house in Clacton.'

'If I write the message during my break, I can catch the post,' I said more to myself than to Judith.

'Do you have the book? With Eric's message in it?'

I nodded. 'It's in the staffroom.'

Judith put her hand on my shoulder. 'Even if none of the other messages get passed on, Eric's wife reading his last letter makes the whole thing worthwhile.'

'Do you think so?'

'I do.'

I smiled. 'I'll send it today.'

'When you're finished do you think you could pop by the huts?' she asked. 'I know the men would like to know what you've done and I'm pretty sure they'd rather hear it from you than from me.'

My cheeks reddened as I thought about Harry and I nodded. 'Of course.'

*

So, at the end of my shift I went to the hut once again. Today the mood among the airmen was more sombre and I wasn't surprised. They'd lost Vinny and Eric in quick succession, not to mention all the men and women who'd been killed by the bomb. There had been so much loss.

'I wanted to let you know that I've written out Eric's message to his wife, and I'm going to post it on my way home.' I looked round at their faces. Less full of fun today and more etched with worry.

'I tell you what,' the airman called Davey said, 'I'm not sure about the others, but knowing I've left a letter that my family can read if ... you know, that makes me feel better. More secure.'

'That's good to know.' I felt tears prickle my eyes again and wondered briefly if I would always feel this way when I thought about Billy. 'My brother ...' I began but my voice cracked. 'He, erm ...'

The baby-faced airman who was always reading the newspaper, had been sitting on top of his bed. Now he stood up and came over to me. 'Got him, did they?'

I nodded. 'Dunkirk,' I whispered.

'What was his name?'

'Billy.'

'Well, I reckon we should have three cheers for Billy. What do you reckon, lads?'

'Nice one, Malcolm,' said Davey. 'Hip hip …'

I laced my fingers together as these kind, funny, brave men all cheered for my brother. The nurses joined in too. I was so moved that when they were done, I couldn't speak. I simply held out my hands, trying to say thank you without speaking.

'Nurse Watson?' I turned to see Harry, in his bed, looking at me with concern. 'Are you all right?'

I gave him a little smile. 'That was just so lovely, it made me all emotional.'

He sniffed. 'You're not the only one,' he said. 'But don't tell the others – they'll tease me rotten.'

'Ah, they were all wiping their eyes,' I told him.

'Life is short,' Harry said. 'And you'd think we'd be used to it by now, but somehow it's always a shock.'

'I think when it stops being a shock, that's when you stop being human.'

'True.' He smiled at me and again I felt that connection between us, like I knew him.

'Nelly, my friend, she says that we should live our lives to the fullest, because we never know when they will end.'

'Nelly's right.'

I knew I should go, because it was getting dark, but I didn't want to leave. Instead I sat down next to his bed.

'How are you feeling? How's your leg?'

Harry hadn't broken his leg but he'd wrenched it so badly he'd damaged some of his ligaments.

'The leg is not great,' he said with a rueful grin. 'But I'm getting the casts off my arms soon.'

'How wonderful. Isn't that a lovely Christmas present?'

Harry looked surprised. 'I'd forgotten that it's almost Christmas.'

'It's only a week away,' I said. 'Nelly and I have decorated our flat with holly.' I lowered my voice. 'She stole it from the park.'

He laughed and I was pleased. 'She is living life to the fullest.'

'She really is.'

His expression darkened a bit and for a second he looked like a little boy who'd lost his favourite toy. 'It's going to be rotten being here on Christmas Day.'

'Oh, blimey. It's Christmas,' said Davey, overhearing. 'What's it like here at Christmas? Will you be working?'

'I will be.'

'Will you bring us presents?' asked baby-faced Malcolm.

I laughed. 'Aren't you a bit old for Father Christmas.'

'Never,' Harry declared.

'I quite like working on Christmas Day,' I told them. 'Well, I always have before now. I can't imagine the Luftwaffe will let up, even if it is December 25, so it'll just be like a normal day.' I remembered the Christmases we'd had at the hospital before the war. 'We usually have carol singers,' I said. 'And the children on the ward get presents. Just something small. And my very first year of nursing, it snowed on Christmas Day, which was really magical.'

'What's your favourite bit of Christmas?' Malcolm asked.

I thought for a moment. 'Carols,' I said. 'They're so beautiful. What's your favourite?'

Malcolm rolled his eyes at the silliness of my question. 'Presents,' he said and I laughed.

Harry cleared his throat. 'Come on, then,' he said to the room.

'God rest ye merry gentlemen,' he began to sing. He had a nice voice, clear and tuneful. One by one, the rest of the airmen joined in. It wasn't always in tune, and some of them didn't know all the words, but it was the nicest carol I thought I'd ever heard.

As they finished singing, I clapped madly and the other nurses all joined in. 'You're all full of Christmas spirit already,' I said. 'Thank you all.'

'Will you come and see us on Christmas Day?' asked Malcolm.

I answered him but it was Harry I was really talking to. 'Just try and stop me,' I said.

I found Nelly waiting for me just inside the main hospital entrance.

'They sang carols for me,' I said as I approached. 'The lovely airmen sang.' She turned to face me and I saw she was looking cross and harried, which was most unlike her. 'What's wrong?'

'I just saw that Jackson,' she said.

I threw my head back in frustration. 'Here? At the hospital?'

'Think he's come to meet you?'

'He knows my shifts,' I said, looking out at the dark sky and shaking my head. 'He is always there. Everywhere I go. And I know he's looking out for me, but it's so annoying. I'm fine. I don't need him.'

Nelly made a face. 'He annoys me and I'm not the one he's following around like a lovesick pup.'

'Urgh, not lovesick,' I said with real force. 'Oh gosh, do you think he's lovesick?'

'He's something all right.'

'Oh, Nell, what should I do?'

'He's not here now, is he?'

I looked around. 'I don't think so.'

'Then let's walk home as fast as we can, and try to stay out of his way for now.'

We wrapped our coats round us a little tighter as we went out into the dark, cold evening.

'I'm so pleased I've got you, Nelly,' I said. 'I don't know what I'd do without you.'

'Same here.' She nudged me with her shoulder. 'Now tell me about these carols.'

Chapter 17

Stephanie

Present day

'Honey, I'm flattered you're asking for my help and of course I'll do what I can, but I'm not sure I can be of any use.' Tara held her hands out, as though she was the one begging for support, and shrugged. 'I'm a bartender, not an artist.'

'I don't need you to paint,' I said, with a chuckle. 'I just need you to help *me* paint.'

'Clean your brushes?'

'Stop it. You know what I mean. I'm hopeless by myself; I need you to give me a shove when I'm struggling to get started, or to put a sketchpad in my hand.'

'Shut up,' said Micah mildly. He was sitting at the table with Tara and me. I'd summoned them both to an emergency meeting to discuss me getting the grant and actually having to put my ideas into action. Now he looked at me and shook his head. 'You're not hopeless. You look after all them old people at that home, and your nan. And you work here and that. And you help me all the time.'

Embarrassed and touched by his praise I kicked him under the table. 'You shut up,' I said with affection.

'The kid speaks sense,' Tara said. 'You're more than capable of pulling this off alone.'

All the bravado I'd felt when I'd spoken to Mr Yin about my plans had deserted me. I just felt sick all the time so I'd rung Tara in a panic this morning, begging her to help. Micah had appeared in the kitchen as I was talking to her on the phone, so he'd come along with me to The Vine.

'Shall I get us some drinks?' Tara said.

I looked at my watch. 'It's a bit early, T.' It was Sunday morning and the bar wasn't even open yet.

'I meant coffee.'

'Oh yes, coffee would be good.' Probably for the best. I'd barely slept last night worrying about the mural and how I was going to pull it off. I'd made a list of everything I'd need to make it work, so I could take it to my meeting with the council. But I'd got scared when I wrote "scaffolding and ladders" and hadn't written anything else. And I had absolutely no idea how to do the rest of the project – a notebook for residents to write in I could just about manage, but finding Elsie? I hadn't a clue where to start.

Tara got up and made us all coffees. The hissing of the machine made it hard to talk for a minute, but as she put our drinks down in front of us, she said: 'Is Finn coming?'

'No, why?'

'Because this whole project is linked with his historical stuff, and he's cute, and I think he should be here.'

I looked down at the froth on top of my coffee. Tara had drawn a heart in the milk.

'What did he say when you told him you'd got the grant?' Tara asked.

'I've not told him yet.'

'Stevie, why not?'

'Because he's busy and I didn't want to bother him,' I said. 'His students have got their exams and there's a lot of marking to do.'

'It's Sunday,' Micah pointed out.

'So?'

'So message him now and tell him. They won't be doing exams today and he might be glad of a break from marking.'

'I don't know what to say.'

'Oh for heaven's sake, it's not you who's doing an exam.' Tara picked my phone up from the table and briskly entered my passcode without even asking me what it was.

'Hey,' I said. 'How do you know that?'

'Sweetie, you always use your birthday.'

'Max's birthday,' I muttered, realising as I said it how ridiculous it was. I didn't even need Micah rolling his eyes to tell me.

'There.' Tara handed the phone back to me.

'What did you do?'

'Messaged Finn.'

My heart thumped hard as I opened the message. Tara had written: "Great news! Got the grant so my mural is happening. Having a chat about it all now at The Vine if you fancy joining us. Could do with your help. Coffees and croissants on me."

'Are there actually croissants?' Micah said hopefully, reading the message over my shoulder.

'Micah,' I tutted. Then I looked at Tara. 'Are there?'

'In the kitchen.'

Micah did a little fist pump and I turned my attention back to the screen. The message wasn't horrendous. In fact, it was just the right balance of friendly and needy. Way better than I'd have written. Which only made me feel more hopeless.

'I feel sick again,' I groaned.

'Can I have your croissant?' Micah said.

My phone buzzed and I dropped it like it was hot. Tara swooped and picked it up.

'He's coming,' she said in triumph.

'Here? Now?'

'Here and now.'

She showed me Finn's reply, which was a GIF of a little boy dancing. Underneath he'd written: "On my way."

'I look awful,' I wailed. 'I don't want to see him.'

'Pull yourself together.' Tara looked stern. 'You look fine. It's fine. Everything's fine.' She narrowed her eyes at me. 'But maybe drag a brush through your hair.'

'Tara!'

'I've got some bits in the office. Go and check your makeup, do your hair, and I'll sort the pastries.'

'All right,' I said. 'Thank you.'

Feeling jittery, I headed to the office where Tara had a mirror on the wall. My reflection wasn't as disastrous as I feared. The eyeliner I'd put on before I left home was still in place. I brushed my hair and then tied it back when it went frizzy because I'd brushed it too much, then took it out again because it was too severe and my ears stuck out.

By the time I'd found a stretchy leopard-print headband in one of Tara's desk drawers and put that on, I could hear laughter coming from the bar, and smell pastries. Finn must have arrived.

I took a deep breath. This was ridiculous. I had a silly crush on him – that was all. He'd come to hear about the mural, not to see me, and I had to get a hold of myself.

But when I walked into the bar and saw him sitting there, my stomach flipped over in a most alarming way and I felt my cheeks redden.

'Hi,' he said, looking at me with what seemed to me to be approval. 'I like your hair.'

'Oh, thank you,' I said, flustered. 'It's Tara's.'

'Your hair?' Finn frowned and I rubbed my nose, feeling silly. 'No, the headband.'

Finn laughed and I felt better.

'I was telling Finn that you're having a meeting next week about the mural,' Tara said as I sat down in the only empty seat, which happened to be next to Finn even though it was where Micah had been sitting before I'd gone into the office.

'I am,' I said, grateful of the distraction from the knowledge that his long legs were only inches from mine. 'With the council people.' I told him all about the meeting and my plans, and Micah chimed in with some surprisingly useful suggestions. Finn listened intently, nodding along and asking some thoughtful questions, until I ran out of steam.

'That's it, really,' I said eventually.

'It's amazing,' he said. 'Honestly.'

I fiddled with Tara's headband. 'Do you think so?' I said. 'I'm worried I've bitten off more than I can chew.'

'Absolutely not.' Finn looked straight at me and I felt my face flush again. 'You've got this.'

Flustered, I bit into a croissant, dropping flaky pastry down my top.

'I actually brought something that might help,' Finn said, as I brushed the crumbs away. He reached down under the table and brought out a box, like the type companies store old files in.

'Moving in?' Tara joked.

Finn chuckled. He took the top off the box and gestured for me to look inside. 'It's the book,' he said triumphantly.

'You showed me that before,' I said, a little confused. 'Remember?'

'Well, yes, but I thought you could keep it while you're making your plans. It's easier to read the real thing than the scans on a screen.'

'Are you serious?' I couldn't believe he was trusting me with them. 'Isn't it valuable?'

'Not in a monetary sense,' Finn said. 'But as long as you don't spill anything on it, or set fire to it …'

'Or lose it,' Micah said helpfully. 'Or leave it on the bus.'

I glared at him. 'I'd love to look at it,' I said to Finn, over-whelmed by the gesture. 'If you're sure?'

'Of course.'

'I've been looking at the messages online but I think it'll be easier to get a proper sense of Elsie from the real thing.' I was beginning to get excited. 'How long can I keep it for?'

'I'm still in the middle of marking exams, so a couple of weeks?' Finn said.

'Perfect. This is so kind of you, Finn.'

He pushed his hair away from his forehead and smiled at me.

'Will you be all right getting it home?' he said. 'It's quite heavy. Are you on your bike?'

I'd not thought about that. I screwed my nose up. 'I am and I don't have my rucksack with me.'

'I'll give you a ride,' Tara said. 'No problem.'

'Thanks, Tara.'

Finn looked at his watch and, worried he was going to leave and I wouldn't know when I'd next see him, I said: 'Perhaps it would be easiest to keep the book at Tall Trees? I could put it in your cupboard and then if you do need it for some reason, you'll know where to find it.'

'Sounds good,' said Finn.

Pleased, I leaned back in my chair as there was a knock on the door of the bar. Tara got up to let Barney, the chef, in. He'd arrived to get the Sunday lunches started.

'Just going to sort the menu, honey,' Tara said, disappearing off into the kitchen after him.

'Oh my days,' Micah said suddenly. 'I need to go. I'm meant to be going to watch my sister play football. Will you be okay?'

'Of course,' I said, touched that he'd checked. 'Go. I'll catch up with you later.'

He pulled his hood up, even though it was a sunny day, and put his earbuds in. Shutting out the world as he was heading outside, I thought. It wasn't easy being a teen these days.

He slouched off, giving me a cheery wave as he walked past the window of the pub.

And then there was just Finn and me.

'So,' he said.

'Yes?' I looked at him, fighting the urge to brush his hair off his face.

'You said you needed my help?'

'Oh,' I was flustered suddenly. 'Yes, I did. I want to find out what happened to Elsie. I think it would really help give the project legs, you know?'

Legs? Oh, Stevie.

But Finn smiled. 'I'll make a historian of you yet.'

'Well,' I admitted, 'I don't have a clue how to begin. I know you said you didn't have a death certificate. I wondered if you could show me how to look for stuff like that?'

'Of course.' Finn's eyes shone. 'I brought my laptop just in case.'

He got his computer out and I watched as he brought up a website called myancestors.co.uk.

'Like I said, I did a bit of research into Elsie ages ago when we first got the book, and found her birth certificate and her employment record, but I've not looked her up since.'

'Could the information have changed?'

'Maybe,' said Finn. 'But I doubt it.' He typed in Elsie Watson and hit return and up came the results.

'There are a few,' he said, 'but obviously you can discount the ones whose dates don't match, and then it's easy enough to find our Elsie because she was born round here.'

'In South London District Hospital?' I said, wondering if Elsie had entered the world in Tall Trees. But Finn shook his head as he clicked on one of the entries.

'At home, actually. Here she is. Elsie Watson, born 28 August 1919. Place of birth: 17 Cedars Road. Parents: Agnes and Anthony Watson.'

'I know where Cedars Road is,' I said, delighted. 'It's near my dentist.'

Finn laughed.

'So we have her birth certificate, but nothing else?' I said, frowning at the screen. 'No marriage certificate? No children? No death certificate?'

'No.'

'And is that strange in itself?'

'It is a bit.' He sighed. 'She might have moved abroad.'

'When did she leave the hospital? Did you say you had her employment record?'

'Here.' Finn typed a few words, then he pulled up another page on his screen. 'See, it has the same address: Cedars Road. Her next of kin is her brother William Watson. She trained at the hospital between 1936 and 1938, when she qualified.' He pointed to the screen. 'She left in 1941.'

'Is there like a central database of nurses? Could we see if she went to another hospital in England?'

He shrugged. 'There is, but it would just show that she was a registered nurse, not where she worked.'

Disappointed, I felt my shoulders slump. 'I've hit a brick wall already.'

Finn shook his head. 'Not necessarily. The interesting thing about social history is there's always another way round. Maybe the direct route hasn't worked, but you'll find another way.'

'Do you think so?'

'I know so. It's happened to me loads of times. And you often find out all sorts of other interesting stuff while you're looking.'

'Where should I start?'

'Perhaps find out more about the history of the hospital? See what you can find out about its role during the war?'

'Can you help me?'

'There's nothing I'd like more,' he said with a grin, and again I felt my stomach flip. 'But, I can't.'

'Work?' I tried to sound casual and not show how disappointed I was.

155

'Exams and assessments. But I'll have more time in a couple of weeks. So how about you get started and I'll help when I can?'

'Sounds good,' I said.

Finn checked his watch again. 'I have to go, I'm sorry. I've got a rescheduled tutorial, even though it's Sunday.'

'Every day's a work day,' I said with a smile.

He got up from his seat, and patted Elsie's book. 'I'm sorry to leave because I'd loved to have gone through the book with you.'

'I'd have liked that too,' I said, hardly able to believe my own boldness. 'When you have an hour spare, drop me a message.'

Finn held my gaze a fraction longer than was necessary. 'I will.'

Chapter 18

Finn had told me to find out more about the hospital during the war, and I knew exactly how to do it. There was a book – the one Helen had snatched from under my nose from the mobile library – and I was going to find it. I couldn't for the life of me remember what it had been called, so simply ordering it from Amazon or finding it in the bigger library in the town centre wasn't an option. I had to get it from Helen.

She'd been keeping herself to herself since she'd arrived at Tall Trees. That wasn't unusual; it often took new residents a while to settle in. But though I'd tried to get to know her a bit better and find common ground, she wasn't very responsive. Maybe though, chatting about local history would give us something in common. She was clearly interested in it.

So I thought I'd go and see her in her room – she didn't spend much time in the communal areas – and spend some time with her. It would be useful for me and my quest to find Elsie, but it would also – hopefully – make her feel more at home.

So I knocked on her door after dinner one evening. It was one of those awful summer days where it's muggy and unpleasant all day and then lashing down with rain all evening. Helen's window was open and I commented as I went in, 'I'm glad Cyril got it open for you. These rooms can get stuffy. You're not getting damp, are you?'

She was sitting in her armchair next to the window, reading a Katie Fforde novel that I'd seen on the bookshelf in the lounge only yesterday. She obviously did spend some time in the communal areas then, despite what I'd thought.

'I like listening to the rain,' she said. 'It reminds me of home.'

'Dublin?'

'That's right.' Helen's face was turned away from me, looking outside to where the heavy raindrops were bouncing off the terrace. She looked very peaceful and, I thought, content.

'What brought you to us?'

Like a door slamming shut, her expression changed.

'Personal reasons,' she muttered.

There was a short, awkward silence.

'Do you still have the books you got from the mobile library?' I asked, looking around her room. Ah, there they were. In a pile on top of her bookshelf. 'Is that them?'

Helen got up. 'What was it you wanted?'

'I wondered if I could have a look at one of the books?' I asked, feeling oddly like I was asking something outlandish. 'The one about hospitals.'

She looked right at me. 'There isn't one about hospitals.'

What on earth? I knew that I should let it go, but I could see the book on top of the pile. *Bombs and Bandages*, it was called. I didn't understand why this woman was being so difficult but I wasn't going to give up.

'Just the one on top.' I took a step towards her and she moved so she was standing in between me and the bookshelf.

'Would you excuse me, I ned to get ready for bed,' she said.

'It's not even six o'clock.'

'I'm tired.' She looked at me, her eyes unblinking. 'Goodnight.'

Totally bewildered, I admitted defeat. 'Goodnight,' I said.

I stood for a minute outside her closed door, wondering why

she was so determined to stop me looking at the book. Maybe she was just contrary? I didn't blame her, really. I had plans to be quite a grumpy old woman myself one day. But that didn't help me now.

Unless … I could do contrary too. And now I'd remembered what the book was called.

I pulled my phone out of my tunic pocket, and leaning against the wall in the corridor, I looked up the local library. Ah-ha! Success. You could search for books and reserve them online. Quickly, I typed in *Bombs and Bandages* and pressed enter and there it was. Two copies. One was on loan – of course it was, it was in Helen's room right next to where I stood. And the other was available. I clicked on the link to reserve it.

"Please enter your membership number," it said.

I knew I'd been a member of the library once but I had no idea where my card was, nor what my membership number was.

Undeterred, I checked the opening hours on the website and for once, luck was on my side. Today was the day they stayed open later. I hit the phone number and waited for it to ring.

'South London Library, Sindhu speaking.'

'Sindhu,' I said, starting to walk down the corridor so Helen wouldn't hear me from her room. 'It's Stephanie from Tall Trees. Could you reserve a book for me?'

*

Sindhu did what she had to do – she even found my membership number for me – so the following morning, before I had to be back at the home, I went off to the library.

I'd not been there for ages, not since I'd been thinking about art therapy and looking up courses, but it hadn't changed. Sindhu saw me arrive and took the book out from under the counter.

'I wasn't sure what you needed,' she said, handing it over. 'So I reserved you a computer too. It's the one on the end.'

159

'I'm doing a community art project,' I told her proudly. And slightly nervously because saying the words to new people made it seem very real and very intimidating. 'It's based on the history of Tall Trees.'

'Wonderful,' she said. 'I didn't know you were an artist.'

I opened my mouth to say I wasn't really, like I always did now, but instead I said: 'I am.'

'Good for you,' said Sindhu. 'Give me a shout if you need anything.'

I went over to the desk she'd reserved for me and sat down. The book had a white cover with several black-and-white pictures on the front of hospital wards and nurses with funny headdresses on. I studied those photos for a moment then flicked through to find more inside – I was definitely more of a pictures person than a words one.

The photographs were fab. There were some amazing shots – one of a man, clearly badly injured, being cared for by a nurse, who was leaning over and lighting his cigarette. Another showed a newborn baby being cuddled by its mother, in what seemed to be a hospital bed inside a cave. Somewhere in the depths of my memory I remembered going on a school trip to the caves that weren't far from here and the guide telling us that people used them as an air raid shelter. I shivered. What a horrible thought. Although, far nicer than being bombed, I supposed.

I flicked through photos of the big hospital that was still used today, though now it was much more modern with a large extension, and the one that had been demolished to make way for luxury flats. And then I found Tall Trees. There was a photo of the building, very similar to the one Finn had showed me, with the poplars standing straight at the side.

There was another shot of some doctors, discussing a patient while he looked at them over the top of his newspaper in a most disdainful fashion. I squinted at the window behind them, trying to work out where in Tall Trees they were, but I couldn't get my bearings.

And then I struck gold.

There was a photograph of the outside of the building, the entrance looking very different from the modern large porch we had now, with its double-glazed windows. Next to the doorway, stood five nurses in a row, seemingly waiting for something. They weren't posing for the picture – they looked like they'd been snapped in the middle of doing something. They were wearing white dresses with crisp, clean aprons over the top and the funny caps, like in some of the other photos.

I read the caption: "Nurses at South London District Hospital await the arrival of more casualties from the East End, January 1941. From left to right, Matron Virginia Morris, with Staff Nurses Lucille Lewis, Enid Prendergast, Elsie Watson and Petra Bateman."

'Oh my goodness,' I said aloud. A man sitting at the computer next to me gave me a hard stare.

'Sorry,' I muttered, wriggling in my chair with excitement and trying to stay quiet.

I looked at the photograph, wishing I could zoom in on the page. Elsie was looking straight at the camera, a slight frown on her face as though she was wondering why the photograph was being taken. She was so young, I thought. Young and pretty, though her expression was serious. I touched my finger to her likeness briefly. *What happened to you?* I wondered.

There was a whole chapter on nursing during the Blitz. I read it carefully, marvelling at how stoical and brave the medical staff had been. Towards the end of the chapter, there was a mention of Petra Bateman – one of the women in the photograph with Elsie. She had worked at South London District Hospital until it closed in 1970, I read, and had been given a special award for service at a ceremony to mark the closure. There was a photograph of Petra Bateman, clutching what looked to be a glass paperweight.

On a whim, I turned on the computer and typed in "South London District Hospital", then added "closure" and "1970".

Up came the same photograph of Petra that I'd seen in the book. I clicked on it, and it took me to an article in a local history journal. It was in closely typed, tiny font, which didn't make me want to read it. But at the bottom was another picture of Petra alongside another woman about her age, and a younger woman with the same sharp cheekbones that Petra had. They looked extremely 1970s, with long dresses and big hair and I assumed the younger woman was Petra's daughter. I zoomed in and gasped. Was the other woman Elsie? It certainly looked like her. Older, of course, but there was a definite likeness. I studied the photograph in the *Bombs and Bandages* book. Elsie was standing with one arm across her body, holding on to her opposite elbow. And in the picture from the 1970s, she was standing in the same way. I was pretty sure that was my Elsie. I felt a bubble of joy inside. She didn't die in the war, then? This was brilliant.

Feeling like I'd really achieved something, I took a photograph of the picture on screen with my phone, which was very low-tech but would have to do. Then I thanked Sindhu for her help, and I went outside with my *Bombs and Bandages* book and called Finn. As the phone rang, I felt the first stirrings of panic. I hoped he wasn't teaching or doing anything that meant he couldn't talk. I didn't want to interrupt …

'Stevie,' he answered, sounding friendly and welcoming and I relaxed a little bit.

'You're not busy, are you?'

'No, just marking some exams and losing the will to live. So it's nice to have a distraction. What's up?'

'I'm pretty sure that Elsie didn't die,' I blurted. 'Not in the war, anyway.'

'How do you know?'

'I don't know for sure, but I saw a photograph from a nurses' reunion thing in 1970.'

'Where are you?' Finn said.

'Just outside the library.'

'I'm in the café on the corner near Tall Trees,' he said. 'The one with the green awning. Fancy a coffee? You can tell me everything.'

'I'm on my way.'

*

I cycled so fast that I was all sweaty and out of breath when I got near the café, so I slowed right down and took it easier. I didn't want Finn to see me with a red face and damp armpits. Though my hair was flat from my helmet and my nose was shiny, so I thought he really wouldn't be seeing me at my best anyway. Oddly, though, I found I didn't care. I just wanted to tell him what I'd found out and see his face light up with the thrill of it all.

What was happening to me?

Finn was out in the café garden in a shady corner. He stood up when I approached and gave me a hug, which I hadn't been expecting but I liked it even though I was a bit worried about being sweaty and gross. He looked a bit flustered when he let go and I liked that too.

I ordered a cold drink from the waitress because I was overheating after my bike ride, and grinned at Finn.

'Tell me everything,' he said.

'I found a photograph of nurses from the hospital at a do in 1970, and I'm pretty sure this is Elsie.' I showed him the picture I'd snapped on my phone. 'See?'

'It could be her,' said Finn thoughtfully.

I must have looked disappointed because he added quickly: 'It's definitely a good start. What's next?'

'I thought I should go back to the book. I wondered if any of the nurses wrote messages. Maybe there's a clue in there?'

'Brilliant,' said Finn. 'You're turning into a historian in front of my eyes.'

I snorted. 'It's not a real thing,' I said, giving him a wink. 'I keep telling you.'

Chapter 19

Elsie

January 1941

For the first time since Christmas, Nelly and I had the night off at the same time. Nelly had briefly mentioned going out somewhere, but even as she said it, she was beginning to laugh, because we were both so tired that we could hardly stand, let alone dance. She was exhausted with her new role in the operating theatre, and the raids had barely let up with more people arriving at hospital every night with terrible, life-changing injuries that pushed all of us nurses to our limits.

I wasn't a great cook, but I'd managed to rustle up a stew that was, I had to admit, more veg than meat, but it smelled good. We ate early, because we wanted to be finished before the siren went off.

It was a full moon tonight. When I'd been walking home earlier, two women sitting at the bus stop had been looking up at the sky as I passed.

'Bombers' moon,' one of them said to the other.

The other woman had shuddered. 'Barely a cloud in the sky,' she said. 'No clouds and a full moon.'

'Bound to be a bad one,' her friend agreed. 'Best get home, fast as we can.'

I'd hurried down the road, eager to get to safety. And now I was chivvying Nelly along, as I washed up our dinner plates, but she was peering into the mirror that hung over our fireplace.

'Percy said my freckles are sweet,' she said, leaning forward.

I leaned backwards away from the sink, so I could see her in the lounge. 'Nell, watch yourself there. Your skirt's dangling into the fire.'

'Do you think I look like a little girl?'

'No, I don't. And I really don't think Percy does either.'

Nelly was actually beautiful. I always thought she looked like a film star. Like Vivien Leigh, perhaps, with her pale skin and dark hair. And her freckles just added to her beauty, in my opinion.

Nelly sighed theatrically. 'All the Malones are cursed with freckles.'

'Cursed or blessed?' I said, rolling my eyes as I put the last plate on the drainer and, after drying my hands, went into the lounge.

'Do you think I should grow my hair?' Nelly twirled one of her gleaming curls around her finger and examined it closely. 'Sure, it's not as shiny as it used to be.'

'That's because you are hungry and tired and it's full of brick dust and smoke.'

Nelly turned to me and gave me a beaming smile. 'You're right,' she said. 'I'm a silly vain old thing.'

'Not old,' I said. 'But vain, undoubtedly.'

Nelly grinned again.

'Come on, let's get ready.' I was feeling nervy and on edge. I gave the blackout curtain at the kitchen window a tug to make sure it was properly closed.

Nelly nodded. 'It's still early.'

'I know. I just feel uneasy.'

'Bombers' moon, isn't it?'

'It's so clear tonight.'

And as if I'd made it so, the siren suddenly began to screech. Nelly and I both jumped.

'Early,' she said. 'Come on, then.' She tugged my sleeve gently. 'Check the gas, and I'll grab our coats.'

'No coat needed, darling,' Nelly drawled. 'I'll get my robe.'

For Christmas, Percy had given Nelly the most beautiful robe. It was made of some silky brightly coloured material with fringing on the sleeves. It was ridiculously over the top but she loved it. And I loved Percy for choosing it for her, because it was absolutely perfect for Nelly.

It was very glamorous – like something you'd see in the pages of a magazine and definitely designed for women who wafted round fabulous apartments in New York rather than maisonettes in South East London. Since Christmas she'd put it on whenever there was a raid 'so I look glamorous if I'm ever in need of being rescued'. I thought she was mad because it was a bitterly cold winter. I preferred to wrap up warm in my coat and as many layers as I could fit underneath.

I darted into the kitchen and made sure everything was turned off. Nelly pulled on her robe and, because she was prone to boredom stuck inside the shelter for hours, collected a pile of books and a newspaper, and a pack of cards. Then we went downstairs, and I put on my coat as we went. Mrs Gold came out of her front door just as we reached the bottom.

'Oh, girls, lovely,' she said. 'Mr Gold's at work and I wasn't sure if I'd be alone in that blasted shelter tonight.'

She was struggling holding a pile of folders full of papers, and with her coat draped over her shoulders. On top of the pile were the gloves Nelly and I had made her as a Christmas gift. Touched that she was using them, I went to her and helped her into her jacket.

As she pushed her arm into the sleeve, I noticed that several of the documents she was trying to stuff into the folder on top were stamped "Confidential". And one of them appeared to be in German.

Mrs Gold saw me glance at the papers and shoved them in, shutting the folder firmly. 'Awfully boring,' she said. 'I can't believe I have to bring typing home from the office. We're terribly short-staffed.'

I looked over her shoulder through her front door, which opened directly into the Golds' lounge, and where I couldn't see any typewriter. Mrs Gold shut the door with a bang. 'We should hurry,' she said.

The moon was so bright outside, it was like daylight. The bombers would have no trouble finding London tonight.

We walked round to the back of the house, then stood for a minute in the garden, feeling the sharp evening air on our cheeks.

In wonder, we looked around the garden, hearing shouts from other houses as people hurried to their shelters.

A car went by, grabbing my attention, and I looked along the side return next to the house and into the street. There, on the other side of the road, was Jackson. At least I thought it was Jackson, standing stock-still on the pavement, looking up at our house. I gasped. But then a cloud covered the moon and the garden went dark. And when the cloud moved away again, there was no one there. Perhaps I'd been imagining it.

The distant boom of the anti-aircraft gun, which was only a couple of miles away, told us the planes were approaching. Then, from overhead, we heard them. Louder than they'd ever been so far. As one, we all turned and looked up, to see them coming from the south, in awful, sinister formation.

'We need to get into the shelter,' Mrs Gold said. She sounded rattled, which was unusual. She set off down the garden, and Nelly and I followed.

The plane engines were louder now, and Nelly grabbed my arm in fright as we heard the whistle that meant a bomb had dropped.

'The railway line will be shining in the moonlight,' she said. 'It's going to be so easy for them tonight.'

'Inside,' Mrs Gold said briskly. She yanked open the door of the shelter and went down the few stairs and we followed. It was freezing inside and smelled dank and damp. I thought that for as long as I lived, if this war ever ended, I would never again go underground. No tube trains. No houses with cellars. I would stay above ground in the fresh air.

Mrs Gold lit the lamp and we blinked in the dim light. I sat down on one of the narrow beds. It was so early – we would be here for hours. I wondered if it had been Jackson I'd seen outside the house, and if it was, where he was now. Home safely, I hoped. Though I didn't like him I didn't wish him ill.

Another crash made us all jump.

'Blast,' Nelly said, going through her pile of entertainment. 'I don't have the poetry book Percy bought me. I definitely picked it up, it was on top of everything else.'

'Perhaps you dropped it?' I said, privately thinking she'd read those poems a million times already and surely she knew them all off by heart by now?

Nelly clutched her chest. 'I stumbled when we were in the garden,' she said. 'When that cloud covered the moon for a moment, I lost my footing. Maybe I dropped it then?'

'Oh well,' said Mrs Gold. 'It'll still be there in the morning. Who fancies a game of gin rummy?'

'I'd rather have a gin,' said Nelly gloomily. She tilted her head, listening to the planes overhead. 'I'll just go and have a quick look. It'll be on the path, I'm sure.'

'Nell, I don't think that's a very good idea,' I said.

'It's fine, Elsie.' She tutted at me, and I looked at Mrs Gold, who shrugged her shoulders as if to say "what can you do?"

Nelly pushed open the door and went up the two steps to the garden. 'God,' she said. 'Look at this.'

'What is it?' I leaned out of the entrance to see what she was talking about and gasped as I saw the stream of planes overhead. The engines were deafening and I thought about the people in the East End, knowing they were coming – probably hearing them already – and bracing themselves for the destruction to come. 'Maybe we should go to the hospital,' I said, to myself really. 'We'll be needed.'

'Not now. It's not safe.' Mrs Gold had squeezed in next to me and was looking up at the sky, white-faced. She raised her voice over the sound of the planes and shouted: 'Come on, Nelly, come back.'

Nelly's book was lying on the path, quite close to the house, its white cover gleaming in the moonlight.

Nelly called something over her shoulder but I couldn't hear her properly. The planes overhead were even louder now, their engines roaring. They were so low I wanted to duck down and cover my head with my arms.

'Nelly, come back,' I yelled, but I knew she couldn't hear us.

She ran along the path, scooped up the book, and turned back to us, holding it high in triumph. There was a whistling sound from overhead and an enormous, blinding flash. It felt, for a second, as though all the air had been sucked from where we stood, with a whooshing sensation. Everything was silent and the world slowed down, and then it rushed back at me, with a horrifying roar and a blast of hot air that was so powerful it knocked me off my feet and sent me flying into the back of the Anderson shelter.

And then everything went dark.

*

I was dazed for a moment, not completely sure what had happened as I heard the bangs and thuds around me. But then the horror engulfed me again and I struggled to my feet.

'Nelly,' I gasped.

Mrs Gold was getting up too. She had blood trickling down her face. She put her hand to her forehead and then glanced at her fingers, dark with sticky liquid, and she looked at me with a confused frown. I knew I should help her, but …

'Nelly,' I said again.

Like a cloud passing from the sun, Mrs Gold's bewildered expression cleared.

'Oh Lord, Nelly,' she said.

As one, we both rushed to the door of the shelter – which was gone, blown off by the force of the blast, it seemed – and in absolute shock and dismay, we looked out on to a scene of devastation.

The air was filled with smoke and dust and it was difficult to see what was happening. I screwed my eyes up against the grit that was flying around everywhere and tried to make sense of it all. Our house hadn't been hit. At least, I could see it silhouetted against the orange flames that were burning and knew it was standing. But I couldn't see Nelly.

Bitter smoke hit my throat and made me gasp for air and I coughed violently.

'Here,' Mrs Gold nudged me and pushed a scarf into my hands. 'Use this.'

I tied the fabric over my nose and mouth and made to crawl out of the shelter. But Mrs Gold gripped my thighs. 'We should stay here,' she said.

I looked at her over my shoulder. 'I need to find Nelly.' I kicked my legs so she'd let go, and clambered up on to the lawn – what was left of it.

'Nelly?' I bellowed. But there was so much noise – sirens, and shouts, and screams and crashes – that I could barely hear my own voice.

And then ahead of me a figure rose up. So scared and diso-rientated was I that for a crazed moment I thought it was an angel with fiery wings, coming to take me to the afterlife, with an unworldly cry. But I blinked and I suddenly understood it was no angel – it was Nelly. My lovely, darling Nelly with her robe alight and flapping in the wind. And she was howling in fear and pain.

'Get the blankets,' I screeched over my shoulder to Mrs Gold. 'Quickly!'

Keeping low to the ground I scurried along the garden to where Nelly stood screaming, and without thinking, I grabbed her round her shins and rugby-tackled her on to the grass. I was acting on instinct, and I just knew I had to stop the flames however I could.

I could barely see a thing, but I heard Mrs Gold next to me, her breathing ragged and raspy, and I reached up so I could take the blanket she pushed towards me.

With Nelly on the ground, I covered her now silent body with the blanket and rolled her up, pushing her this way and that, until I was certain the flames were out, talking all the time in case she could hear me. 'It's going to be all right, Nell,' I muttered. 'You're going to be fine. It's all going to be all right.'

Nelly was still and quiet and my heart was thumping so hard in my chest, I thought I might be sick or pass out, but I unwrapped the blanket and put my hand to my best friend's breastbone and felt, with utter, glorious relief, the rise and fall of her breath.

'She's alive,' I said. 'She's alive.'

I felt rather than saw Mrs Gold scramble to her feet and disappear. 'Come on, Nelly,' I said. 'Keep breathing. Keep going.'

Nelly's breaths were shallow and gasping, and I was frightened for her. I knew we had to get her to hospital. I couldn't see her properly because of the smoke and dust, but I knew she had to be terribly burned. And, I thought, looking around me, it wasn't safe to be here. The fence was ablaze, one of the trees in the garden was burning like a fiery torch, and our neighbours' house was gone. Simply gone.

'Elsie?' Mrs Gold was back, this time with some other people. 'Elsie, these women will help Nelly.'

'Oh, thank God,' I breathed.

Unsteadily I got to my feet. There were two ambulance drivers there – women I vaguely recognised from the hospital – and behind them two firewomen, pointing their hose at the fence to make sure we could get out of the garden safely.

'She's breathing,' I said, trying to sound professional. 'She's alive. But I think she's burned. She was alight.' My voice caught on the words. 'She was burning.'

'You did well,' one ambulance woman said. 'You saved her. We can take her now.'

'Mrs Gold needs help too,' I said. 'She's bleeding.'

I heard Mrs Gold's protests that she was fine, but I ignored them. 'Help them both,' I said urgently. And then, all my energy spent, I sank to the ground and cried.

Chapter 20

Nelly was alive. She was alive and I was so glad. But her burns were worse than I could have imagined.

'She was wearing some sort of housecoat,' one of the emergency doctors explained to me, early the morning after the raid. I knew him – his face was familiar to me and he called me Nurse Watson so he clearly knew me too – but my mind refused to call up his name.

'The housecoat caught alight and stuck to her body as it burned,' he went on.

'It was a robe,' I muttered. 'Not a housecoat.'

The doctor looked at me oddly but he carried on. 'She's got burns to the right of her torso,' he said. 'Her right arm, her right leg, and the right side of her face. It's too early to tell but she's probably going to lose the sight in her right eye. Her hair caught fire, which is why her face is so badly injured, and her ear is damaged so we think she may well have some hearing loss. Also …'

'Enough,' I cried holding my hands out. 'Enough. She's alive.'

'She's alive for now,' the doctor said carefully.

'Is she to stay here?'

'She isn't stable enough to move.'

'Is she conscious?'

He gave a vehement shake of his head. 'She is sedated. The pain …'

His voice trailed off and I breathed in deeply 'Can I see her?'

'You can. She's in the side room off ward 2.'

Ward 2. Of course she was in ward 2 – the ward where the sickest patients were cared for. It was a frightening place full of artificial lungs and still figures with masks and bandages covering their faces. I had known that Nelly would be there, but it was still a shock to hear the doctor say it.

'Nurse Watson,' the doctor said. 'Don't …' He screwed his face up. 'Don't get your hopes up. Nurse Malone is very poorly.'

'I know.'

I thanked him, and hurried off along the corridor towards ward 2.

'Elsie?' A voice made me turn and there was Mrs Gold, her pretty face streaked with soot and a large dressing on her forehead.

I wasn't sure I'd ever been quite so pleased to see anyone in my whole life. I rushed to her and she rushed to me and we threw our arms around one another and clung on for dear life.

'Where's Nelly?' she said. 'Is she here? Is she alive? I've been so scared, Elsie.'

I untangled my arms from Mrs Gold's, smelling the smoke from her clothes as she moved. 'She's not good,' I said in a small voice. 'She's very badly burned.'

'Oh Lord.' Mrs Gold hung on to my hand. 'Have you seen her?'

'I'm on my way now, but she's sedated. She won't know I'm there.'

'She might,' Mrs Gold said with conviction. 'You girls are so close, she might sense you.'

I wasn't sure about that, but it was a nice idea, so I nodded.

Mrs Gold brushed her hair away from her face. 'Is she going to make it?' she asked.

I wanted to reassure her, and tell her Nelly would be fine. But I didn't have the words. I opened my mouth to speak and instead found myself sobbing.

Mrs Gold gathered me into her arms again, and soothed me, stroking my back like I was a little girl who'd fallen over in the playground.

'I know,' she said. 'I know. You've lost so much.'

'My brother,' I gasped through sobs. 'My brother died. And now Nelly ...'

Mrs Gold let me cry, guiding me to a bench in the corridor and pulling me to sit down next to her. Then she simply sat with her arm around me while I wailed. And when, finally, I was exhausted, she handed me her handkerchief, which was embroidered with little white flowers and was surprisingly clean considering what she'd been through.

I wiped my eyes and blew my nose.

'What can I do?' Mrs Gold asked. She sat up a bit straighter, wiping the soot from her forehead and adjusting the collar of her coat. Suddenly she looked like someone who was in charge and I liked it. 'I know people, Elsie,' she said. 'What do you need? Should we get Nelly moved to another hospital? Guy's, perhaps? Down in Kent?'

I shook my head. 'She can't move; she's not strong enough.'

'Are there any doctors she should see?'

'Everyone here is marvellous.'

Mrs Gold nodded. 'Well then, what about you? Mr Gold tells me our house is intact, thankfully, though he says it reeks of smoke and it's damp from the water the fire brigade used. I assume yours is the same. Would you like to go home, or would you rather come and stay with us?'

'I don't know.' I was bewildered by everything that had happened. I couldn't imagine going home without Nelly but I didn't think moving in with the Golds would help either.

'Anything you need, Elsie. Just ask and I will do my best.'

I looked at Mrs Gold curiously. Her hair was a mess and her face was still dirty despite her efforts, but I still had the impression she was someone who could make things happen.

'I want to carry on with the book,' I said in a hurry. 'I want everyone in the hospital to write messages and memories. I want them to make sure they say the things they might not get a chance to say otherwise.'

Mrs Gold put her hand on mine and nodded.

'If Nelly …' I began. Then I stopped, because I didn't want to say the words. 'Nelly has been a good friend to me. She was by my side when Billy was killed and she's never really left. I want to tell her how grateful I am and now I'll have the chance.' I breathed in, feeling my throat scratch from soot and smoke. 'But other people won't get that chance to say the things they want to say – just like Billy and I didn't. I can help them.'

'I think that sounds like an important task,' Mrs Gold said gently. 'But for now, I think you should go and see Nelly.'

I nodded slowly.

'You're not working today, are you?' she said.

'No, Matron has given my shift to someone else.'

'Good. Come home after you've seen Nelly. You need sleep.'

'And a wash,' I said looking in dismay at my mucky clothes.

Mrs Gold sighed. 'I think these clothes are just fit for the bin.'

'It doesn't matter.'

'No, you're right, it doesn't.' She smiled at me. 'Come along. Pop your head in on Nelly because I think it's important you see her …'

The words "just in case" hung heavily in the air and Mrs Gold took a deep breath. 'Then come home. Albert will be worrying about us. You can come back and see Nelly again later.'

'All right,' I said, feeling a rush of affection and gratitude towards her. She was a good person. 'Thank you.'

We both stood up and Mrs Gold kissed me on the cheek and headed off towards the hospital entrance.

Much more slowly, I walked down the corridor to ward 2. The matron was there, but she wasn't familiar to me. She looked at me when I entered.

'Can I help? Visiting hours aren't until three o'clock.'

'I'm Nurse Watson from ward 7.'

She looked at me up and down, taking in my ragged appearance. 'I'm Nelly's friend,' I said hurriedly before she sent me away. 'Nelly Malone. The doctor said I could see her.'

Matron's expression cleared and she nodded. 'Of course,' she said. 'This way.'

I knew where Nelly was, but I followed her anyway, once more grateful that someone else was in charge.

'No more than five minutes,' Matron said, opening the door to the side room. She checked the watch pinned to her tunic. 'I'm timing you.'

Left alone, I stood still by the door, looking at Nelly where she lay on the bed. Only the slight rise and fall of her chest told me she was alive. She had a white mask over her face covering one eye completely, and leaving only one part of one cheek and her other eye exposed. It made her look other-worldly, like a ghost or a spirit. She had a tube in her mouth and a noisy machine helping her breathe and a drip sending fluids into her arm. Her body was completely bandaged, except for one forearm and one hand, which lay still on the sheet. I breathed in sharply, assessing her with a nurse's eye though I wished I hadn't. This wasn't good. Poor Nelly was in a bad way and I was astonished – but glad – she had survived.

I took a moment to compose myself and then stepped towards her. 'Well, isn't this typical,' I said in a jovial voice. 'Nelly Malone causing trouble for everyone again. You've got doctors running round all over the place looking after you, and I've heard your Percy is frantic. I'm sure he'll be in to see you soon.'

I looked at her. The eye that I could see stayed shut.

'Please get better, Nell,' I begged, my voice catching. 'I've got so much to tell you.'

Did I imagine it or did her eyelid flicker?

'Time to go,' Matron said from the door.

'Her eyelid moved.'

'She's probably due some medicine,' Matron said, efficiently checking the chart at the end of Nelly's bed. 'We're keeping her sedated because of the pain.'

'Can I come back later?'

'Visiting hours are three until five, and then again from eight o'clock.' Matron's expression switched from professional to sympathetic and she reached out and squeezed my arm. 'We're doing everything we can for her.'

'What ...' I took a breath. 'What treatment will you give her?'

The matron grimaced. 'We've been using saline baths to clean burns. It seems to be effective, but it's painful for the patients.' She blinked. 'It's all painful. We gave her a general anaesthetic so we could clean her wounds when she first arrived, but we can't do that every time.'

Slowly, I let out my breath. 'What about infection?'

'It's a big risk, you know that.'

I nodded.

'And the fluid loss is a worry too. But we know what we're doing. We're going to look after her.'

'I know.'

She ran a practised eye over me. 'And in the meantime, you need to look after yourself,' she said. 'Go home, sleep, wash, eat, and come back later. But only for an hour. Are you back on the wards tomorrow?'

I nodded and Matron gave me a quick, kind smile. 'We need you, Nurse Watson. Take care of yourself.'

Feeling close to tears again, I nodded. 'Thank you,' I muttered.

*

I was so tired, I wasn't sure I could face the short walk home, but I had no choice. So simply concentrating on putting one foot in front of the other – left then right, then left again – I headed back to the house.

All around me were signs of last night's raid. The recovery teams were still there, checking the damaged houses. There were many piles of rubble that told me houses had been hit and some fires were still burning. I thought it must have been one of the worst raids this area had suffered so far and shuddered at the thought there could be more to come.

Along with the recovery teams and the ARPs, there were lots of people milling around in the streets, looking more than a little lost. I wondered if their houses had been destroyed and where they would go. I'd heard that some people who'd been bombed out were living in the caves, a couple of miles away in Chislehurst. I couldn't imagine spending all my time underground, but at least they would be safe. Perhaps if we'd gone to the caves when the siren had wailed, Nelly would …

But no. I couldn't think about that now. I had to get home. Left, right, left.

My pace slowed as I approached the corner of our street, nervous about what I would see. I felt a bit sick, and my head was pounding, and I wasn't sure if it was because of the smell of smoke that hung in the air, or because I was hungry or scared.

A milkman, his face dirty with soot, walked past me as I rounded the corner. He was holding four bottles of milk, and looked so normal and everyday that I almost felt I was dreaming for a second. 'Morning! Lovely day,' he called cheerfully.

Bewildered, I looked up at the sky. Was it morning? It seemed so. It was cold but bright and the weak wintry sun was trying its hardest to break through the smoke.

Life went on, I thought in bewilderment. The sun came up every day and the milk was delivered and the buses rumbled along bomb-damaged streets taking people to their jobs. It didn't seem possible, and yet it was happening right in front of me.

Feeling my shoulders tense, I walked towards our house, wondering how it would look. I could see the damage to our neighbours' building already. But ours seemed to be untouched, standing strong despite the carnage around it.

And there, sitting on the wall outside was Jackson. And he'd seen me, and he was rushing towards me, and my treacherous feet carried me in his direction. Left, right, left.

'Elsie, oh Elsie, I've been so worried.' Jackson's breath was quick and his Adam's apple was bobbing up and down in his throat. 'The siren went and I knew it would be a bad one, because it was such a clear night, and I wanted to come and check on you because I knew that was what Billy would have wanted, and I rang your doorbell, but the siren was so loud and that must have been why you didn't hear it, and I knew you weren't at work because it wasn't your night shift …'

So it had been him I'd seen outside our house.

Jackson was still talking: 'And I saw Nelly come out of the shelter, so I knew you were there.'

'You saw Nelly?'

'Yes, but the bombs were falling and I had to go.'

'Why didn't you stop her?'

'Stop her?'

'Send her back to the shelter.'

'I was just worried about you, Elsie.' Jackson reached out and cupped my cheek in his hand. 'You're the only one I care about.'

Sickened, I ducked my head away from his hand.

'Don't be like that,' he said. 'I'm trying to help. I promised Billy.'

He reached out again and this time I reached out and pushed his hand away roughly.

'Elsie,' he said. His voice held a warning tone, like he was my father and I'd done something wrong. 'I'm only being nice.'

'Don't be nice. I don't want you to be nice.'

'But I told Billy ...'

'Stop it,' I said. My voice was shrill and my throat hurt but I had to say this. 'Stop talking about Billy and stop following me around.'

'Elsie ...'

'Go away, Jackson,' I shrieked. 'Go away and leave me alone.'

Chapter 21

Jackson didn't go away. Not for a while. He sat on the wall outside the house while I ran a bath and peeled off the skirt and jumper I'd been wearing since we went into the shelter. It seemed like a lifetime ago. My clothes were grubby and reeked of smoke. I thought I'd put them into the tub to soak when I'd got out.

As I tested the temperature of the water, I peeked out of the window and to my relief, saw Jackson had gone. Thank goodness. He didn't scare me, not exactly. Or at least he hadn't scared me before today. But he was just around all the time, and I'd definitely seen a flash of something in his eyes – irritation, perhaps, or anger even – when I'd pushed his hand away that made me feel a flutter of unease. Mind you, it had been a long and difficult day, and perhaps I was imagining things. He wasn't a bad bloke, really, was he?

Quashing my misgivings, I got into the bath and tried to relax into the water. But it was cold and I couldn't turn my worries off, so I simply gave myself a good scrub with a tiny amount of soap, and then got out again. I put on my dressing gown, dropped my smelly clothes into the tub and sat down in front of the fire to dry my hair. It seemed strange doing these everyday tasks while Nelly was so poorly. But what else could I do?

*

Even though Jackson had gone, when there was a knock on the door, I was still cautious because I knew he'd come back. He always did.

'Mrs Gold?' I called before I opened it.

'It's me.'

I let her in and she put her hand on my shoulder and gave it a little squeeze. I had a sudden flush of embarrassment about my threadbare dressing gown and bare legs, but she didn't seem to notice. She'd changed her clothes and washed her face, and the wound on her head had a clean plaster.

'How is Nelly?'

'She was asleep.' I couldn't begin to tell her the things the nurse had told me.

'Before I left the hospital earlier, I popped into your ward. And I spoke to a lovely nurse there. Bateman her name was. I asked her to make sure your book carried on being passed round.'

'You did that?'

'It's important, like you said.'

I gazed at Mrs Gold, thinking how lucky I was to have her as a neighbour.

'What's next?' she asked.

'I'm going to go back to the hospital later to see Nelly,' I said. 'I'll take some of her things. When she wakes up she'll want her things. A book, perhaps. And her hairbrush.' I put my hand over my mouth as I remembered Nelly's awful burned hair. 'A book,' I said again firmly.

'I can help you get some bits together.' Mrs Gold bit her lip. 'Is there anyone we should tell?'

'Her mother in Dublin,' I said. 'I've been wondering how is best to do it. Should I send a telegram?'

Mrs Gold nodded. 'Better than a letter, I think.' She grimaced. 'Quicker.'

I didn't want to think about why it was important Nelly's mother knew as soon as possible. 'I'll go to the post office tomorrow,' I said.

'No need,' Mrs Gold said. 'Albert can arrange that for you from his office. Do you have the address?'

'In the kitchen drawer. There are some letters from her mum there.'

Listlessly, I wandered into the kitchen and dug about in the drawer until I found the most recent letter from Mrs Malone. I noticed that it had been opened. Apparently, Nelly had read it after all and I was glad. Really glad. I knew her mother's address would be at the top of the letter, but I didn't take it out of the envelope because I couldn't bear to see her writing, or catch a glimpse of the words she'd written begging Nelly to come home because London was too dangerous. How terrible for a mother to be proven right in such an awful way. Instead, when I went back into the lounge, I handed the envelope and its contents to Mrs Gold and she tucked it into her bag. 'I'll get Albert to send a telegram this evening.'

'Thank you,' I said. 'For doing all this.'

Mrs Gold snorted. 'You girls have kept me company all these evenings in the shelter,' she said. 'And you helped me when I needed you.' She smiled at me, and I thought how pretty she was. 'My family are far away, and I miss them. I'm glad that we're friends.'

'We are.'

'When are you going to go back to the hospital?'

I looked at the clock on the mantelpiece. 'Maybe around three? I'll get all her things together.'

'You go and get yourself dressed and then let me help you gather some bits and bobs for Nelly. What first? A book, you said?'

I went to put on some clothes, then we bustled around finding Nelly's belongings. I knew she wouldn't need much, and that the nurses in her ward would prefer to keep things simple. But I wanted her to have a few personal effects at least. I took the book from her bedside table and a rather stern-looking photograph of her mother and father, and Mrs Gold found a nightgown in a drawer, which I thought Nelly probably wouldn't wear because she was so completely wrapped in bandages, but I let her put it in the bag anyway.

I was extremely tired, but I didn't want to take a nap because I was worried I'd feel worse if I closed my eyes. I'd catch up on sleep later. When I'd seen Nelly again and made sure she was still ... well, still with us.

'I wish I could come with you, but I have a lot of work to do,' Mrs Gold said as I pulled on my coat and got ready to go. 'Will you be all right?'

I nodded. 'I'll be fine.'

'Don't stay too late at the hospital, will you? We'll need to be in the shelter tonight.' Mrs Gold shuddered. 'Albert will be home too.'

'I won't,' I said. 'Nelly's still sedated anyway so she won't be chatting. But I always think there's a chance patients know their visitors are there.' It felt wrong to be thinking of Nelly as a patient.

Mrs Gold gathered me into a hug and gave me a kiss on the cheek. It was nice to be taken care of for a while, rather than being the one doing the caring. 'I think you're right,' she said.

'I'd better go if I want to be back before the siren.'

*

The hospital was quiet. It always felt less chaotic in the early evening, but I knew it was simply the calm before the storm with the patients settled and all the nurses and doctors taking five minutes to catch their breath before the raids began.

Occasionally – and I did mean occasionally, because it had only happened twice or three times – there wasn't a raid and then the calm continued all night. I allowed myself to hope, briefly, that would happen tonight. Because however bad Nelly's physical injuries were, I knew that when her sedation was reduced and she woke up, she would be bound to find the sound of the bombs very frightening. And though some of our patients managed to get to the basement shelter when the raids began, the ones who were bedbound – like Nelly – wouldn't move.

'Back again?' asked Matron as I got to Nelly's ward.

'I brought some things for Nelly.'

'Not working tonight?'

I shook my head. 'My matron swapped my shifts around. I'm back tomorrow.'

'I'm glad.' She looked at me with her head tilted to one side. 'You need rest.'

'I know.'

'You can go in. She's still sedated but Doctor Gilligan said he's upped her pain relief so we might be able to bring her round tomorrow.'

'That's wonderful news.'

'There's still a long road ahead,' Matron warned. 'You know the odds.'

I did. I knew that patients as badly burned as Nelly rarely survived. But I wanted to have a little bit of hope.

'I understand.' I shifted the bag from one hand to the other because it was getting heavy. 'I won't stay long.'

This time I was prepared for the sight of Nelly, of course, but it was still a shock to see her there on the bed, swathed in bandages. I drew my breath in sharply.

'Hello again,' I said, forcing myself to speak cheerily though my voice shook a little. 'Still asleep, are you? You've always loved a bit of shut-eye.'

I glanced at Nelly but she didn't move, other than the rhythmic rise and fall of her chest.

'I brought some things for you.' I put the bag on to the chair next to the bed, and began unpacking, talking Nelly through everything.

'Here's the photograph of your mum and dad from your bedroom,' I said, popping it on to the cabinet. 'They look very stern, I think. Probably they're saying, "What were you doing

187

prancing about the garden in an air raid, Nelly Malone?" That's what my parents would say, if they were here.'

I rubbed my throat, trying to steady my voice, which was high-pitched and croaky. 'Mrs Gold made me bring you a nightie, bless her. I'll put it in your cupboard and when you get those bandages off it'll be ready for you.'

I opened the little cabinet and shoved the nightgown inside, not wanting to think about how long it could be before Nelly wore it. 'She's been ever so good, Mrs Gold. She's such a nice person, don't you think?' I left a pause for her to reply, but obviously, Nelly stayed silent. 'She's a diamond; that's what my dad would have said. Mrs Gold, a diamond.' I tried to laugh at my weak joke but somehow it came out sounding more like a sob.

'I'm working tomorrow, so I'll come and see you when I can,' I said hurriedly. 'Hope you have a good night.'

I put the empty bag under the bed safely out of the way. 'You'll need this when you come home again,' I said firmly. 'To carry all the bits and pieces I've brought you back again.'

I paused by the door and blew her a kiss, then left the room, feeling guilty that I couldn't do more to help her. I was a nurse, for heaven's sake. And yet I felt so helpless.

Chapter 22

I felt better after a night's sleep. Desperately worried about Nelly, of course, but more able to deal with it all. Mr Gold had sent a telegram to her mother in Ireland and he'd told me he had the car from work for as long as he needed it so he would drive me wherever I needed to go. He was being so kind, just like Mrs Gold was. But when I said as much to Mrs Gold, as I got ready for work the next morning, she pooh-poohed my sentimentality.

'Where I come from, people help each other out,' she said. 'It's just what we do. I think Londoners are no different. You helped me, now I help you.'

'Where are you from?' I asked curiously, but she didn't answer. Instead, she put her hands on my shoulders and looked at me.

'Are you sure you're up to going to work?'

I honestly wasn't sure. I'd been a nervous wreck when the bombs had started falling, but Mrs Gold had tucked me into my bunk tightly, like I was a little girl, and she and Mr Gold had stayed awake in the shelter, playing cards and talking quietly between themselves, until I fell asleep. I'd been so tired that I hadn't even woken with the thuds and wails of the raid, except once, when I turned over on the hard bunk and half-woke. But even then I must have still been dozing, because though I could hear the Golds chatting in low voices, I couldn't understand what they were saying.

Now though, I felt a bit stronger. I was glad I was on daytime shifts for now so I didn't have to cope with a raid *and* patients, and I was keen to see Nelly. So even though I was nervous about going back to the wards, I nodded.

'I'm fine.'

'Good girl,' said Mrs Gold, like my mother always used to. It made me laugh because I was not a girl, and she was really only a few years older than I was.

'Are you going to work?' I asked. 'Will you be all right, with your head?' She was dressed for the office in a neat suit and shoes that I wouldn't be able to walk in. She even had stockings on – sheer shiny nylons that were very different from the thick woolly monstrosities I wore under my uniform.

'I'll be fine,' she said, touching her hand to the plaster on her forehead. 'This is nothing, really and Albert has the car, so he can drive us.'

'Be careful,' I warned.

She nodded. 'You too.'

I was worried Jackson might appear somewhere on my journey to the hospital but thankfully, he wasn't there. Though the streets were busy with emergency workers and families who'd been bombed out, and the WVS volunteers dashing about with mugs of tea and blankets, so perhaps I just hadn't seen him.

In any case, my mind was on Nelly.

My train was delayed because there was debris from the raid on the line, so I ended up getting a bus to the hospital, which took ages, and I had to rush to my ward, worried I was going to be late to start my shift.

As I hurried along the corridor, Matron appeared. 'Nurse Elsie Watson,' she bellowed down the hall at me.

'I'm here,' I called, trying to walk even faster, because running was strictly forbidden. 'I'm coming.'

But Matron came towards me, and held her hand out to stop me and for an awful, heart-wrenching moment I knew absolutely what she was going to say. Nelly was dead. I was sure of it. Because Matron had never sought me out in the corridor before and I couldn't ever imagine it happening again.

My legs buckled beneath me and I reached out to steady myself on the cool, distempered wall.

'Is it Nelly?' I asked, my voice quiet and small in the busy corridor.

Matron had arrived at my side and now she took my arm and I leaned on her, grateful for the support.

'She's awake,' she said.

My vision blurred and I thought I might faint for a second. Then it cleared and I looked at Matron, whose own eyes were filled with tears. 'She's awake,' she said again.

'Is she going to be all right?'

'It's still too early,' Matron said. She was a large woman with a big bosom and a heavy tread. She rarely smiled or laughed, was sharp-tongued when she had to be, and she was very good at her job. I respected her but I could never have said that I liked her. Now, though, she seemed more human. 'Too early to be sure,' she added. 'You should go and see her.'

'Now?' I was surprised. 'But my shift is about to start.'

'Nurse Bateman will cover until you're back,' she said. The tiniest of smiles crept across her lips. 'She wasn't busy last night so she's fine to stay.'

Nurse Bateman – Petra – was sweet, but she was a devil for taking ages to move patients or fetch files from the records office. If there was an opportunity for her to skive off work for five minutes, she took it. I was amused to know that Matron had spotted her habits, too. 'Thank you,' I said.

'Half an hour,' Matron said. 'I need you back on the ward by half past eight. Don't make me send Nurse Bateman to fetch you.'

'I won't,' I said, half over my shoulder because I was already turning to go. 'Thank you.'

Not caring about any rules about not running, I pounded along the corridor to Nelly's ward, and burst through the door. It was a different matron in charge today, but she obviously knew I was coming because she looked up at me and smiled.

'Here to see Nelly Malone?'

'Is she awake?' I gasped. 'Is she talking? Will she be all right?'

She got up from behind her desk and came round to where I stood. 'Don't get ahead of yourself,' she warned. 'Nelly is very poorly. She's off the sedation but she is still on a lot of pain medication. She's drifting in and out of consciousness, but I think she'll know you're there and be glad of it.'

'That's what I think,' I said. 'I always think that.'

She nodded. 'She can't speak.'

'Because of the oxygen?'

'We think her airway was scorched by the flames. She's responding to our words but can't make a sound herself.'

I put my hand to my mouth. 'That could heal though? With time?'

'She's very badly hurt,' the matron said softly. 'Her burns are extensive and there is a high risk of infection.'

'Can I see her now?'

'Five minutes, no more.'

Nervous about what I would find, I walked into the side room where Nelly lay. She looked just the same as she had the night before. But as I neared her bed, her eye – the one I could see that wasn't covered in that awful expressionless mask – flickered open.

'Hello,' I said.

She looked at me and her breathing changed, just a little, as if she were trying to speak.

'Don't try to talk.' It sounded so painful, I didn't want her to hurt herself. I took her fingers in mine, averting my eyes from her bandages and her terrible shaved head. Weakly, almost imperceptibly, I felt her hand squeeze mine.

'Oh Nelly,' I said, almost dizzy with relief. 'You've given me the most awful scare, you sod.'

Her fingers moved again and her eye met mine.

'We've got to get you better, love. And get you home. Because you know how untidy I am. There are already dirty plates in the sink. Piled high they are.'

I laughed, but it sounded forced and fake. Nelly's eye closed and her fingers went limp in mine. Without thinking, I shifted my hold so I could feel her pulse. There it was, beating nicely. A little fast, perhaps, but there all the same. She was asleep. I felt light-headed with relief.

'I have to go or Matron will be furious,' I said. Nelly stayed still. 'I'll come back later. I'll try to find the book, shall I? We can have a look at what people have been writing.'

Wiping a tear from my eye, I kissed Nelly's hand and then headed off to my own ward to start my shift.

*

Much later, after hours on my feet and after spending half the day rearranging the ward to squeeze in another two beds, much to all of our disbelief and concern, I handed over to the night staff.

'I owe you for this morning,' I told Petra. She looked at me impassively through her dark, sleepy eyes and then grinned.

'Nah,' she said. 'Nelly's one of us, isn't she? How's she doing?'

'On the mend,' I told her confidently, half-hoping that if I said the words, they'd be true.

'Glad to hear it.'

'And thank you for passing the book on. Do you know where it's got to?'

'Last I heard it was going down to theatre.'

*

I found the book in the holding ward next to the operating theatre in the basement. It was strange down there, dim and gloomy in the corridors and ward, and then brightly lit in the theatre itself. I wasn't sure how Nelly coped being down there all the time. I was glad I didn't work in that bit of the hospital. Apart from anything else, the part of nursing I liked the best was talking to my patients and getting to know them. I wasn't cut out to be a theatre nurse. Unlike Nelly who loved the precision that was involved.

With a shudder, I went along the gloomy hallway following the daubs of white paint that had been splattered on the walls to lead the way. It was odd down here. There were a few cupboards that were used for storage and a slightly larger room that had the emergency generator in it. I knew it had been used a few times when the power had gone out during raids. And next to that was the boiler room, which was the warmest place in the hospital. When I'd been a student nurse, we'd had the most awful cold snap with deep snow and freezing temperatures. I remembered there had been ice up the inside of all the windows at home and in the hospital and we would be shivering constantly on the wards. We nurses used to dash down to the boiler room in our breaks to thaw out our frozen fingers and sometimes we even sneaked off for a snooze down there if we'd been tired after a hectic shift. I gave a little snort of laughter. I'd had no idea back then what a hectic shift was really like.

Walking past the boiler room, I went into the holding ward. There weren't many patients in there, but one – a man in his fifties with a bushy moustache – was sitting up in bed scribbling furiously in the book. His skin had a greyish tinge and he kept stopping to breathe in sharply. He was obviously in pain. I exchanged an alarmed glance with the nurse hovering by his bedside and she rolled her eyes. 'Mr Hobbs here has appendicitis,' she said pointedly. 'And they're ready to take him into theatre, but he's got something to write first.'

I made a face. 'Sorry,' I said. 'That's my doing. It's my book.'

'Oh well done.' She beamed at me. 'It's such a good idea. Make sure you look after it, won't you?'

'I will.'

Mr Hobbs finished his writing with a flourish and snapped the book shut. 'There,' he said, leaning back against his pillow in exhaustion. 'Message for the wife, just in case, you know?'

'I know,' the nurse said fondly. 'Having your appendix out is a routine op, though. I'm sure your wife won't be reading that note.' She patted his arm in reassurance and took the book from him. 'I'll get a porter to take you through to theatre.'

'I'll find Frank for you, if you like,' I said, taking the book as she held it out to me. 'I'm heading up to the wards now.'

'No, not Frank, the new chap. He's around somewhere – I just saw him.'

'If I see someone, I'll send them down. Good luck, Mr Hobbs.'

He nodded to me and with the book under my arm, I hurried off again, totally forgetting to look for a porter in my eagerness to get to Nelly.

*

She was awake when I got to her room. Another nurse was there, adjusting her sheets, and I greeted her.

'Nelly's awake, aren't you, love?' she said. I didn't recognise her and I didn't like how she raised her voice a bit and spoke as though Nelly was simple.

She turned to me. 'She can't talk but she's responsive.'

'It wasn't her brain that was burned,' I said sharply and the nurse narrowed her eyes at me like an irritated cat. 'Sorry. It's been a long day.'

The nurse nodded in understanding though she still looked a bit annoyed.

'Brought the book, Nell,' I said. 'Thought we could look at it together.'

'Don't tire her out,' the nurse warned.

'I won't.'

I waited until she was outside the room and then I sat down next to Nelly's less injured side, smoothing the book's cover with my fingertips. I opened it on a random page. 'Let's have a look, shall we? It's been all over the hospital.'

Next to me, Nelly's eye widened slightly. 'Want me to read some of the notes?' I asked. Her fingers twitched.

'Your wish is my command.'

I read a few of the cheerier messages. The ones that were memories or funny anecdotes. I didn't want any of the gloomy last words for loved ones. Not today. When I came across the note Mr Hobbs had left, I scanned it, wondering what had been so important but feeling a bit like I was invading his privacy as I did. The note made me chuckle.

'Listen to this, Nell,' I said. 'This chap was writing before he had his appendix out earlier on. I thought it was a loving message to his wife, but it's instructions about how to feed his chickens.'

I laughed but Nelly looked as though she was drifting off to sleep, so I thought I should leave her be.

'I'll get off,' I whispered. 'I'll come back tomorrow.'

She opened her eye fully and tapped her fingers on the bedclothes to show she was pleased.

'We need to work out a code, like two taps for no and one for yes,' I said. 'Just until you can talk again.'

Nelly tapped once and I grinned. 'You've got it already.'

I went to shut the book but as I did, I noticed some of the pages were stuck together. Poking out of the top of the pages was a scrap of paper, like a bookmark. 'Oh, look at that,' I grumbled. 'Not everyone is as careful as I am.'

Using my hand like a letter opener I ran it between the pages and peeled them apart. They separated easily. I rubbed my finger and thumb together. It felt slightly gritty, like … I sniffed my finger … and it smelled like tea. Was it a drink that had sealed the pages together? Perhaps one of the patients had spilled something. But it was only on the edges of the paper and it felt more deliberate than accidental.

'This is odd,' I said aloud to Nelly, whose eye was still open. 'Look, someone's stuck the pages together. Do you think they wanted their message to be private?'

She tapped her finger lightly on her sheet and I nodded. 'I think you're right. I feel a bit bad now, that I've found it. But … oh. Oh goodness.'

I felt my cheeks burn as I looked at the scrap of paper that had been marking the page. It said "To my favourite nurse" in tiny writing. 'I think this might be a message to me, Nelly.' Was it? Or was I being presumptuous? And who had written it?

Nell tapped her hand on to the bed impatiently, but I ignored her, lost in my own thoughts. With a lurch of discomfort I wondered if somehow Jackson had found the book and written me a note. But I scanned it, and realised with a great deal of relief, that wasn't the case.

'It's not from Jackson, I'm sure. But it isn't signed,' I said to Nelly. She drummed her fingers again. I shook my head.

'I'm not even convinced it's for me.'

Nelly thumped her hand on the bedclothes and I grinned. 'Shall I read it aloud?'

'*If we were in normal times, I would ask you to a dance or to the pictures,*' I read. '*But times are not normal and I worry that they will never be normal again.*'

I paused and glanced at Nelly to make sure she was all right. She was still, but her eye was open. She was listening. I carried on. '*I think you're lovely, and I'd like to get to know you. Your idea to pass this book around the wards was so clever and thoughtful – I want to know more about you.*'

I paused, pleased to have confirmation that the note was definitely meant for me. '*But I know it's awkward with you being a nurse and me a patient so I thought we could use this book to share our thoughts. What do you reckon?'*

I felt hot again on my cheeks. Could it be from Harry? Or was I being ridiculous? 'It's sweet, I think,' I said to Nelly. She tapped her finger once. 'But I don't know who it is. It could be anyone. It could be one of the old men from upstairs, or a youngster playing a prank. Should I write back?'

Nelly tapped her finger with a surprising amount of vigour. 'That's a yes then?' I said with a chuckle.

She tapped again. 'Fine,' I said. 'I'll write back and stick the pages together again.' I thought for a moment. 'But with no idea who's written this note, I've got no way of knowing when it would find its way to him. I'll just have to send it off round the wards again and see what happens.'

Nelly breathed in deeply and I looked at her. 'Are you loving this?' I said to her. 'It's right up your street, isn't it?'

She tapped her finger and I grinned. 'Has Percy been in to see you?'

There was a pause and then she tapped again, twice this time. I kicked myself for asking. 'He'll come,' I assured her. 'He's a good bloke.'

Nelly made a noise, deep in her throat. A sort of moan.

'You don't want him here?' I said.

She tapped her finger twice again.

'All right,' I said. I understood that she didn't want Percy to see her looking so badly hurt. 'You tell me when you're ready to see him and I'll let him know.'

She walked her fingers along the sheet and clasped my hand in hers.

'And I'll reply to the message,' I said, wanting to distract her. 'I promise.'

Nelly squeezed my fingers and then let go.

'We need to take Nelly for a bath now.' One of the nurses stood in the doorway.

Nelly moaned again.

'Now?' I said. 'Really?'

'I'm afraid so. We'll give you some painkillers, Nelly. I know it's not nice, but it's important to keep your burns clean.'

A tear trickled out from Nelly's eye. 'Be brave,' I said to her. 'Do you want me to stay?'

She took my hand again but the nurse shook her head. 'We can't have too many people in the room. The risk of infection is too high.'

'Sorry, Nell,' I said.

She made the horrible moaning sound again and I wanted to cry for her.

'The porter's on his way,' the nurse said. 'Let's get you ready, shall we?'

I kissed her hand and said goodbye, hearing her moans follow me all the way along the corridor.

Chapter 23

Stephanie

Present day

I couldn't concentrate on Elsie's book at Tall Trees, because I didn't get a minute to myself. I sat in the staffroom but there were people coming and going the whole time and I kept losing my place.

One of the other carers, an annoying woman called Rowena who was one of those people who was always right when everyone else was wrong, sat next to me and told me a long, convoluted story about how she'd got a parking ticket and she was fuming. Then, when she finally got up and left, another carer – Vir – sat down next to me to eat his lunch. I was so nervous about getting crumbs, or Coke, or both on the precious pages that I shut the book with a snap.

'Can you tell Blessing I'll be back before my shift?' I said to Vir, who was watching *Squid Game* on his phone and wasn't, as far as I could tell, paying any attention to me whatsoever. 'Thanks.'

And then, feeling slightly reckless and indulgent, I got an Uber to The Vine.

It was, thankfully, quiet there. Tara was behind the bar, and she raised an eyebrow as I arrived.

'You've brought the book to a bar?'

'I'm not going to dunk it in the drip tray,' I said. 'I thought I could sit in a corner and read it. It's crazy at Tall Trees and I don't want to go home by myself.'

'Take your pick of corners,' said Tara with a grin. 'I'll bring you over a coffee.'

'No,' I said. 'What if I spill?'

'Glass of water?'

'And a portion of chips?' I said hopefully.

Tara laughed and I took the book over to a corner booth. Wriggling on the bench seat to find a comfy position, I opened the first page and, enjoying the peace and quiet, began to read.

It was astonishing. I'd read some of the notes and letters before, of course, on the online version and I was glad because it meant I was prepared for the waves of emotions that the writing gave me. Some of them were so very sad, others were funny. All of them were touching.

About halfway through, I found a beautiful little pencil sketch of a nurse and gasped in delight to see it was Elsie herself. She had been drawn side-on, her headdress billowing behind her like a veil. She was so young, I thought. So young and very pretty.

'Is that her?' Tara leaned over my shoulder as she put a bowl of chips down in front of me. 'She was pretty.'

'She was.'

'How are you getting on with tracking her down?'

'Haven't found her yet. But never say never.'

'And how are the plans for the mural coming on?'

I made a face. 'I'm hoping reading these letters will give me some inspiration.' I screwed my nose up. 'And I need to get my own book for the Tall Trees residents to write their messages in. There's a lot to do.'

Tara smoothed my hair in a motherly fashion. 'Just don't take on too much, will you? With this place and Tall Trees and your nan, and now this project, you'll be run ragged.'

'Can you cut my shifts for a few weeks?' I said. 'Not yet, but when the grant money comes through? And not completely, because I still want the job.'

'As it's you,' Tara said with a grin, 'I'll get one of the students to cover your hours. They'll be glad of the work over the summer.'

She bustled off back to the kitchen and I turned to the book again, wondering if there was anything inside that might give me a clue about what had happened to Elsie. Finn said himself that he hadn't finished going through the whole book yet, not properly, so it was possible he'd missed something.

I closed the book wondering if I should read from the back instead of the front. With my thumb, I flicked through the pages, hearing the satisfying buzz of the soft paper as it fluttered. Until it stopped on some pages that were stuck together.

'Oops,' I muttered, opening the book on the right bit. There were two pages stuck together, quite near the front. Had something been spilled on these pages to make them sticky? I wondered. Very carefully, hoping they didn't tear, I began to peel them apart. They actually separated quite easily because they were only stuck around the edges – making me think it had been deliberate.

'What have you been hiding, Elsie?' I said, pulling the last bit apart and opening out the pages. I was looking at a spread of two pages, which were completely covered in tiny writing. Two different people's handwriting, I saw. And one of the hands was familiar. I leafed back through the book until I found the note Elsie had left about the bomb in Stepney and nodded in satisfaction. It was definitely Elsie's handwriting, though she'd not initialled her notes as she'd done elsewhere. I rubbed my eyes, wondering where to start with the tiny writing and then gasped aloud as I saw the words: "You are my sunshine. My heart aches for you and my arms feel empty when you're not in them."

'Elsie, you saucy minx,' I said in delight. They were love notes.

'Look at this,' I called over to Tara, who was bottling up. 'I've found something exciting.'

'What is it?'

She slid into the booth opposite me and peered at the book. 'God, there's no chance of me being able to read that. I'm at the stage when I have to take a photo of labels so I can enlarge them.'

'It's love letters,' I said. 'And please go to the optician.'

She ignored me. 'Who from?'

'From Elsie,' I said, thrilled. 'This is her writing, see?' I pointed to a paragraph where Elsie had written: "This is all very nice but how do I know who you are if you don't tell me?"

'That doesn't sound very romantic,' said Tara squinting at the page. 'She sounds wary.'

I scanned the writing. 'No, it gets better,' I said, jumping to the second page. 'Look, they've obviously met up by this point, because he's written that he doesn't want to cause her any trouble so he'll hide his feelings when he sees her, even though ...' I turned the page back towards me so I could see it better. 'Ooh, even though the memory of their kiss keeps him warm at night.'

'Elsie!' Tara exclaimed.

'This is adorable,' I said, reading more declarations of love from Elsie and her mystery man. If it was a man, of course. 'Maybe it's a woman, she's writing to?' I suggested. 'Maybe that's why it was a secret?'

'Maybe,' said Tara. 'Looks like a man's writing though.'

'Really? How can you tell?'

She shrugged. 'I just can.'

'Do you mind if I grab some paper from the office?' I said. 'I might read this properly and copy all the notes out.'

'Sure.' Tara sighed in a most unlike-Tara fashion. 'I wonder if they got together in the end? Elsie and her letter-writer? Maybe they ran off together. Maybe that's where she went?'

'Since when did you have such a sentimental streak?'

'Since forever,' she said. 'I just hide it well.'

'Very well.'

She laughed. 'This is lovely though, isn't it? Like a romcom.'

I looked down at the densely packed words. 'I just hope it has a happy ending.'

Chapter 24

Elsie

1941

There were only two of us in the shelter because Mr Gold was at work again. I thought it was a very strange office job he had, which involved him staying out all night, but everything was strange nowadays.

It was freezing cold, so Mrs Gold and I were huddled together under a blanket, both of us with our winter coats and hats on. We looked like Eskimos, she said, and I remembered a picture in an old book my mother used to read to me and agreed.

'Show me this note then,' she said. 'I'm dying to see what it says.'

I pulled the book out from under the blanket and arranged it across our laps, leafing through to find the right page. Mrs Gold moved the lantern so it shone brightly on the paper and I read the note aloud.

'Oh my,' she said, her eyes shining in the candlelight. 'This is really romantic.'

I wasn't so sure. 'Is it?'

'Isn't it?'

'I was worried, you know. Worried that somehow it might have been Jackson who wrote the note.'

'The odd chap who's always hanging around?'

I nodded. 'He seems to be fixated on me for some reason.' I gave a little self-conscious giggle even though I didn't think it was funny. 'He was annoyed that Mr Gold gave me a lift to the hospital, and then he came to meet me from the hospital and walked me home. It wouldn't surprise me if he had somehow got hold of the book and written the message to me.'

Mrs Gold frowned. 'He's a strange one all right. Nice enough on the surface but he always strikes me as slightly sinister. But it seems a bit of a stretch to think he'd have weaselled his way into the hospital to write you a note.'

'He gets everywhere,' I said darkly. 'The night Nelly got injured in the raid. He was just standing out there on the street. I thought I'd imagined it, but he told me later he'd been there. It's like he thinks he needs to be looking out for me all the time. As if he …' I trailed off, not wanting to say it.

'As if he owns you?' Mrs Gold said. 'I've known chaps like that before. Give him a wide berth is my advice. Maybe he'll join up? He's the right age.'

'He tried, but he failed the medical. He said he was going to try again, though.'

'Well hopefully they'll let him in this time. They probably need all the help they can get, those poor buggers, with so many casualties …'

Her words hung heavily in the air and she put her head back in exasperation. 'Lord, I'm sorry, Elsie. I didn't mean he'd be replacing your brother.'

'It's fine,' I said. 'Honestly. I just want Jackson to leave me alone.'

Mrs Gold nodded in understanding and bent her head to examine the note more closely. The writing was small and not easy to read in the dim light. 'He says he's a patient.'

'I know, but I thought perhaps if it was Jackson, he could have just fibbed that he was a patient.'

'He doesn't strike me as the duplicitous type,' Mrs Gold said, thoughtfully. 'I feel if this note had come from him, he'd have signed it in large letters across the page. Plus, someone who wasn't a patient would have no reason to keep quiet. You wouldn't get into trouble for having a sweetheart who was nothing to do with the hospital, presumably?'

She was right. I told her so and she grinned. 'I think this note has come from someone else. Someone with genuine feelings for you. Do you know who it could be?'

I felt my cheeks burn because I was still wondering – hoping – if it could be Harry. I thought about him all the time and I'd felt a real connection to him. The only thing I didn't know was whether he felt the same.

'You do!' Mrs Gold said in triumph. 'Have you spoken to this man?'

I nodded. 'A little.'

'Then I have an idea. Why not ask him to tell you something you talked about that only you and he would know.'

'That's clever,' I said. 'You're clever.'

'I like puzzles.'

'I can see that.'

'So what are you going to write?'

'Perhaps I'll just say that I want to be sure who he is, and then ask about our conversation.'

'What if someone else reads it? Would that be a problem?'

'He stuck the pages together round the edges,' I said. 'I think he used tea to dampen the paper and make it stick. He stuck a little scrap of paper out of the top so I'd know it was for me.' I felt absurdly proud of my crafty correspondent.

'Now who's the clever one?' Mrs Gold nudged me. 'Do you have a pencil?'

*

With my message to the mystery writer carefully etched on the page below his, in writing that was just as tiny and neat as that above, I sealed the pages together again. And when I went to the hospital the following day, I took the book with me. Close to the entrance I spotted Frank the porter. Perfect.

'Frank, do me a favour would you?' I called. He came over, looking more rested than he had for a few weeks.

'What do you need, love?'

'Could you drop the book off somewhere as you're going round the hospital?' I tried to act casual. 'There are still lots of people who've not written in it.'

'Course I can.' He grinned at me. 'Anywhere in particular?'

'It's not been to ward 8 at all yet,' I said, thinking about how I could let everyone write in it, and also ensure it got back to the huts just in case my mystery writer was indeed Harry. 'But it doesn't matter too much where you start it off because there are new patients arriving all the time.'

'We had some new arrivals in the huts overnight,' Frank said, nodding. 'I've just started my shift but apparently there are some pilots that have been brought in. More burns, by the sound of it.'

I made a face, thinking of Nelly's moans as she prepared for her treatment. 'So many burns.'

'It's the dogfights,' Frank said. 'I think they'll be sent on this time because they're worse than the other lot. But reckon it won't be long before we get more in. Those huts are getting lots of use.'

'Poor sods.' It was a sobering thought that the new wards were already full. It seemed to me that things would get worse before they got better. If they ever got better. I stared at my feet, thinking about all the sisters like me who'd lost brothers, and children who'd lost fathers, and wives who'd lost husbands.

'That's where I was heading now actually.'

'Where?' I looked up at Frank.

'The huts.'

My gloom lifted a little bit.

'Well, perhaps they'd like to write if they're up to it,' I said. 'Thanks, Frank.'

'No problem at all, Elsie.' He took the book I was holding out, and put it on the trolley he was pushing, which was laden with bandages and saline for baths and bottles of iodine. I felt a bit sick knowing what was in store for those men.

He gave me a jaunty wave, then disappeared off through the door.

We'd had lots of new patients overnight, brought down from East London, so I was very busy all day and didn't get a moment to think about the book. Which was a blessing really, I thought. For me and my patients.

After I'd handed over to the night shift, I went to try and track down the book, which wasn't hard because Frank appeared, holding it aloft triumphantly.

'Got loads more to write in it,' he said. 'There was even a bit of a tussle at one point. Everyone's really keen to get involved. I wondered …' He stopped.

'Do you want to write in it, Frank?' I asked.

He nodded. 'I wouldn't mind, but I wondered if it was just for the patients?'

'Not at all,' I reassured him. 'Do it now, if you like?' I was itching to see if my mystery letter-writer had replied but even so, I wanted Frank to have a chance to write his own message.

'Not today,' he said. 'I'll have a think about what I want to say. I might jot down some thoughts about working here, during all this.'

'That would be perfect.'

He handed me the book and I thanked him, and headed off to see Nelly.

She was the same. Her nurses had propped her up a bit so she was more upright. I suspected it was to help her breathe because she was still on oxygen and her breathing was slow and laboured thanks to the smoke she'd inhaled, and her airway being burned.

But it made her look more "with it" despite her white face covering and her body still being swathed in bandages.

She was awake when I crept into her room and I was glad.

'How are you today?'

She gave me a thumbs-up sign with her hand, like the pilots did in their cockpits, and I grinned, pulling her chart out from the end of her bed and scanning it quickly. She was still on a high dose of pain relief, but they'd reduced her sedation during the day. What worried me slightly was that nothing was happening really. Nelly wasn't being transferred to a different hospital like the new pilots were, which made me think the doctors were still nervous to move her. I turned the page in her notes, trying to see if there was anything in there that would give me a clue about what the doctors had planned, but Nelly tapped her hand on the bed impatiently, so I shut her notes instead.

'I've got the book,' I said. 'I wrote a note to him, a sort of test to see if I could work out who he is, but I've not looked to see if he's replied yet.'

Nelly tapped on the bed again.

'I wish you could talk,' I said. 'I miss hearing your voice.'

She gestured to herself with her finger, and I thought she was saying "me too". But that gave me an idea.

'I don't want to tire you out, Nell,' I said. 'But what about if I write out the alphabet in the book and you can point to the letters and spell out words?'

She did a thumbs up again so quickly I turned to a clean page in the book and wrote large letters from A to Z.

'Now we can chat,' I said.

I moved my chair closer to her and held the book near her hand. With an amount of difficulty that made me wince for her, Nelly spelled out "R … E … A … D".

'Bossy,' I said. 'All right, then.'

Leafing through the pages I found the one that was sealed, slid my hand inside to open it and flattened out the paper, feeling my heart thump. And there, under my writing, was another message.

'He's replied,' I said. 'Oh, Lord. I can't look. What if it's Jackson?'

Nelly put her hand against mine in reassurance and feeling calmer I dropped my gaze to the writing.

'*The first day we met, we spoke about my uncle,*' I read. So pleased I could have got to my feet and done a little dance right there and then, I beamed at Nelly. 'We spoke about his uncle,' I declared. 'I know exactly who this is!'

Nelly tapped the bed furiously, until I brought the page of the book with the letters on back to her. "W … H … O," she spelled.

'It's Harry,' I said, hugging myself in delight. 'Lovely, sweet Harry the airman. You were right.'

Nelly gave the tiniest nod, which was about all she could manage, with her head bandaged as it was. She was trying her best to stay awake, I could tell, but she was flagging.

'I'm wearing you out,' I said. 'I'm sorry.'

She tapped the bed again and I moved the book towards her. She breathed in, and it sounded so painful that I winced.

"D … Y … I … N … G," she tapped.

Full of horror and sadness, I stared at her.

'No,' I said. 'No, Nell. You're not dying. You're going to get better and come home and we can have fun the way we always have.' My voice shook as I said the words, because for the first time since the raid, I understood, that they weren't true. Nelly was very weak and she was very badly injured and even with the doctors and nurses all doing their best to care for her, I didn't think she would ever come home again.

'Anyway,' I said, trying to keep my tone light. 'You are the expert in matters of the heart. I need your help with this Harry business, because I don't have a clue.' I tried to laugh but it was shrill and echoed round the room. Nelly turned her face away from me.

'I'll go.' I leaned over and kissed her, feeling completely desolate. It was so unfair that my vibrant, funny friend was ebbing

211

away from me. That Nelly, who would have loved to be a real part of these notes and this mystery romance – if that's what it was – couldn't even tell me what she thought. There had been many times during our friendship when I'd been despairing about Nelly's tendency to fall in love at the drop of a hat, but now I wished with all my heart that she'd one day do that again. Looking at her now, her whole body wrapped in bandages, and her breath laboured and whimpering, it seemed unlikely.

'You're going to come home, Nell,' I whispered fiercely. But I knew I was lying.

Chapter 25

I hugged the knowledge that my mystery note writer was Harry to myself all night, alone in the shelter. I didn't know where the Golds were. I usually hated being in the shelter on my own and I was still nervous and jumpy when I heard the bombs falling, but for once I didn't mind. I liked having my secret to keep me company.

I wrote a reply in the book, telling Harry I knew who he was and – surprised by my boldness – that I was glad it was him. It was nice, writing things down. I wasn't sure I'd be as confident face to face. I'd never been one for flirting and romance, like Nelly was; I was too unsure of myself. I liked to dance and I liked spending time with men, but I'd never really had a sweetheart. War had broken out just as I was beginning to spread my wings, and all the men my age went off to fight, and I spent all hours at the hospital anyway. But now, there was Harry.

I thought about his open, boyish face and wrote my reply. I told him how much I'd appreciated the patients cheering for Billy, and that I understood how his mother felt about his uncle dying in the last war, because of how I'd lost my brother – though I didn't name Billy of course. I was still aware that someone might read our messages. I told him how lost I'd been feeling since Nelly had been injured in a raid. The words poured out of me like a bottle had been uncorked. I had someone to talk to – at last.

And it seemed the same was true for Harry. Over the next few days, we wrote back and forth every day. Sometimes twice a day. I had an inkling he'd given Frank a nudge and was encouraging him to bring the book backwards and forwards to the hut.

Sometimes Harry would comment on how I looked: "I like how your hair is escaping from your cap today," he wrote. "It makes me want to reach out and tuck it in. I wish I could touch you."

I ached to touch him, too. It wasn't something I'd experienced before. I even dreamt about being in his arms one night and wrote about it the next day.

"I feel the same," he replied. "I want to go to sleep with you in my arms."

He called me Angel in the notes, which I rather liked. It was flattering and exciting and a lovely distraction from the awfulness of everyday life in the hospital and Nelly's injuries and Jackson, who I'd not seen for a few days but who was always there in the back of my mind because I expected to find him round every corner.

On the fourth day after I'd started writing to Harry, I was back on night shifts. I'd got to the hospital early so I could visit Nelly. She seemed to be in a lot of pain so they'd upped her sedation again and her doctors were concerned. I had written a letter to Nelly's mother, assuring her I was visiting Nelly every day and that she was able to communicate when she was awake, feeling I was perhaps misleading poor Mrs Malone into thinking Nelly was less injured than she was. But I couldn't quite bring myself to tell the truth.

I was desperate to see Harry. I'd not managed to come up with a reason to visit the huts for days, so when I got to my ward, earlier than I thought because Nelly had been asleep, I jumped when Matron asked if I'd take some blankets over.

'They're patching up their patients, shoving them out the door and filling the beds again so quickly laundry can't keep up,' she explained. 'This damned blanket shortage isn't helping anyone, and I can't find a porter for love nor money, even though Frank told me there's a new chap.'

I held my arms out so she could pile blankets on top. 'The new porter?'

'Apparently, but I've not seen him yet. Is that all right? Can you manage all of those?'

I could have managed a hundred blankets because I was so keen to get to the huts. 'No problem,' I muttered over the top of the woolly pile.

'Please be careful on the stairs,' Matron said. 'Handover is in half an hour.'

Taking care so I didn't slip, because I couldn't really see where I was going, I carried the blankets over to the hut. Judith was there and I was pleased because I liked her.

She took some of the blankets from the top of my teetering pile and handed them to another nurse to put straight on to beds.

'I'm glad I've seen you. I wanted to tell you that my husband got a note from Eric's wife,' she said.

'Really? What did she say?'

'She said to thank you from the bottom of her heart for passing on Eric's last letter,' Judith said. 'She wanted you to know how important it was, and how much comfort it gave her.'

I put my hand to my chest, not sure what to say.

'Your book is very special, Elsie,' Judith carried on. 'You should be proud of yourself.'

'Oh stop,' I said. But I was pleased. 'Thank you.'

Relieved of the last blanket, I shook my arms out and subtly turned my head to see Harry.

But he wasn't there.

His bed was empty, neatly made up with crisp sheets and no sign of Harry anywhere else in the ward. My stomach lurched and I tasted bile in my throat. Where was he? Had he … was he …?

Swallowing the bitterness away, I cleared my throat. 'The lad who was in that bed?' I said, trying to keep my tone light. 'Has he gone back to his base?'

Behind my back I crossed my trembling fingers. Much as I didn't want Harry to have gone without us even having the chance to properly meet, I was terrified that something awful could have happened. Patients who looked to be on the mend did sometimes take a turn for the worse. Look what happened to Eric. And Vinny.

'Nah,' said Judith. 'He's not gone yet, though it won't be long.'

I stared at her, not properly understanding. Was Harry ill?

'He's just off for his daily walk to strengthen his legs with one of the RAF doctors,' she explained seeing my startled expression. 'It's an assessment of sorts, I think. He's doing so well, I think he'll be back at his base later this week.'

My knees almost buckled beneath me. 'I thought he'd died,' I said. 'I thought he wasn't here because he'd died. Like Eric.'

Judith gave me a slightly odd look.

'No, he's fine,' she said carefully.

Recovering my composure slightly, I forced a smile. 'Wonderful,' I said through gritted teeth. 'And he's off back to base soon? That is good news.'

Behind me the door to the hut opened and as though we'd conjured him up like a genie from a lamp, Harry appeared. He looked tired but in good spirits and the way his face lit up when he saw me, made my heart jump.

'Nurse Watson,' he said. 'Have you brought the book back again?'

The book! No, blast, I didn't have it. In fact, I wasn't sure where it was.

'Nurse Watson brought some clean blankets this time,' Judith said. 'How was your walk?'

'Good,' Harry said. He looked at the tall, rather severe-looking doctor who was with him. 'Doc said I'm doing better than expected, isn't that right?'

'He's my ideal patient,' the doctor said with a smile. 'Does what I tell him to do.'

'Any news on when you'll be leaving us?'

Harry looked at Judith when he answered but I knew he was talking to me really. 'The day after tomorrow,' he said deliberately. 'I've got one more day here. One last day before I head back to base.'

'Then you need to make the most of it,' I said, making my voice sound like I was joking though I really wasn't. 'See the sights of the hospital on your walks.'

'I will indeed,' Harry said. 'Though I'll be alone tomorrow because the doctor is off to assess someone else.'

Was I imagining it or did he put a little emphasis on the word "alone"?

Harry's gaze met mine and my heart thumped. He was such a nice man, I thought. Kind, and brave, and very handsome. He gave me the tiniest of tiny winks and I thought, *cheeky too.*

'So, you've got your last day all planned out?' I said. My voice shook a little bit.

'I have. It's important to make the most of every day because life is short. The war has made me realise that. And your book, of course, Nurse Watson.'

'My book.'

'Yes,' Harry said, looking at me like he was trying to pass a message through his widened eyes. 'Your book.'

'I don't know where it is,' I said, slightly desperately. 'Do you need it?'

'I'd like to write a final message, if that's possible? Could you track it down for me?'

'I think it's in the children's ward,' Judith said. 'I heard some of the nurses were helping the kiddies write messages.'

'I'll find it.' I checked the watch pinned to my tunic. I had time before I had to be on my ward for handover. 'I'll go right now.'

'Nice to see you, Nurse,' Harry said. 'I do hope I get to say goodbye.' He looked straight into my eyes. 'Properly.'

Feeling completely light-headed and giddy, I hurtled down the stairs, over to the main building, and along to the children's ward. It was the only part of the hospital that was quiet now, with most of the littl'uns having been evacuated. But there were a few children in there and I liked the idea of the kids getting their chance to write too.

Panting and sweaty from my 100-yard-dash across the hospital, I pushed open the doors to the ward and told the matron who I was.

'I need the book,' I said, trying to control my breathing. 'One of the airmen is off back to his base and he needs to write a message.'

'Of course,' Matron said. 'It's here. Some of the children have written the most adorable messages. Have a look.'

She opened the pages, and found some drawings done by her patients. They absolutely were adorable and on any other day I'd have loved to have read the messages carefully, and admired the wonderful penmanship, and chatted with the children who'd written them. But not today. Today I wanted to write a note for Harry and make sure he'd get it.

I made some suitably impressed noises, and then gathered the book in my arms. 'So sorry,' I said. 'I really need to go.'

The matron looked slightly taken aback at my lack of enthusiasm for her patients' talents, but she said goodbye and bustled off down her ward. I took the book into the corridor and, feeling slightly sneaky, headed for the ladies' toilet. Not the staff one, the public one. I didn't want to bump into any nurses. I went into a cubicle, sat down on the closed toilet seat, and opened the book to the page where Harry and I had been sharing our notes. He'd not written anything since I'd last seen it, but that didn't matter, because I knew what he wanted. He wanted us to meet. And I wanted it too, more than anything.

Finding a pencil in the pocket of my dress, I tapped it against my lip and thought. "I thought you were dead," I wrote. "Your bed was empty and I thought you had died, and it was awful. We have to make the most of the time we have together."

I took a breath. I knew what I was going to suggest was wrong but somehow, it also felt absolutely right.

"I'm on a night shift again tomorrow," I wrote. "But I can come to the hospital in the afternoon. In the basement, near the operating theatre is the boiler room. Meet me there if you can. I'll wait from three o'clock."

It seemed risky, writing the arrangements down so boldly, but Harry was leaving, and the awful truth was that I might never see him again. So what choice did I have?

I wet my hands in the sink, and dampened the edges of the pages so they'd stick together again, then checked my watch. My shift was starting in a couple of minutes and Matron would have my guts for garters if I missed handover. I didn't have time to take it back to the hut and I didn't want to risk the book going walkabout round the hospital and not making it to Harry in time. If I could catch Frank, I could give it to him. His shift would just be starting too, so with any luck he'd be in the little porters' room.

I headed out into the corridor and along to the room and knocked on the door, nearly crying with relief when Frank opened it, buttoning up his porter's coat.

'Hello, Elsie love,' he said. 'What can I do you for?'

'I'm dashing up to my ward now, but I wondered if you can take the book to the huts, please? I'd really appreciate it. One of the airmen is moving on and wants to write a message.'

'I'll do that for you,' said a familiar voice. I froze as Frank opened the door wider, to reveal Jackson inside. He too was wearing a porter's coat.

'Jackson?' My voice was squeaky.

'Surprise,' he said.

'What are you doing here?'

'I work here.'

'Didn't you tell her, Tim?' Frank said. 'You silly goat. I thought you was good mates? That's what you said.'

'I've not seen much of Elsie recently,' Jackson said. He looked

219

straight at me and I felt – ridiculously – that he was accusing me of something. 'She's been very busy.'

'Well, Nelly's so poorly …' I began, then trailed off wondering why I felt I had to explain my whereabouts to him.

'I'll take the book for you,' he said, holding out his hands. I did not want to give him the book. I didn't want his hands on it. I had a horrible feeling if I let him have it, I'd live to regret it. But I knew if I said no, then there was no chance Harry would get my message.

You're being a fool, Elsie, I told myself sternly. *Jackson's harmless. Give him the book.*

'Are you sure you know where to go?' I said. 'Maybe Frank should …'

'Of course I know. I've been working here ages now. It's nice, being able to look out for you.'

I stared at him. What did he mean "look out for me"?

'Give the book here,' Jackson said.

Reluctantly, I held it out and he took it. 'The huts?'

'That's right.'

He tucked the book under his arm, his eyes never leaving mine. Did he look triumphant or was I imagining it?

'I'll get right on to it,' he said.

Chapter 26

Stephanie

Present day

'It's honestly the sweetest thing,' I said to the eager faces gathered round me in the Tall Trees lounge. 'My friend Tara says it's like a romcom. Even my teenage neighbour is gripped by it and he says he's not interested in romance.'

'So these people wrote each other letters in the pages of the book?' Val said. 'But they didn't know who they were?'

'Like internet dating, when people aren't who they say they are,' said Kenny with a throaty chuckle. 'Catfishing they call it.'

Not wanting to think about how Kenny knew so much about catfishing, I spoke up. 'At the beginning, he knows Elsie, but she doesn't know who he is, so not surprisingly she is really wary.'

'Clever woman,' Val said approvingly. 'Can't be too careful.'

'She asks him lots of questions, about conversations they've had, so she's obviously sort of piecing it together.'

I looked down at the pages on my lap, where I'd typed out all the tiny, densely packed writing. It had taken me ages to get through it but I'd got there eventually and it was so wonderful that I couldn't stop telling people about it. I'd started off telling Val as I made her tea that morning, and somehow I'd ended up in the middle of a group of chairs with residents clustered round wanting to hear the story.

'Look, he says they can get to know each other through the pages, because he's a patient and she's a nurse and it's not appropriate for them to spend time together. But before she agrees, she asks for clues about who he is and whether they've talked.'

'And he says yes,' Val put in, because she had already heard this bit. 'So she says, tell me what we talked about.'

'Don't rush, Val,' Kenny said crossly.

I laughed. 'He tells her they talked about his uncle the first time they met, and that's obviously enough for Elsie, because she immediately starts opening up.'

'She knows who he is,' Joyce said. She moved her chair a little bit closer to mine. 'Who is he?'

'I don't know,' I admitted. 'I only know it's Elsie because I recognised her writing from little notes she's made under some of the entries. None of these letters are signed and the writing is terribly small.'

'It might not be Elsie at all,' a voice said from the other side of the room. I glanced over to see Helen sitting alone by the television. It was muted but she was staring at the screen anyway, though I had the impression she was listening carefully to our conversation.

'Sorry, Helen? I didn't quite hear what you said.'

'I said, the notes might not have been left by Elsie at all.'

I was a bit put out by that suggestion. 'Well, I've got no proof, but like I say I recognised the writing.'

'You said the writing was very small.'

'It is.'

'So you might be mistaken.'

'I suppose so.'

'Oh give over, Helen,' said Joyce. 'It doesn't matter really, does it? What matters is the story.' She turned to me. 'So what happens once she knows who he is?'

'This is the cute bit,' I told her. 'They start sharing stories about each other.'

'Like what?' Kenny moved his chair this time. Honestly, they'd all be sitting on my lap soon.

'Mostly about the war actually. Elsie ...' I emphasised the name deliberately to annoy Helen who was still pretending to be engrossed in *A Place in the Sun* even though she couldn't hear it. 'Elsie talks about losing her brother. She's still being cautious, and I can see she doesn't want to get into trouble so she doesn't name him in the letters, but we know that Elsie did have a brother who died.'

Joyce gave Helen a little triumphant look over her shoulder. 'What else?'

'Shall I read something?' I asked. 'It's my favourite bit.'

'Yes please.' Val looked pleased and I was glad that hearing these stories from long ago was perking her up a bit.

'It's the chap writing here. He says he knew he couldn't join the Army because of what happened with the seagull. He writes that it was the seagull that made him realise he didn't want to kill anyone directly.'

I knew I was milking it, but I paused for dramatic effect and out of the corner of my eye, I noticed Helen stiffen. She was definitely listening.

'What happened with the seagull?' asked Mr Yin slightly breathlessly.

I cleared my throat and began to read. '*I grew up in Lytham St Anne's ...*'

'That's a seaside resort in the north-west,' Joyce told Mr Yin. 'We used to go there on our holidays. My brothers would play football in the sand dunes for hours.'

I glared at her and she stopped talking. 'Sorry,' she muttered.

'*We lived in a big house right opposite the beach. It was a bit run-down and bits were always falling off it, because of the winds that came racing across the sea and battered the front of the house.*'

'He's quite poetic, isn't he?' Kenny commented. 'Nice turn of phrase.'

Wondering if I'd ever get to the end, I carried on: '*One day I came home from school to find my mother in a state. She said there was a seagull in the back garden that had a broken wing and that it was hopping about and squawking. She asked me to go out with a spade and finish it off.*'

Helen was sitting bolt upright in her chair, no longer pretending to watch telly. I had no idea why she was being like this, but there was nothing I could do about it. '*I went out into the garden,*' I said, reading carefully. '*But I couldn't do it. I couldn't bash that seagull over the head and kill it.*'

'It would have been kinder to put it out of its misery,' Kenny said, folding his arms. 'Leaving it injured would just mean it would get taken by a cat or a fox.'

'Ah but he didn't.' I grinned at the expectant faces around me, and carried on reading: '*I picked it up and took it into the house. We had a little spare room that overlooked the flat roof of our kitchen. So I put the seagull in there with some bird seed, and left the window open. I thought it would recover and fly off.*'

'Did it?' asked Joyce.

I chuckled. 'No,' I said. 'He says it stayed in the spare room for three years. Three years! Its wing didn't heal so it couldn't fly but our mystery man cared for it, and let it hop about on the roof every day, until it died peacefully.'

At the other side of the room, I thought I saw Helen wipe her eyes. But she had turned away from me so I couldn't be sure. Strange woman, I thought.

'He sounds like a real sweetheart,' Val said fondly. 'What a lovely chap.'

'Did Elsie reply to the story?' Kenny asked.

'Yes, she did.' I looked down at my notes. 'She replied, saying he should be a vet.'

'I wonder if he ever was.' Val looked sad. 'We don't even know if he made it through the war.'

'That's why I feel this is so important,' I said. 'Elsie was doing a lovely thing for her patients – recording their thoughts and memories and emotions. And that's why I want to do the same for you. Why I thought we'd do our own Tall Trees book. And I'm planning to incorporate some of the words from Elsie's book into my mural.'

'It's such a good idea. I've already thought about what I'm going to write. I'm going to start with a message to my son and daughter ...'

There was a screeching sound as an alarm in one of the rooms went off. One of the residents must have had a fall or got themselves in trouble. I jumped to my feet and put my notes and the book itself, which I'd had on my lap, on to the chair where I'd been sitting.

'I'll be back shortly,' I said.

*

But I wasn't back shortly. It was a couple of hours before I managed to get back to the lounge because one of our sweetest residents – a lady called Jill – had slipped getting out of bed and broken her hip and – we thought – one of her arms. She was very elderly and frail, and she was scared, and Blessing and I were terribly worried about her. So we phoned for an ambulance and stayed with her until the paramedics arrived, which took a while. It was a nice day but it was chilly in her room, so we managed to put a pillow under her head, and covered her in a blanket to keep her warm and I sat on the floor next to her, to chat.

To distract her, because she was in awful pain and we couldn't give her anything to take the edge off until the professionals arrived, I told her about Elsie and her mystery sweetheart and held her hand, and then I went and fetched some paper and she very sweetly dictated some messages to her family for me to pass on. The messages made us both emotional but I felt Jill was almost enjoying it. Or rather, she was appreciating the opportunity. The thought made me feel warm inside.

When the ambulance came, the paramedics took over and I stood up, stretching out my limbs. I felt a bit tearful because I thought Jill probably wouldn't come back from hospital. She was so frail now, like a baby bird, with a froth of fine white hair on her head. I couldn't see her recovering from this fall. I hoped she'd said everything she needed to say.

'Come and have a cup of tea in my office,' Blessing said. 'It's always tough, but she'll remember how kind you were.'

'Thank you.' That did make me feel a little better. I sat down in the chair opposite Blessing's desk and she smiled.

'Jill had a big family. Her daughter was here yesterday, you know? She's almost eighty herself.'

'Really?'

'Really. Jill had her when she was just eighteen. She has grandchildren and great-grandchildren, and her great-great-grandson was born in lockdown.'

'She told me about that,' I said, thinking back. 'She said she was pleased she'd got to meet him. She had me write some messages for her family. Can you pass them on?'

I handed over the pieces of paper and Blessing nodded, looking satisfied.

'Of course. What a nice thing to do.'

I liked that so many of our residents had big families to visit. I always felt a bit sorry for my own nan, who only ever got to see me. And my father on the rare occasion he dragged himself over from Portugal. I wondered if Max would ever get to visit her again. Not that he'd been a regular visitor before he went to prison.

'Do you know much about Helen?' I asked. 'The newish resident? Does she have family?'

Blessing made a face. 'Not that I know of. She's never had visitors.'

'That's quite sad.'

'Perhaps her family are all in Ireland?'

'Then why come to this home? She could have stayed in Ireland, surely?'

'Who knows why anyone does anything?' Blessing said. 'How are you feeling now?'

'I'm all right. Better than Jill.'

'She'll be fine. She's being looked after. Go home early if you like, your shift will finish soon anyway.'

'That's kind of you, thank you,' I said. 'I'll just grab my bits from the lounge and then get off. I've got some preparation to do for my grant meeting anyway.'

I hurried off back to the lounge. The chairs had all been put back to how they were and two of the other carers – Franklin and Vir – were supervising a very rowdy pub quiz. I couldn't see the book or my notes anywhere.

Joyce and Mr Yin were poring over their answer sheet, their heads close together. I tapped Joyce on the shoulder.

'Where did the book go, do you know?' I asked.

She looked startled. 'I thought you took it?'

'I've been with Jill this whole time.'

'It's not there now.'

'I know that,' I said patiently. 'The chairs have all been moved. I just wondered if you saw where someone put it. Did Franklin put it aside?'

Joyce shook her head. 'It wasn't there when they came to set up for the quiz. I know that for sure because Vir stacked all the chairs up to carry them and I thought how strong he was. He wouldn't have been able to stack them if the book had been there.'

'Did you see where it went, Mr Yin?'

He looked at me, his brow furrowed. 'No,' he said slowly. 'Because after you ran off, there was a kerfuffle.'

The word sounded lovely in his accent. I smiled. 'What sort of kerfuffle?'

'Someone saw a mouse,' Joyce said. 'And let me tell you, Val pretends to be all strong and bolshie, but she was up on her chair, holding her skirt above her knees before I had time to catch my breath. Kenny had to help her down because he was worried she was going to break her ankle. He got Cyril's stepladder in the end. And that funny woman from the end room – Marge is it? She was shrieking.'

'Where did the mouse go?' I asked, looking around me gingerly. I wasn't a fan of rodents myself.

'No idea,' said Joyce. 'I'm not even sure there was a mouse. No one else saw it, and I know they move fast but there were a lot of us in here at the time.'

I rolled my eyes. 'So, there was the mouse kerfuffle and then after that the book had gone?'

Joyce gave me a hard look. 'Are you implying that the mouse kerfuffle was a distraction so someone could take the book?'

I actually hadn't been implying that at all, but now she'd said it, it made total sense.

'Who else was in here when the mouse appeared?'

'Just us,' Joyce said. 'All of us who'd been listening to you talk. Marge. And that Helen woman of course. She's the one who saw the mouse in the first place. She must be really scared of them because she just vanished.'

'Hmm,' I said.

'Hmm?'

'Oh nothing. Sorry to interrupt your quiz. I'm sure the book will show up.'

Joyce looked like she was going to question me further but then Mr Yin nudged her. 'How many actors have played James Bond?' he hissed.

Joyce narrowed her eyes. 'Just on screen or on radio, too?'

Leaving them having a fierce whispered argument about 007, I headed out into the hallway and leaned against the wall. To my surprise, I wasn't panicking. Yes, I'd lost the book and yes, Finn had told me to pretty much guard it with my life. But I had a suspicion Helen was behind all this. She clearly had a problem with the book, or with me, or – I thought suddenly – perhaps it wasn't me but my project? I thought about Blessing saying that Helen didn't have any visitors. Perhaps the idea of people leaving messages for their loved ones was making her feel bad because she didn't have any family to write to.

'Oh, bless her,' I said, feeling guilty. She was prickly and a bit strange, but I resolved to be nicer to her. Starting right there and then, in fact.

I headed for Helen's room and knocked on the door. She was sitting at her little table in the window. Her room looked out over the road, instead of the garden but I knew some people liked that – they liked watching the passers-by and the traffic trundling along the street.

On the table next to her was the book. She looked up at me as I entered, and then at her hand, which was resting on the cover. I thought she looked as though she'd been crying, but I couldn't be sure.

'I've got your book,' she said. 'There was a bit of confusion in the lounge earlier and I took it for safekeeping.'

'A kerfuffle.'

A flash of amusement crossed her face. 'A kerfuffle, indeed.'

'Did you read it?' I asked. 'The book?'

She screwed her nose up. 'Sure, what would I want with that sentimental nonsense?'

There was a small, slightly awkward pause.

'Can I take it?'

She pressed her hand down on the book, like she was welding

it to the table, but then she let go and I darted forward, picked it up and clasped it to my chest.

'Thanks for looking after it,' I said.

She closed her eyes briefly, as if she didn't want to see me, then turned her attention to the view out of the window once more.

'They're doing a quiz in the lounge, if you fancy it?' I said.

'Thank you, but no. I have things to do.'

'Well, if you change your mind, you know where we are.'

She didn't reply.

With the book still clutched in my arms, I left her to it.

Chapter 27

The grant money arrived. I couldn't quite believe it. I kept checking the balance of my bank account to make sure it was still there. And then I immediately opened a savings account and transferred it all so I didn't have a reckless moment and spend it all on something frivolous.

In fact, the first thing I bought when the money landed in my account – even before I started thinking about buying paint or equipment for the mural – was a book. I'd found one online that looked similar to Elsie's thick notepad and when it arrived, a couple of days later, I was delighted because it was perfect.

Everything was perfect, in fact. I had the grant money and because it was helping with my living expenses, I could start paying off Max's credit card bill with my wages. I felt lighter. Happier. More solid than I had since before Max had died. Wasn't it amazing what a bit of financial security could do? For the first time since he'd scarpered to Portugal, I felt a glimmer of sympathy for my father. He'd had money and then he'd lost it. That couldn't have been easy.

My meeting with the grant bigwigs had gone without a hitch, because it turned out the woman organising it all was an artist too – see how I was thinking of myself as an artist again – and her father was in a care home, so we had lots to talk about, and she was already talking about expanding the book project to other homes in the area.

So now I was all set. I had the money, I had the book, I was making progress in finding Elsie. Now I had to properly design the mural and get the residents on board with writing messages.

I'd arranged with Blessing to gather the residents in the lounge so I could explain my project properly and let them know what I wanted them to do. I just hoped they'd all want to be involved.

With my spirits high, and the sun shining, I cycled to the home, locked my bike up and ran my eye over the end wall where my mural would soon be without even the faintest twinge of panic. It was like a new beginning, I thought. A new me.

My good mood didn't even falter when it took me twenty minutes to get all the residents together in the lounge. It was like herding cats, honestly. As soon as I thought I had them all in one place, someone would go to the loo, or to get a cup of tea, or pop back to their room to find some biscuits. It was a nightmare. But eventually, I had almost all of the residents together, custard creams in hand. Even Helen was there, though she refused to sit down and instead lurked at the back, leaning against the wall. I was glad she was joining in, because I was trying to be more sympathetic towards her since Blessing had told me she'd had no visitors.

Feeling nervous all of a sudden, I stood up at the front of the room.

'I wanted to tell you a bit about my ideas,' I began.

'Speak up,' bellowed Kenny. 'We're not as young as we were.'

A ripple of laughter spread around the room and I rolled my eyes.

'Shhh,' said Joyce loudly just as I started talking again and I shut my mouth immediately.

'Not you, love,' she said with a hearty chuckle. 'This lot. You carry on.'

Now the laughter was less of a ripple and more of a wave. Amused, I drank the tea Val had made for me with her special teabags and waited for them to stop. When the chatting faded away, I shook my head. 'You are all like naughty children,' I told them sternly. 'But you're very funny. Now just don't talk for five minutes while I explain. Can you do that?'

'Course we can,' said Kenny.

'Good.' I grinned at them all. 'Some of you know I'm going to be painting a mural on the end of the building, telling the story of Tall Trees, during the Second World War, in particular when it was a hospital. I'm using some words from Nurse Elsie Watson's book that she got her patients to write in when she was nursing here during the Blitz.'

'Can we help paint?' Joyce asked.

'Would you like to?'

'Oh, I'd love to.'

Pleased, I nodded. 'Absolutely – the more the merrier.' I looked round at them all, thinking about what Finn had said. 'Actually, I used to teach art for a while. I did wonder about holding some classes here. Would anyone be interested in those?'

There was an immediate clamour of enthusiasm. 'Amazing. I'll speak to Blessing and put a sign-up sheet on the board.'

This was going much better than I'd expected. I felt boosted by their eagerness.

'Alongside the mural project, I thought it would be nice if we made our own book,' I said.

I paused as the door to the lounge opened and Finn came in. My heart gave a little jump. I'd not been expecting to see him and it seemed I was very pleased about his unexpected arrival. He went over and stood next to Helen who gave him a cursory, dismissive glance.

Finn gave me a thumbs up and I smiled at him, feeling my already good mood get a little bit more sunny.

I turned back to the group. 'I love talking to you all. I love hearing your stories and your opinions and your takes on the world. I want you to write them down.' I picked up the book I'd ordered online and held it up. 'This is going to be the twenty-first-century version of Elsie's book. I'll pass it round and you can all write in it.'

'What do we write?' asked Vince, one of the residents from the top corridor.

'That's the beauty of it,' I said. 'You can write anything at all. Messages for your loved ones. Memories. Poems. Jokes. You can draw a picture if you like. Anything goes.'

'Anything?' said Kenny. He made the word sound rude and I rolled my eyes again.

'Within reason, Kenny,' I said, using my stern voice again.

He winked at me. 'Roger that.'

'Right then,' I said. 'Who wants to go first?'

Val raised a hand. 'Could I take it? I've got some things I want to write. Things I should have said a long time ago and never got the chance.'

'Of course you can.' I took it over to where she sat and gave it to her along with a pack of pens I'd bought. 'Take as long as you want, and when you're done, just pass it on.'

Val looked pleased. 'I will,' she said. Then, to my surprise, she took my hand in hers. 'This is a good thing, Stephanie. I told you that you're one of the good ones.'

I looked up to the ceiling, trying to stop the tears that had sprung into my eyes from falling. 'Thanks, Val.' I raised my voice. 'Thanks, everyone. Come and see me if you've got any questions, and I'll put that sign-up sheet on the board today.'

'Sign-up sheet?' Finn said, appearing next to me. He leaned over and kissed me on the cheek and I breathed in the closeness of him, feeling slightly light-headed.

'I asked if anyone was interested in art classes.' I stood up a bit straighter, pulling my shoulders back. 'Lots of them were. And Joyce wants to help with the mural.'

'That's why I'm here actually,' Finn said.

'For an art class?'

He chuckled. 'No, to offer my services. Exams and marking are over; I've got no students and no teaching until the autumn. I thought you might need a hand.'

'With finding Elsie?'

'Finding Elsie, painting the mural, passing round the book – whatever you need.'

'Are you serious?' I was delighted.

'Absolutely.' He frowned, his hair falling over the top of his glasses. 'But I can't draw. Please don't ask me to do anything artistic.'

'I could definitely use your help,' I said. 'But first I've got something to show you and I think you're going to love it.'

I took him over to the corner of the room, where I'd left Elsie's book on the table, and we both sat down.

'There were a couple of pages stuck together and I managed to pull them apart.' Finn looked alarmed and I shook my head. 'Carefully,' I reassured him. 'And it turned out, they'd been stuck together deliberately. Because look what I found …'

I'd put a Post-it Note on the correct page so I found it easily and opened the book up in front of Finn.

'What's this?'

'Love notes,' I said in glee. 'Love messages between Elsie and a mystery man. It's the most gorgeous thing. She's quite cautious at first, gets him to give her clues about who he is.'

'Smart lady.'

'I know – she'd be good on Tinder, wouldn't she?' I looked up and met Finn's gaze just as I said "Tinder" and blushed. 'Anyway, she clearly knows him. He's a patient and she's a nurse so they don't use names – she's still being wary.'

Finn had pushed his glasses up on to his head and was studying the tiny writing. 'This is astonishing,' he said, half to himself. 'I can't believe I missed this.'

I shrugged. 'There's a lot of other stuff in the book and you said yourself you'd not been through the whole thing. I just got lucky.'

'Give me the gist,' Finn said eagerly. 'So Elsie knows who this chap is?'

'It seems so, and they go on to share stories about themselves. And then here ...' I tapped the page at the right message. 'Here is where Elsie scribbles a meeting place. It's not nearly as neat as her other messages so I wondered if she was in a bit of a hurry when she wrote it.'

'Did they meet up?'

'I think so – because then the final message is him saying his arms feel empty without her in them. He says she's his sunshine – like the song. And then the messages stop. I thought at first he was a soldier because he talks about going back to the war, but he also says he didn't want to join the Army.' I swallowed. 'I wish we knew who he was. I'd love to know if he made it home safely.'

'If he was a soldier, then we might be able to track him down,' Finn said, his eyes lighting up. 'Military records are brilliantly helpful.'

'I wondered if he could have been in the air force,' I said. 'You said there were airmen at the hospital weren't there?'

Finn pointed his finger at me. 'There were,' he said in delight. 'There was an annexe here, which had a Red Cross ward.'

'A Red Cross ward?'

'A temporary building, like school huts. It was initially built for the injured airmen from the bomb at Biggin Hill but it was used throughout the whole war.'

'When was the bomb?'

'November 1940,' he said.

I felt a little shiver of excitement run through me. 'So it does fit. Maybe Elsie's fella was one of the airmen?'

'Maybe he was.'

'Could you find out?'

'Probably.'

I clutched his arm. 'Please tell me he survived, and he and Elsie lived happily ever after.'

'I didn't have you down as the romantic type.' Finn looked amused.

'Normally I'm not but Elsie's got me hooked.' I grinned. 'And, if we can work out who the mystery man is, then perhaps he'll help me find Elsie. It would be so perfect to find her.'

'Wouldn't it just?'

He turned to me and we looked at each other for a second. I felt something fizz between us and resisted the temptation to reach up and brush his hair back from his face. Then he grinned and my stomach flipped over. Oh dear, I had it bad for my professor.

'Come on then,' he said.

'Where?'

'I thought you wanted my help with your mural?'

Only a tiny bit disappointed that he'd not meant to whisk me away for a romantic date, I got up from the table. 'The scaffolding is meant to be arriving tomorrow, but they keep changing the days so I'm not holding my breath,' I said, as we walked down the corridor.

'How are you going to paint it?' Finn said. 'It's so big and high up.'

'I'll show you.' I led him into the staffroom where I had my large folder stashed alongside the lockers. 'Look.'

I took out my final version of the mural. 'This is my design.' I smoothed it out on the table and stepped back so I could see it properly.

'Talk me through it.'

I glanced at him. 'You're such a teacher,' I teased. 'I remember my lecturers at college saying that.'

'It's just good to hear it in your own words.'

I smiled. 'So obviously the frame around the edge is made up of the tall trees. Then in the background is the outline of the hospital itself. Over here I've got silhouettes of soldiers ...' I paused. 'But actually I might change that now, tweak it so they're more like airmen. There are planes overhead and a searchlight, showing the Blitz. And then all around the bottom, I'm going to pull out quotes from the book. I've been keeping a list of my favourite bits.'

'Do you have enough to choose from?'

'So many. Some funny bits, some sad, some inspiring.'

'It sounds wonderful.' Finn stared at the picture, rubbing his nose. 'I have a question.'

'Go on.'

'How do you get it from here on to the massive wall?'

'I'll draw squares on the picture, and then on the wall, and just copy each square. It's easier than doing it all in one. I'll do the outline first then fill it in. That's when I think I'll need the most help.'

'So you don't need me right now?' Finn sounded disappointed.

'Not really,' I admitted. 'But thanks for offering.'

'I am very keen to help,' he said. 'Honestly.'

'I know.'

Finn fixed his gaze on the picture on the table. 'I like spending time with you.'

'I like that too,' I said as, much to my annoyance, the door to the staffroom opened and Franklin came in.

'Dunno what you've done to that lot, Stevie, but they're all totally overexcited. Took me half an hour to get them all in the right place for the talk from the local history chap.'

'There's a local history chap?' I said. 'What local history chap?'

'Oh bugger, that's me,' Finn said, looking alarmed. 'I'd totally forgotten. I have to go.'

'See you later?' I tried not to sound too hopeful and needy because Franklin was still there, and I was embarrassed to bare my feelings when he was listening.

'Definitely,' said Finn. 'Just let me know when you need help with the painting.'

That was much later than I'd meant – days and days away, rather than hours or minutes. But I just nodded. 'Will do.'

Looking faintly harassed, Finn hurried off with Franklin, and I started putting away my sketches. Then I had an idea. Perhaps it was ridiculous but I'd never know if I didn't try.

I left the staffroom and walked quickly down the halls to Val's room, hoping she'd be there and not at Finn's talk. She was there, sitting at her little table, much to my relief.

'Stephanie, hello,' she said, giving me one of her rare smiles. 'I've just been writing in your book.'

'Are you done?'

'Just this minute.'

I bit my lip. 'If you're sure you're finished, then could I take it? But only if you're sure.'

'Of course.' She gave me a sly look. 'Are you writing your own message?'

I thought about fibbing and making up a reason why I needed it, but my mind was blank.

'Sort of,' I said.

'Here you are.' She handed me the book and the pens. 'I hope he replies.'

My cheeks flamed. 'What? Who? What?' I stammered.

'Your young man with the floppy hair. Is that who you're writing to?'

I looked at her through narrowed eyes. 'You're too sharp for your own good, Valerie,' I said. Then I sighed. 'I'm thinking about it.'

'Life is too short to spend it thinking,' Val said. 'Just do it, Stephanie. Trust me.'

'Really?'

'Really.'

She pulled the other chair out from under the table and patted the seat. 'Sit down and write it now.'

'Here?'

'Yes, here. Or you'll go away and stew about it, and it'll never get done. Come on.'

I sat down and opened one of the pages near the back. I'd been thinking about what to write, but now, with Val's eyes on me, I couldn't remember what I wanted to say.

'What should I write?'

Val got up – quite slowly and painfully. I watched her with a carer's eye, making sure she didn't pull a muscle. When she was upright, she said: 'I'm just off to the loo.'

I thought she probably didn't need the loo at all, but she was giving me some privacy, bless her.

I picked up a pen. "Just do it," Val had said.

Trying not to overthink it, I drew a little series of pictures. First of all, I drew Harry Potter, with his floppy hair and scar. I hoped Finn would know that meant the message was for him. Then I drew some vine leaves with grapes – meaning The Vine. That was self-explanatory. I added a clock showing 7 p.m., and then a calendar with Thursday's date circled. And finally, not wanting to sign my name, I paused. When Max and I were little we'd write notes to each other like this. He would draw a volume dial with the sound turned all the way up – to Max – for him. And I'd draw a little old-fashioned television with an S on the screen. S-TV – Stevie. It was naff, but it was all I had. I quickly sketched it out.

'All done?' Val emerged from her bathroom, looking serene.

'All done.' I closed the book before she could see what I'd written. 'Thanks, Val.'

'What are you going to do now?' she asked.

'Now I'm going to leave it in Finn's cubbyhole and hope he replies,' I said.

Chapter 28

Elsie

1941

I wished Nelly was with me as I got ready to go to the hospital the next day. I wished it so hard it almost hurt. I thought about the times we'd got ready for dances together, Nelly choosing her lipstick according to which would stay strong with all the drinks she intended to sip, and men she intended to kiss. Not worrying about getting home before the sirens went off. Billy coming to meet us from the hall, teasing us about which fellas we'd been dancing with, and walking us home safely afterwards.

For the thousandth time I marvelled at how quickly and how totally life could change. Now I was down to my last tiny sliver of lipstick, and Nelly had no use for the cherry red Yardley I'd bought her for Christmas. I had no one to see me home because Billy was gone, and I was getting ready alone because Nelly was so ill.

And, I wasn't going dancing, of course. I was going to work. Sort of.

A little shiver of excitement ran through me as I brushed my hair to make it shine. I was going to see Harry. Just him and me. And even if this romance – was it even a romance? – came to nothing, then at least we'd given it a go. Taken a chance. The war had taught me many things, but living each day as if it were my last was possibly the most important lesson of all.

Even though we were meeting in a dusty old room in the basement, I didn't want to meet Harry in my uniform with my face bare and my hair pulled back. So I packed a bag neatly with my clothes for later, and a cloth so I could wash my face before I started my shift. Matron did not look kindly on nurses who wore makeup on to the ward.

Then I put on my best dress. I'd had it since before the war, and it had a pretty flowered pattern. I liked how it swished around my knees.

But when I checked my reflection I thought I looked fine for a dance or a party, but not for walking through the streets of South London in the middle of the afternoon.

So I pulled it off again and put on skirt and a sweater because though I wanted to look nice, I didn't want to look like I'd tried too hard. Goodness this was difficult.

'Oh Nelly,' I said aloud, looking at my reflection as I rubbed the end of my kohl pencil along my eyelid. 'It's so typical of you to desert me in my hour of need.'

Makeup done, I gave myself a last look in the mirror, put on my coat and hat, picked up my bag and headed out of the door.

I was nervous about how I was going to make it to the basement without being spotted. I thought if anyone saw me, I'd say I was taking a message to theatre. And me not being in uniform wouldn't matter because I could just tell everyone I was visiting Nelly. But I still felt worried. I wasn't even sure Harry would be there. I'd look a right lemon if he didn't show up, I thought, as I walked towards the station. I didn't know if he would want to come. Or if Jackson would have delivered the book as I'd asked.

I stopped walking suddenly. What if Jackson showed up and

Harry didn't? What if he'd intercepted my message and would be waiting for me instead?

My breathing quickened, making little puffs of cloudy air in front of me. Surely that was impossible? He had no way of knowing I'd written that note, nor that the note was even there. Despite the uncomfortable way he made me feel, I didn't think he was a bad man. Not really. Not deep down. Did I?

'It's fine,' I muttered to myself firmly. 'It's fine.' I would check the boiler room first, before I went inside, I thought. There was a little window on the door to let in light. I'd peek through there and make sure Harry was inside before I went in.

Feeling more certain, I climbed the stairs to the station platform.

*

I got through the hospital corridors without seeing anyone I knew – everyone was so busy all the time that they were dashing around all over the place and no one noticed me heading downstairs.

I walked along the hall to the boiler room feeling half excited, half scared. I stopped for a second to gather myself, and then peeked through the little window.

To my utter relief and delight, I saw that Harry was there. He was wearing his uniform trousers and a loose white vest and he looked just as nervous as I felt.

I took a deep breath and opened the door, feeling every one of my nerves vanish as soon as he turned and smiled at me.

'Elsie,' he said. 'You came.'

'I was worried you'd not be here,' I told him, fighting the urge to run to him and throw myself into his arms because this was really the first time we'd met properly. 'But here you are.'

'Here I am.'

We both stood a little way apart from each other. I felt a bit awkward suddenly, not sure what to do or say.

'Should we …' I began, just as Harry said: 'I've got an idea.'

I laughed. 'This is a little odd, isn't it?'

Harry's shoulders relaxed. 'So odd. I feel like I've known you all my life and also that we've never met.' He grinned at me and again I felt a pull towards him, wanting to feel his arms around me. 'What were you going to say?'

'Just that we could lock the door,' I said, feeling my cheeks burning. 'I don't mean … well, you know? I just thought we don't want anyone finding us in here.'

'Good idea.'

I turned the key in the lock and feeling more comfortable turned back to Harry. 'What were you saying?'

He looked at his feet. 'I had an idea, but you might think it's silly.'

'What's the idea?' I liked the way he spoke, his northern accent making the words sound warm and loving. Or perhaps that was just how I was hearing them.

'I thought that as we can't get to know each other the normal way, going out to the pictures or having a drink and that, we could do it all now. Here.'

'In the boiler room?'

'Told you it was silly.'

'No, it's interesting. What do you mean?'

He looked up at me and smiled again. 'Don't laugh, but I thought about what we'd do if it was a normal night out. So, first up, I'd pick you up from your house and take you for a drink.'

'All right.'

Harry gave me his arm, and I looped my hand through it, and feeling faintly ridiculous I walked alongside him as he strolled round the boiler room. It was so small it only took three strides to get across the whole room, and we had to steer round a table that was in the corner, but we walked up and down a few times.

'Lovely weather we're having,' he said, looking up at the ceiling. 'Glorious sunshine.'

I giggled. 'Very unusual for the time of year.'

'Ah here we are,' Harry said.

'Where are we?'

'We're in the Three Crowns.' He looked at me and I beamed up at him, enjoying myself now. 'It's my favourite pub in Lytham. Right on the seafront, it is. You can hear the seagulls calling, and if the tide's in …' He tilted his head. 'Yes, you can hear the waves.'

'Do you miss it?' I asked. 'The sea?'

'I do. I like being near water.'

'I've only ever been to Hastings,' I said. 'Oh, and I went to Pevensey once with my brother. He was sick because he ate too much ice cream and then went on the carousel.'

'I'll take you to Blackpool,' Harry said. 'It's really something. You can have a ride on a donkey.'

'Well we're here now,' I said, sweeping my arm around the boiler room. 'In the Three Crowns.'

Harry looked aghast. 'We are not in Blackpool,' he said firmly. 'We are in Lytham St Anne's, thank you very much.'

'Sorry,' I said. 'Lytham.'

'Have a seat.'

Harry showed me to the corner of the room where he'd arranged some tatty blankets into a neat pile for me to sit on.

Obediently, I plonked myself down and arranged my skirt around my legs.

'What would you like to drink?'

'Gin and orange,' I said.

'Coming up.'

Harry went over to where he'd left a bag – I'd not noticed it when I first came in – and pulled out two glasses. They were the glasses patients had next to their beds. Then he also produced a glass bottle half-filled with water.

'Where on earth did you get that?'

'Pilfered it off the nurse's desk in my ward,' he said with a wink. 'Gin and orange, was it? I'll have a pint.'

He poured some water into our glasses, handed me one, then sat down next to me.

'Cheers,' he said. We clinked our glasses together. I was having more fun than I'd had for ages. I felt a sudden wave of guilt for being happy when poor Nelly was suffering upstairs but I pushed it aside. Nelly was the biggest lover of fun I'd ever met. She'd adore all this.

'I'm having a very nice time,' I said.

Harry was sitting close to me and I could feel the warmth of his body through my jumper. 'I'm glad. I wanted it to be special, in case ...'

'I know,' I said. Surprising myself I took his hand in mine. His fingers were soft and curled round mine like they were meant to fit together. 'What are we doing next?'

'I thought we'd go to the pictures.'

'How ...'

'What was the last film you saw?'

I thought about it. 'Nelly and I went to see some terrifying thing in the summer. Now what was it called? *Gaslight*, that was it. It gave us the proper shivers.'

Harry arranged himself more comfortably on the pile of blankets and put his arm round my shoulder. 'Tell me about it,' he said.

'I remember it started with a robbery,' I began.

'No, wait,' Harry said. 'Newsreel first.' Adopting the clipped tones of a Pathé presenter, he said: 'A wounded airman from Biggin Hill is returning to base after being cared for at the South London District Hospital. He says his injuries were worth it because he met a beautiful nurse.'

'Oh, stop it,' I said, giggling.

'Time for the film, then. Tell me the story.'

A lot had happened since Nelly and I were last at the pictures, but I found that sitting there in the snug boiler room, Harry's arm around me, I could remember all the details of the thrilling film we'd watched.

Harry listened carefully, asking clever questions, and pointing out things I'd not thought of. By the time I'd finished I really felt like I'd seen it again.

'Did I explain it well enough?' I asked. 'I'm afraid I've spoiled it for you now.'

Harry grinned. 'I'd seen it anyway.'

I gave him a good-natured shove. 'And you asked all those questions?'

'I liked hearing you talk.'

'What's next?' I said.

'Now we go dancing.' He stood up and pulled me to my feet. 'Come on.'

'There's no music.'

Harry cleared his throat. 'You are my sunshine,' he began to sing. He took me in his arms and we swayed together, our bodies pressing into one another as he hummed in my ear.

I gazed at him and he kissed me. All my senses sprang into life like a jack-in-the-box bursting open. It felt as though all my nerve endings were tingling and my hair was standing on end. I could smell the hospital soap on Harry's skin, and feel the heat of his breath on my face. I'd kissed boys – men – before of course, but never like this. My head was spinning and I thought Harry felt the same way because when we broke apart he looked quite dazed.

'Blimey, Elsie,' he said. 'Blimey.'

He kissed me again, for a long time. At some point – I wasn't sure when – we sat down again and we kissed until we were both lying down on the pile of soft blankets, Harry's weight on top of me. Until he suddenly sat up. 'We should, erm, stop,' he muttered, adjusting his top self-consciously. 'Sorry. I didn't mean to. You know.'

I chuckled at him being so flustered. 'It's fine,' I said. 'Honestly.' I sat up too and ran my fingers through his tousled hair. 'You're going away again tomorrow, and that means we might never get the chance to be together again.'

Harry touched his nose to mine. 'Not if I have anything to do with it.'

'But, Harry, you might not have anything to do with it. That's the awful, horrible thing.'

'I know.' He rested his forehead on mine and we gazed at one another. I thought I could stay there, looking into his eyes, forever. I took a breath.

'Let's not stop,' I said, almost unable to believe what I was saying. 'Let's not.'

'Are you sure?'

'If you are?'

'I've never been more sure of anything in my whole life.'

*

Much later, I realised someone might be missing Harry.

'The Red Cross nurses think you've gone for a walk and you've been ages,' I said. 'You really should go.'

'I suppose you're right.' Harry sounded reluctant. He sat up and pulled on his shirt. 'You will write to me, won't you?'

'Of course I will. It's really the only way I know how to communicate with you.'

Harry chuckled and I was pleased. I liked making him laugh.

'What time are you leaving tomorrow?'

He shrugged. 'They'll just come and get me when they're ready.'

I felt a hard knot of despair settle in my gut. 'I'll miss you.'

Harry leaned over and kissed me again. 'I'll miss you too, Sunshine.'

A sudden noise from the door made us spring apart. 'What was that?' I said. I looked over and thought I saw a face at the little window. 'Was someone there?'

Harry held his finger up, telling me to be quiet and we both stayed silent, listening. Eventually he shook his head. 'Must have just been someone walking past,' he said. 'Nothing to worry about.'

'You go first and I'll follow,' I said. 'We can't leave together.'

We kissed again and Harry went towards the door, pausing with his fingers on the handle, looking away from me. 'I'm not going to turn round because if I see your face now, I might never go,' he said. 'And then there would be a whole court martial thing, and I'd probably get shot, and it would be a big old mess.'

I laughed. 'Please don't do that then.'

'I just want you to know that today has been the best day of my whole life, no question. And I'm going to see you again, Elsie. I promise. You're my sunshine.'

He opened the door and he was gone, just like that.

I sat there for a while, wondering if I'd dreamt that perfect afternoon. Then I gathered all my things – my bag and coat – and let myself out of the boiler room. I had to get changed into my uniform, I thought, and visit Nelly and obviously I had to go and start my shift, and then ... 'Oh,' I said as I walked round the corner and came face to face with Jackson. 'Lord you made me jump.'

He gave me a strange sort of wolfish smile. 'What are you doing down here?' he asked. 'Down here in the basement?'

'Theatre,' I blurted. 'Taking a message to theatre.'

He looked me up and down. 'You're not in uniform.'

'No,' I said. 'Neither are you.'

He wasn't wearing his porter's coat and he didn't have his trolley or a wheelchair or a patient.

Jackson straightened up to his full height and with a slight desperation I found myself trying to work out if I could duck past him and carry on down the corridor. But he was quite a large man, and I didn't want to squeeze alongside him. There was a brief pause and then slowly, he stepped aside.

'Have a good shift,' he said. 'Don't work too hard.'

I hurried past him then stopped as he added: 'You must be exhausted. All these extra hours you're putting in.'

What did he mean by that? Extra hours? Did he know I'd been at the hospital all afternoon?

I didn't want to ask so instead I just walked away, feeling his eyes on me the whole time.

Chapter 29

Stephanie

Present day

'Oh my days,' Micah said, helping himself to a bowl of my Coco Pops. 'You asked him on a date.'

'Not a date as such, I just asked him to meet me.'

'For a date?'

'Do your parents not feed you?' I said, snatching the cereal box away from him before he finished the whole thing.

'Not enough.' He grinned at me then started shovelling Coco Pops into his mouth. 'So what did he say?'

'Who?'

'Finn. What did he say when you asked him on a date?'

'I didn't ask him.'

Micah looked at me over the top of his spoon, milk dripping on to the floor.

'None of this is making sense.'

'Please wipe that up,' I said. 'It makes sense to me and that's what's important because I'm the one going.'

'On the date.'

I laughed despite myself. 'Yes, on the date. Now can you please leave me alone and let me get ready?'

Micah put his empty bowl into the sink. 'What are you going to wear?'

'Are you seriously asking me that?'

He fixed me with a steely glare. 'Do you want my help or not?'

'Not, actually.'

'Fine. Wear that blue sparkly thing.'

'My one and only party top?'

'Is it blue and sparkly?'

'It is.'

'Then that's it. Wear that one.'

'Okay.'

'By the way,' he said in an offhand fashion. 'I joined art club.'

'At school?'

He rolled his eyes. 'Obvs. Don't make a big deal of it.'

I bit my tongue and instead just said: 'Sounds good.'

Micah looked pleased. 'And I was thinking about those letters and that?'

'What about them?'

'You should write to your brother.'

I stared at him. 'What? No.'

'Not for him. He sounds like a loser. But for you. Might make you feel better.'

'I doubt it.'

He shrugged. 'Then it don't matter. You're just the same as you were before.'

'I thought you were going?'

'You know I'm right.'

I shook my head, but I was laughing. 'Get out of here, and let me get ready.'

He headed towards the door. 'Good luck on your date, Steve,' he said. 'Text me when you get home, yeah?'

'It's Stevie,' I called as I heard him clattering down the stairs outside. I smiled to myself. He was a sweetheart, bless him. And a nice distraction from the nerves that were crippling me. What if Finn hadn't seen the message? What if he didn't turn up? What if he'd seen it and he still didn't turn up?

'Maybe I should cancel?' I said aloud. But then what if I messaged him to cancel and he hadn't seen the note and he didn't know what I was talking about? I'd have to explain and how embarrassing would that be? I shoved my hand in the Coco Pops box and dropped a few bits of crunchy rice into my mouth. Ah, I'd have to go to The Vine. But I wouldn't wear my sparkly top – I didn't want to look as though I was trying too hard. God this was impossible.

In the end I put on my best jeans and a plain black vest top. But then I thought I looked like I wasn't trying hard enough, so I added some glittery flip-flops and dangly earrings.

'Urgh,' I said, looking at my reflection. But I had to get to The Vine on time because if Finn did turn up, I didn't want him to think *I* hadn't turned up.

I picked up my bag and headed outside to walk to the bar – for once I wasn't going to cycle – but when I got downstairs, Bernie was just getting into his car. I'd not seen him for ages, so I stopped to say hello.

'Need a lift?' he asked and I accepted gratefully because it looked like it was going to rain again and I was, after all, wearing flip-flops.

*

My nerves vanished as soon as I got to The Vine. Finn was sitting at the bar, wearing a very nice shirt and as soon as he saw me, he looked so pleased and also relieved, that I didn't feel worried anymore.

'God, I was convinced I'd totally misinterpreted that message and I'd be sitting here like a lemon,' he said getting up off his stool to greet me with a kiss on the cheek.

'I was convinced you'd not see the note, or you'd see it and pretend you hadn't,' I told him.

He looked serious for a second. 'Why on earth would I do that? I was really pleased you'd invited me out.'

I ducked my head, embarrassed by his compliment. 'Shall we sit down? Tara reserved a table for us – it's the one in the corner.'

Finn held out his hand and I took it. It felt completely natural to entwine my fingers in his.

'Lead the way,' he said.

*

Admittedly, I'd not been on loads of first dates, but the ones I had been on – even with men who I went on to have proper relationships with, like my last boyfriend, Si, – had been awkward and clunky. I'd talked too much, or not enough, worried about what to order, laughed too loudly or in the wrong places, and gone home and agonised over every word and every look.

But with Finn things were different.

Maybe it was because we'd already spent time together, or because we had Elsie and her mystery man to talk about, but there were no uncomfortable silences, no jokes that I didn't get or silly comments for him to roll his eyes at. We just had a really good time.

'I've found a list of the casualties from the bomb at Biggin Hill,' Finn told me over our first round of drinks. 'Lots of women.'

'Women pilots?'

He shook his head. 'No, there were female pilots during the war, but not at Biggin Hill. These were from the Women's Auxiliary Air Force. They'd have been providing support to the base.'

'So perhaps Elsie's secret lover was a woman?'

He shook his head. 'The women and the most seriously injured

254

men all went to a different hospital – closer to Biggin Hill. They must have had space for them. It was only the men who came to South London District Hospital. They were supposed to be the less injured chaps, but I believe some of them did die.'

'That's so sad, but I guess it'll help us narrow it down even further.'

'Indeed.'

'As long as our bloke isn't one of the ones who passed away.'

'I don't think so, because you said he talks about going back to the base.' He smiled at me. 'I might have missed that page in the book altogether if it hadn't been for you. I was concentrating more on the messages from others, and what they told us about the Blitz in South London, but you went straight to Elsie.'

'It sounds weird but I feel sort of connected to her,' I said. 'Like with her brother, and not having parents. I mean, obviously my brother and my parents aren't dead, but they are …' I thought about the right word. 'Absent. And I like the idea of saying the things you want to say before it's too late.'

A picture of Micah telling me to write to Max popped into my head and I pushed it away.

Finn was looking at me.

'What?' I said.

'This project – the mural and the new book – they're important, you know? It's a good thing that you're doing.'

'Well, it's not like I'm saving lives. But I think it'll be nice for the residents.'

He nodded. 'I'm sorry you had such a lot of bother with your family,' he said, reaching across the table to take my hand again.

I dropped my gaze from his, enjoying the feeling of his skin against mine. 'Thank you.' I grinned at him. 'Tell me about your family. Are they normal?'

*

Finn did not live close enough to The Vine, or to me, to walk me home. But he did it anyway and I was glad. We strolled through the mild evening, chatting about everything and nothing.

When we reached the black gates that led to Bernie's driveway I stopped. 'This is me,' I said.

Finn's jaw dropped. 'You live here?' He gazed through the fence at the large house at the end of the drive.

'Yes and no.' I reached up and turned his head to the side so he was looking at the garage. 'I live up there.'

He frowned. 'Because you look after the cars overnight?'

'Because when Max went to prison, everything got a bit messy for a while and I needed somewhere to live, and my dad called in a favour from an old friend. He lives in the big house with his family – he's Micah's dad, you met Micah – and I live in the granny annexe.'

'And your dad's in Portugal?'

'He is.' I screwed my nose up. 'He's not exactly what you'd call a "hands-on" dad. I've not seen him for a while.'

Finn nodded, his eyes taking in the house and the garage.

'You're very independent,' he said. 'It's impressive.'

I gave a snort. 'Well I've had to be. I've got no one else to rely on.' I felt a sudden wave of self-pity. 'Everyone just leaves anyway.'

Finn put his arm round me and pulled me close to him. I melted into him, thinking how well we fitted together.

'I love how you don't need anyone to look after you,' he said into my hair. 'But you should know that I'm definitely not going to leave you,' he said. And then he kissed me and it was strange because I'd wanted it to happen all night really and I'd felt the attraction between us fizzing and crackling the whole way home, so I'd have thought it would be like fireworks or a fuse being lit. But actually, what I thought was: 'Oh, there you are.' It was as though I had been waiting for him, but I hadn't even known it.

And because of that, when he said goodnight, I wasn't even disappointed that he wasn't coming in. There was no rush.

He stayed by the gate until I'd reached my front door.

'I'll message you,' he called, waving to me as he sauntered away. I saw his face lit up by his phone screen – obviously looking for an Uber – and for the millionth time that day I thought how nice-looking he was. Not *Love Island* perfect perhaps, but handsome all the same.

Inside my flat I shut the door and leaned against it dreamily like a heroine in a romcom. I felt as though Finn's arms were still around me, holding me close, making me feel cared for. It was a good feeling.

My phone rang in my back pocket, buzzing against the door and making me jump, which broke the mood a little. I pulled it out. It was Tara.

'Tell me everything,' she said when I answered. 'Every gory detail. How was it? Is he there? Can you talk?'

I kicked off my sparkly flip-flops and walked barefoot into the kitchen to turn on the kettle. 'It was lovely. He's not here. I can talk.'

'He's not there? I thought you two were hot for each other. He kept touching your arm.'

'Were you watching us the whole time?'

'Pretty much.' Tara sounded unapologetic.

I sighed happily. 'He's perfect, Tara. Funny and clever and gorgeous. And he gets me.'

'He'd better,' she said. 'How did you leave it?'

'He said he'd message me.'

'Has he?'

'Give him a chance – he won't even be home yet.'

'Well, he'd better not mess you around, that's all I'm saying. If a guy says he's going to message my friend Stevie, I want him to message.'

*

257

And he did. Just not in the way I was expecting. When I got to Tall Trees late the following afternoon to start my bedtime shift, I found the new book in my locker. And when I opened it up, there was a message from Finn underneath my little sketches.

He'd started with a fairly rubbish approximation of my telly with an S on the screen. It made me smile.

"I can't draw," he'd written. "But I wanted to say I had a lovely time. Are you free on Friday? I thought I'd take you to a museum. Never let it be said I don't know how to show a girl a good time!" He signed off with a little fish and an arrow pointing to its fin. Which was, I thought, extremely cute.

Hugging myself in delight, I wrote underneath: "Yes please. I love museums. What time and where?"

I took the book and walked along the hallway to leave it in Finn's cubbyhole, passing Helen on the way.

'Still doing that, are you?' she said. 'My mammy always said there was no point flogging a dead horse. I thought everyone would have lost interest by now.'

'Everyone's on board,' I said airily, though I'd been so excited about Finn's message that I hadn't checked to see who else had written. 'It's going very well, thank you.'

'Humph,' said Helen, striding past me towards her room at such a pace that I was reminded again how fit and active she seemed compared to some of our residents.

Refusing to let her grumpy demeanour ruin my good mood, I hurried off to leave the book for Finn. If I was quick, I'd have time to pop in and have a cup of tea with Nan before I had to go and get Val ready for bed.

Chapter 30

Elsie

1941

Harry had gone. He'd gone back to Biggin Hill and though it was just a few miles down the road, he may as well have been in France or in Russia or on the moon. He'd been gone for seventeen days and each one seemed longer than the one before. I'd written to him, and he'd replied, but while our letters had seemed thrilling at first, before we'd spent proper time together, now they seemed a poor substitute for being in his arms.

And Nelly was in a very bad way. They'd given her another saline bath, because they were worried about her burns becoming infected. But it had been so painful, I'd heard her unearthly moans echoing down the corridor as I walked along with a patient. The sound had made my blood run cold. The pain of the bath had sent Nelly's body into shock. The doctors had sedated her heavily – like they had when she was first injured. She'd been kept asleep for more than a week, and though I went to visit, of course, I missed her so much. I felt totally alone.

I even missed Mrs Gold, who seemed to be working every hour of the day and night and wasn't around much. When our paths did cross I didn't feel much like chatting because all I could think about was Nelly and how awful it was to know she was suffering in such a horrible way.

Of course the one person I didn't get the chance to miss was Jackson. He was everywhere. He was working the same shift pattern as I was, so he was at work when I was at work and he was always there to walk me home, or to take the same train as me.

I tried leaving home early or late, I tried taking the bus, I tried everything I could to avoid him, but he would always track me down. He was always there. It was odd that I'd never had so much company – unwanted though it was – and I'd never felt so very alone.

I was grateful when I switched to night shifts again, for I knew we'd be rushed off our feet, and I hoped that being so busy would mean I had less time to fret over Nelly and to miss Harry.

I left for my shift very early, partly to avoid Jackson and partly to visit Nelly. I was worried about her and another good thing about working nights was that I could see her during the day. Her sedation had been gradually reduced and I hoped that today she'd be more awake. I planned to find the book and take it to show her – she seemed to like hearing the messages that people had written and had particularly loved the pictures drawn by the children. If she was up to it, I wanted to see if we could "chat" some more using the alphabet, too.

Of course, I couldn't find the book. Someone told me it had been on ward 10, so I went there, but the nurses there said it had been taken down to the theatre because someone had specifically requested it. I felt nervy when I didn't know where the book was. I knew I had been taking a risk to write such personal messages to Harry. I'd even thought about tearing those pages out, but I couldn't quite bring myself to do it.

I went all the way down to the basement only to find that it had gone somewhere else with one of the doctors. I decided that I didn't have enough time to track it down, so I'd visit Nelly first. But actually, when I arrived at her ward, she was with the doctors and I couldn't go in to her room. Instead I peeked through the door, trying to see what was going on.

Her usual doctor was there, and so were two others and a nurse, too. I was glad there was a nurse there because I knew some of the doctors tended to talk about patients as if they couldn't hear and I thought the nurse would stop that happening.

'Three of them?' I said to one of the nurses nearby. 'Is that good or bad?'

She made a face. 'I've never seen those other two before. They're from a different hospital, I think. Doctor Gilligan wanted a second opinion.'

'Are they moving her?' I was worried about that. I really wasn't sure Nelly would stand up to a journey.

But the nurse shook her head. 'She's not stable. I don't think she'd make it. You ask me, she'd not make it out the front door of the hospital.' Her eyes widened as she remembered I was Nelly's friend and not just another nurse. 'Sorry, forgot she was your mate.'

'She's very ill – I understand that.' I swallowed. 'She's getting worse, isn't she?'

'It's not good,' the nurse admitted. Though then she shrugged. 'But she's still here.'

I nodded, as the door to Nelly's room opened and the doctors and the nurse came out. They all looked grave and my stomach gave an unpleasant lurch as I took in their expressions.

'Doctor?' I said. 'Can I …?'

Doctor Gilligan held his finger up to me, letting me know to give him a minute. The nurse who had been in the room with him rolled her eyes at me, and went off to file the notes she was holding.

'Appreciate you coming down,' the doctor said to the other

men, slapping one of them on the back. 'George, just shout if you need me to repay the favour, won't you? Love to Erica and the children. And Marcus …' He shook the other's hand vigorously. 'Great to meet you at last. Let's hope the blasted Army get rid of that anti-aircraft gun soon and let us back on the golf course, eh?'

I watched their exchange, thinking that men spoke a different language to women, even though we were all using English.

The other men went off down the hall, and Doctor Gilligan turned to me. 'Nurse,' he said.

I opened my mouth to ask him what he and his friends had been discussing and found that no words came out. The other nurse stepped in.

'This is Nurse Watson,' she said. 'She's Nelly's friend.'

The doctor's slightly cross expression softened into sympathy, which actually made me feel a little worse. 'Shall we sit down?' he said.

I shook my head. 'Just tell me.'

'Nelly sustained burns to more than half her body,' he began. I got the impression he was giving me the information he'd prepared for his visitors. 'She has severe damage to her airway causing her respiratory distress. She's lost a lot of fluid and her wounds are beginning to get infected. The pain of any treatment we can give her is so extreme that her body shuts down each time we try.' He squeezed his lips together. 'If the burns don't kill her, the treatment might.'

'I know,' I said in a small voice. My jaw was clenched so tight that it hurt. 'She's not going to get better, is she?'

He paused and then slowly he shook his head. 'I'm afraid not.'

I breathed in sharply. Hearing the words meant I could no longer ignore what I'd known all along. 'How much time?'

'Her burns are too extensive and her organs will soon begin shutting down,' the doctor said. 'A month or so? She's fought so hard so far.'

'A month?'

'Of course, if she develops an infection, which I'm afraid is likely, then it could be quicker.'

My legs buckled and I felt the nurse grab my arm and guide me into a chair. 'Put your head between your legs,' she said. 'It's the shock, is all.'

I did as she told me, breathing in deeply as I tried to take in what he'd said. My lovely friend. My happy-go-lucky, lively, funny Nelly only had a few weeks left to live? And what awful, painful weeks they would be. Her organs failing. Her airway swelling. And the awful, dreadful pain.

Slowly I lifted my head, feeling the room spin. 'Will she know what's happening?' I asked.

'As you know, she has periods where she is conscious and responsive,' the doctor said. 'She will understand what's happening. In some ways, that's a blessing. She can say her goodbyes.' He looked at me. 'Perhaps you could write something for her, in your book. That might help?'

'Are you going to tell her?' I said. 'That she's dying?'

The doctor gave me a little half-smile. 'I think she already knows, don't you?'

*

I sat there for a while, as he continued on his rounds and then, aware that time was getting on and I had to start my shift soon, I forced myself to my feet and into Nelly's room.

She was awake. And to my distress, she was crying. Tears were trickling from the only eye I could see, dripping down her face and on to the bedsheets. She was making a soft, painful moaning noise that rasped in her throat. When she saw me, she reached her hand out and held on to mine.

'I know,' I said. 'I know.'

I sat down on the side of her bed, even though I knew I wasn't supposed to, and I held her hand and I stroked her hair and I let her cry. I couldn't imagine what she was feeling but I knew I wanted her to know that I would be there for her in the weeks to come.

'I'll write to your mother,' I said eventually. 'I'll write a message for you.'

Nelly squeezed my fingers.

'Would you like a priest?' Nelly had never been much of a churchgoer but I had occasionally seen her holding on tight to her rosary beads when we were in the shelter and the bombs were falling nearby.

Nelly didn't respond, though she was awake.

'Is that a no?' She squeezed my hand.

'No priest, got it.' She squeezed again. 'Do you want me to get the book?' I asked her. 'You can show me the letters.'

This time she squeezed even harder.

'I will,' I said. 'I couldn't find it earlier, but I'll go down and ask Frank to keep a lookout for it too, and I'll come back after my shift.'

Still holding her hand, I leaned over, carefully avoiding putting any of my weight on her burns, and put my cheek to hers. 'I'm going to be right here, all the time,' I said. 'Don't be frightened.'

Nelly turned her head towards me slightly and I felt her breath on my skin. I blinked away my own tears, because I had to be strong for her. She'd been with me when I found out that Billy had died. She'd seen me through the nights when I'd cried and cried. Now I had to be brave for her.

'I'll be back in the morning,' I said. 'Get some rest.'

I blew her a kiss from the door of her room and hurried off to find Frank before I started my shift. Predictably, just as he was always around when I wasn't looking for him, now I wanted to speak to him, he was nowhere to be seen. I went to the porters' room, hoping he'd be there – and that Jackson would not.

But much to my disappointment it was Jackson who was inside, reading a newspaper and eating a sandwich. He was laughing with another porter who'd just finished his shift and when I walked in, they both looked up at me with annoyance, as though I'd interrupted something fun.

'I was looking for Frank,' I said.

Jackson looked around where he was sitting in overexaggerated fashion. 'He's not here.'

The other porter laughed. I thought about how when we were children, and Billy was with his friends, he would be mean to me and our mother always said he was showing off.

'Thanks anyway,' I said.

Jackson stood up. 'No, don't go. Sorry I was silly. I can help you.'

I didn't want him to help me but now I couldn't leave without seeming to have taken umbrage at his joke. I sighed. I always felt so unsettled when I was around Timothy Jackson. I really needed to learn how to deal with him better.

'I'll get off,' the other porter said. He aimed a playful punch at Jackson's upper arm.

Quick as a flash, Jackson put his hand out to block the hit. 'Just try it, mate,' he said with a hearty bellow of laughter.

The other man chuckled. 'Just testing,' he said. They both looked very pleased with themselves and I was reminded of how the doctors had all slapped each other on the back earlier on.

'Don't go on my account,' I said quickly, because I didn't want to be left alone with Jackson. But the porter picked up his coat anyway. I turned to Jackson, my words tumbling out. 'I wanted to ask if you'd keep an eye out for the book. Because I need it and I'm not sure where it is.'

Behind me, the door to the porters' room slammed shut as the other man left and there was a sudden quiet. Jackson grinned at me.

'Course,' he said. 'Got something important to write?'

I shook my head. 'It's not for me, it's for someone else.'

'One of the airmen?' The way he said "airmen" made it sound like an insult.

'No, it's for Nelly.' I cast around for the right words. 'She's not doing so well.' My voice cracked and immediately Jackson was at my side.

'Oh, Elsie,' he cooed, wrapping his arms around me. 'Oh poor you.'

I tried to wriggle out of his embrace but he held me tighter. 'Poor, poor you,' he said. He was stroking my back and then suddenly his hand edged lower down until he was caressing my buttock. Again I tried to wriggle away but he held me fast. 'Shhh,' he said into my ear. 'I'll make you feel better. Doesn't that feel nice?'

My cheek was pressed against his chest, the button on his porter's coat digging into my skin. Now his hand trailed up my side and brushed against the edge of my breast. 'Shhh,' he said again. 'There, there.'

With his grip loosened I saw my chance. I wriggled again and this time managed to untangle myself from his arms. 'I have to go,' I said. My cheek was burning where it had been pushed against Jackson's body and I put my hand up to feel it. Jackson reached out and put his hand over mine and then suddenly he kissed me, pushing his mouth roughly against my lips.

I froze, hoping if I didn't react he'd stop and sure enough, he pulled back. 'Elsie,' he groaned. He looked at me, in what seemed to be admiration. 'You really are something. I never knew you were like that.'

I wanted to ask what he meant. What was I like? But I also wanted to be out of the porters' room before he could kiss me again, so I dived for the door. 'I have to go,' I said again. And then I ran.

Chapter 31

I was off my game all shift. I felt shaken and out of sorts and I kept making silly mistakes. I kept thinking about the tears that had rolled down Nelly's cheek, and the way Jackson had pushed his lips against mine and how I could taste the pickle in the sandwich he'd been eating and smell the stale sweat on his coat.

There was no raid that night. No bombs fell. There were no sudden arrivals of terribly injured patients. Much to my surprise – and slight disgust at myself – I was sorry. It wasn't that I wanted people to die or be hurt as the bombs rained down, but I knew that if it had been a normal night, I would have been so busy I wouldn't have had time to brood about Nelly and how to cope with planning for a life without her, or to fret about when I'd next see Jackson.

Instead, I took temperatures and changed dressings and ferried patients down to the operating theatre – keeping a lookout the whole time in case Jackson appeared, of course – and volunteered to do every task Matron needed doing, so my mind was kept busy.

When the day shift arrived and we had done our handover, I went straight back to see Nelly. I was hoping desperately that the book had shown up and that Jackson had done as he had promised and delivered it to Nelly's ward.

To my relief, he had – or Frank had. The book was on Matron's desk when I arrived. I felt dizzy for a second with gratitude that I didn't have to see Jackson again and I gave Matron a huge smile.

'The book's here,' I said.

'That new porter brought it.'

I made a face and she nodded. 'He's a bit strange, isn't he? Looks at you like he wants to eat you.'

Sour bile rose up in my throat. 'Can I see Nelly?' I said in a strained voice. 'How is she?'

'Go on in. She's had a bit of an unsettled night. The night matron said she was quite distressed.'

Bracing myself, I went into Nelly's room, with the book tucked under my arm. 'Morning,' I said.

I could see she was agitated immediately. Her hand tapped on the bedclothes and her eye was wide open.

'What is it? What's the matter?' I went to her side and held her hand. It felt cold. 'Are you warm enough? Do you need another blanket?'

Nelly moved her head slightly saying no.

'Can you tell me what's wrong?'

I took the book and opened it to the page where I'd written the alphabet, holding it up so Nelly could see. Straightaway she started tapping the letters, her hand moving so fast that I couldn't keep up.

'Slow down,' I said. 'Let me write it.'

I took a pencil from my pocket and as she tapped on the letters, I wrote them down.

"Dying," she tapped. Again. My breath caught in my throat. It was so horrible seeing the word on the page.

'Your injuries are very severe,' I said, sounding more like a professional than a friend. I tried again. 'Dearest, you've been hurt so badly.'

Nelly tapped the page once more. "Scared," I wrote down.

'I know.' I stroked her cheek gently. 'Me too.'

"How long?" she tapped.

I couldn't lie. I knew she would know and that would upset her even more. 'A few weeks.'

A tear fell from her eye and she tapped furiously at the page.

'Hold on,' I said, scribbling down the letters. 'Let me catch up.'

She tapped again. I wrote down: "Kill me."

'Nelly …'

Urgently she tapped the page where I'd written her message.

'Nelly, you don't mean that.'

She nodded slowly and deliberately. "I do," she tapped. "It hurts."

'I'm a nurse, Nell. We can't take a life – you know that.'

She tapped again. "Friend."

'I am your friend, and I'll do whatever I can to help you, but I can't do that.'

Once more she pointed to where I'd written: "Kill me."

'No,' I said.

She turned away from me, dropping her hand from the book and I saw in her eye a look of absolute despair.

'Nelly?' I said. She didn't respond. 'Nelly, this is a big thing you're asking of me. If anyone found out …' I bit my lip. 'I don't want to hurt you, Nell.' My throat was thick with tears. 'I don't want you to die. And it's illegal, Nell. I could go to jail. I could hang.'

Slowly Nelly turned her head so she was looking at me. She tapped the page of the book where I'd written "dying" and then where I'd added "it hurts".

'I know.' I looked up at the ceiling. 'I know. But you're not a horse with a broken leg, Nell. I can't just put you out of your misery.'

She took my hand. Her fingers felt cold and bony. She was disappearing before my eyes, already a shadow of the woman she'd once been. Deep in her throat she made a whimpering sound. And then she let go of me and tapped the page once more, spelling out "P … L … E … A … S … E".

269

'I can't make a decision now. I'll need to think about it,' I said. 'I don't even know how I would …' I paused. 'But I promise I will think about it.'

Nelly gave a tiny nod and turned her face away from me again. It seemed our conversation was over.

*

I picked up the book in shaking hands, and left Nelly's room. As I went to go out of the ward, Matron stopped me.

'Can I take the book?' she asked. 'I was telling my friend Prue about it – she works on ward 3 but she's been off because her husband was killed. She said she'd like to have a look. Maybe write something herself.'

Aware of Nelly's messages tucked away at the back of the book, I knew I should say no, but Matron was holding her hands out, and I couldn't think of a reason to say no that wouldn't sound odd. 'Of course,' I said in a shaky voice. Nelly's messages were garbled and scribbled because I'd been writing the letters any which way as she tapped them. I'd just have to hope if anyone came across them they'd think they were doodles. Because if anyone read her request …

I took a deep breath and handed over the book to Matron as a yawn overcame me. Goodness I was tired all of a sudden. I needed to get home and have some sleep before I was due back at the hospital. I wasn't sure I'd get so much as a wink, though, with Nelly's request weighing heavily on me.

Sluggishly, I pulled on my coat and hat and, my mind on poor Nell, walked along the corridor and outside into the frosty air.

'Elsie, you've been ages.'

It was Jackson. Of course it was. He was sitting outside the hospital on the wall and when he saw me coming he jumped on to his feet, barring my way. I was so tired, so worn out with it all, that I barely registered the primal tickle of fear at the back of my neck. With what seemed like too much effort, I raised my eyes to his face.

'Hello.'

'I've been waiting for you,' he said. 'You should have told me you'd be late.'

I frowned. 'Why?'

'Pardon?'

'Why should I have told you I'd be late?'

'Well, it's polite, isn't it?' he said.

I looked at him. My best friend had just asked me to help her die, and here was this sorry excuse for a man, standing in front of me, talking gibberish. Speaking clearly as though he were hard of hearing, I said: 'I don't know what you're talking about, Jackson.'

'Are you tired?' He looked sympathetic. 'Long night? You're the one who's not making sense.' He reached out and took my arm, gripping it more tightly than I thought was necessary. His expression changed from caring to cross. 'It's polite to tell your fella where you'll be, and when. It's good manners. Surely even you understand good manners?'

Now the fear was right there, jolting me out of my tired stupor.

'Jackson,' I said carefully. 'You're not ... We're not ...' I searched for the right words that would make it clear I wasn't his girl, and I didn't want to be his girl, but in a way that wouldn't upset him. Because, I realised now, I was afraid of him.

'Not what?' he said. His voice had an edge that made me feel nauseous.

And then from across the street came the parp of a car horn and a voice called: 'Elsie! Elsie, over here!'

Like a miracle, there was Mr Gold in his car, with Mrs Gold hanging out of the window waving madly. 'Elsie!'

'Goodbye,' I said to Jackson, not meeting his eye. I yanked my arm out of his grip, feeling it ache where he'd been holding me and then I darted across the road, Mrs Gold opened the door and I half jumped, half fell into the car.

271

'We were just passing and happened to see you,' Mrs Gold said. 'What luck.'

I put my head back against the seat in relief. 'Thank you.'

'Friend of yours?' Mr Gold asked, watching Jackson out of the window.

'No,' I said firmly at the same time as Mrs Gold cried: 'Good Lord, no.'

Mr Gold lit a cigarette and then pulled away from the kerb. 'Has he been bothering you, Elsie?' he asked. He caught my eye in the rear-view mirror. 'Want me to have him arrested?'

'Albert,' said Mrs Gold in a warning tone.

There was a tiny pause and then Mr Gold laughed heartily. 'Only joking,' he said. He glanced at Mrs Gold who was looking straight ahead. But strangely I got the impression he hadn't been joking at all.

There was a slightly awkward silence and then Mrs Gold said in a jolly voice: 'I once pretended to be having women's troubles to get poor Elsie away from that man.'

Mr Gold chuckled. 'Poor sod,' he said. 'Bloke like that's bound to be terrified of a woman's monthly ups and downs.'

Somewhere in the back of my mind, something about what he said rang a bell. Had I forgotten something important? But I was too tired and on edge to think properly.

'Isn't it a treat to have the car again?' Mrs Gold was saying. 'I feel like royalty being driven around.'

'It's lovely,' I agreed.

'Mrs Gold and I have been at work, but I need to go on elsewhere, so I'll just drop you ladies off at home and dash off.'

'Fine by me,' Mrs Gold said. 'Elsie and I can have a cuppa and a chat, can't we, Elsie?' She turned round in the front seat and beamed at me. 'Or do you have to sleep?'

'I do, but I'm a bit on edge after my shift,' I fibbed. Actually, I wanted time to think about Nelly. 'So, a cup of tea would be nice before I hit the sack.'

At home, I went into the Golds' flat. It was a nice place, but it was oddly impersonal. There were no photographs on display, or little knick-knacks anywhere. Then again, they'd only moved in relatively recently and they worked long hours, so perhaps that wasn't so surprising.

Mrs Gold filled the kettle and put it on the stove to boil, and when she'd made the tea, she brought me a large mug where I sat on her sofa, and looked straight at me.

'You've got the weight of the world on your shoulders today, Elsie. What's up? Is it that chap?'

'Yes,' I said. 'But he's only part of it.'

'Tell me.'

I looked at her, longing to pour my heart out about what Nelly had asked of me. But something was stopping me. 'Is Mr Gold a policeman?'

Mrs Gold looked startled. 'No, why? Oh, because he said he'd have that man arrested? No. He's not a policeman.' She leaned forward and lowered her voice. 'Do you need a policeman?'

I shook my head vigorously, making my tea slop up the side of the mug I held. 'No.'

'What's wrong?'

I took a breath. 'Remember the letters in the book?' I said. 'From the mystery chap. He's a pilot. His name's Harry.'

'You tracked him down.' Mrs Gold's eyes were gleaming with pleasure.

'I did. He's gone now. Back to base. But we still write to each other.'

'Yes.' It was clear Mrs Gold had no idea where I was going with this.

'In one of his letters, he told me a story about a seagull.' I smiled, remembering. 'He grew up near the sea and his mother saw a gull with a broken wing on the beach. She asked Harry to put it out of his misery and he went off with his cricket bat.'

'Good gracious,' said Mrs Gold, putting her hand over her mouth.

'No, he didn't do it. He couldn't. He took the seagull home and looked after it.' I gave a little laugh. 'He looked after it for three years.'

'Three years!' Mrs Gold hooted with laughter. 'That's wonderful.'

'But he knew the seagull could recover, you see?'

'Yes, I see.' She frowned. 'I think I see.'

'Perhaps if it had been more badly injured, he'd have done things differently. If the gull had been in pain, and had been dying slowly then he might have changed his mind.'

'Perhaps.'

I put my mug down on the coffee table. 'People think death is peaceful but it isn't,' I said. 'I've sat with patients when they've died and it's not how people think. It's not like going to sleep. It's unpleasant and upsetting and frightening. And sometimes it takes days and days.'

Mrs Gold nodded. 'I've seen people die,' she said carefully. 'Quicker is better. Merciful.'

I looked at her sharply. 'Do you think?'

'I know.' She sighed. 'My father fought in the last war. He said that when men were badly injured and they knew there was no chance they could survive, their own soldiers would sometimes shoot them, rather than let them suffer.'

I was horrified. 'They did that? They shot their own men?'

'I believe so. It wasn't official of course, but they knew it was kinder that way.'

'When Billy died his commanding officer wrote to me, and one of the things he said was that Billy went quick,' I told her. 'They were bombed, you know? As they were evacuated. They were like sitting ducks.' I took a shuddering breath in. 'But it was a comfort to know he hadn't suffered.'

Mrs Gold put her own mug down and took my hands in hers. 'Has something happened at work, Elsie?'

'Sort of.' I looked into her clear blue eyes and wished I could tell her everything, but the knowledge that this awful, terrible thing I was considering wasn't just merciful but also illegal, stopped me. Instead, I simply said: 'You've helped me so much.'

'Have I?'

'Yes.' I stood up. 'Thank you.'

Chapter 32

Stephanie

Present day

Biggin Hill museum was the sweetest, smallest museum I'd ever visited. Finn had picked me up from Tall Trees after my morning shift in his car – an old Mini that was so perfect for him I was positively gleeful when I got in – and driven us up to the old airfield, explaining that it was the perfect place to try to track down Elsie's mystery man. The former RAF base where Fighter Command had flown from during the war was now a swanky airport for private jets. I always wondered which celebrities were landing and taking off whenever I went past.

The museum itself was a small new building at the side of the RAF chapel. When Finn and I went in, he was greeted like an old friend by the chap who was on the desk.

'Good to see you,' he said, shaking Finn's hand vigorously.

Finn grinned at him. 'Likewise. This is my erm, my ah, my Stevie.'

I smiled to myself. He obviously didn't want to call me his

girlfriend – we weren't there yet – but didn't want to "friend-zone" me either. I liked it.

'Stevie's an artist,' he added. He sounded quite proud, I thought.

'Finn and I are working on projects that have overlapped,' I explained.

'I hear you have a mystery to solve,' the man said. He looked at Finn. 'I've got all the casualty lists out for you. They're in the reading room.'

'Cheers,' said Finn, slapping him on the back in a manly fashion. 'Shall we have a look round first?'

We wandered around the little museum, reading the displays about the men and women who had worked there during the war. It made fascinating reading, especially when I found the displays about the bomb that had fallen.

Then we went into the reading room and discovered Finn's friend had put out all the records we needed.

'Ah-ha,' said Finn looking blissfully happy at the idea of wading his way through old documents. 'Here we go.'

His idea – and I had to admit it was a good one – was to simply read the names and information about the men who'd been injured in the bomb and try to whittle it down.

'There were twelve men injured in the bomb who went to South London District Hospital,' he said. 'Some will be too old to be Elsie's chap – we know roughly how old he is by some of the things he's said in his notes to her.'

I nodded, taking the book out of the tote bag I'd brought it in and putting it on the table. 'We can always check again if we have to, but I know he mentioned in one of his notes that he doesn't remember the last war.'

'Great,' he said. 'So let's have a look. I think he'd have to be early to mid-twenties in 1940. If he was any older, I reckon he'd have some memories of the war. The end of it at least.'

We trawled through the list of casualties, discarding the men that were too old. That got rid of half of them, another was

277

Polish – apparently there had been a lot of Polish pilots at Biggin Hill – so we got rid of him too because we knew our man came from Lancashire.

With five left, Finn logged on to his laptop and called up the RAF records that he had a subscription for.

'Now we have names,' he said. 'We can find their address when they enlisted and hopefully the address they returned to at the end of the war, too.'

'We know Elsie's fella was from Lytham St Anne's because of the seagull story.'

'Exactly.'

He checked the first couple of names and I watched him, hunched over his laptop typing away.

'He's not Eric …' he said. 'Nor George.'

I opened Elsie's book, planning to flip to the page where she'd shared her notes to her mystery man. But I had it upside down so instead of opening the front cover, I opened it right at the back. I swivelled it round and started leafing through from the back instead, and stopped as I found a page that had been scribbled over. Urgh, had someone at Tall Trees done that?

The messages, pictures and poems in Elsie's book were higgledy-piggledy over the pages. Some pages had just one letter on them. Others had a few squished in together. But they weren't untidy – just making the best use of space, like when people signed a birthday card at work. This page, though, was more like the doodles I always did when I was on the phone, writing down random words from my conversation that made sense at the time but none at all when I looked at it five minutes later.

I tutted, gazing at the messy page. There was the alphabet written out from A to Z. And then around the letters were words scattered here and there in scribbled handwriting. That seemed, I thought to myself looking closer, not unlike Elsie's writing.

'What is this?' I muttered. I read the scribbled words. "Friend," one said. Another said: "Dying," and another "it hurts." I shivered, even though it was warm in the room where Finn and I were. This was so odd.

'Look at this, Finn,' I said. 'Weird messages in what I think is Elsie's handwriting.'

I showed the book to him and he pushed his glasses up on to his forehead so he could see better close up. 'What is this?' he said. 'Are you sure Elsie wrote these?'

'Not sure but I think it's her writing.' I squinted at the letters again. 'Hmm, it's hard to tell though. Everyone wrote so beautifully back then.'

I leafed through the pages until I found Elsie's notes to her bloke, and flipped back and forth studying the writing carefully. 'I think so,' I said. 'Look at how she loops the ends of her Ss? It's the same in both.'

'I agree.' Finn nodded. 'But what does it mean?'

'Oh God, look. She's written "kill me".'

We both looked at each other in surprise.

'We don't have a death certificate for Elsie, and Petra saw her in the Sixties, so we know that no matter what she says on these pages, she wasn't dying.' I frowned. 'But maybe she thought she was?'

'Could this be a game of some sort?' Finn suggested. 'Like a weird version of hangman?'

'A very weird version of hangman.'

I flipped back and forth again, and Finn said: 'Hang on.'

He put his finger into the page to stop me moving them. 'Look, there's another message on the other side.'

Sure enough on the other side of the page where the alphabet was scrawled, was another – neater – message in Elsie's writing.

'Mammy, I am sorry I didn't get to say goodbye,' I read aloud. 'I love you all very much.'

'What is this?' I said. 'Is she writing on behalf of someone else? Someone whose injuries were too bad for them to write themselves?'

'Maybe so,' Finn said. He sat up a bit straighter. 'Perhaps the person who was dying?' He flipped the page back to the letters and tapped the page with his finger. 'And perhaps this person couldn't speak so they were spelling the messages out letter by letter.'

I stared at him. 'Bit far-fetched isn't it?'

He shrugged. 'I saw a documentary about assisted dying where the chap involved was paralysed and he spelled words out on this computer thing by blinking.'

'Say that again.'

'He was paralysed and he—'

'No, the first bit. Assisted dying did you say? What if this patient was asking Elsie to help them die?'

'Now who's being far-fetched?' Finn raised an eyebrow.

'It literally says "kill me",' I pointed out.

'So you think Elsie was running round the hospital seeing off patients? Like some angel of death?'

'No I do not,' I said frostily. I felt very protective of Elsie. 'I think this person might have been special to her.' I gasped. 'What if it was our mystery airman? What if he was badly injured, couldn't speak and he asked Elsie to put him out of his misery?'

Finn shook his head. 'The same airman who wouldn't kill a seagull? Plus he was fit enough to meet Elsie in secret and be sent back to his base. He wasn't dying.'

'No he wasn't,' I said delighted about that. 'Maybe a friend then? It says "friend" there on the page. Or a family member, even?'

'Maybe,' Finn said doubtfully.

We both stared at the book for a second, at a loss as to what to do next, and then he spoke.

'Perhaps if we find her fella that will help us? It's the only lead we've got at the moment anyway.'

'Perhaps. Who's next on your list?'

'Harry Yates,' he said, typing the name. There was only one result. Finn clicked on it and let out a little shout of triumph that made me jump.

'Harry Yates, born 1919, address 14 Stewart Crescent, Lytham St Anne's.'

'That's him. That's Elsie's bloke.'

'Sounds like it.'

'What else does it say?' I leaned over and he put his arm around me and pulled me close. It felt totally natural to rest my head on his shoulder as I gazed at the screen. 'Does it tell you where he went after the war?'

'Let's have a look,' said Finn. He clicked again. 'Yes, his address is Dublin, in Ireland.'

'Dublin?' I sat up. 'Ireland?'

'Maybe he had family there.'

'Or maybe Elsie went there,' I said. 'Maybe that's why we couldn't find her death certificate – because she died in Ireland.'

'Why would she go to Ireland?'

'To be with Harry?'

'We're going round in circles,' Finn said. 'I'm not registered on any Irish genealogy sites, but I'll get myself an account and then we can search for Elsie and Harry on there.'

'Perhaps they got married in Ireland and lived happily ever after.'

'I hope so.' Finn still had his arm around me and now he pulled me closer again and we kissed. 'I'd like them to have a happy ending.'

I felt so completely happy that I almost expected little birds and butterflies to appear around us like in a Disney fairy tale. I grinned at Finn. 'Me too.'

And then, there it was. The little niggle in the back of my head that told me not to relax. That if I was feeling happy now, something bad was bound to happen. *Remember when you were happy about your exhibition*, it told me. *Remember how you thought everything was working out and then Max turned up and you messed everything up? Remember, remember, remember …*

I took a deep breath in and Finn looked at me, concerned. 'Okay?'

'Might just get some air,' I said. 'I'll wait outside.'

I picked up the book and hurried out to the front of the museum where I sat on a bench and gazed up at the two Spitfires that were displayed next to the entrance. My breathing was recovering now and I was pleased that I hadn't panicked. *See*, I told myself. *It's all going to be all right. Finn's here. You're here. It's all fine.*

While I waited for Finn to say goodbye and thank you to the staff at the museum, I looked at the odd notes I'd found. "Kill me" was such a blunt, awful thing to read. Such a blunt, awful request for someone to make.

Who was it? I wondered. Who had asked Elsie to do such a terrible thing? I turned the page over and looked at the message there.

'Mammy, I am so sorry I didn't get to say goodbye,' I read under my breath. Mammy? What was that? Did Geordies say "Mammy"? Or was it Scousers? I was sure someone I'd spoken to recently had said it. I looked up into the sky, trying to think.

'Ready to go?' Finn appeared next to me. 'Are you working later?'

'I have the night off as it happens,' I said. 'I was planning a Netflix binge with some takeaway pizza.'

'Want some company?'

I looked at him, this lovely clever man who seemed to want to spend time with me, no matter what we were doing, and I nodded. 'Yes please.'

'I can bring wine.'

'Yes please,' I said again, and he laughed.

I got up from my bench and followed him to his car and just as he unlocked the door I remembered where I'd heard "Mammy" recently.

'Irish,' I said, getting into the passenger seat. 'Mammy is Irish.'

'Your mammy?'

I chuckled. 'No, the note in Elsie's book that's addressed to "Mammy"? On the other page to the alphabet?'

'What about it?'

'Mammy is what some Irish people call their mums. You know grumpy Helen at Tall Trees? I'm sure she mentioned her mammy the other day and she's Irish.'

Finn started the engine and winked at me. 'So Ireland could be a link between Elsie and Harry and the person who was dying,' he said. 'We just have to find out what it means.'

*

Finn stayed the night. We watched *Casablanca* and ate pizza and talked for hours about Harry and Elsie and whether they could have gone to Ireland together, and it was lovely. And then we went to bed and that was lovely, too. Really lovely. We slept with our legs tangled up together and again I thought that I was completely happy – and this time I didn't have the fear that it was all about to go wrong.

I woke up early to find him getting dressed, tiptoeing around the room.

'Are you going?' I felt a lurch of fear. 'Stay. I don't have to be at Tall Trees until later.'

'I'm going to go into work and use the uni logins for the Irish genealogy sites,' he told me. 'It's best to get in early before the summer school students arrive at the library.'

'Oh that's exciting.' I sat up in bed and he came and sat next to me, giving me a long kiss. 'Although,' he said. 'There's no rush.'

I was dozing when he eventually left again. He kissed me and said he'd ring me later. I half heard him leave, and then I nodded off again. I only woke up when my "just in case" alarm went off – a night of very little sleep had obviously caught up with me.

Contentedly, I stretched out, smelling Finn's aftershave on my pillow and then went off for a shower. And when I came out, my doorbell was ringing. I paused, my head on one side listening.

Was it my doorbell? No one ever visited me. In fact, I hadn't even known the flat had a doorbell.

Rubbing my wet hair with the towel, I tied my dressing gown around me more securely and went to answer. And there, on the doorstep were two police officers – a man and a woman. They were talking but when I opened the door they both stopped.

'We're looking for someone called Stevie?' one of them said.

I dropped the towel, and stared at them, feeling my legs beginning to shake. Suddenly I was back in the gallery where I'd been when the police had arrived to tell me the news about Max.

'That's me,' I whispered. 'I'm Stevie.'

'Do you know Mr Finn Russell?' the policeman said.

'What's happened? What's wrong?'

The police officers exchanged a glance. The female officer spoke in a kind tone. 'I'm afraid he's been involved in an accident,' she said.

Chapter 33

Elsie

1941

I had made my decision. I was going to do as Nelly asked. And it was the worst thing I could ever have imagined. In fact, it was far beyond anything I could ever have imagined – before the war at least. Before the nightly raids and the destruction of our normal lives. But somehow it also seemed less bad than watching Nelly die a slow and painful death. Seeing her limbs withering beneath the dressings, or watching her being submerged in baths of saline water, hearing her moan with pain, and knowing none of it would help.

Once I'd decided I would help her die, I felt lighter, as though a weight had been lifted from me. But that lightness didn't last long. This was a huge thing I was doing. I knew it would be a decision that would stay with me for my whole life. And that was assuming no one ever found out what I had done. It was something I would have to learn to live with. But I knew in my heart that if the roles had been reversed, I would have wanted Nelly to do the same for me. And I knew she would have agreed.

Fortunately, I had two days off after Nelly had asked me to help her die, and I decided to spend them getting everything ready. I knew I had to act fast, because the awful truth was Nelly was suffering terribly and I wanted it to stop. I wanted her to be at peace.

'A few of us are going to the pictures tomorrow,' Petra said as we left the hospital. 'Afternoon showing, then a couple of drinks afterwards and home before the siren goes. Fancy coming along?'

I smiled at her. 'I'd love that,' I said honestly, wishing I could go and do normal, fun things like Nelly and I used to. I wondered if I ever would again. 'But I have to help a friend.'

At home I dug out some of my old books from my nursing training and pored over the sections on medicines. Nurses couldn't prescribe of course, but we handed out the drugs that the doctors had allocated for patients. We had access to the medicines cupboards and with everyone so busy at the hospital, things weren't as tightly controlled as they once had been, or indeed, as they should be.

I thought the best way to let Nelly slip away would be to give her more morphine than she needed. But because she was already on lots of painkillers, she would be used to the medicine and I needed to be sure that the dose I gave her would work.

I looked at the pages in my book and rubbed my head, thinking hard. Nelly was small and slight – even more so now – but she'd have a tolerance to the medicine. I scribbled down some sums on the back page of the textbook and then added a bit more to be sure. That would do it, I thought.

But how to get hold of it? I couldn't go and take what I needed from the drugs cupboard in my own ward. Someone would notice it was missing. Instead, I thought, I would have to take little bits from all over. But the good news was, I had access to every ward in the hospital thanks to my book. No one would pay any attention to me wandering around. No one would even notice what I was doing.

Morphine came in tiny glass bottles and lots of patients were given it, because we had so many badly injured people to care for who needed proper pain relief. I planned to take a walk round the wards just when I knew the nurses would be doing their rounds with the medicines trolley and swipe a bottle here and a bottle there.

So, the following day – when I was still on my break from the ward – I headed to work. Thankfully there was no sign of Jackson. He was on the same shift pattern as me more or less – nurses and porters' shifts weren't exactly the same – and though that usually made me uneasy, this time it made things easier.

I found the book quickly in one of the women's surgical wards. I checked my watch – almost time for the drugs round – and decided to hang around for a while. So I chatted to a few of the patients about the book, staying out of the way of the nurses as they bustled round, checking charts and getting the medicines ready. And then, when the trolley was prepared, I said goodbye and walked casually towards the door. As the nurse with the medicines looked at the chart she was holding, I reached out a hand without breaking stride, picked up one of the little bottles of morphine and slipped it, unseen, into my pocket.

Then I did the same in the ward along the corridor, popping in and pretending I'd got the wrong ward, so I didn't have to linger. And finally I did it on a ward upstairs, where I pinched two more bottles from their trolley too.

And then, with the book clutched in my arms and my pockets rattling with the bottles, I went to see Nelly.

'She's very low,' the nurse on the ward said as I went in. 'Hopefully seeing you might cheer her up.'

I doubted that, but I nodded and pushed open the door to Nelly's room.

'It's me,' I said quietly because her eye was closed but I knew she wasn't asleep. Sure enough, she blinked a couple of times and then opened her eye and looked at me.

'Do you feel awful?'

She nodded slightly.

I pulled the chair over from the corner of the room and sat down next to her.

'I've been thinking about what you asked me,' I said. I took a breath. 'I'll do it.'

Nelly breathed in sharply. She felt for my hand and squeezed it tightly.

I leaned over so I could speak into her ear. 'Morphine,' I said in a low voice. I looked up at the metal stand where a glass bottle was dripping fluid into Nelly's vein. 'I thought about putting it into your fluids ...'

Nelly shook her head.

'No, I know that wouldn't work. I changed my mind. I'll inject you.'

I felt Nelly relax. 'But I need to know this is what you want. I thought we could come up with a signal so if you want me to stop at any time, you can let me know.' I thought about that. 'Maybe hitting the bedclothes with an open hand like this?' I showed her and she copied.

'That's it. Do that if you want me to stop.'

Nelly nodded.

'I can't do it today because I need ...' I paused, trying to collect my thoughts. 'I need to prepare myself. And I think it'll be easier when I'm working.'

Nelly nodded again.

'But I brought the book and I thought you could tell me what you want to say to your mum?' I felt tears prick at my eyes again as I thought about Nelly's mother, across the Irish Sea, worrying about her daughter and knowing she'd never see her again. 'If you tell me, I'll write down the message.'

Wiping my eyes, I tried to sound efficient. 'Shall we get started then?'

Being cautious, I'd sealed the pages where I'd written Nelly's request. But now I opened it again so she could use her alphabet.

Slowly she tapped out her message, and I wrote it down. "Mammy, I am sorry I didn't get to say goodbye," I wrote. "I love you all very much."

'They love you too,' I said to Nelly. 'I know that from your mum's letters, and her stories about your family. They love you so much.'

A tear trickled down Nelly's cheek.

'And so do I,' I said. 'I love you too. You're the best friend I ever had and I don't know what I'll do without you.' I was crying properly now. I wiped my eyes again and tried to carry on. 'When Billy died, you were there for me, looking after me. And you always make me laugh. And you taught me how to put kohl pencil round my eyes and how to get the last bits out of a tube of lipstick.'

I looked down at my handkerchief clenched in my fist and leaned closer to Nelly. 'Nelly, I think I might be expecting,' I said in a quiet voice. 'I think I'm having a baby.'

Nelly's eye widened. She took my fingers in hers and squeezed.

'I don't know what to do,' I said. I'd not properly let myself think about this added complication yet. It seemed too huge to contemplate, but it also seemed like a tiny chink of sunlight on a very dark day. And I wanted Nelly to know.

Nelly reached for the book again. I held it up and she tapped out the word. "L ... I ... V ... E," she spelled. "For me."

'I will. I promise.'

Nelly's chest was heaving in a way that looked very painful and she was making a sort of whimpering sound in her throat. 'Don't get upset,' I urged her. 'Please don't. I didn't want to make you sad. I just want you to know that I'm a better person because I knew you. That my life is better because you were in it.'

I sniffed, searching in my pockets for another handkerchief because mine was soggy with tears, and feeling the little bottles of morphine clinking together. 'Thank you, Nelly,' I whispered. 'I'm sorry my baby won't know you. I'm really going to miss you.'

I leaned over and kissed her head, and she stroked my hair awkwardly with her good hand, and then I left her room without looking back.

Chapter 34

Stephanie

Present day

'We know it's a shock,' the policewoman said gently. 'But Mr Russell is going to be all right.'

'What happened?'

'He was turning left out of a junction. There was a queue of traffic on the opposite side of the road and someone decided to nip out on to his side of the street. They would have hit him head-on if he hadn't reacted so fast. As it is, his car's a write-off, but we've just had word that he is okay.'

'Head-on?' I said faintly. 'How badly hurt is he?'

'Cuts and bruises, I think. A bang on his head and a broken arm from yanking the steering wheel.'

I put my hand up to my head, thinking about how fragile life was. 'Why did you come here?' I asked. 'I'm not his next of kin or anything. Why me?'

The policewoman smiled at me. 'He was unconscious when the ambulance arrived, and yours was the most frequently called number on his phone. I think they've tracked down his mum now, though.'

'Okay. Good. Where does she live?'

'She's on her way from Manchester, apparently.'

'We can take you to the hospital,' the policeman said. 'Drop you off.'

'No thank you. I'll get some bits together and then make my own way.' I forced a smile. 'Thank you for coming to tell me.'

I showed them out and then went to sit on the sofa. I was shivering though the day was warm.

'Head-on,' I muttered to myself. Head-bloody-on. Finn could have been badly injured. He could have died. Sudden nausea overwhelmed me and I sprinted to the bathroom where I threw up violently.

When my stomach was empty of last night's pizza and wine, I sank down against the wall of the bathroom and cried and cried. I wasn't ready for this, I thought. I wasn't ready for the feeling of liking someone and risking that those feelings could be taken away. I was too fragile, too raw.

Feeling weak and pathetic I got up from the floor and went into my bedroom. I took off my dressing gown, put on my pyjamas and crawled into bed, but the sheets smelled of Finn, so I got out again, pulled the sheet off, and put a clean one on. I didn't have the energy to change the duvet cover, so I just flipped it round.

Huddled under the covers, I messaged Blessing telling her I had a tummy bug and couldn't come to work, then I did the same to Tara. Both of them replied saying I should stay away for twenty-four hours, and I was glad.

Then, hating myself, I messaged Finn. "I'm sorry," I wrote. I pressed send, then I blocked his number and deleted him from my contacts, like the big old pathetic coward I was.

I pulled the duvet right over my head and went to sleep.

*

I didn't leave the flat for an entire day and night. I heard Micah come in at one point. He knocked gently on my bedroom door and I called out to him. 'I'm sick,' I lied. 'Don't come in, you don't want to catch it.'

'Should I call someone?' he asked. 'Let someone know?'

'No,' I said through the door. 'There's no one.'

Eventually on the second day, I knew I had to get up. I gave myself a little pep talk. Finn wasn't dead. This wasn't the same as what had happened with Max. Finn wasn't hurt. And nothing bad had happened. Except for me realising I wasn't really in a good place to start a relationship. I was too messed up. I had to let Finn go and that way it would all be okay. I just hoped I wouldn't bump into him at Tall Trees. I thought I might ask Blessing to put me on evenings and nights for a while, just so I could stay out of his way.

I did, though, still have Elsie's book. I knew I should return it. I was working later that day so I'd just have to bite the bullet and give it back.

But first, there was something else I needed to do.

Micah's suggestion of writing to Max had stuck in my head. I couldn't stop wondering if he was right – if it would make me feel better. This thing with Finn and the police turning up had brought back all the horrible feelings of that time, and I thought that perhaps I should write them down.

Maybe I'd never send it, but I felt I needed to get the thoughts out of my head.

I got dressed and sat down on the sofa with a notepad and pen.

"Dear Max," I began. And then, much to my surprise, the words just started to come, flowing on to the page more easily than I'd expected.

"I'm sorry I said all those awful things to you when we argued," I wrote. "I was angry and frustrated that you'd showed up on my doorstep again just because you needed help. But you're not a loser and I'm not sorry you're my brother. I called the police after the burglary because you took everything I had and I needed to claim on the insurance." I underlined "everything".

"I am not the reason you went to prison, Max," I wrote. "That's all your doing. I'm sorry for the things I did that were wrong, but you did wrong things too. I hope when you get out, we can be friends again because I miss you. And so does Nan."

I signed the letter with the little sketch of the television with an S on the screen, even though it made me think of Finn and that made me sad. Then I added: "PS: I am keeping your leather jacket." I thought I deserved it.

I reread it. It was fair, I believed, and I did feel better actually. In fact, I found I wanted Max to read it.

I pulled out my phone and Googled "how to write to a prisoner at HMP Portsmouth" which was where Max was. I found the address, copied it on to an envelope and put the letter inside.

I almost changed my mind as I plopped it into the post box near Tall Trees, but by then it was too late anyway. It had gone and I had no way of getting it out again. Feeling bold, I crossed my fingers that Max would understand and continued on to the home, carrying Elsie's book carefully in my backpack.

When I arrived at Tall Trees, I pulled on my metaphorical big girl pants and went straight to Finn's cubbyhole.

'Is he in?' I asked Vanessa who was hunched over a textbook containing some incomprehensible chemical formula.

She looked up at me. 'No, he's gone.'

'Gone to the uni?' I walked round the back of the reception desk and into Finn's cupboard. 'Oh.'

'See?' Vanessa called, turning her attention back to her book. 'Gone.'

Finn's tiny office was completely empty. There were no papers anywhere, no reference books or pictures pinned to the walls. It was as though he'd never been there at all. I felt sick again but I swallowed the nausea down.

'Did he say why?' I asked, coming out of the cubbyhole again.

Vanessa shrugged. 'Just that he wasn't working here anymore.'

'Did he mention me? Or the book.'

She looked over her shoulder at me, her expression unreadable. 'No.'

'Okay,' I said.

Rattled and unsure what to do with Elsie's precious book, I took it to the staffroom and left it there for now.

'How are you feeling?' Blessing stuck her head round the door.

'Better, thank you,' I said.

She looked at me critically. 'You don't look better.'

'Thanks.'

'You're looking very peaky.'

I felt peaky, but I gave her a fake smile. 'I'm fine,' I said.

'You'll need to be. I've put you down for bingo in the lounge. It's starting in …' she looked at her watch '… five minutes ago.'

Stifling a groan, I gave her a thumbs up and went off to see what was going on in the lounge.

It was busy in there – bingo was always popular – and when I walked in, Joyce said loudly: 'About time.'

I ignored her, walking over to the table where the bingo set was already laid out. 'Do you all have cards?'

There was a murmur as they all waved their cards at me.

'Dabbers?' I said and they all murmured again.

'Where were you?' Joyce said, appearing next to my table as I tipped the numbers into a bag.

'I was looking for someone.'

'That Finn?'

'No.' I dropped the bag and number tiles spilled out over the floor. Tutting, I crouched down and began scooping them up again.

'He's gone, you know?' Joyce said, watching me reach for the number 22, which had slid under the table. 'Does that mean he's not helping with the mural anymore?'

'I don't know, Joyce.' My fingers reached the number and I

pulled it out, shoved it in the bag, and got to my feet. 'Why don't you go and sit down and I'll start the game?'

She ignored me.

'Because I think we're going to need him,' she said.

I bristled. 'We don't need him, because it's my project.'

'But he knows all about the book, doesn't he?'

'I do too.' I sighed. 'Joyce, what's the problem?'

'No one's written in the book.'

I looked at her. 'The new book?'

'Yes, the new one.' She ran her fingers through her hair. 'Blessing said you weren't well, and I thought it would be nice for you if I took it round a bit and got folk to write in it so when you got back, all you'd have to worry about would be the mural. So I got hold of it, and took it round to everyone.'

I smiled at her. 'That was kind of you, thank you.'

'No one will write in it.' She lowered her voice. 'Not even Mr Yin and he does everything I ask.'

'Really?'

'Really. All that's in there is a letter from Val and some funny doodles.'

I felt my cheeks flush at the mention of doodles. 'No one else has written anything?'

'Nope.'

'Why not?'

'Some people said they felt it was an invasion of their privacy. Others said something about data protection laws.'

'I'm not sure those apply here,' I said.

'I know, but that's what they said. Kenny said you were going to put the letters on the internet for everyone to read.'

'No, where did he get that from? That's not true.'

'Kenny doesn't think so.'

'Where's all this come from?'

'I don't know.' She thought for a moment. 'You know how rumours spread.'

I sat down at the bingo table and put my head in my hands. 'The book is a big part of this project,' I said into my fingers. 'It was the main reason the council picked my application over others. The mural on its own isn't good enough.'

'I'll write in it,' said Joyce.

'That's so sweet, thank you.' But I knew that Joyce and Val didn't make a project on their own. I needed most of the residents to take part if it was going to be a success.

I clapped my hands together to get the bingo competitors' attention. 'Hello, everyone,' I called.

Gradually the chattering stopped and they all looked at me.

'We're going to be starting bingo in just a second, but first I wanted to remind you to take five minutes and write in the book that's been going round.'

Joyce had gone back to the table where she'd been sitting with Mr Yin. Now she held up the book with a flourish, like the ring girls at a boxing match.

'What about data protection?' one of the men from the end of the corridor called. He had a very red face and an aggressive manner.

'I don't think that's relevant.'

'You don't think, or you don't know?' he said. Pleased with himself, he glanced to his friends and they all nodded in approval. I almost expected them to high-five him.

'I know it's not relevant. We're not holding any data that needs protecting.'

'Looks like data to me.'

'Well it isn't.'

'But it does feel like a breach of privacy,' one woman said softly. She was sitting alone at the front of the room with several bingo cards spread out in front of her.

'Oh give over, Maud,' Joyce said crossly. 'Don't write anything private then. It's not blooming hard.'

Maud scowled at Joyce. 'I'm worried about what you're going

to do with our work. If you're using it elsewhere then it should be copyrighted. I heard you were going to take our words and put them in your painting.'

'I'm not using it anywhere,' I said, beginning to get annoyed. 'The only words I'm using on the mural are from Elsie's book. Not this one. Look, I didn't want to upset anyone. I just thought it was a nice way of recording memories or thoughts.'

'So you're not putting it on the internet?' Kenny's brows were knitted together.

'No, not on the internet. Not on the mural. The messages you write won't be anywhere except the book.'

'Ah, I must have misunderstood.'

'I think so. Who told you it was going on the internet?'

'Tobias,' he said, glancing to the red-faced man.

'Who told you, Tobias?'

Tobias blustered a bit, because he didn't like to admit to getting information from anyone else, and then admitted it had been Maud who'd told him.

I fixed Maud with my steeliest glare. 'And where did you get it from?'

She folded her arms. 'From that new woman, Helen. And she said she'd heard it from you. So it must be true.'

Helen? Again?

'Oh, for heaven's sake,' I said. 'Let's not ruin this project for the sake of one disgruntled resident who's upset because she's got no one to write a message to, shall we?'

Maud looked annoyed. 'You shouldn't speak about the residents like that, Stephanie. We pay your wages, don't forget.'

I gave her a thin-lipped smile. 'I don't ever forget,' I said. My anger at Helen causing trouble again – not to mention my anger at myself for treating Finn the way I had – was bubbling away under the surface and I tried to push it away before it burst out of me.

'Shall we get on?' I said. I stuck my hand in the bag of number tiles and pulled one out.

'Two fat ladies,' I called half-heartedly. 'Eighty-eight.'

'Give it some welly, Stephanie,' Kenny said. 'No need to be so miserable.'

I tried my best, but the mood in the lounge was sombre despite the residents quacking for "two little ducks" and whistling at "legs eleven". It seemed I'd ruined bingo too, like I'd ruined everything else.

When the game was over, I gloomily packed it all away. Joyce was deep in conversation with Mr Yin, her hand resting on the book, and I hoped she was trying to persuade him to write a message. Goodness, if he was worried about privacy, he could write in flaming Chinese and none of us would be able to understand it anyway.

'Stevie?' Blessing stood next to me. 'I've just had a call from the dementia unit. Apparently your nan's asking for you.'

Well if anyone deserved to write in my book, it was my grandmother. 'Is it okay if I pop over?' I asked Blessing. She nodded, so I walked over to where Joyce and Mr Yin sat. 'Could I take this?' I said, putting my hand on to the book.

'Absolutely,' said Mr Yin.

I picked up the book and clutched it to my chest. Then I went to talk to my grandmother.

Chapter 35

Elsie

1941

It was a strange feeling to go to work the next day, knowing that as well as helping my patients, patching them up and possibly saving their lives, I would be taking a life.

My footsteps were heavy as I went towards the hospital, thinking that when I returned home, Nelly would be gone. But my heart was strangely light. Deep down, I knew I was doing the right thing. Nelly would no longer have to suffer the excruciating saline baths, or be forced to lie awake at night thinking about how slowly she was going to die. I was helping her – I knew that. I was helping her to avoid a terrible, painful, awful death. And I had made my peace with that. Almost.

The thought of putting the morphine into the syringe and pushing it into Nelly's vein made me wince. It was so ... physical. It was why I'd wanted to put it into her fluids at first, and why I'd been going over and over in my head if there was another way for her to take the drug. But there was nothing. It had to be morphine, and it had to be an injection.

I was working the night shift and I planned to go to see Nelly as soon as I finished. I thought that among the hustle and bustle of the morning rounds and the nurses handing over, I could do what I had to do and be gone again before anyone noticed.

And in the back of my mind was the knowledge that Jackson tended to wait for me beside the main entrance after a night shift. The last thing I wanted was him lurking in the corridors, getting in the way of me doing what I'd decided to do.

As it happened, though, events got away from me. The early part of my shift was quiet because the planes were coming in from the east tonight, following the river to their targets instead of the railway line. We could hear the anti-aircraft guns booming and our planes roaring overhead, but the bombs weren't dropping so close to us. That meant that while we would no doubt have patients arrive in their buses later on, for now things were, if not calm exactly, then calmer than they'd otherwise have been.

And then I had a stroke of luck, if you could call it that. One of our patients, a sweet woman called Mrs Chalmers, took a turn for the worse. She had lost a leg in a raid, a few nights earlier. She'd been recovering but now she was going into shock and things were so bleak for her, that her doctor thought she would do better on ward 2 where there were more nurses to give her more concentrated care.

Matron phoned down to see if there was a bed available and when the ward confirmed they had space, she phoned for a porter to take Mrs Chalmers away. I wanted to make sure she'd had a chance to write in the book, before she got too poorly. I had a bad feeling that she wouldn't be returning to our ward. But I didn't want to ask her outright, because she looked pale and afraid and I didn't want to make things worse for her.

'She wrote a message you know,' one of the other nurses said out of the corner of her mouth as we gathered Mrs Chalmers' possessions. 'You did right by her.'

Pleased that the book was working exactly as I had intended, I made myself scarce in case Jackson arrived to take her, skulking at the back of the ward where I was unlikely to be spotted. But it was Frank who came and I was relieved. It was silly how I had started planning my days around whether I was likely to see Jackson, but he just made me feel so on edge, I couldn't help myself.

Frank took Mrs Chalmers down to the other ward, and we went about our business. But then, just as the phone rang to tell us casualties from the East End were on their way, Frank came back from ward 2.

'Elsie?' he hissed. 'Come here.'

With half an eye on Matron, who was on the phone looking grim-faced at whatever news she was receiving, I went over to where he stood.

'Your Nelly's not looking good,' he said. 'Nurse down there said she was suffering bad with the pain tonight. She thought you might want to go and see her.'

'Now?'

He nodded. 'If you can spare five minutes before the buses arrive.' He lowered his voice. 'Nurse said she thought she was giving up. Like she didn't want to live anymore.'

Well, that was true enough.

Matron had hung up the phone and was briefing the other nurses. I nodded to Frank. 'I'll pop down now,' I said. 'Thanks for that.'

The buses were on their way, Matron said. And they were full to the brim. It was going to be a difficult shift – that was clear. I put my hand in my pocket and felt the bottles of morphine I had in there and I made a decision.

'I'll go and bring the patients in,' I said. 'But could I go now and pop in on Nelly on the way? Frank said she wasn't great.'

I thought Matron might say no, but she was fond of Nelly, too, and her eyes softened as she said: 'Of course.'

Hardly believing that I was simply going to visit Nelly, give her a lethal dose of morphine and then leave again, I walked quickly down my ward and out into the corridor.

My heart was thumping and my legs felt weak. I could stop this, I thought. I didn't have to do this. I could end it now and tell Nelly I wasn't going to do as she'd asked.

As she'd begged.

And yet, my legs kept moving towards Nelly's room.

The nurses in the ward were efficiently preparing beds – they were obviously expecting some more patients too. One of them looked up and gave me a little wave, but they barely acknowledged me as I slipped into Nelly's side room and shut the door behind me.

'Nell?'

Nelly's eye blinked open.

'Were you sleeping?'

She shook her head gently.

'I've come …' I said. My voice shook. 'I've come to do as you asked.'

Nelly reached out and took my hand, squeezing my fingers tightly.

I looked down at her hand on mine, noticing that her fingertips were dusky purple and her knuckles were swollen. She didn't have long, I thought. Even if I didn't do this now, there was no doubt that she was dying. But this way the end would be quick and painless. She would fall asleep and she wouldn't wake up and I would be by her side.

'I have the morphine,' I said, speaking slowly and clearly, but quietly. 'If you want me to administer it, please squeeze my hand once for yes and twice for no.'

Nelly squeezed once. I felt dizzy suddenly and I was glad she was holding me. I looked round at the closed door of her room.

303

It was shut tight, but on a whim, I pulled the chair from next to the bed to block it. Just in case. Through the window I could see nurses bustling past. No one would bother us, I thought.

'I'm going to prepare the dose now,' I said. 'Remember we discussed you hitting the bedclothes if you want me to stop? Don't forget.'

Nelly's fingers stayed still. Carefully I let go of her hand and laid it on the sheet. Then I went to the end of her bed and checked her drug chart to see how much morphine she'd been given. I'd done my sums over and over but I wanted to be sure. Satisfied I knew how much to give her, I filled the syringe I'd brought with me, put it on a tray, and went back to her bedside.

'Nelly,' I said, stroking her hair and speaking softly. 'It'll just be a sharp scratch and then you'll go to sleep. I'll be here the whole time.' I swallowed. 'Can you hit the bedclothes if you want me to stop?'

I fixed my eyes on her hand. It didn't move.

Fighting the urge to throw the syringe into the waste bin and run away, I cleaned her arm, and then I tried to pick up the syringe, but my hands were trembling so violently that I couldn't even do that.

'Sorry,' I murmured. 'Sorry.' I took a deep breath, clenching my hands into fists and then releasing them. When I felt less shaky, I tried again. This time I fumbled a little but picked up the syringe.

'Last chance,' I said. 'Do you want me to stop?'

Nelly's hand twitched and I froze, my eyes never moving from her fingers. But instead of hitting the sheets, she brought her hand up towards her mouth, touching her fingers to her chin briefly and them taking them away. I smiled. She'd had a deaf patient on her ward a few months before who had used sign language and we'd all picked up a few things. "Thank you," Nelly was signing.

'You're welcome,' I whispered. 'Ready?'

Nelly gave a tiny nod.

'I love you, Nell.' I said. Then with a deep breath, I put the syringe into her arm and pushed the drug into my best friend's vein.

When I was done, I leaned over and kissed her head, noticing her eye was closed already and her breathing was slowing. Quickly, I cleared away the mess, dropping the syringe and bottles into the waste bin and putting the tray back where I'd taken it from. As I worked, I counted Nelly's rasping breaths. One ... two ... Slow, slower, slower. I reached out and felt her pulse. It was very weak now and I could barely feel it, though her wrist was thin and frail and her skin was so pale that her veins were visible. Around her nose and mouth was some frothy liquid. I knew that meant her lungs were failing. Very gently, I wiped it away and bent over her, listening for another breath.

None came.

I watched for a moment, to see if her chest would continue to rise and fall. But it didn't. She was gone.

I breathed in deeply, a painful, juddering breath. I wanted to throw my head back and wail because Nelly was dead and I had killed her and I would miss her. But instead I wiped my eyes and straightened my dress. There were patients to attend to and jobs to do.

I went to the door of the room, and looked over my shoulder. Nelly was lying still, her face no longer twisted in pain.

'Goodbye, Nell,' I said aloud. 'See you again someday.'

I shifted the chair out of the way of the door. Then I straightened up, opened the door and saw, with a start, that Jackson was standing a little way outside the room, looking in.

'Elsie,' he said.

Our eyes met and I knew without a shadow of a doubt that he had been watching the whole time. He knew what I'd done.

Chapter 36

Stephanie

Present day

When I arrived at Nan's room, the doctor was just leaving.

'Hello there,' she called as I came along the corridor.

I hurried over. 'Is she all right?'

'She's fine now. She was a bit flustered earlier. Confused. Go on in – I'm sure she'll like to see you.'

Nan was asleep in her chair. I sat next to her and waited for her to wake up. I put the book on the floor next to me, then I took out my phone and typed a message to my dad.

"I'm with Nan," I wrote. "She's fine but she won't always be fine." No point in beating around the bush when it came to my dad. "You should call her."

I pressed send and put the phone back in my pocket. And when I looked back at Nan, she was awake. She looked right at me.

'Max is in prison,' she said.

Her words hit me like a hammer blow and made me gasp. How did she know? 'He is, Nan.'

'Can't say it's a surprise. He attracts trouble like honey attracts bees.'

I laughed.

'He wrote to me.'

Startled, I looked at her closely, wondering if she was getting confused again. 'Really? Are you sure? Where's the letter, Nan?'

She blinked at me, and I scanned the room. On the bedside table was an envelope. I picked it up and waved it at her.

'Can I look?'

'What is it?'

'A letter.'

'I don't get letters now,' Nan said. 'No one writes letters anymore.'

I slid the paper out of the envelope. There was one page addressed to Nan. It was typical Max. Full of bravado and charm and perfect for Nan, I thought. And then, tucked inside the envelope was another page. This one was folded into quarters and had my name on the front. I breathed in sharply and for a bewildering moment I thought Max had already replied to the letter I'd only just sent him but that was impossible.

'I wrote to Max today,' I told my grandmother, who was watching me. 'Our letters must have crossed.'

'Right pair of Charlies,' she said.

Feeling my heart thump, I unfolded the note. Inside, Max had drawn his version of my television. Beneath it, he'd written: "Sorry." And beneath that, he'd drawn the volume dial turned up to max. I turned the page over but it was blank on the other side. That was it. He was a man of few words, my brother. But it turned out that one word was all I needed.

I smiled at Nan.

'Max said sorry,' I said.

'He likes cheese on toast for his tea.'

I shook my head. 'That's dad, Nan. That is Geoff, your son Geoff.'

'Geoff.'

I reached out and took her hand. Her skin was like soft paper, like the pages of a well-loved book, and the veins on the back of her hand stuck out. I thought how lucky I was to have her.

'Nan,' I said. 'I wanted to say thank you for looking after me and Max. I don't know what we'd have done without you when Mum left.' I paused, trying to gather my thoughts. 'You'd done it all, hadn't you? You'd already brought up your kids. And then you got landed with us. It can't have been easy. But you did it and we love you so much, Nan.'

She turned her head slowly and watched me as I spoke.

'My son Geoff is a waste of space,' she said. I stifled a laugh. That wasn't something I would write in the book for her. 'But oh, he's a charmer.'

I laughed out loud this time. 'He is, Nan.'

'Could sell snow to the Eskimos that one.'

'Like your mum,' I said.

She looked right at me. 'He's just like my mum. Gift of the gab.'

I smiled but she wasn't finished.

'He's got twins, you know? Twins. Stephanie and Max. Always together. Thick as thieves. Always off whispering together. A right pair of Charlies, I call them.'

'That's right, Nan,' I said, enjoying her being so talkative for once. 'Remember when we swapped clothes and you pretended you didn't know which of us was which?'

She gazed at me from watery eyes.

'I love those kids with all my heart,' she said firmly. 'Proud as punch of them I am.'

I swallowed a sob. She'd never said anything like that before.

'I'm proud of you too, Nan.'

She nodded. 'Max is in prison.'

'He is.'

'He'll come and see me when he gets out.'

'He will.'

On my lap, my phone beeped with a message from my dad. "FaceTime me, please."

He'd never been one for long gushy messages.

I pressed call on his number and when he answered and the call connected, I saw he was on the beach.

'Working hard,' I said with a grin, using his own catchphrase. 'Or hardly working? I can't believe you're on the beach.'

'I'm not on the beach, I'm having a beer next to the beach,' he said, holding up his glass so I could see it. 'Can you speak up? It's hard to hear you.'

'I'm in Nan's room, so I don't want to disturb her.'

'She's deaf as a post; she won't be bothered.'

'Dad,' I chided. I got up and went outside the door so Nan wouldn't hear. 'Listen, I've been doing this art thing, about saying stuff you want to say before it's too late.' I paused. 'I wrote to Max.'

Dad was quiet for a minute. Then he said: 'I hope you didn't apologise.'

Surprised, I said: 'Well, I did a bit.'

'The only person to blame for Max being in prison is Max,' Dad said firmly.

'You're right,' I agreed. 'But I still felt bad. I thought everyone blamed me.'

'Not at all,' Dad said. 'Though I do blame your mother a bit.' I laughed. 'Did he reply to your letter?'

'He won't have got it yet,' I said. 'But the funny thing is, he wrote to me, here at the same time. He wrote to Nan and me.'

Dad rolled his eyes. 'And did he apologise to you?'

'He did.'

He nodded. 'Good lad.'

Feeling calmer than I had since Max went, I said: 'Do you want to speak to Nan? I know you've not always had the best relationship, but I'm learning how important it is to say what you want to say. Before it's too late.'

'You're right,' Dad said. He sounded surprisingly choked up. 'I suppose I should have a quick word.'

'She might not know you,' I warned.

Dad nodded. 'I understand.'

I went back into Nan's room and held the phone up so she could see. She looked at the screen, but she didn't react, until Dad spoke.

'Hello, Mum,' he said.

Nan frowned. 'My Geoff's got himself a girlfriend. Proper sort, she is. Legs up to her armpits. Flaky as a bloody steak pie. Don't trust her as far as I can throw her.'

'Nan!' I exclaimed, shocked at her description of my mother. But Dad laughed.

'I should have listened to you, Mum. Saved myself the bother.'

'He's a good boy, my Geoff,' said Nan. She squinted at the screen. 'He looks like you. But younger.'

Dad chuckled. 'Thanks, Mum,' he said softly. 'I'll call again next week, eh?'

'Waste of bloody space,' Nan muttered.

'Stevie, can we speak outside again?' Dad said. I took the phone away from Nan's face and went back to the doorway. Dad sighed. 'You're a good girl, looking out for her like you do. She loves you to pieces – you know that. You and your brother.'

'Yes,' I said, honestly. 'I do know that.' I ended the call, feeling teary, and went back inside to sit with Nan.

*

'Oh, honey, I'm so pleased Max wrote to you,' Tara said the next day.

I smiled. 'I owe Elsie one,' I said. 'I wrote to Max, and he wrote to me – though that was coincidence I suppose, I can't really give Elsie credit for that. And Dad spoke to Nan, and she said some funny stuff about my mum, and she said she loved us. And my dad even said I was good for looking out for Nan and he was grateful.'

'Well, who'd have thunk it,' Tara said. 'Everyone's saying things they should have said years ago.'

'Thanks to Elsie.'

'Talking of Elsie, how's that gorgeous Finn?'

'Ah.'

'Ah?' She looked at me through narrowed eyes. 'What does "ah" mean? I don't like the sound of that "ah".'

I put my head into my hands. 'We broke up.'

'What? You'd barely gotten started.'

'I know.'

'What did you do?'

I thought about lying and saying it wasn't me, but Tara was looking at me in the way she had that made me admit everything I'd ever done wrong, so I said: 'He was in an accident and I couldn't handle it. Not after all the stuff with Max. I know I'm pathetic but it just felt like it was too soon.'

'Is he okay?'

'Yes.' I groaned. 'I think so.'

'I don't get it, Stevie. Why did you break up with him?'

I looked up at the ceiling. 'Because I like him too much,' I muttered. 'And I was scared it was all going to go wrong.'

'Oh, honey.' Tara gave me a friendly and slightly despairing nudge.

'I know. I'm an idiot. But I was so scared, Tara. The police came to my flat and it was just like …'

'Like when Max stole your stuff?' She sounded sympathetic and that made me want to cry. I pinched my lips together and nodded.

'What happened with Max was terrible,' Tara said carefully. 'But you can't live your life worrying things are always going to go wrong, Stevie. That's no life at all.'

'It's too scary,' I whispered.

'I know.' She smoothed a strand of my hair off my face. 'But all the good stuff is a little bit scary. I was terrified when I first came to London. More so when I opened this place.' She looked round. 'I'm still a bit scared about it actually.'

I gave a little laugh. 'God, Tara. How are you so wise?'

'Because I've been a bartender my whole adult life and I've heard a lot of people's problems,' she said with a grin. 'How was Finn when you saw him?'

'I've not seen him.' I winced. 'He cleared his stuff out of Tall Trees.'

'All of it?'

'Pretty much. Except for Elsie's book. I was going to give it back but he'd left already.'

'So you have it still?'

'I do.'

Tara gave a knowing nod. 'Because Finn is a good guy and he knows you need it for your project.'

'Ah,' I said.

'No, not another "ah". What now?'

'I'm thinking of pulling out of the project.'

'No way,' said Tara firmly. 'What's going on with that?'

I shrugged. 'I'm not really feeling it anymore,' I said vaguely. 'I've not managed to find Elsie, and the residents at Tall Trees are totally not into it. No one's written in the new book so that's a non-starter. I've not even started painting. The whole thing is dead in the water, Tara. Just like me and Finn.'

'Really?' Tara sounded unconvinced.

'Really.'

'Except you just sorted out your family troubles because of Elsie. You all said the things you wanted to say. Do you think you'd have done that before you'd seen Elsie's book?'

'No, maybe not,' I said truthfully. 'But …'

'But nothing.' Tara prodded my arm. 'You've seen first-hand how the idea behind the project helps people and now you're

312

going to stop other people benefiting?' She tutted loudly. 'I didn't think you could be so selfish, Stevie.'

'But they don't want to take part.'

'Then you have to convince them why it's a good idea.' She grinned at me. 'Plus, if you pull out now, you'll have to pay back the grant money.'

I'd not thought of that. 'I've spent some of it already,' I said.

Tara slid off her bar stool and stood up. 'Well, there you have it. I guess your project's still on.'

*

I still wasn't convinced, though. I went home and slept all morning and woke up feeling even less certain about the project. I lay in bed, and called up the contract I'd signed on my phone, reading through the terms and conditions and discovered that, unsurprisingly, Tara was right. If I pulled out now, I'd have to repay the £10,000. I couldn't bear the idea of going back to having money troubles.

'Bugger,' I breathed. Perhaps then I could change the project? Abandon the idea of using Elsie's book as inspiration and not face the slog of changing the residents' minds about the new book? Give up trying to find her. I could just do a mural based on the Industrial Revolution or the Battle of Hastings or some other random moment in history, and forget about Elsie and the Blitz.

But I scanned the Ts and Cs again. "The project must be broadly as outlined below," I read. "Any large-scale or conceptual changes may result in the withdrawal of funding."

It seemed my hands were tied.

Feeling sluggish and gloomy, I put on my Tall Trees uniform and went into the kitchen to see if Micah had left me any food before I went to work.

*

When I arrived at Tall Trees later on, I found myself scanning the car park for any sign of Finn's Mini. But of course, it wasn't there. It was probably still in the garage or at the scrapyard after his accident. I realised I was disappointed.

'Make your mind up, Stevie,' I told myself. But the truth was, I was missing Finn already and beginning to think Tara was right. Maybe the good stuff was always a bit scary?

I locked my bike up, averting my eyes from the large expanse of wall that I was going to have to paint, and made my way to the entrance.

As I was going in, two women were coming out carrying boxes. I held the door open for them.

'Oh,' said the older of the two, glancing at my name badge. 'You're Stephanie.'

'I am.'

'I'm Jill's daughter, and this is my daughter.'

I smiled at her. 'I'm sorry about your mum.'

Her eyes filled with tears. 'We're going to miss her,' she said. 'But Blessing told us you sat with her when she'd fallen. And she said it was you who wrote the messages for us.'

I waved my hand, telling her it was nothing. But she put the box she was holding on to the ground and gathered me into a hug, which was unexpected but actually quite nice. 'Thank you,' she said as she let go. 'It was so kind.'

Her daughter nodded. 'We'll treasure those messages. It was a really lovely thing to do. So thoughtful.'

I looked over their heads at the bare wall, waiting for my mural, and thought about the empty pages of the book inside Tall Trees.

'I'm glad it helped,' I told them.

'It really did.' The older woman bent down and picked up her box again, which I now saw was full of Jill's bits and pieces from her room. I would have to do the same with Nan's stuff one day, I thought.

'You should do that for all the residents here,' Jill's grand-daughter said to me. 'It would be so special.'

'That's a very good idea. I'll think about it.'

I said goodbye and went into the building, thinking about Nan and Jill and Elsie. The book was special, I thought. It was.

'Penny for them,' said Joyce as I wandered into the lounge, clearly still looking thoughtful.

I looked at her. She was sitting beside the window with Mr Yin and – to my surprise – Val. They were all having a cup of tea and drawing the flowers in the garden.

'You're drawing?' I said in astonishment.

'We thought we'd get a head start on your art classes,' said Val with a grin. 'Mr Yin found a video on YouTube.'

I blinked at them. 'How's your arthritis?' I asked Joyce, whose knuckles were often swollen.

'Not great,' she admitted. 'But Blessing got me some chunky pencils like the kids use at nursery and I'm getting on okay with those.'

I smiled at them all. 'That's good,' I said. 'Because I'm definitely going to need your help with the mural.'

'You're doing it then?' Val gazed out of the window and then down at the drawing pad in her lap.

'Yes,' I said firmly.

'I thought as Finn's done a disappearing act, you might have gone off the idea.'

'I did.'

'But you've changed your mind?' She looked up at me with a smile.

'I have.'

'Good.'

'I might need your help though.' I sat down in a spare chair next to them and leaned forward. 'I've been a colossal idiot.'

'Broke up with him, did you?' Joyce rolled her eyes.

'How did you know?'

'I saw him taking all his stuff out of his cupboard.'

'Nothing gets past you, does it?'

She looked proud. 'Nope.'

Mr Yin gave Joyce an admiring glance. 'What do you need us to do?' he said.

'Nothing big,' I told them. 'Just give me a hand with the mural, convince all the other residents to write in the book, and help me find out what happened to Elsie.'

The three of them all glanced at each other and then nodded at me.

'You forgot something,' said Val with a cheeky look in her eye.

'Did I?'

'You need to win Finn back, too.'

I shook my head. 'I think that ship has sailed, Val.'

'Absolutely not,' she said. 'He likes you a lot. Any fool can see that.'

'He does,' Joyce agreed.

I laughed. 'I'm not sure.'

'I'm right,' Val said. 'You'll see.'

Chapter 37

Elsie

1941

Jackson stood a little way in front of me, his eyes glittering with triumph. He looked taller somehow. More straight-backed. Defiant.

I wanted to walk away, but somehow my feet wouldn't move. I looked over at the other nurses but they were still preparing the beds for the new arrivals. How had so much changed in my life in such a short space of time?

Jackson gave me a small, wolfish smile. 'Shall we go and have a chat?'

I took a deep breath. 'I have to wait for the buses.'

'I think this is more important, don't you?'

His complete lack of empathy made my fear recede and replace it with annoyance. 'No, I don't,' I said. 'People need my help.'

'Help like how you helped Nelly?' He looked past me into Nelly's room and I found myself shifting slightly, hoping to block his view, even though he was taller than I was.

'Nelly's sleeping.'

'Is she?' He smiled that wolfish smile again. 'Shall we get one of the nurses to go and check?'

I felt sweat bead on my forehead.

'I have to go.' I made to walk past him and he reached out and took my arm.

'Come with me,' he said in a low voice.

'Jackson, I don't know what you think you saw, but I promise you …' I trailed off as he showed me he was holding the book.

'Where did you get that?'

'The good thing about being a porter is you can go anywhere in the hospital and no one asks why,' he said. His tone was triumphant. 'I took it from your bag in the staffroom.'

'Jackson …' I cursed my stupidity in leaving the book with its incriminating messages where he could get it.

'I wondered why you kept sending the book to the Red Cross hut,' he said. 'But now I know. I read the messages you'd written at the back. They were sweet. Touching.' He put his face close to mine. 'Shocking.'

'I didn't write any messages,' I lied. Again I glanced over at the other nurses but they were all busy and not even looking in my direction. 'That wasn't me.' My protests sounded weak and unconvincing to my own ears.

'Come on,' Jackson said. He gave me a little nudge in the small of my back and obediently I started walking.

'Where are we going?' I said over my shoulder.

'Basement.'

'The operating theatre?'

He snorted. 'No,' he said. 'The boiler room. I know you know where that is.'

Suddenly the hospital felt very cold. I wrapped my arms around myself as we walked down the stairs, hunching over like an old woman. I wondered if Matron would be concerned about where I was or if she'd think I was still waiting for the buses.

'Hurry up,' Jackson said, nudging me again. 'Stop dragging your feet.'

'I have to go and meet the buses,' I said pathetically. Jackson ignored me.

We got to the boiler room and Jackson opened the door. No one was around – everyone was getting ready for the arrival of the new patients. He herded me inside and shut the door behind us. For a second he just looked at me. I hung my head, because I didn't want to see his face.

'Oh, Elsie,' he said. 'You really have been up to all sorts, haven't you?'

Now I looked up. 'I don't know what you're talking about.'

'I think you do.'

I didn't reply.

'Billy would be horrified by your behaviour,' he went on. He sounded agitated and that scared me even more than his calm defiance. 'And I hold myself responsible too, you know. I took my eye off the ball, and look what happened? But I can make things right again. Make everything better.'

'It's fine, Jackson,' I said, trying to placate him. 'You've done nothing wrong.'

'No. But you have.'

'I haven't.' I shook my head but I couldn't help thinking I sounded unconvincing. 'I've not done anything wrong.'

'You killed Nelly.'

The bluntness of his accusation stunned me. I took a step back further into the boiler room, my hand over my mouth.

'I didn't.'

'I watched you do it,' he said. 'You took a syringe and you injected her. And I know you're not her nurse because you don't work on that ward. And I know you killed her because I read it in here.'

He brandished the book in my face and I shrank back even further, trying to get away from him.

'And that's not all.'

I opened my mouth but no words came out. I felt clammy with fear.

'I saw you in here,' Jackson went on. He took another step towards me and I retreated. 'I saw you in here with a man.'

I stared at him in absolute horror. He had been watching me all the time. Everything I'd done. Everything Harry and I had done. He'd seen it all.

'I saw you and him together,' he said. He stepped towards me again and this time when I walked backwards, I hit the wall. I pushed my back against the cold bricks, wishing I could disappear through them. Jackson wasn't in a hurry. He carefully put the book down on a table that was at one side of the small room and came towards me. I felt his breath hot against my cheek. 'I saw you kissing,' he said. 'I saw him unbutton your dress. And I saw you …'

'Stop it,' I almost shouted, wondering if I could make a grab for the book. 'Stop this. You're mistaken.'

Jackson put his hand on my cheek. 'I'm not mistaken,' he said matter-of-factly. 'You're ruined, Elsie. Damaged goods.' He put his face right up to mine and I saw some spittle on his lips. 'You're a slut.'

I was crying now and he wiped away my tears with a thick thumb.

'Don't get upset. I can help you.'

'No.'

'We'll get married.'

'No.' I was firmer this time.

'I promised Billy I'd look after you,' he said. 'And I didn't and now I need to put things right.' He gave me that wolfish smile again. 'And now I know what you like.'

He put his hand on my leg, just where my skirt ended. And then gradually he moved it upwards to the top of my stocking. His rough hands grazed my bare skin and I tasted bile in my mouth.

'Elsie,' Jackson said, his voice gruff. I tried to turn my head away, but he pushed his lips against mine. His hand was getting higher up my leg and I felt my whole body trembling.

'No,' I moaned. 'No.'

'Don't worry, Elsie. We're getting married. It's fine.' Roughly now he shoved his hand in between my legs. 'You're mine now.'

I felt his fingers pushing into me, poking and hurting me. 'Stop it,' I whimpered. 'Please, stop.'

But he didn't. He leaned against me, and I felt his groin grinding hard into my thigh as he let out a little moan of pleasure. I turned my head slightly and realised his eyes were closed and I saw my chance. I put my hands against his chest and shoved him hard. He stumbled backwards and I darted past him.

Somewhere up above us, I heard the air raid siren begin to wail. I reached for the book and gasped as Jackson grabbed me round the waist before I could get it.

'Don't,' he warned.

'There's a raid.'

'We're safe down here, silly.' He pressed his lips against mine again and I struggled to get away. He held me tighter as I wriggled.

'Jackson, please,' I begged. 'Don't hurt me. I'm having a baby.'

Suddenly he let go. 'You're having a baby?'

'Yes.'

I pulled myself back away from him, keeping my eyes fixed on me. 'Billy's nephew or niece,' I said carefully. 'He'd want you to look after them, wouldn't he?'

For a brief, giddy second I thought it was all going to be all right. But then he hit me, smack across the face. Before I'd properly realised what had happened, I found myself sprawled on the floor of the boiler room, my head spinning and my face burning. I reached up and felt my nose bleeding.

In shock and disbelief, I looked up at Jackson who was towering over me. 'Look what you made me do,' he said.

A huge thud made us both jump. Dust fell from the ceiling, making my eyes sting. 'There's a raid,' I said again. 'We need to go.'

'We're going nowhere.' He began to unbuckle his belt. 'You're my girl, and you've betrayed me.'

'I'm not your girl,' I said frantically. 'I'm not and I never will be.'

'Then I'll tell everyone what you did. You'll go to prison.' His eyes widened. 'You'll hang for what you did to Nelly.'

'No one will believe you.'

Jackson picked up the book from the table and held it over his head in triumph. 'I've got the evidence,' he said. 'I'll show the police this book and they'll know I'm telling the truth. You're a slut and a murderer and you'll do whatever I tell you to do.'

I knew then that there was no way out for me. That I would be forced to do what he wanted or lose my job and my freedom and maybe even my life. I tried not to show my fear, but I couldn't keep back my sobs.

Jackson gave me a look of utter disdain. 'You brought this on yourself, Elsie,' he said. He tucked the book under his arm and turned his attention back to his belt. 'You're lucky to have me. Other men wouldn't be so understanding.'

I whimpered, as he began unbuttoning his trousers, sliding myself backwards towards the wall in a futile attempt to escape from him.

And then there was an enormous deafening roar, and the room began to shake. I let out a shriek of fright.

'It's the raid, Jackson. We've been hit.' In panic, I began crawling across the floor to shelter beneath the table in the corner and watched as Jackson looked up to the ceiling in surprise. Then he was gone, vanished into a cloud of dust that fell from above. There was another roar and the clatter of falling masonry, the thump of more bombs falling and somewhere I heard the whoosh of flames igniting. Beneath the table, I curled up into a tight ball, trying to protect my abdomen though I knew it was in vain, and I waited to die.

Chapter 38

Stephanie

Present day

My team were smashing it out of the park. Honestly, if it hadn't been for Joyce, Val and Mr Yin – and the others – I'd have abandoned the mural altogether. It just seemed such a big job, and impossible to even start. But the residents had given it some extra oomph and then they'd kept things going and they wouldn't let me give up.

'Ta-da!' Joyce said, when I got to Tall Trees a few days later. She handed me the new book and I looked in astonishment at the pages, which weren't yet filled but weren't nearly as empty as they had been.

'How on earth did you do this?' I asked, flicking through. 'This is wonderful.'

Joyce giggled. 'We decided to fight fire with fire.'

'What does that mean?'

'We started our own rumours about the book.'

'What kind of rumours?'

Joyce exchanged a mischievous glance with Val. 'I heard some celebrities were writing in it,' she said, her face the picture of innocence.

'That Richard Osman from *Pointless* wrote a message, you know,' Val said. 'And that lovely Gary Lineker.'

'Gary Lineker?' I scoffed.

'You'd be amazed who wanted to see if the rumours were true,' Joyce said. She lowered her voice. 'Kenny was first in the queue after we spread that one. And of course, once they had the book, then it made sense for them to write their own.'

'Especially when they heard that there would be a cash prize for the most heartfelt entries,' Mr Yin said, totally straight-faced. 'And that a television crew were thinking about making a documentary about it.'

'A documentary?' I was almost speechless with the cheek of them.

'For Netflix,' Val said in triumph and the three of them collapsed in giggles.

'I can't say I approve of your methods, but the results are impressive,' I said, leafing through the pages and admiring the many messages inside. 'I owe you. Maybe I'll add you all to the mural.'

All three of them looked thrilled at the idea. 'Us?' said Mr Yin. 'Really?'

'Yes, why not?' I said. I nodded, thinking. It wouldn't be hard to include some of the residents. I already had an idea about how to fit them in. Though perhaps I should include them all – even grumpy Helen. I didn't want to annoy anyone.

'So now you just have to paint the mural,' Joyce pointed out. 'We can't help with that bit.'

'When's the scaffolding coming?' Mr Yin asked.

I made a face. 'I've not got a date yet. I keep chasing but they're dragging their heels a bit.'

'And when does the mural need to be done by?'

I groaned. 'The council have planned a big unveiling at the end of next month.'

'Next month?' Joyce raised an eyebrow. 'We'd better get on with it then.' She called over to where Kenny sat in the corner of the lounge. 'Didn't you have a building company, Ken?'

'I did indeed. My grandson Kyle runs it now.'

'Can you get Stephanie some scaffolding.'

'Course.'

'Today?'

Kenny looked at his watch. 'Today might be pushing it but I reckon I can get it for tomorrow. Would that work for you, Stephanie?'

I stared at him. 'That would be amazing.'

'Consider it done, love. I'll go and give him a call now.' He grinned at me, as he pulled himself up out of his chair. 'Oh, and I wrote in that book of yours. Just a few instructions for Kyle and that.'

'Great,' I said, giving the others an amused glance. 'Thank you.'

'It's a good idea.'

'It is.'

He shuffled off looking pleased with himself.

'What else do you need?' Joyce said. 'Paint?'

'I've got all that.'

'And the design's finished?'

'It is.'

'So you just need to get cracking.' She clapped her hands together. 'Get on with it then.'

'Well, I really need to wait for the scaffolding.'

'There must be something else you can do in the meantime,' Val pointed out. 'Have you found Elsie?'

'No.'

She tutted in a way that made me feel like I'd let her down.

'And have you heard from Finn?'

'No.' My heart jumped at the mention of his name and I

325

wanted to squirm with the guilt and sadness that thinking about him brought. 'I really don't think there's anything I can do about that. I really messed it up.'

'You should write him a message, like Elsie did for her fella,' Joyce said.

'I did.'

She looked chuffed.

'But that was before I made a total arse of everything.'

'Well, why not write him another one?'

'He wouldn't even see it.'

'He would if you put it on the mural.' Joyce looked triumphant. 'Write it in letters six feet high. He won't be able to miss it.'

I laughed, but it was a sad laugh. 'I'm not sure there's much point.'

'How far did you get when you were trying to track down Elsie's mystery man?' Mr Yin asked, a frown on his face.

'Not far. We found his name and that's it really.' I swallowed. 'Finn was going to look him up. I'm at a bit of a loss now. It seems I don't have the skills for historical research. Finn was the one who was doing it really.'

Val looked at me with her sharp eyes. 'Maybe this could be a way for you to make things up with him?'

'What do you mean?'

'I mean, if you find out what happened to Elsie, you could give him that knowledge as a kind of present.' She nodded, thinking things through. 'Have you invited Finn to the launch?'

'No, of course not.'

'I think you should.'

'I think you should mind your own beeswax,' I said only half-joking. Val made a face at me.

'This whole thing's about not leaving it too late to say the things that matter,' she pointed out. 'And here's you, doing exactly that.'

I scowled at her, knowing she was right.

'What do you know so far?' Joyce said, clearly wanting us to stop bickering. 'Start from the beginning.'

I settled back in my chair. 'Elsie was a nurse here, before the war and then through the Blitz. But she disappears from records, around the time of the bomb that hit this building.'

'She wasn't killed in the bomb?' Mr Yin frowned.

I shook my head. 'Her employment record says she left the hospital in 1941 and we couldn't find a death certificate.'

'Was the building badly damaged?'

'Part of it. Where the new wing is now. Lots of the patients were moved to other hospitals nearby and many of the staff went too.' I took a breath. 'And that's when Elsie must have left.'

'But you don't know where she went?'

I shook my head.

'Was she reported missing?' Joyce asked.

'No, not as far as I know. But I don't think she had much family.' I bit my lip. 'She had a brother who died in the war.'

'And what about her chap? The one who saved the seagull?' Val leaned forward. 'What have you found out about him?'

'Bits and bobs,' I said. I filled them in on Harry and how he'd gone to Ireland at the end of the war. For some reason I didn't mention the odd writing in the back of the book. The messages saying "kill me" and the sad note begging "Mammy" not to cry. I felt like I would be betraying Elsie by sharing those, though I didn't really know why.

'Why Ireland?' Val said, jolting me out of my thoughts.

I shrugged. 'We wondered if Elsie had gone there during the Blitz and he'd gone to be with her at the end of the war.' I screwed my nose up. 'Could she have travelled anywhere though, in that time?'

'Ireland was neutral in the war,' Val said. 'I'm not sure how easy it would have been to get there though.'

'I didn't know that.' I was a bit ashamed of how little I had known about the war. 'Anyway, Finn was going to look Harry up on some Irish genealogy sites. See if he could find his death certificate.'

'You could look him up.'

'I don't know how.'

Joyce gave me a look that suggested she was terribly disappointed in me. 'Have you never watched *Who Do You Think You Are?* on the television?'

I shook my head. 'I've never really been interested in history before now.'

She snorted. 'It's all online. Where's your phone? Give it here.'

Obediently I handed it over and she took it then gave it back to me straightaway. 'It's far too fiddly for me, you do it. Search for Irish death certificates.'

I typed it in the search bar. 'There are a few sites,' I said, showing the others.

'Just pick the top one,' Val said impatiently.

I did as I was told. 'I have to make an account.'

'So make one.'

It took me a little while but eventually I managed to type Harry's name into the search and bingo! It brought up a death certificate from 1985.

'Here he is,' I said in delight. 'He died in Ireland.'

'Does it say who registered the death?' Joyce leaned over, trying to see. 'When my Tony died I registered the death, so my name's on his certificate.'

I turned my phone sideways and enlarged the picture. My heart began to pound. 'It does,' I said. 'It says informant: Helen Byrne.'

'Helen Byrne?' Joyce looked bewildered. 'But that's our Helen's name. Grumpy Helen. Does it say what connection she has with Harry?'

My head reeling, I nodded, slowly. 'It says she's his daughter.'

Chapter 39

Elsie

1941

When I woke up, I had no idea where I was. My head was aching and there was a strange glow coming from up above me.

Am I dead? I thought for a second. And then I blinked my eyes open and saw the glow was torchlight shining through a hole in the ceiling.

'Stay still!' someone shouted. 'We're coming to get you. Are you hurt?'

I tried to speak but my face was covered in dust and my mouth was too dry. I was in the hospital, I remembered with a rush. In the basement. With Jackson. Oh Lord, Jackson. I tried to turn my head to see where he was but I was surrounded by rubble and could barely see two inches past my face. I had no idea where the table I'd been sheltering under had gone but it wasn't above me any longer.

Up above, an ARP warden with HR written on his helmet was being lowered down beside me on a rope ladder.

'All right, love?' he said cheerily as he came to a halt next to where I lay. 'I'm just going to check everything's safe before the rest of the crew come down, then we'll get you out of here. Boiler room is it?'

Whistling a jaunty tune, he quickly but thoroughly checked over the boiler and turned the large wheel on the front. The boiler, which had been making a very loud, very alarming clattering sound, fell silent.

'That's better,' the man said. He shouted up to the people above. 'All clear!'

Then he turned to me. 'Anyone else down here with you.'

I tried to swallow but my throat was dry as a bone. 'Jackson,' I whispered. 'Jackson.'

'Another nurse?'

'No,' I croaked. 'Porter.'

The small room was full of people now, moving rubble from around me and talking in low voices. One of the men helped me to my feet. 'You've barely got a scratch,' he said in wonder.

'I was under a table,' I told him. I looked round. 'But I don't know where it's gone.' The book had vanished too. Covered in rubble and bricks. Gone forever, I hoped.

'Can you climb the ladder? There's someone up top who'll check you over.'

'I think so.'

He helped me on to the ladder and with trembling arms I managed to haul myself up very slowly. As I reached halfway, there was a shout from below.

'Over here!' one of the men called. 'We've got him.'

'Is he alive?' another asked.

I stopped on the ladder, not sure whether I was hoping Jackson would have survived the blast or not.

'He's alive!' came the call. 'We need a stretcher here.'

I began climbing again, and someone reached down to help me up and then I was outside. It was still dark, though I could see the glow of morning in the distance. Or was that a fire burning? I couldn't tell. Dazed and disorientated, I looked around. I was at one end of the hospital, or what had once been one end of the hospital. Now there was nothing. But to my amazement, I could see the rest of the building was intact.

I couldn't tear my eyes away from the destruction. The heavy rescue ARP wardens were swarming across the rubble like ants, checking gas pipes and stopping water leaks, but I couldn't see any casualties. Was everyone dead?

I stumbled and someone caught my arm and guided me over to sit on the ground next to an ambulance driver.

'Hello there,' he said. 'We're just going to check you over. What's your name, love?'

I tried to speak through dusty, cracked lips but found I couldn't. He handed me a cup of water and I gulped it gratefully.

'Elsie,' I said. 'I'm a nurse.'

'Then you can keep an eye on me while I do my job,' he said.

He gently checked my arms and legs, which were bruised and battered. My left ankle was swollen and painful but I didn't think it was broken. Then he felt my head carefully where I had a huge egg-sized bump. He gave me a cloth to wipe my face and I was astonished when I saw how dirty it was.

'You're ever so dusty,' he said. 'You look like a snowman made of brick dust.'

I looked down at my uniform, which was completely covered in reddish dirt from the rubble. My hair felt thick with it and my eyes were gritty. One of the ARP wardens went past me, carrying a rope, and I stopped him.

'Where are the patients?' I asked, almost not wanting to know the answer. 'Where is everyone?'

'The bomb took out the end of the building,' he said. 'But by chance everyone got out before it fell. Apparently, the only thing down that end of the hospital was the operating theatre and the canteen and all the staff had gone to the entrance for a meeting or something.' He shrugged.

'To meet the buses,' I told him as my memories from the night before suddenly resurfaced. 'The buses coming from the East End.'

'Well, isn't that something,' he said. 'It's like a miracle. Could have been a lot worse.'

The shock of it all hit me like a truck and I covered my mouth with my hand as I recalled Jackson threatening me in the boiler room. And Nelly. Oh Lord, Nelly. I stifled a sob.

'Is that painful?' the ambulance driver asked, prodding my ankle. I nodded, but it wasn't why I was crying. My whole body just felt numb. Nelly was dead, and Jackson knew I'd killed her, and I didn't know if he was going to tell anyone. I thought about the way he'd looked at me in the boiler room – pure disdain and disgust – and I knew that if there was any way he could use what he knew against me, then he absolutely would.

The ambulance driver who'd been examining my ankle, looked up as shouts told us they were bringing Jackson up to ground level.

'You need your ankle bandaged, and I'd like that cut on your head cleaned, too,' he said. 'I'm going to go and help with the chap who was trapped. Can you go to the ambulance over there and say Martin sent you to be patched up?'

'I will, thanks.'

He watched me stand up. 'All right?' he said. 'Can you walk?'

My ankle was painful but not so much that I couldn't put weight on it. I nodded. 'I can hop over there. Go and help, go on.'

I hobbled a little way from where I had been sitting and then paused to watch as they brought Jackson up. He was completely covered in dust, as I was, and he was on a stretcher, motionless but breathing. As I looked at him, I felt nothing but repulsion. Hatred even. I was glad he was hurt, and the thought frightened me.

Walking as quickly as I could with my swollen ankle, I limped towards the ambulance Martin had sent me to, but instead of stopping, I carried on straight past and into the darkness of the street. I needed help, but not from them.

It took me ages to get home because I couldn't go fast, and two people stopped me to ask if I needed help but left me alone when I assured them I was fine. But eventually I reached our street and to my utter relief, I could see a light on in the front window, which meant Mr and Mrs Gold were home and awake.

Half sobbing, I hobbled up the path and banged on the front door, I saw the curtain twitch and Mrs Gold peek out, wearing her dressing gown and with curlers in her hair, and then she was there, opening the door and catching me as I virtually fell through into the hall.

'Elsie, oh my God, Elsie,' she cried. She shut the door behind me and helped me into the lounge. 'Sit down.'

'I'm so dirty.'

She waved her hand. 'It doesn't matter, sit down.'

I fell back on to the sofa.

'What happened?' she said. 'Was the hospital hit? Are you hurt? Why are you here? You need to be looked after.'

Her questions were coming too fast for me to follow. I put my dusty head against the back of the sofa and began to cry.

'Oh, Elsie,' Mrs Gold said. 'Oh my dear girl. It's all over now. It's over and you're all right.'

I nodded silently, still crying.

'Was it awful?' she asked, putting her arm around me. 'Were there many injured? Oh Lord, is Nelly all right?'

I breathed in deeply. 'Nelly's dead.'

Mrs Gold gasped and tears sprang into her eyes. 'Oh no. I'm so sorry, Elsie.'

How to explain? I looked at her. 'Do you remember you told me you would do whatever you could to help me?'

'Of course.'

'I need your help now.'

'Tell me.'

Slowly I began to explain about how Nelly had made her request in the pages of the book, and I'd agreed.

'It was a terrible thing to do,' I said. 'A terrible thing.'

Mrs Gold shook her head. 'It was the right thing to do. She was suffering dreadfully and she wasn't ever going to get better. You were merciful.' She patted my hand. 'I think you're very brave.'

'That's not all of it, though.'

Her eyes widened as I told her about Jackson watching.

'I don't know why I didn't think he'd be there,' I said, my voice shrill. 'He's always there. He's everywhere I go. He told me he'd watched Harry and me. Together.'

'That awful man,' Mrs Gold said, her face pale in the early morning light. 'There's something off about him. I've always said so.'

'He scares me,' I admitted. 'He scares me so much.'

'What did he say when you saw him after Nelly ... after she'd gone?'

'He said he'd seen everything and he had proof. He had the book.' I swallowed. 'He made me go down to the boiler room with him. It's where Harry and I ... you know.'

'Did he hurt you?'

Bitter bile filled my mouth as I thought about being trapped in the room with Jackson. 'A bit,' I said. 'He told me we were going to get married. He said I was a slut and that he was going to tell everyone what I did to Nelly.' My words were coming fast, falling over each other as I remembered. 'He said I was going to hang for what I'd done. Unless I ... unless I let him ...'

Mrs Gold took my face in her hands and made me look at her. 'Did he rape you, Elsie?'

Slowly I shook my head. 'I think he was going to. But the bomb fell.'

'And where is he now? Is he alive?'

'They got him out. He was breathing.'

'Where's the book?'

'I don't know,' I said desperately. 'I don't know. It was in the room with us. Maybe Jackson still has it, maybe not. Maybe the ARP squad will find it. And then everyone will know.'

I stood up, wincing as pain shot up my leg from my ankle. 'I don't know what to do,' I said, running my fingers through my gritty hair and watching dust drift down to the rug. 'I don't know how to make this better. Perhaps I should go to the police station and tell them everything? Tell them what I did.'

'Absolutely not.' Mrs Gold stood up too. She took my hands in hers. 'You listen to me, Elsie. You did the right thing with Nelly. She was suffering terribly, and you did the best thing for her. This is a war, and any man on the battlefield would have done the same.'

I nodded, feeling my racing heartbeat begin to calm.

'We can sort this out,' she assured me. 'We can make this right.'

'How?' I wailed. 'I killed my best friend. How can we ever make this right?'

'You ended her suffering like the compassionate, caring nurse you are,' she said firmly. 'And I think deep down you know you did the right thing. Don't you?'

I nodded. 'She was in such awful pain.'

'There we are.' Mrs Gold was thinking hard. 'We need to tell her family.'

'Yes, I have a message for them.' I put my hand to my head. 'Nelly wrote it in the book, but I remember it. I can write to her mother.'

'Or,' said Mrs Gold, 'you can go to Ireland and tell her yourself.'

It was such an outlandish suggestion that I almost laughed. 'Of course I can't go to Ireland. There's a war on, or hadn't you noticed?'

'Ireland isn't in the war.'

I snorted. 'How would I get there?'

'Do you want to go?'

I thought about Nelly's letters from home, about her enormous family and her mother's conviction that there were plenty of jobs available in the hospitals in Ireland. Then I thought about how my nerves jangled every time I heard a thump, even if it was someone dropping something heavy. How tired I was from the nightly raids. How I'd lost Billy, and now Nelly, and how Harry wasn't here, and I was alone. And I thought about Jackson and his threats. I knew no one would be likely to believe his accusations on their own, but if he somehow still had the book then things could be different.

Slowly, I nodded. 'Could I work? Could I register as a nurse in Ireland?'

'I don't see that being a problem.'

'I would feel bad, leaving the hospital and London when they need so much help.'

'You've given more than your fair share to the war,' Mrs Gold said. 'I think you deserve a break.'

Suddenly, going to Ireland seemed like the answer to my prayers and I thought I couldn't bear it if I couldn't go. That I couldn't stay in London for a second longer.

'I want to go to Dublin,' I said. 'But how?'

'We can get you on a ship. Merchant Navy probably.'

I stared at her, open-mouthed.

'Don't ask questions,' she said. 'I can't tell you the answers anyway.'

'But …'

She gave me a little smile. 'Don't ask questions,' she repeated. 'So, are you going to Ireland?'

'I am.' But then a sudden thought occurred to me. 'No. I'm not.'

'Why ever not.'

I put my face in my hands. 'I'm pregnant,' I mumbled. 'At least, I think I'm pregnant. I wrote to Harry and told him a few days ago.'

'Has he replied?'

'Not yet.'

Mrs Gold gave a brisk nod. 'Do you think he'll stand by you?'

I thought about Harry and the lovely things he'd said. The way he'd held me so tightly and told me all about his family. And slowly I nodded. 'I think so.'

'This is all going to be all right,' Mrs Gold said. 'Do you trust me?'

What else could I do? 'I do.'

'First things first. I'm going to go and wake up Albert. We're going to need him.'

She told me to sit down and then disappeared off into the bedroom, where I heard them talking in low voices. I sat very still, my mind racing. What was happening? Could I really look Nelly's mother in the eye and tell her that her daughter had died? But actually, I thought, I could. I could tell her Nelly wasn't alone, that she went peacefully and that she wasn't in pain. That was all true. Maybe we could organise a memorial for her. Put up a headstone, even. I wondered if I could ask Mrs Gold to make sure Nelly had a proper funeral. I knew that her family would want to know she'd been properly looked after. And as for me and the baby, well … If I was wrong about Harry then perhaps I could buy a cheap ring like Mrs Marsden who'd been on my ward back when the bombings first started, and tell everyone I was a widow. There was so much to do. I felt sick with the worry of it all.

Eventually, Mrs Gold came back into the lounge. She'd got dressed and looked very smart in a suit with proper stockings.

'Why don't you go and have a bath and a sleep?' she said. 'Albert and I have some things to organise this morning. Can you pack a bag, make sure you have anything important – documents and whatnot – but don't take too much. We'll need to leave this afternoon.'

'My head's spinning,' I said.

'You'll feel better after a snooze. Come on, up to bed with you. I'll strap up that ankle for you later on.'

'Thank you,' I said as I struggled to my feet and headed for the door.

'You're welcome.' Mrs Gold adjusted the cuffs of her blouse.

'Mrs Gold?' I paused by the front door. 'You're not really a secretary, are you?'

She smiled at me. 'Don't ask questions,' she said.

Chapter 40

Stephanie

Present day

I was completely stumped. Totally bamboozled. Nothing made sense.

'What does this mean?' I said to Mr Yin, Joyce and Val, who all looked as blank as I felt. 'Is this Helen Byrne the same person as our Helen? Or is it a coincidence?'

'No such thing as coincidence,' Val said. 'I thought she was a bit young and sprightly to be living here in Tall Trees.'

'She is eighty, Valerie,' Joyce pointed out. 'I saw her date of birth on her library card. She was born in 1941, same as me.'

'But why would she come and live here?'

'I can't see any reason for her to lie about needing care,' Mr Yin said reasonably. 'This must be a coincidence. Helen is not an uncommon name.'

'Nor is Byrne, really,' Joyce said.

Val scoffed. 'This is not a coincidence. You're all deluding yourselves.' She folded her arms crossly.

'Right,' I said, standing up. 'There's only one way to find out for sure. I'm going to ask her what's going on. Just me,' I added as the others all stood up too – more slowly but with just as much determination.

'Really?' Joyce was disappointed.

'I want her to open up, not make her clam up by going in mob-handed,' I said. 'She's done nothing wrong.'

'So you think,' said Val.

'Stay here and I'll come back as soon as I've spoken to her.'

'If you're not back in thirty minutes, we're coming to get you,' Joyce said.

'She's not dangerous.'

'Isn't she?' Val looked mulish and I couldn't help laughing as I made my way down the hall to Helen's room.

I knocked but I didn't bother to wait for an answer, I just opened the door and went inside. Helen was sitting in her armchair, Elsie's book on her lap. She looked up with a start as I went in and shut the book with a thud. She looked guilty, I thought. Guilty and upset.

'Did you take the book from the staffroom?' I said, remembering how I'd stashed it in there for safekeeping.

Helen looked cross. 'Yes, I did.' She stared straight at me. 'So what?'

'Were you going to return it?'

'No.' She was defiant, but I didn't know why.

'Are you Harry Yates's daughter?'

She breathed in sharply as though she'd not been expecting the question. Then she nodded. 'Harry was my dad.'

'So what do you want with Elsie's book?'

'I want to destroy it.'

Shocked, I lunged towards her intending to grab the book, but she predicted what I was going to do and pulled it away from me.

'Stop it,' she said. 'Or I'll pull my alarm cord and Blessing will come.'

'You can't destroy the book – it's a piece of history. Why would you want to do something like that?'

She gave me a little sad smile. 'Because it was the last thing my mother asked me to do before she died. She made me promise.'

'Who's your mother?' I asked, though really I already knew.

'Her name was Elsie Watson. Though of course she became Yates when she and my father got married.'

'But you're Helen Byrne? Are you married?'

'I was for a while. I kept the name, ditched the husband.'

I sat down in the armchair next to her with a heavy sigh. 'I think you'd better tell me everything.'

Helen nodded. 'I think you know most of it.'

'At the moment I feel like I know nothing. Can you start from the beginning?'

Helen got up and went to her bookshelf where she found a photograph album. She came back and opened it on her lap at a faded black-and-white photograph. I recognised the woman immediately as Elsie. She was holding a baby wearing a knitted cap and she looked happy.

'That's Elsie,' I said. 'Your mum. She was so young.'

'She was only in her early twenties when I was born,' Helen said. She flipped the pages and opened the album at the back, showing me a photograph of a small, elderly woman – Elsie again. She was sitting on a chair, wearing a party hat and she was surrounded by people, all smiling. I spotted Helen in the picture, standing just behind her mother, her hand on her shoulder.

'This was at her ninety-fifth birthday,' Helen said, her eyes shining. 'She lived to be ninety-seven.'

'Crikey.' I looked at her. 'You've got good genes. I thought you were too sprightly to be at Tall Trees.'

Helen gave me a little sideways glance but she didn't argue.

'My mother lived in Dublin for more than seventy years, but she always considered herself to be a Londoner and she kept up with news from home. She loved the internet. She used to read the *South London Echo* online. She was better with technology than I am.'

I chuckled and Helen went on. 'A couple of months before she died, she got very distressed about something she'd read. She was babbling, making no sense. I was really worried about her – I thought she'd had a stroke or a funny turn. I stayed with her that night and she had bad dreams that made her cry out in her sleep. And in the morning she told me why.'

'Why?' I breathed, leaning forward.

Helen rubbed her forehead. 'When my mother was nursing she had a best friend called Nelly. That's who I'm named after, in fact. Nelly was badly injured in an air raid and she died during the Blitz.'

'That's so sad.'

'My mother moved to Ireland in 1941. She'd lost Nelly and she'd lost her brother and she was expecting me – I'd always assumed that she just wanted to get away from the bombing and the memories. She always said she'd come to see Nelly's family and deliver a final message from her friend and then she liked it in Dublin so much that she stayed there.'

'But there was something else?' I said, thinking about the scribbled messages in the back of the book.

'There was. My mother told me she'd read online that when they'd been digging out the basement of this hospital, they'd found a book full of messages written during the Blitz. She was shaking when she told me. Terrified.'

'Because she knew that the book proved that she'd done something wrong,' I said, suddenly putting it all together. 'She'd killed Nelly. A mercy killing.'

Helen looked startled. 'That's right.' She turned the pages of the album again and showed me a picture of Elsie arm in arm with another young woman, whose eyes flashed with fun. 'This was her.'

'She looks nice.'

'Mammy always said she was a handful,' Helen said looking at the photo. 'She loved her very much – that was clear from how she spoke about her. And when she went to Ireland, she didn't mean to stay with the Malones. But Nelly's mammy took her in and made her part of the family. I called her Granny.'

'So Elsie didn't want anyone knowing what she'd done?' I said.

'She was so worried it would change everything. Of course, Nelly's parents are long dead, and her siblings are all gone too now, but we're all intertwined. I have three brothers younger than me and one of them married Nelly's niece. Mammy thought the family would break apart if the truth came out.'

'Poor Elsie, worrying about it all in her final days.'

'She made me promise I'd travel to England and find the book and stop anyone finding out.'

'So you came to Tall Trees?'

She looked sheepish. 'It took a while to organise.'

'You left behind your life in Ireland to fulfil your mum's dying wish?'

A shadow crossed Helen's face. 'I did.'

'You must have loved her so much.'

'She was the best person I've ever met.' Helen lifted her chin. 'She was a wonderful nurse. An amazing mother. My father adored her. My brothers have dozens of children and grandchildren and they all loved her too. I know that if she helped Nelly die, then she did it for the right reasons. I don't want her memory tarnished.'

'Do you have children? A partner?'

'No children,' Helen said. 'I have a partner. Or I did.' She sighed. 'Her name's Julia and we've been together for twenty-five years. She thought I was bonkers doing this. I'm not sure she'll still be at home when I get back.'

On a whim I reached out and patted her hand. 'We'll talk her round,' I said. A thought struck me. 'Why did Elsie have to leave? If Nelly was dying anyway, no one would have suspected your mother had helped her along. It seems so extreme.'

'Someone saw her.' Helen looked like she was going to cry. 'This chap called Jackson had a bit of a crush on her. I think nowadays he'd be called a stalker. He followed her around and he'd got himself a job at the hospital and he saw what she did.'

'God,' I said, putting my hand over my mouth.

'He threatened my mother and she was scared. So she left.'

'But he didn't tell,' I said. 'Because Elsie came back when the hospital closed to see her friends.'

Helen shook her head. 'He was the only casualty in the bomb that fell on the hospital. He survived the blast but died a few weeks later. Of course, my mother didn't know he'd died until a few months had gone by. And by then she was hugely pregnant with me and settled in Dublin.'

'How did she get to Ireland?' I frowned. 'Could you just flit about during the war? I thought it would be like lockdown?'

'Apparently, there were a couple called the Golds who lived in the flat downstairs from my mother who helped her.' Helen chuckled. 'Mammy said they claimed they were just civil servants but when she needed them they sprang into action. She thought they worked in intelligence or something.'

'Spies,' I said, delighted. 'Really?'

'That's what Mammy claimed. We'll never know.'

'That's amazing.' I sighed. 'What a story.'

Helen ran her fingers through her hair. 'But you see why I couldn't let anyone see those messages? No one should know what my mother did.'

'I think she was brave.'

'Me too.' She smiled. 'But it's just too complicated. I was going to scribble all over them, or tear them out when there was the kerfuffle in the lounge, but I got reading the notes between my parents and then you showed up.'

'Sorry,' I said with a grin. 'How about if we rip the pages out now? Well, not rip – that's a bit drastic. I could cut them out with a craft knife? We can make it neat so no one will notice unless they're looking for it. And then Elsie's secret will be safe but we'll still have the other messages.'

'Would you do that?'

'I would. I think it's important to keep the love notes between your parents. They're so special.'

'They are.'

'Then it's settled.'

'I've not been very nice to you.' Helen looked down at her knees. 'I didn't mean to be rude, but I was so worried about you finding the truth. I thought if I made things difficult for you, you'd give up.'

'I nearly did.'

'I'm sorry.'

I shrugged. 'It's okay. I understand why you did it.'

'I saw that historian chap had given it up. I watched him move all his things out of that cupboard they'd put him in.'

'That was my fault,' I said, wincing. 'I've got a lot of making up to do.'

Helen looked at me. 'You and me both.'

We laughed and I thought how nice she was and how much I'd misjudged her.

'Would your brothers or your nieces and nephews come to the unveiling of the mural?' I asked. 'Or Julia?'

'I'm sure they would love to.' She looked pleased. 'Not sure about Julia though.'

'Perhaps you should ask her?'

She shook her head. 'It's still a bit raw.'

I didn't want to push it so I nodded.

'Fair enough.'

'Stephanie?' I looked up and saw Joyce, Val and Mr Yin hovering around the doorway to Helen's room.

'Is everything okay?' Val said pointedly.

Helen shot me an amused glance. 'Everything's fine,' she said to the others. 'I was just telling Stephanie about my mother.'

'Helen's mother was Elsie,' I said, laughing at their shocked faces. 'And her father was Harry.'

Joyce flung her arms out joyfully. 'This is wonderful,' she said. 'They lived happily ever after.'

'I was just about to tell Stephanie about how my parents found each other again,' Helen said. 'Do you want to hear the story?'

'Of course we do.' Mr Yin looked excited. 'Shall I put the kettle on?'

Chapter 41

Elsie

1941

Mrs Gold arranged everything. As I was packing a bag, with a few possessions, she arrived home. I heard her coming upstairs and opened the front door to let her in.

'You look better,' she said as she followed me back into my bedroom. 'Are you doing all right?'

'I feel really calm.' I shook my head. 'I don't know why.'

She leaned against the doorframe and studied me. 'Sometimes, when the worst things you can imagine have happened, you stop being frightened.'

'I've got nothing left to lose.' I felt a shiver of self-pity and Mrs Gold straightened up and came over to where my suitcase lay on the bed and began looking through what I'd packed. 'Now, that's not true, is it?'

I smiled. 'I suppose not.' I let my hand drift down to my abdomen. 'And I have Harry.'

'You don't need three sweaters, Elsie. It's April, for heaven's sake.'

'I feel the cold. And Ireland's chilly – Nelly always said so.'

'It's rainy. You'd be better with a mackintosh.'

'I have one. It's hanging up behind the door.'

Mrs Gold went to get it and began folding it up. 'There's a boat leaving from Liverpool on Thursday, sailing to Dublin,' she said.

'So soon?' Today was Monday.

'I'd have preferred it to be sooner, but the only other ship is going from Fishguard and that's not as straightforward to get to from London.'

She opened her handbag. 'These are your train tickets. Albert and I will take you to the station and I'm going to travel with you.'

'To Dublin?'

'No, just to Liverpool, I'm afraid. But I'll see you on to the ship.'

I threw my arms around her and hugged her and after a moment when I thought she might push me away, she hugged me back.

'I owe you,' I said.

'You owe me nothing, darling. Now, what about shoes?'

*

It was a strange feeling, saying goodbye to the house I'd lived in since I was a child. I took a photograph of my parents, one of Billy in uniform, and another of Nelly and me when were student nurses, and slipped them into my bag. And then I stood for a moment in the lounge, looking round and wondering if I'd ever come back. I had no plans beyond finding Nelly's family. I thought perhaps I could find a job at a hospital in Dublin for a while. Mrs Gold had said she would sort out tenants for my flat.

'It'll give you an income for when the baby's born,' she'd said. 'I'm sure someone from work would move in.'

I was staggered by how kind she was being. And more than a little overwhelmed at how she was making things happen. But she was staying infuriatingly tight-lipped about how she had so much authority.

'Are you ready?' she called. 'Albert has just pulled up in the car and the train leaves at four.'

I looked round the lounge again, thinking of happier times with my parents and with Billy. 'Coming,' I said.

Mr Gold was hurrying up the path, looking a little flustered as Mrs Gold and I went to meet him. He came into the hall and looked up at us where we stood on the stairs. 'It's all arranged,' he said a little breathlessly. 'It's all done.'

'Really?' Mrs Gold clapped her hands. 'You saw him?'

'I did.' He reached into his inside pocket and pulled out a letter. 'This is for you,' he said holding it out.

I went down the last few stairs and put my suitcase on the floor so I could open it. My heart was fluttering because I recognised the writing on the front of the envelope. It was from Harry.

"My darling Elsie," he'd written. "Well, isn't this a turn-up for the books? Just this morning I received your letter telling me you are expecting. I'm so pleased, Elsie."

My breath caught in my throat as I read the words. I'd been worried he'd be cross or – even worse – indifferent. But of course he was pleased. He was a lovely man, wasn't he?

"And then, as I was thinking about how I would ask you to marry me first chance I got, I was called into the flight sergeant's office and given emergency leave to go to Liverpool."

'What's this?' I said looking up at Mr Gold. 'What does this mean?'

He grinned at me. 'Harry's got twenty-four hours. That's all I could arrange, I'm afraid. But it's enough to get him to Liverpool and back.'

I looked at Mrs Gold, where she stood on the stairs looking thrilled to bits, and then at Mr Gold, and then back at the letter.

"Will you marry me?" Harry had written.

'We're getting married?' I said in wonder. 'Are we?'

'If you want,' Mr Gold said. 'It's not strictly legal, but we'll sort out the paperwork when you're safely in Ireland. But only if you want to.'

'No pressure,' Mrs Gold added. 'Do you?'

I could hardly believe how I'd gone from wretched despair to absolute happiness in just a few hours. 'I do,' I said.

*

And after that it was like a whirlwind. Mrs Gold and I got on the train at Euston and we were soon speeding our way up north. I'd left London before, of course. I'd been to Pevensey and Hastings, and I remembered going to visit a great-aunt who lived near Hever Castle, but I'd never been to the north of England before. It was hard to tell where we were because the station names had all been removed, and it was often slow going as we stopped to allow a goods train to go ahead of us. But we eventually reached Liverpool, dusty and dirty. Mrs Gold had the address of some rooms where we were to stay and to my relief – because I was tired and starting to feel more than a little queasy – they weren't far from the station.

The landlady let us in. She was wearing a dressing gown and had her hair in a scarf. She obviously knew Mrs Gold because they kissed hello and she didn't ask any questions about who we were or why we were there. Instead, she showed us to a basic room with two hard single beds, and said: 'Lav's down the hall. No baths. No smoking in the bedrooms.' She looked at us both with a steely glint in her eye. 'No men.' Her accent was strong and I had to concentrate on what she was saying, though I got the impression she was doing the same when I spoke.

She turned to go and then winked at Mrs Gold, pointing in her direction. 'And you,' she said. 'Behave.'

'Never,' Mrs Gold said, flopping on to one of the beds.

The landlady went off down the hall and I watched her go,

peeling off her housecoat to reveal a smart skirt and jacket underneath. A few minutes later we heard the front door slam and I looked out the window to see her leaving, bag tucked under her arm and her hair in victory rolls. I turned to look at Mrs Gold with a quizzical look but she just shrugged. 'No questions, darling.'

*

I was to meet Harry off the train at lunchtime the following day and I found I was sick with nerves. Mrs Gold said she had something to attend to, so I went by myself. I had to sit down on a bench because my legs were shaking so much and the smoke and heat in the station made me light-headed. Harry's train was due just after twelve but it was gone one o'clock and I was beginning to worry he wasn't coming. Maybe he'd changed his mind, I thought. Maybe this was all a huge mistake. We barely knew each other. I let out a small sob. I was pregnant and alone. What was I thinking?

Or maybe something had happened? I thought, my mind flitting from one awful scenario to another. Had he been flying last night? Was he hurt? Was he dead? Feeling my palms beginning to sweat, I tried not to panic. I gulped some deep breaths, working out a plan. I didn't know where Mrs Gold had gone but I knew where the church was, where we were supposed to be getting married later. I checked the large clock. In just a couple of hours from now. What if we missed our slot? I took another deep breath and shut my eyes for a second, steadying myself.

And when I opened them again, there he was. Standing right in front of me, in his blue uniform, his cap under his arm. My Harry.

He opened his arms wide and I stood up and fell into his embrace, all of my worries and fears vanishing as we laughed and kissed and spoke over each other.

'You look so pale. Are you eating enough? You have to eat for two now,' he told me, stroking my hair and looking at me.

'I thought something had happened. I was so worried. Are you all right?' I babbled at the same time.

Eventually we stopped jabbering nonsense and simply gazed into each other's eyes.

'Is this madness?' I said.

'Complete madness,' Harry agreed. 'But strangely it makes total sense.'

'You're absolutely sure you want to get married?'

'Absolutely sure.'

'Because there's something I need to tell you and I'm worried you might change your mind.'

Harry frowned. 'Will I need a drink?'

'Possibly.' But then I shook my head. 'But let me tell you first. I've been stewing over it for ages and I want to get it over with.'

For the first time, Harry's smile faltered. We sat down on the bench where I'd been waiting for him and I tried to think of the right words to say.

'Nelly died,' I said.

'I'm so sorry about that. She was a lovely woman. I know that's why you're going to Ireland.'

I shook my head. 'You don't know all of it.'

'Tell me.'

I looked into his sweet face and then down at my knees, and I spoke in a rush. 'Nelly was dying and she was in so much pain. So much, Harry. It was awful. It was going to be long and agonising.' I took a shuddering breath. 'She asked me to help her, to help her go quicker. And I did. I gave her morphine so she'd just fall asleep and not wake up.'

Harry was quiet. I braced myself, but he didn't speak for ages. I shot him a glance but he was looking up to the ceiling where pigeons darted in and out of the smoke.

'Do you want to find the police station?' I said eventually in a small, scared voice.

Harry looked at me, finally. 'What for?'

'To tell them what I did.'

He looked at me with his brows furrowed. 'What you did, Elsie, was really brave.'

'It was illegal.'

He shrugged. 'Maybe. But it wasn't wrong.' He reached out and stroked my cheek with his thumb. 'She was suffering and you stopped it.'

'I can't ever tell anyone what I did.'

'No,' he agreed. 'We'll keep that to ourselves.'

'I thought you wouldn't understand, because of the seagull.'

He grinned at me. 'I think I do understand because of the seagull.'

Weak with relief I leaned against him, and he kissed my temple.

'Right then,' he said, checking his watch. 'I've got four hours until I need to be back on the train so I thought maybe we could go and find a pub, and then this afternoon if you're not busy, we could go and get married. What do you reckon?'

I laughed. 'I reckon that sounds like a plan.'

Chapter 42

Stephanie

Six weeks later

I was a total mess of nervous energy. I wasn't sleeping. I was barely eating. But it was strange. It was good. It wasn't like when Max had disappeared and I was curled up inside myself, frightened about what could have happened. This was different. This time I was throwing my energy outwards.

'Outwards?' Tara said with a raised eyebrow. 'That sounds like hippy-dippy bullshit to me.'

I punched her arm. 'You're meant to be supportive,' I said. 'Which shoes? These ones that make me feel like Kate Middleton, or the trainers?'

'Trainers,' Tara said without hesitation. 'Can you even walk in the other ones?'

'Not really.'

'Trainers. What are you wearing?'

'I thought that floaty dress and Max's leather jacket if it's chilly?'

'Perfect.'

'Not too scruffy? The mayor's coming.'

'The mayor of London?' Tara looked impressed. 'That's so cool.'

'No, not him. The local mayor.'

'Oh.' She shrugged. 'Still good, though.'

'Will you do my hair?'

'If you like.'

'And my makeup? I'm too nervous.'

'Sure.' She looked at me closely. 'Have you heard from Finn?'

'No.' I buried my head in my wardrobe. 'Now where did I put that dress?'

'It's hanging on the door,' Tara said. She was sitting on my bed and now she lay back against the pillows and watched me.

'Nothing at all?' she said.

'No, stop asking.' I'd sent Finn an invitation to the unveiling of the mural. And I'd added a little note to the back of the card, saying: "Have BIG news about Elsie. Will tell you when I see you. Please come."

But he'd not replied. Instead of fretting about it, I'd thrown myself into painting the mural – with a lot of help from the Tall Trees residents who'd picked up brushes and more than done their bit. Everyone had got involved: Joyce, Mr Yin, Kenny, Helen – even Blessing. Val had taken it upon herself to organise the catering for the event and was spending her time writing lists and haranguing Tara who was holding the after-party at The Vine for me. I'd thought Tara and Val would clash horribly but actually there was a mutual admiration there that warmed my heart.

'And the Irish visitors have all arrived, have they?'

'They have. Micah's been showing them round, bless him. He's going to fetch them from their hotel later and herd them all to Tall Trees.'

'He's a sweetheart.'

'He is. He's helped me so much.'

'I think it goes both ways.' Tara clapped her hands. 'Right, go and get in the shower and then we'll sort your hair and makeup.'

Obediently, I picked up a towel from the radiator and made for the door, then I paused.

'Do you think he'll come, Tara?'

She smiled at me. 'Go on, or we won't have time to do your hair.'

That was a no, then.

*

The residents at Tall Trees were in a frenzy of excitement. The noise level was more like a primary school than a retirement home with laughter echoing through the corridors. Tara and I exchanged a glance and I felt a little flutter of pleasure.

In the lounge, Val was holding court, directing Franklin and Vir who were handing round canapés and drinks. Joyce was wearing a lime-green suit and looked like the queen, and Kenny's very buff grandson Kyle had arrived and was charming all the elderly ladies. Blessing had said she would go and get my nan before the unveiling, so she could be involved too. There was a real buzz of fun and anticipation in the room.

'This is all for you,' Tara said giving me a nudge. 'You did this.'

I gave her a tight smile as Val rushed up and swept her away, asking questions about prosecco glasses and sausage rolls. I went to walk into the room and found I couldn't move. I was paralysed with fear – frozen to the spot. "This is all for you," a voice in my head said. "Do you really deserve it?"

I stood at the door, watching the activity around me with wide eyes, fighting the urge to run away. My breath began to quicken and I pushed my palm against my chest, trying to force myself to breathe normally. But it was too late. My skin was prickling and I knew I was about to panic. I glanced behind me, wondering wildly if I could make a dash for the door, but a group of men in suits – one wearing the thick gold chain of office that told me he was the mayor – was approaching and I didn't want to barge past the dignitaries and ruin everything.

Trapped, I felt my forehead grow clammy and my head spun as shadows crowded into my vision. And then suddenly someone looped an arm through mine, holding me steady. I glanced round to see Micah looking at me in concern.

'Okay?' he said.

I couldn't speak. I just shook my head, pressing my lips together.

'Right. Follow my breath,' he said. 'In, out, come on. In and out.'

I tried to do as he said, as the crowded room swirled round me.

'Watch me,' Micah said. 'Look right at me. In, out, in, out.'

Slowly my breathing became more regular and steady and my vision cleared.

'Thank you,' I said to Micah.

'Better?' he asked.

I nodded. 'Did anyone see?'

'Nah, they're all too busy looking at that man's guns.' He nodded towards Kyle who was surrounded by eager Tall Trees residents and he gave me a wide grin. 'I brought a mate.'

For the first time I noticed another teenaged boy standing slightly self-consciously to the side. 'This is Oz. We do art club together. He's like a major history geek.'

'Nice to meet you,' I said, pleased that Micah was making friends now. Maybe we really had helped each other.

Not wanting to embarrass him in front of his new mate by giving him a hug, I instead gave Micah's arm a grateful squeeze. 'What would I do without you?' I said.

'You wouldn't run out of cereal so fast.'

'There is that.' I laughed. 'Go and get yourselves a drink and some food.'

The boys didn't need to be asked twice. They vanished off in the direction of the buffet and ever so casually I surveyed the room, looking for Finn's floppy hair. But there was no sign of him.

'Stephanie?' Helen was there looking proud as punch with her three identical-looking brothers. She introduced me to them all and I was touched when they all bundled me into an enormous hug.

'We're so grateful to you for telling Mammy's story,' one of them said when he let me go.

'It's a wonderful tale to tell,' I said. I swapped a little glance with Helen, who gave me a nod. We'd cut the incriminating pages out of the book and then Helen and I had stuck them in the shredder in the office. No one would ever know about what Elsie had done, and that was fine.

'Your mother was a clever woman,' I said now, truthfully. 'She lost so much and then gained a whole new family when she went to Ireland.'

'Do you know she arrived in Dublin a week or so before the Belfast Blitz?' one of the brothers said. 'They weren't prepared for bombings, and they didn't have enough ambulances or fire engines.'

'Or hospital beds,' said another brother. They'd obviously heard this story many times before.

'So, when the bombs fell, a load of ambulances and fire engines went up from Dublin to help,' the man carried on. 'They put aside all political differences and just helped out. Mammy volunteered at the hospital, because they were short of staff obviously as so many people had gone up to the north. And that's how she got given her job there after Helen was born.'

'That's amazing,' I said, thinking with a pang how much Finn would love to hear that tale. 'I'll have to do another mural to tell that story.'

The men all laughed heartily, then one of them pulled out his phone, which had buzzed with a message.

'Just arriving,' he said to me in an undertone. I nodded.

'Helen?' I said. 'I think there's someone here to see you.'

I guided her towards the door, just as a woman with silver-streaked short hair, dark-rimmed glasses, and a gorgeous necklace walked in.

'Julia,' Helen gasped. 'How did you …'

Julia laughed. 'Someone called Stevie phoned me,' she said. 'Begged me to come over and "make amends before it was too late".'

'I did say that,' I admitted.

Helen fixed me with a steely glare. 'Before it's too late?' she said pretending – at least I hoped she was pretending – to be insulted. 'I've got years left in me.'

'Then make the most of them,' I said. I watched as she and Julia embraced and, feeling a little teary and emotional, I went in search of some prosecco. With a glass in my hand, I stood at the edge of the room. Micah and Oz were talking to Kenny, who was animatedly demonstrating some sort of football move. I hoped he wouldn't hurt himself – he wasn't as steady on his feet as he thought he was. Joyce and Mr Yin were standing beside the windows, elegant as anything, sipping their drinks. Blessing and Vanessa were dressed in their best, looking gorgeous and laughing like drains, which was making everyone around them smile. Val was rushing around, rosy-cheeked, and looked happier than I'd seen her in months. It was perfect. I felt like everything was coming together.

But not quite.

Suddenly I wanted to see the mural and check it was all okay before I had to share it with the world. Well, maybe not the world but the mayor and the residents. I put my prosecco on a table and slipped out of the door and round the corner to the end gable.

The mural had been covered with a thick curtain, sort of like a changing room in a clothes shop, ready for the grand unveiling, but I wanted to see it before then. So I ducked underneath the fabric to look at it.

It was quiet in there with the material muffling the sounds of the cars swishing past on the road, and the laugher and chatter from the lounge. The light was dim but I could see enough. I stood there, breathing deeply and looked up at the mural.

I'd painted trees, like the ones that had given Tall Trees its name, on each side, framing the space. There were silhouettes of soldiers and airmen, and planes in the sky, and I'd included some poppies and nurses and doctors. I'd added an NHS rainbow as a nod to the difficulties of the last couple of years, too. And then right in the middle, I'd painted Elsie in her nurse's uniform, holding the book in her arms. Slightly behind her, I'd added Harry. Handsome and proud in his RAF garb. Above them the sun shone and I'd twisted the words "You Are My Sunshine" into its rays.

In fact, if you looked closer you could see there were words all over the mural. In the blades of grass beneath the soldiers' feet, in the petals of the poppies and on the leaves of the trees. There were hundreds of messages taken from Elsie's book.

And finally, on the trunk of one of the trees, so it looked like an old-fashioned etching in the bark, I'd painted my own special message. I'd copied Finn's small fish with the arrow pointing to its fin, drawn my little TV with the letter S on the screen, and then beneath them both I'd painted: "Sorry."

Of course, none of that meant anything at all if Finn didn't see it. But I still held out the hope that perhaps he'd go past one day on the bus or walk by and glance over and perhaps read the message I'd left for him. I would just have to wait.

'I don't know where she's gone,' a voice said on the other side of the curtain. It was Blessing. I froze, hoping she wouldn't look behind the material. 'She's probably just in the loo or something. I will go and find her for you.'

I stayed very still and quiet as I heard her footsteps fade away. She was probably talking to one of the councillors, I thought. I'd have to go and do the networking bit in a minute. I couldn't hide out here much longer. I'd wait a couple of minutes to make sure they'd gone inside and then follow.

But suddenly there was a tugging at the curtain and there was Finn.

'Stevie!' he said with genuine surprise. 'I erm, I didn't know you were here.'

'I was just looking at the mural.' I felt my cheeks flame. 'Before the big unveiling.'

Finn looked up at the painting in awe. 'It's absolutely wonderful,' he said. 'You've done such a good job.'

He put his hand out and touched Elsie. 'Here she is,' he said. 'Our girl.'

'She moved to Ireland,' I told him in a hurry, desperately wanting him to know everything. 'She went to find her best friend's family and pass on her dying message. And she stayed. Harry followed and they got married.' Finn's eyes widened and so did his smile.

'They had a happy ending,' he said.

'Better than that.' I bounced on my feet, glad I'd worn the trainers. 'Grumpy Helen is Elsie's daughter!'

Finn's jaw dropped. 'What on earth?'

'She didn't want us to read some of the messages,' I said vaguely with a wave of my hand. 'But it's all sorted now. Her brothers are here too. They're so proud of their mum.'

'And rightly so.' Finn looked up at Elsie's portrait and then he turned back to me with a smile. 'You are my sunshine,' he said. 'That was Elsie and Harry's message.'

'It was.'

We stood side by side for a moment, gazing up at the pictures. I felt my knuckles graze his.

'I've really missed you,' I blurted, keeping my eyes fixed on the mural. 'I was so scared when you had your accident. I thought everything had gone wrong, like it did with my exhibition and with Max.'

Finn turned to look at me. 'I know,' he said. 'I realise that now. I was hurt when you didn't come to the hospital. Hurt and embarrassed, I think. I assumed I'd misread it all and there was nothing between us.'

I snorted. 'There was definitely something between us.'

He smiled. 'I should have thought more about all the stuff that had happened to you.'

'I was pretty brutal, though,' I admitted. 'I could have been nicer.'

He sighed. 'Ironically, we could have communicated better. Perhaps we should have written messages like Harry and Elsie.' He looked back at the painting and I heard him breathe in sharply as he spotted the little fish. He reached up and touched it with his fingertips.

'You did this?' he said.

I nodded. Finn trailed his hand across the arrow pointing to the fish's fin, and then the television and finally he traced the word "sorry".

'I'm sorry,' I said.

He turned to me. 'It's beautiful.' Then he grinned. 'Much nicer than my effort.'

He put his hand in his pocket and pulled out a stack of Post-it Notes. One by one he peeled them off and stuck them on to the mural. On the first one he'd made a pretty rubbish effort at drawing the telly. Then he'd drawn his own version of his fish. And finally, he'd written: "You are my sunshine".

I was so thrilled I could hardly speak. 'Really?' I squeaked. 'Really and truly?'

Finn took me in his arms. 'I've been miserable without you, Stevie.'

'I've been miserable without you.'

'You are my sunshine,' he said. And then he kissed me.

I melted into him, thinking this was really the best message of all.

'We should probably go inside,' Finn said eventually.

'I know,' I groaned. 'They'll be wanting to do the unveiling. Can't we stay here a bit longer?' We kissed again and somewhere far away I could hear voices, chattering and laughing … and counting?

'Three, two, one …' someone shouted. The curtain dropped and there stood the mayor and the councillors, all the residents of Tall Trees, my nan in her wheelchair, Tara, Micah, and the photographer from the local paper, all clapping and cheering.

Sheepishly, Finn and I broke apart as Val spoke up, a note of triumph in her voice. 'I told you he liked you,' she said.

Acknowledgements

This is the third novel I have written during the Covid pandemic and I can't tell you how pleased I was to be writing about my local area instead of faraway places that were only available via Google Earth. It was so fascinating to research the Blitz in the suburb of London where I live but as always, I took a few liberties with the facts!

South London District Hospital didn't exist but it is based on the real-life hospitals in Beckenham, Bromley and Farnborough.

Biggin Hill is a real place, of course. Now it is a commercial airport but in the war it was a base for Fighter Command. And it was indeed bombed with a loss of 39 lives. The bomb actually fell in August 1940 – just before the Blitz began. This didn't work with the timeline of my story, so the bomb in my book is a couple of months later.

The museum at Biggin Hill, where Finn and Stevie go to do their research is a real place. It's tiny but a treasure trove of history and if you're ever nearby, I really recommend you pop in. The staff have an amazing knowledge, love to answer questions and are so friendly and enthusiastic. And the tea room is brilliant!

When I decided to write a novel based around nursing, I failed to consider the fact that I have absolutely no medical nowledge whatsoever. Thankfully, my fabulous friend and paramedic extraordinaire, Claire Tinker, came to the rescue. She talked me through the kind of injuries poor Nell could endure and put it all in terms that someone with only biology GCSE to her name could understand. She also put me in touch with her friend Louise Cox – another expert paramedic – who sent me all sorts of articles about burn care during the Second World War, answered all my questions, and helped me enormously while condemning Nelly to a slow and painful death!

I also have my husband's friend Charles Kloet to thank for Harry's story about the seagull that lived in his spare room for three years. It really happened!

And so to Elsie. As Mrs Gold says in the story, it is true that during the First World War many nurses kept scrapbooks for their patients. One of those nurses was called Elsie Harvey and she worked at a Red Cross hospital in Beckenham throughout WW1. She called her scrapbook her 'autograph album' and her soldier patients wrote marvellous things in it. There are messages to families, drawings of Elsie herself, rude poems, accounts of battles at Ypres and others. And even one rather lengthy account of a football match in the trenches.

I stumbled on Elsie's book when I was helping my son with a history project (thanks, Tom!) and her real-life story inspired my Elsie. The original Elsie's book is now in the Imperial War Museum and you can view the pages online if you are interested. https://www.bromleyfirstworldwar.org.uk/content/people/autograph-album

Thanks, as always, to my family – Darren, Tom and Sam. Also to my agent, Felicity, and my editor Abi and her assistant Audrey, who have championed Elsie and Stevie wonderfully. And, of course, to my fabulous readers. I hope you enjoy this story. Please let me know what you think!

Keep reading for an excerpt from
The Secrets of Thistle Cottage ...

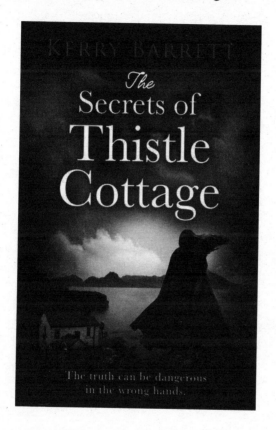

Edinburgh Daily News
Friday, April 3

Breakfast television presenter Alistair Robertson has pleaded guilty to two charges of sexual assault and one of attempted rape.

The star appeared at the High Court in Edinburgh yesterday, April 2, and was warned that he would face a custodial sentence.

Adjourning the case for a week, Judge Lady Morpeth said: 'You were in a position of trust and you used that power to assault women who looked up to you.'

Robertson presented Good Morning Scotland *for ten years and was voted the nation's favourite TV star three years in a row. He was a runner-up on* Celebrity Masterchef *and was tipped to be in the line-up for next year's* Strictly Come Dancing.

He shares his million-pound house in Edinburgh's swanky Marchmont area with his wife, Tess – a top lawyer – and their teenage daughter.

Outspoken Tess (pictured leaving court) has been under fire since she tweeted that 'silly girls should think about their actions before ruining people's lives'. The tweet has since been deleted.

Comments:

Hanny said: Disgusting pig. They should throw away the key.

Scottydog said: I hope his victims get some closure now they know he's locked up.

Alphamale said: Me too has gone too far. Soon you won't be able to compliment a girl without her crying rape.

LittleJohn said: Earn £200 a day from home. Click here for more information.

Royalfan23 said: These women knew what they were doing. Bet they were out for revenge because he turned them down.

Rugbylad09 said: Look at her, the sour-faced bitch. Can't blame him for looking elsewhere.

Muffinman said: Face like a slapped arse.

Survivorandlovingit said: Victim blaming is the lowest of the low. She needs to get in the bin.

Proudmum said: She should be ashamed of herself. What kind of woman looks the other way when her husband is up to all sorts.

Sayit said: Agreed. She's a disgrace. Like a Poundshop Hillary Clinton. Imagine putting their daughter at risk like that. I heard the victims were in their teens.

Stayalert said: Paedo scum.

Mumstaxi said: This comment has been removed for legal reasons.

Prologue

Summer, 1661
Honor

I did not like the new laird and he could tell.

I remembered him as a sour-faced boy and surly young man, who was cruel to his wee brother and bullied the local children, but I'd hoped his time away from North Berwick would have softened him. He'd got married, I'd heard, and I thought losing his father might have made him realize that riches meant nothing – that family was the most important thing.

But it seemed Gregor Kincaid as an adult was just as unpleasant as he'd been as a child.

He stood at the front of the meeting hall, chest puffed out, and I felt a prickling on the back of my neck that warned me not to trust him.

Gregor had only been the laird for a few weeks but he had big plans for the town. Plans he was outlining to the meeting.

'The returns are impressive,' he was saying.

'Aye, for you,' said Mackenzie White, tipping the brim of his hat back so he could look Gregor in the eye. 'No for the town.'

'That's not true. Bringing larger ships into the harbour will put North Berwick on the map.' Gregor threw his arms out wide, his enthusiasm obvious. 'Making us a trading port with direct connections to the colonies will increase opportunities for everyone.'

'We'd have to dredge the harbour,' Mackenzie said. 'Make it deeper.'

'That's right.'

'And what about the fishermen?'

I sat up straighter. My husband John had been a fisherman. He'd run a fleet of boats from the harbour and when he'd died he'd bequeathed each boat to the men who'd worked for him. They had a trade and an income for life thanks to my John – as long as our town remained a fishing port.

'Fishing could continue,' Gregor said.

The prickling on my neck got stronger and I spoke. 'You can't run clippers and fishing boats from the same harbour,' I said. 'The fish won't bite. The men would have to go north to Fife or even further.'

Gregor's eyes fell on me, in my usual seat at the back of the room, and he raised an eyebrow in recognition.

'Widow Seton,' he said.

'Yes.'

'I believe the fishing would not be affected.'

'You are wrong. Bringing tall ships into this harbour would change the town forever.'

'She is right,' Mackenzie said. 'It's one or the other. And fishing was here first. It gives us a good living and we would be fools to change it.'

There was a swell of murmuring in the room and Gregor cleared his throat for silence, giving me a small, mocking smile.

'Why are you here at this meeting? It is for burgesses only, not women.'

I lifted my chin. 'I am a burgess.'

Gregor laughed but his brother, Davey, touched his arm and nodded. I didn't know Davey well either. I'd not seen much of either of them since they were boys. Like Gregor, Davey too had grown and left, but he'd returned before his father died, with his small son and tales of a wife who'd died tragically. The town gossips told me he had a fondness for playing card games and, penniless, had been forced to come home to North Berwick with his tail between his legs. I had no idea if it was true, but despite the stories, I thought Davey more worthy of respect than his boorish brother because I remembered him as quite a sweet-natured lad back when we were all young. His brother had always been a bully.

'Widow Seton was left her position as burgess by her late husband,' Davey explained now. 'She has the same voting rights as the men.'

Gregor's face went red. He turned to Mackenzie, who'd lowered his hat again. 'You went along with this?'

Mackenzie just shrugged and I hid my smile. I knew the men would never question John bequeathing me my position in his will – that would mean questioning their own inheritance.

'We should vote,' Davey said. I suddenly had another memory of him as a child, forced to soothe the ill temper of his older brother. Poor Davey, having to make room in his life for this coarse, bad-mannered man. I caught his eye, hoping he knew I was behind him, and he smiled at me, showing me he appreciated my support.

'All those in favour of dredging the harbour to accommodate large clippers and other ships,' Gregor said.

A few hands were raised.

'All those against?'

This time, there were many more hands raised – including my own.

Gregor snorted. 'You will believe the insane ramblings of a woman over my own plans?'

There was silence.

'Very well,' Gregor said. His voice was light and casual but I felt a darkness descend over the room like a shadow and I shivered in the sudden chill. 'I trust you all know the teachings of good John Knox about women holding positions of authority?'

The men all stared at him blankly. We all knew of John Knox's beliefs, of course. He may have been dead and gone these last one hundred years, but his teachings lived on in the changes to our churches and our lives. And no more so than in the mistrust of women who rose above their station. I fixed my eyes on Gregor and he looked back.

'Beware,' he said. Was he talking to me personally? It felt that way. But then he looked around the room. 'Be careful who you trust and who you follow. For witches come in many disguises.'

There was a gasp from the other council members and my heart lurched in fear. This didn't sound like a warning. This sounded like a threat.

Dear Reader,

We hope you enjoyed reading this book. If you did, we'd be so appreciative if you left a review. It really helps us and the author to bring more books like this to you.

Here at HQ Digital we are dedicated to publishing fiction that will keep you turning the pages into the early hours. Don't want to miss a thing? To find out more about our books, promotions, discover exclusive content and enter competitions you can keep in touch in the following ways:

JOIN OUR COMMUNITY:

Sign up to our new email newsletter:
http://smarturl.it/SignUpHQ

Read our new blog www.hqstories.co.uk

 https://twitter.com/HQStories

www.facebook.com/HQStories

BUDDING WRITER?

We're also looking for authors to join the HQ Digital family!
Find out more here:

https://www.hqstories.co.uk/want-to-write-for-us/

Thanks for reading, from the HQ Digital team

If you enjoyed *The Book of Last Letters*,
then why not try another heart-wrenching
historical novel from HQ Digital?

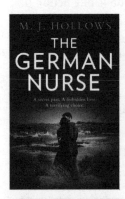

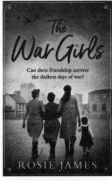